A Secret Place

PATRICIA RAINSFORD

PENGUIN BOOKS

PENGUIN BOOKS

Published by the Penguin Group
Penguin Books Ltd, 80 Strand, London WC2R ORL, England
Penguin Group (USA) Inc., 375 Hudson Street, New York, New York 10014, USA
Penguin Group (Canada), 90 Eglinton Avenue East, Suite 700, Toronto, Ontario, Canada M4P 2Y3
(a division of Pearson Penguin Canada Inc.)
Penguin Ireland, 25 St Stephen's Green, Dublin 2, Ireland
(a division of Penguin Books Ltd)
Penguin Group (Australia), 250 Camberwell Road, Camberwell, Victoria 3124, Australia
(a division of Pearson Australia Group Pty Ltd)
Penguin Books India Pvt Ltd, 11 Community Centre, Panchsheel Park, New Delhi – 110 017, India
Penguin Group (NZ), 67 Apollo Drive, Rosedale, North Shore 0632, New Zealand
(a division of Pearson New Zealand Ltd)
Penguin Books (South Africa) (Pty) Ltd, 24 Sturdee Avenue, Rosebank, Johannesburg 2196, South Africa

Penguin Books Ltd, Registered Offices: 80 Strand, London WC2R ORL, England

www.penguin.com

First published by Penguin Ireland 2007
Published in Penguin Books 2008

1

Copyright © Patricia Rainsford, 2007
All rights reserved

The moral right of the author has been asserted

Typeset by Rowland Phototypesetting Ltd, Bury St Edmunds, Suffolk
Printed in England by Clays Ltd, St Ives plc

ISBN: 978-1-844-88011-9

'It is such a secret place, the land of tears.'
Antoine de Saint-Exupéry,
The Little Prince

Prologue

He fiddled with the volume control on the steering wheel and a loud guitar wail filled the car. Ah, now – that was better. The Stones were one great band that was for sure and some music just had to be listened to loud, didn't it? Sitting back in his seat, he relaxed a bit. The music filled the inside of the car. Fuck – it was hard to beat it, all the same.

He closed his eyes and he didn't mean to but he must have nodded off because next thing he knew the Stones were back at Track One and he'd been having a dream about swimming in Kilkee with Alan and they were kids and he was winning the race. For once.

He felt like shit, his mouth was foul and his head was killing him. He rubbed his hand over his face and flipped down the glove box, looking to see if there was anything there he could take for his headache – nothing. He muttered curses and jabbed at the stereo controls. Silence replaced the music in the car and he peered into the dark street. Not that he could see anything. It was pitch black out there and now it'd started raining as well.

He thumped the steering wheel. For God's sake. He knew he probably should have worn his glasses. All the squinting wasn't helping the headache much. He hated those bloody glasses – especially since his mother had said they made him look like his father. That was the last time he'd worn them.

He leaned forward to see if he could see anything in the darkness. It made no difference. All he could see were the dark ghosts of the houses on the empty street and the rain gathering on the windscreen. He flicked on the wipers. Still no sign of her.

He looked at his watch – two thirty-five – twenty-fucking-five-to-three. Jesus wept. Well, she knew what'd happen when she did eventually turn up – she'd have to make it worth his while. Still, it was damn annoying. And as if that wasn't enough he knew Caroline had probably phoned while he was out. Phoning and phoning – calling his mobile . . .

He pulled his phone out of his pocket to have a look. It was blank and quiet. He'd forgotten he'd turned it off earlier when he was in Finn's, watching the match. Nothing ruder than a phone blaring during a match. He fucking hated that himself.

But she didn't get that and she'd want to know why he turned it off, considering everything. She'd want to know what he was doing there anyway after all they'd talked about – blah, blah, blah, the usual shite. Ah, well, so what? He'd just say he'd fallen asleep in front of the telly. Didn't hear the phones. She could like it or lump it.

He thought about the girl again. Jesus, she was something herself all the same. Now he'd had a bit of a sleep he was really looking forward to seeing her again. The Lexus was great like that – plenty of room in the front for her to make up to him for all this bloody hanging around.

Why the fuck had he told Caroline he was meeting the girl, anyway? He could have kicked himself as soon as the words were out of his mouth. A few too many Bushmills when she rang last night. That and the shock of it, what with the girl having called just before . . .

If he was honest, she was the last person he'd expected to hear from, so he'd gone and blurted it out to Caroline like an eejit as soon as he heard her voice. Big mistake. She always got so worked up about this stuff – over-reacted every single time. And with no reason – as he was tired of telling her, it was all well under control. Had been for years.

She was such an uptight bitch sometimes, freaking out and ringing Alan, like they couldn't do anything without him. She even said that once when they were fighting. Later she took it back and said she didn't mean it. He wasn't a fool, though. He knew she did. If Paddy Power's was open he'd have put down a bet that she'd already phoned Alan and told him about this as well. Mister Fucking Knowitall. So that was two lectures he was due.

For Christ's sake, what did they think he was? A child? A fucking eejit?

He opened the glove box again and took out the silver hip flask that he'd bought in France. He'd managed to slip it past Caroline when they were in that shop in Paris – she'd been right beside him and she hadn't seen him buying it. That still made him smile.

He filled his mouth with whiskey. That was definitely better. He swallowed, enjoying the feeling of heat as the liquid rolled into his gut. He followed it with a second mouthful – that tasted even better than the first.

He could feel a lot of the tension moving out of his body as it welcomed the top-up. He relaxed – well, most of him relaxed except for that all important area where – as Roddy Hannon always said – you wanted to keep your tension.

He squirmed in his seat and looked out at the dark, deserted street. There was still nobody around and nothing stopping him giving himself a bit of tension relief if he felt like it; but no, he wouldn't – he'd wait. It'd be all the better for the waiting. That little bitch was in no position to object and he had a few ideas about how he wanted her to repay the favour he was doing her.

He looked at the clock on the dash – two forty-five.

Where the fuck was she? Hadn't he just seen a Pink Floyd album in that glove box?

He leaned over and rooted around. There it was: 'Wish You Were Here'. Fucking great album. Music filled the car again and he had another slug of whiskey. If she didn't turn up by the time 'Shine On You Crazy Diamond' was over . . .

The passenger door opened and he started. Jesus H. Christ! The music was so loud he hadn't even heard her coming — after all the waiting. She sat in beside him. She smelled great, like lemons.

'You took your fucking time,' he said, carefully screwing the top on his hip flask. He didn't want to spill any. Stink up the car and draw another lecture on himself.

The girl didn't say anything. He didn't care. He wasn't interested in her using her mouth for talking, anyway. That thought made him laugh — he must tell that one to Roddy.

He tossed the hip flask into the back and it landed near the bag.

'OK now, let's get down to some business here,' he said, leaning back in his seat and unzipping his fly.

She turned her head. He couldn't see her properly in the dark. He was definitely going to have to get contacts — bloody uncomfortable probably but better than being blind or looking like his father. He peered at her but he could only really see her outline. She smelled the same as always, though. He loved that lemony smell — the memories that went with it'd nearly be enough to give him an erection by themselves. He pointed at his lap.

'Get going,' he said.

She didn't say a word. He looked down to pull out the lad. Jesus, there definitely was plenty of tension going on there — he didn't think he was going to need Viagra any time soon. And then he felt something even harder at his temple.

1. Monday 4 April, 5.40 a.m.

Hi Clint,

I went with Kelly after all. Remember I told you about it and how she said she'd go by herself? Anyway, first she goes out by herself to meet him – like she said she would. Then she comes back – after ages – and says will one of us go with her after all? Natalie (as usual) was all, Oh, so now we're suddenly good enough to meet your precious friend. But I didn't give a shit. Just said I'd go.

It was late when we left – after two in the morning, maybe later even. We didn't talk much, walking there, but like I told you already, Kelly doesn't talk much ever – which is fine with me. All she said was he wanted to meet up at the back of the park. So that's where we went – the People's Park.

Remember when we used to go there? Remember rolling down the hill there under that big statue? I haven't been there in years.

Anyway, that's where we had to go. I don't know why she wanted anyone to go with her because when we got there she wouldn't even let me go up to the car. Told me to wait in a doorway. I was pissed off about that but like I said already I didn't care really as long as he gave us the money.

When she told us about it first – Kelly, I mean – she'd said it was simple. He was some guy she had information about and he was going to give her money to keep her mouth shut. Ordinary blackmail – she just had to meet him and collect it and that was it.

Natalie said it was hardly as fucking straightforward as that but Kelly swore it was and I didn't care who he was or why he was willing to give us money as long as he did. Wc aren't going far without money.

So there I was, anyway, standing in this doorway. Freezing. Wet – it rained on us the whole way there. I was just thinking about all the shit that'd gone on while I was watching these two cats riding on the footpath beside me and then I heard this scream. Jesus Christ, Clint – a banshee had nothing on it.

I ran up to Kelly. She was standing beside your man's car up at the corner of the street, just standing there in front of the door – which was wide open, and she was screaming. Fuck it, it was weird!

First I could only see shapes. And hear music – there was a radio or a CD or something on – and then my eyes got used to the dark and I could see your man. Billy Hendrick. I know his name because Kelly told us, though that was about all she told us about him. Well, that and that he was going to give her money.

Anyway, there he was, sitting in his car and the engine was on and he was sort of lying against the driver's door. The glass behind his head was shattered to shit with this dark stain all over it and even I knew it was blood. And all the time the music was playing, so it made it like watching a film.

Kelly'd shut up by then and was like a statue frozen on to the street. Standing and staring. I didn't know what to do but I'll tell you, I knew one thing: there was nothing we could do for the poor fucker in the car. I grabbed hold of her arm and said her name a few times until at last she looked at me, and then she sort of unfroze and the two of us ran.

First we were kind of shaky when we were running – like

6

we were running on ice or something. Stumbling and falling and stuff. But then we got faster. Running and running and running. If we'd run as fast as that on Friday we'd have had nothing to worry about – they'd never have had a chance of catching us.

We went down by the park, and up the back along Lord Edward Street. I kept thinking maybe we should walk when we were passing the army barracks. Running always makes you look suspicious, doesn't it? But we were too far gone by then and I'd say we just couldn't have stopped running even if we'd wanted to.

I kept thinking about the dead guy and the blood and at the same time worrying that someone had seen us. Maybe we weren't the first people who'd come along? Maybe somebody else had seen him there in the car with his brains blown out and called the Guards and they'd come along any minute and see us running away and arrest us. We were fucked if that happened – especially as we were actually innocent for once. Who'd believe us, though?

I was just starting to think we were clear and then we ran around a corner and slapped right into a couple who were snogging the faces off each other in the middle of the footpath. I couldn't fucking believe it. They fell over – actually fell over on to the ground – and the guy was swearing and the girl squealed and I was, Sorry, sorry, sorry, Jesus are you all right, we're awful sorry, you're not hurt are you?

Kelly didn't say anything. Just stood there like a bloody statue again and looked at them. I helped the girl to get up. She was nice – kept saying she was grand. Her boyfriend was a pain in the arse, though, and was going on and on about us not looking where we were going and stuff – like we'd fucking run into them on purpose.

I wanted to tell him what to do with himself but I knew

I couldn't. So instead I acted all friendly and laughed – ha ha. Then I started with all this shit about how we were supposed to be babysitting our small brothers and our mother was at work and due back at half two and we'd ducked out to meet our fellas and how she was going to kill us if she found out.

Your man was still sour but he shut up at least and the girl smiled and said they were fine and that we'd better hurry up 'cos it was twenty past. So after more complaining out of him, and me saying, Thanks and are you sure, and the girl saying, We're grand, really, off you go, we're OK – we went off again. We walked at first but the minute we were out of their sight we started to run.

To be honest I'm a bit worried about running into those people like that, Clint, but I can't see how they'd ever have to tell anybody they'd seen us, can you? It could have been worse, I suppose – we could have run into a couple of cops. Then we'd have been rightly fucked, wouldn't we?

When we got back here to the warehouse we went straight in. Natalie'd left the door open for us – it's one of those doors that's part of a big metal gate. I sort of banged it when I was trying to put on the bolt and Kelly looked at me all cross like I'd done something bad, which made me mad with her then because fuck it, she was the one who'd made us go there in the first place.

Thinking like that made me remember your man with his brains splattered all over the window of his car and the minute I thought about that, I puked. No warning. Just like that. All over my shoes.

I looked at Kelly and all I could say was, Fuckfuckfuck, like a prayer or something over and over again. Then I puked again. And again. When I stopped we went across the yard and into the warehouse.

The minute I came in the door I could see Nat sitting on the floor by the gas heater and I don't know why but the sight of her made me crazy and I started saying all this stuff about how stupid she was to be sitting there and we could be anyone and why didn't she hide when she heard us outside?

Natalie just looked at me like I was mad – which I was – and told me to rise out of her and said that only the two of us'd make that much noise, so why would she be arsed hiding? Then the crazy feeling inside me disappeared all of a sudden and I was freezing and shivering like mad, so I went up close to the heater.

Natalie could see me properly then, in the light from the gas heater, and started being all nice to me and asking me what was wrong and why the fuck I looked like a ghost. I wanted to tell her about the dead guy but for some reason I couldn't make myself say it out, so I just said I'd puked. And then Kelly said it: Hendrick had his head blown off.

Just like that. That's exactly the way she said it. Part of me was glad to hear Kelly talking because she hadn't even made a sound since she'd screamed. But at the same time it was still weird hearing somebody saying it out loud – like it made it more real or something. Not that I think it wasn't real – ah fuck it, I don't know what I think. It was just weird, that's all.

Look, I think that's all I'm going to write for now. I'll tell you the rest later, OK?

Gina xxx

2. Monday 4 April, 9.45 a.m.

'Morning Rob,' Seán said to me as soon as I opened the heavy fire doors into the huge open-plan office area. Phones rang and someone laughed and a low hum of chat and work filled the air.

Seán was perched on a desk, chatting up a blonde innocent. He turned his dark head to say something to the girl and then stood up and stretched before loping towards me, leaving the girl dropping files in the background. I squinted a little against the sunlight that was streaming in through the big plate glass wall at the end of the office.

Three recruits passed. One bumped into me and blushed across his acne into the roots of his new haircut as he apologized. They were being led somewhere by Johnny Gannon, who I'd recently heard had applied for detective. Though he was startlingly baby-faced himself, I figured he must be older than he looked as he was married and had at least one baby. He winked at me and I winked back and tried to smile but it hurt my face.

'Do you think they even shave yet?' I asked Seán, as he fell into step beside me.

'High risk with those pimples,' he said.

I shook my head.

'You look like shit,' Seán said.

'Thanks,' I said.

'And you're late.'

'Really? I hadn't noticed, teacher. Has something big happened in the fifteen minutes since you got here?'

'As it happens the answer is yes. Billy Hendrick,' he said, stopping for effect. 'Shot dead.'

I stopped walking as well and looked at him. Shit.

Seán laughed at whatever expression was now on my face. 'Well, it didn't happen in the last fifteen minutes. It happened some time last night. I was called in but they couldn't get you. Anyway, O'Toole wants you as her right-hand man, I'd say. She just rang. She'll call back in a few minutes – I said you were in the jacks.'

'Thanks.' I reached into my pocket and took out my phone and turned it on. I'd forgotten that I'd turned it off while I was with Rita. 'I didn't think you were you on duty this weekend.'

'I wasn't, but that didn't stop anyone calling me at seven o'clock this morning.'

'Why does she want me?'

Seán shrugged. 'Because you're so special. Jesus, Rob – how am I supposed to know?'

Seán followed me into the tiny kitchenette, where I made myself a cup of tea. I groggily tried to get my head into work mode as I squeezed the last drop out of the teabag with the back of a spoon. Who exactly was Billy Hendrick? It felt as if I should recognize his name but somehow I didn't. It'd been a bad night. I'd had hardly any proper sleep.

'Do you want anything?' I asked Seán.

He waved a cup he was holding at me. 'Already have coffee on the go. Anyway, your man – Hendrick – was shot in the head.'

'Where?' I said, leading the way back through the noisy open-plan office.

'In the head. I just told you,' Seán said, grinning as he followed.

I gave him the finger.

He smiled. 'In his car, a Lexus – ruined now. Brains everywhere.'

'Jesus, Seán, please. It's nine o'clock in the morning.'

'Nine forty-five.'

'So who is he? Do I know him?'

'Maybe,' Seán said. 'He's a solicitor.'

'Alan Hendrick? I thought you just said his name was Billy.'

'The deceased is Billy Hendrick – he's Alan's brother.'

'That's familiar all right – I mean I know Alan unfortunately but I'm not sure I ever met his brother,' I said, opening the door of my office. Seán followed me in.

'Billy was in practice by himself for years. You probably never ran into him. He was never as successful as Alan. Did a lot of ambulance chasing. He only joined forces with his brother a few years ago. Poor old Alan was in the market for help – he's run off his feet.'

'Well, I suppose that's what you get when you represent every low-life in town.'

'Bit of a boom, all right,' Seán said, sitting down and sticking an unlit cigarette into his mouth. 'It's possible that you never came across Billy because he didn't do much criminal work – compensation cases and other bits and bobs. Alan does the hard cases. He probably brought Billy in to free him up for his more important work of defending bollockses.'

The telephone on my desk rang. I picked it up.

'Rob, it's the Super – for you.'

'Thanks, Gloria.'

There was an odd banging noise as Gloria put the call through.

'Rob?'

'Superintendent, good morning, how are you?'

A brief pause on the other end of the line was followed by a sharp cough.

'I'm fine, thanks. I suppose you've heard by now?'

'Yes, yes, I heard. Sorry you couldn't reach me. I didn't realize my phone was turned off.'

Another pause and I imagined Sharon O'Toole's face as she tried not to reprimand me for not being available when I was actually off duty. Tough shit, Sharon.

I didn't say a word – just dropped my head and massaged the back of my aching neck. When I looked up Seán was grinning at me and pretending to smoke his unlit cigarette.

'OK, well, no time to waste, so, I suppose. You know as much as I do if Detective Sergeant Ryan has filled you in – I presume he has?'

'Yes, yes he has.'

'Good. Well, the Bureau are already here – or at least they should be at the scene by now and though Dublin will be sending more people down I want you and Seán to take charge from the start, really.'

'That's fine.'

She let out a long sigh. 'Look, Rob, I don't know how any of this is going to shake out, but if we don't mark out our territory from the start then I have a bad feeling that we'll be taking orders from Harcourt Street.'

'Don't worry, it'll be grand. Seán and I are on our way to the scene now.'

'Good,' she said, her voice reconstituting into its more formal mode. 'I have every confidence in you.'

'Thanks.'

'I'm due at a meeting with the Chief Superintendent in ten minutes. Somehow the papers already have a hold of the story so we might have to have a press conference later. I'll want you both there if that happens.'

'No problem.'

'OK, great. You assemble the rest of the local team and I'll talk to you in a while.'

And then she was gone. My head was really starting to hurt. I fished two paracetamol from my desk drawer and swallowed them with a mouthful of tea.

'How the hell is Sharon, anyway?' Seán asked, tipping back his chair with his feet on my desk.

'Frazzled.' I drank another mouthful of tea. 'The papers are on to her office already.'

Seán rolled his eyes. 'High-profile family.'

I groaned. 'Speaking of which, do we need to contact them?' I was dreading the thought. I knew what it was like to be on the receiving end of that particular visit.

Seán shook his head. 'I've done that already. Wife is away, mother's in a nursing home, Alan is the only other family, so I went round to see him. I was just back when you came in.'

'How did he take it?'

Seán shrugged. 'Hard.'

'Natural enough. How were we alerted?'

'A couple on their way home found the car under a lamp-post in Morris Street.'

'Where is that?'

'Up near the park, near the Mechanics Institute – one of those small, narrow streets.' Seán paused to pretend he was smoking. 'Anyway, they rang it in about half four. Conor Vaughan was on. He rang me to come in and then O'Toole called me as well but I was already on the way. They called you as well – but I told you all of that.'

'Did you call Dublin?'

He shook his head. 'O'Toole did it herself.'

I nodded. 'Well, the Technical Bureau are already here.'

'That was fast – which was why she made the phone call herself, I suppose. Get the boot in early.'

'Anyway, keep going. How did the couple who found him notice that there was something wrong?'

'The passenger door was open and there was loud music.'

'Music?'

Seán nodded and looked at his notes. 'That's what they said. Máirín Healy is the woman and your man – Gerry O'Sullivan is his name – loves Pink Floyd and there was a Pink Floyd CD playing in the car and the passenger door was open. So they had a look.'

'I bet they're sorry,' I said, trying not to think about it.

Seán grinned. 'Maybe somebody shot him for listening to Pink Floyd – I can see that.'

'Very funny,' I said, before I drank the rest of my tea in one long gulp. I hadn't woken at all until after eight so I'd only had enough time to have a quick shower and shave when I got home. 'We need to have a think about the team.'

'Already done.' He tossed me a page of scribbled names. I read through it. They all looked fine to me.

'The powers that be will probably send in people from the NBCI to help,' I said.

Seán grimaced; he could barely tolerate the Technical Bureau guys. I knew the prospect of working with a sizeable contingent of importees from the National Bureau of Criminal Investigation would set his teeth on edge.

'It'll be OK,' he said.

I nodded in surprise.

'We'll outnumber them.'

'That's not what I meant,' I said.

'I know.'

I read the list again but couldn't think of any way to add

to it. I slid it across the desk to him. 'O'Toole will want to approve the list. Fax it to her,' I said.

'Already done.'

'Arrogant bastard.'

He shrugged.

'I'm starving,' I said, having a quick flick through a couple of notes that'd been left on my desk. Nothing else important.

'We can get one of those breakfast rolls on the way to the crime scene,' Seán said.

'Heart-attack food,' I said.

'It'll hardly kill you this once,' Seán said, throwing me a set of keys. 'You drive – I hurt my wrist playing badminton last night.'

I should have known better than to eat a greasy breakfast roll on the way to seeing Billy Hendrick's dead body. As soon as we arrived at the crime scene I could feel that the combination of exhaustion and murder and black pudding in a roll was about to take me down. Even my knees felt funny – which hadn't happened to me since I was a raw recruit at my first murder.

I tried taking loads of deep breaths. That helped a bit. I was really beginning to come to the conclusion that I wasn't cut out for this work. Especially in the past year. And now it looked as if I was going backwards. Christ. I'd definitely have to rethink my life.

A large area surrounding Billy Hendrick's silver Lexus was cordoned off and the whole place was swarming with people. A distinctive, white Garda Technical Bureau van was parked to the side and gloved and suited forensic specialists moved back and forth inside the cordon.

A cross section of officers from the Bureau in Dublin were present. Some I recognized, some I'd never seen before. But as I watched them work I could see that all the various departments were well represented – ballistics, fingerprinting, photography, mapping. There was no doubling up at this scene. No local police collecting evidence. That told its own tale.

Seán walked off and I stood where I was, hoping that it looked as though I was doing something useful. But all I was really doing was observing the activity around me.

Crime-scene technicians combing for evidence, chatting as they worked about houses and holidays and children and who was seeing who. Journalists arriving in their cars with their photographers. Casual passers-by *en route* to work, eyeing the scene as they hurried past. Uniformed police officers and onlookers, crowded together like partners on the periphery outside the crime-scene tape. It struck me as weird that the whole area was full of life – except for the man in the car, of course.

I hate crime scenes. A strange truth for a detective who makes his living out of them. It isn't the gore – not that I like it – but nobody except for the very hardened or the very strange likes the blood and guts. It's something about what it represents. The proof of something I don't want to believe about the human race.

Seán finished speaking to the sergeant in charge and waved at me to follow him inside the cordon. Nothing ever seems to knock a stir out of Seán. He walked ahead of me, asking questions of everyone he passed. As I came closer to the car I could feel the food dancing in my stomach. I swallowed hard and took more deep breaths and then forced myself to look inside.

Billy Hendrick was still in his car. He was slumped sideways, head leaning against the shattered driver's door window, eyes open to the dashboard as if he was checking the time or his speed. The sun was glinting off a pen in the pocket of his grey jacket and a halo of blood fanned out behind his head. The inside of the car smelled of Hugo Boss aftershave and something else I couldn't place. There was a red child's pencil case on the floor in front of the back seat, a deep burgundy leather briefcase on the back seat itself and behind it what looked like a silver hip flask.

I forced myself to bring my attention back to the victim. The entry wound was tidy, black and stellate against his grey face, most of the gore had been saved for the exit. The black star on his left temple suggested that it was most likely a contact wound. Somebody had put the gun against Billy Hendrick's temple, pulled the trigger and blown his brains out. It was intimate.

As I forced myself to keep my attention on Billy Hendrick's dead body, I noticed his penis protruding from his open fly. It was very out of place with the rest of the besuited businessman picture but it possibly explained what had happened.

Maybe one of the local girls had been plying her trade and her pimp had decided to hold up the client. Or maybe his girl hadn't been paying him his share as she should. Trying to cheat him and he wasn't having it. Something ordinary and seedy like that. The pimp follows her and he tries to rob them. Billy Hendrick objects and the pimp shoots him.

Simple and totally wasteful. Most crime is impulsive and thoughtless and in the moment, so it was likely this one wouldn't be any different. Billy should have stumped up for a hotel room – it would probably have been a bit safer. I looked at his dead body again and at the darkened blood behind his head, and the undigested breakfast roll churned.

'No broken glass, no sign of forced entry to the car,' Seán said beside me. I was glad of the excuse to turn away.

'Exactly what I was just thinking,' I said, stepping back from the car to stand beside him. We made our way through the increasing congestion of police and ducked under the blue and white plastic tape.

'Did you notice that he was caught with his trousers down?'

'Well, open, as opposed to down.'

Seán sighed. 'You're so picky. All I'm saying is that he was obviously not sitting in his car waiting for his mother to come out of Mass.'

I laughed.

Seán grinned. 'And considering the open trousers etc. I can think of a few little fuckers who might have done something like this. Kenny Hogan, for example.'

'He's in jail,' I said. 'He was caught in that big drugs bust last month.'

'Well, well, well – didn't know Kenny was expanding the business. But anyway, you know what I mean: he's not the only one capable of something like this.'

'I know. I can think of a few candidates myself. We'll round them up and have a word.'

Neither of us spoke for a few seconds as we watched Tommy O'Malley – one of the uniformed Guards on the periphery – reassuring a slightly hysterical old lady who'd just come out of one of the small terraced houses near by. He said something to the woman and she beckoned to another old lady. Even from the distance it was possible to see that whatever Tommy was saying, the old women were actually being reassured.

'If the press saw that bit of taking care of the community,

do you think we might get some positive publicity for once?' Seán asked.

'No, probably not. Anyway, any theories about the actual shooting?'

Seán nodded. 'Yeah, either they opened the door and leaned in and blew his brains out or the murderer was already sitting in the passenger seat talking to him. The lads agree that either is possible,' Seán said, as we leaned back against a low, red-brick wall and surveyed the scene. Dark clouds were gathering overhead and a breeze that smelled of rain started up.

A tall, thin man with dark hair wearing blue jeans and a khaki parka ducked under the tape. He waved at us. We waved back. Keith Smith, an assistant pathologist. Keith moved around the car and then spoke to one of the uni-formed Guards standing near by.

He pointed as an ambulance pulled up outside the cordon. The Technical Bureau could smell the rain as well as I could and they were anxious to finish before any more evidence was destroyed.

Seán and I watched in silence.

'I wonder what happened?' I said eventually.

Seán shrugged. 'Who knows?'

'One way or another he's definitely dead,' I said.

'No doubt about that,' Seán said, pulling a packet of cigarettes from his pocket and lighting one. 'No fucking doubt about that.'

It was mid-afternoon before Alan Hendrick arrived in my office. I'd expected him earlier. Seán had gone to get some lunch. I was still struggling to digest my breakfast roll.

Alan Hendrick was a tall man, fiftyish, dark hair turning grey in narrow bands, clean shaven, handsome face, regular white teeth, expensive suit and a look of contempt in his eyes. Everybody in the station – no, everybody who worked in law enforcement in the region – hated him.

The very sight of him made you remember all the cases he'd won. All the hours and hours and hours of work wasted in collecting evidence against dangerous bastards who were destined to walk free because they had the money to employ him.

That Monday morning, though, I came closer to feeling sorry for him than was ever going to happen again.

'You're in charge of this case?' he said as he walked into my office unannounced.

'Good morning, Mr Hendrick. How may I help you?'

'I would have expected an incident room to have been set up by now. This is a very serious crime.'

'Everything is being set up as we speak,' I said, struggling past the impulse to tell him what to do with himself.

Alan Hendrick paused as if he was thinking. His face was transparent for once and I could see the pain as if it was a cobweb strung over him. I knew what that was like.

'I'm very sorry about your brother,' I said.

He frowned and his eyes widened; then he coughed and pulled a chair over to my desk.

'Can I sit down?' he said, sitting down immediately.

'Help yourself. What can I do for you?'

He sat back in his chair. His face had changed back to its shellacked self. 'My brother was murdered.'

I nodded.

'Well?' he said. 'What the hell are you people doing about it?'

I sat back in my chair as well, my sympathy evaporating. 'Your brother was shot some time in the early hours of this morning. His body has only recently been removed from the crime scene.'

'I know. I've just identified him.' Alan Hendrick fiddled with the edge of his tie and I felt sorry for him all over again. 'His wife and son are still away – on their way home from Spain – so I went to the morgue.'

His face was almost as grey as his brother's and his eyes unfocused as he remembered what he'd seen. I knew he'd never forget it.

'Look, go home,' I said. 'We'll be in touch as soon as we know anything.'

'No. I want to know what's happening.'

Not that it'll change anything, I thought, but I didn't say it. I knew what that was like as well. That sort of desperate hope that information would somehow fill the huge hole gouged inside you.

'Just the normal routine at the minute,' I said. 'Pathology, crime scene investigation and the usual search for witnesses – who saw him last and so on. We're doing a door-to-door in the area just in case any of the neighbours saw or heard anything that'd help.'

'And what have you found out so far?'

'Not much. Your brother was shot at close range either by a person sitting in the vehicle with him or somebody who opened the door and leaned in.'

'I think I could have figured that out myself.' Alan Hendrick stared at me as he spoke and I watched as the pain on his face dissolved once again, allowing his solicitor's mask to reappear. 'The issue about his trousers being open . . .' His voice tailed off and he swallowed hard. 'I don't want that piece of information in the papers – there's no need for it.'

'I agree.'

'They'll have a field day and he has a wife and child.'

I nodded. 'As I said, I agree.'

'So you're willing to promise me that nobody will say anything to the press?'

'Look, Mr Hendrick – Alan – this has been a difficult day for you and I know you're looking for answers. I promise you as soon as we have any further information . . .'

'Forget that.' He leaned forward, eyes bright with pain and fear and anger. 'I want . . .' he tapped the desk in time to his words. 'I want you now – this minute – to assure me that this private information won't get into the public domain. Because I'm warning you . . .'

The door of my office flew open as if it'd been caught in a gust of wind and a thin, blonde woman stood in the doorway. We both looked at her as she grabbed the hand of a small dark-haired boy dressed in red shorts and a white T-shirt who was standing beside her.

'Detective Inspector O'Connell?' she said, walking straight towards me, the small boy trailing like an appendage. Her eyes were bright blue and set far apart and there was a streak of mascara across her right cheekbone.

Alan Hendrick jumped out of his chair. 'Caroline!'

She stopped and looked at him and it was obvious that she somehow hadn't noticed him before. As she looked up at him her eyes filled with tears until one overflowed down her face, following the line of the mascara streak to her chin. I realized she must be the wife of the deceased.

Caroline Hendrick, née Farrell, according to the information I'd read just before her brother-in-law had arrived. Thirty-five-year-old ex-model, now a wedding planner – whatever that was. Youngest of three children. Originally from Ennis. Ten years younger than her dead husband.

And Dylan. Dylan William Hendrick. Seven years old. Only son of Caroline and Billy Hendrick. Just finishing first class in the multi-denominational Limerick School Project.

Alan Hendrick put his arms around his sister-in-law and pulled her close to his tailored chest. The small boy looked at me. I smiled but he didn't smile back. Why would he? He'd probably been told that his dad was dead.

Hendrick stroked Caroline's head as she cried and looked down at the child.

'I can swim without armbands now, Alan,' the boy said, solemnly.

'That's great news,' Hendrick said as he released his sister-in-law and bent down to pick up the small boy. 'I bet you're a brilliant swimmer.'

The child nodded and settled himself in against his uncle. Caroline blew her nose and sat down in the chair her brother-in-law had vacated. Hendrick held the child high as if he was weightless and the boy's arms encircled his neck.

'Alan . . . identified him?' she said, biting her lip and looking at Hendrick and me. We both nodded. She sniffed and looked upwards and rubbed her flattened palms across her cropped blonde hair. I wished Seán would get back. He was a lot better at this kind of thing than me.

I'd been full of admiration for Gerry Hourigan, who'd had the job of telling me about Rita. Even as he was telling me what had happened I'd been impressed by how well he managed it – and me. I wasn't ever going to be as good as that at dealing with distressed relatives.

Caroline Hendrick looked up at her brother-in-law. 'Can you do me a favour, Alan?'

He nodded.

'Buy Dylan an ice-cream?' she said.

Hendrick looked confused but nodded his agreement. Dylan began bouncing in his arms and his uncle hugged him and laughed and they left the room. As soon as the door closed Caroline Hendrick turned to look at me.

'Do you know who killed my husband?'

'Mrs Hendrick,' I began, 'it's only been a short time since your husband's body –'

'Well, I do,' she said, her calm voice cutting across mine. 'I know exactly who killed my husband.'

3. Monday 4 April

Hi Clint,

I didn't get a chance to write again until now. I told you the stuff – about your man being shot and all last night.

Jesus, it was rough here for a while after we came back. Kelly said it out about him being shot – like I told you – and Natalie was pure weird. First she started laughing and stuff like she thought we might be messing or something. By then I was losing it. I was never so cold in my life, shivering all the time like a kid who'd been swimming. Almost sitting into the gas heater. Useless yoke. I could smell it burning my clothes but it didn't make me any warmer.

Anyway, then Natalie wanted to know who killed him and I said, How the fuck should we know, and Kelly said nothing. Just stared into space. And then it hit me. Where'd Kelly been all night before she came back and asked us to go with her?

I tried to see if there was anything on her face that'd tell me what was going on, but there wasn't. She doesn't have a face, that one – it's more like a mask. Then Natalie started saying this stuff about the dead guy being connected to us and asking Kelly if she'd told anyone she was meeting him. And Kelly just said no. And that was all. And then the three of us stood there for ages – like dummies – around that heater, just staring at those orange and blue flames like they were the most interesting things we ever saw.

After a while I started to feel better and I closed my eyes

but I straightaway could see your man with his exploded head so I opened them fast enough. And then before I knew it I started saying stuff to Kelly. It was like somebody else was talking but it was really me. Did that ever happen to you?

I said all this stuff about maybe she had some idea who might have killed him and did she have any ideas and shit? I mean, when you think about it she's the only one who knew him after all, isn't she?

Anyway, I just kept on with vague shit like that. I mean, I didn't say straight out, Oh Kelly, did you shoot your man? But it was sort of there all the same 'cos I couldn't stop thinking it.

For ages she said nothing and I couldn't stop talking then, 'cos I was – I don't know – fucking nervous or something. Especially because I kept thinking maybe it was her, maybe it was her, maybe it was her. But then she started talking a bit. And it stopped the shit going round in my head.

She said it could have been anyone who shot him because he was such a scumbag. Natalie started laughing when she said that and she said she thought he was a solicitor and I said the same thing and Kelly just kept looking at the heater and she said it again: He was a scumbag. He's no loss – except for our money.

We didn't say anything for ages again after that but at least the stuff had stopped in my head and then Natalie claps her hands together – like a teacher – and says, Ah fuck it, we'll think of something else.

Just like that.

And then we just all went off to bed.

Anyway, after all that I went to sleep, believe it or not – slept like a baby. But as soon as I woke up I started worrying in case the police thought we'd shot Billy Hendrick.

I told you about the people we knocked over, didn't I? Well, between worrying about them saying something to the Guards and thinking that maybe somebody knew he was meeting us or he'd told someone or something, it was going round and round in my head like a chairoplane.

That and trying to stop my head from wondering if Kelly did it.

So I called Tony and told him what had happened. He was great and said, Oh don't worry, Gina, and calm down and just put it out of your head and stop worrying. Nobody'll think ye were involved. Why would they?

So I tried to stop thinking about it. Worrying's a waste of time and anyway when I made myself calm down and think about it properly I was sure nobody knew we were even anywhere near where your man was killed.

I don't know, Clint, but like I'm sorry he's dead and all but maybe it's not such a bad thing. Give the cops something to think about instead of us.

Look, someone wants me. I'll talk to you in a while.

Gina xxx

4. Tuesday 5 April

The last thing I did before I went off duty on Tuesday was look over all the reports relating to the Hendrick case. It'd been a long, hard day. Everything about the case was like walking through quicksand. Though I went through the usual motions, I was really losing confidence in my having the extra energy it'd take to push this particular boulder up the hill.

That day we'd had our first real morning conference insofar as we'd had a full meeting, with all the Hendrick investigation team assembled. The good, the bad and the ugly, as Seán called them.

The energy at the meeting was nervous. We all knew it was a big case. Billy Hendrick wasn't just any old low-life pulled out of the Shannon or killed in a knife fight. And the truth was it was nothing to do with him or the value of his life and everything to do with the political power of those he'd left behind.

At the press conference the afternoon before our Superintendent Sharon O'Toole had arrived with a new hairdo and make-up that even I could see had been applied by a professional. It was the first big murder case that had come along since she'd been appointed a year before. It was both an opportunity for her to shine and equally an opportunity for her to fall on her arse. And she knew it.

Sharon was a large, imposing blonde woman in her early fifties with a cushiony bosom and the hands of someone who'd cuffed more than one little fucker. The press conference was held in the ballroom of an old city-centre hotel.

Sharon could have picked a plusher hotel – this was probably the last unrenovated hotel in town. But the slightly battered, ex-tea-dance environment fitted in with her presentation of herself as a woman of the people. Getting down and dirty in the inner city. If that's what you could call the small collection of faded Georgian buildings and the statue of Daniel O'Connell that constitute Limerick's inner city.

The ballroom was too big for the press conference, so it was mostly empty. The standard-issue long white-tableclothed table across the top of the room created an island in the centre of the maple dance floor with maybe fifty plastic bucket chairs ranged in front of it. Most of the chairs were already full.

'Alan Hendrick,' Seán muttered as we made our way past the rows of local and national journalists already seated. We waved at the ones we knew.

'He probably thinks we all hate him so much we won't bother looking for his brother's killer unless he puts on the pressure,' I muttered as we took our seats towards the end of the long table. Seán nodded.

Sharon and her people were already seated. She motioned to us to sit closer and we did as instructed. I was hoping she wasn't planning to have me speak. I didn't think she would – Sharon didn't like to share the limelight much – but you never knew what she might think looked best.

Almost as soon as we were seated the press conference began.

'It falls to me today,' Sharon began, standing up to address the audience, 'to give you the latest details of the investigation into the tragic death – in suspicious circumstances – of one of Limerick's leading citizens, William Hendrick.'

The whole room fell silent as she spoke and, knowing how terrified she probably was, I was very impressed by her impersonation of a calm and competent Garda Super-intendent. She made her statement with only minimal glances at her notes and after promising to rid our city of scumbags she asked for questions. The journalists began asking their questions and she fielded every one with just the right balance of gravitas and flirtation. And soon it was clear that they were all on her side and Sharon O'Toole was in complete command of the room.

As she spoke, Seán and I sat there looking serious. We nodded to the audience as she introduced us but other than that we let her do all the work. When the press conference was over, the room erupted into chatter.

Sharon stood up immediately and came straight towards us.

'Rob,' she said, shaking my hand firmly as she simul-taneously held my elbow. 'Good job. Good job. We'll get the bastards who did this, don't worry. All we have to do now is keep the lid on that embarrassing bit of evidence with the . . . am . . . trousers and all.'

I smiled and said nothing. There were two chances of that.

Sharon had already moved on to Seán. He tried his woman-killing under-the-eyebrows glance and smile as they shook hands but Sharon was impervious. As soon as she had finished with us she had to leave to attend some other important meeting. Two minutes after she was gone, we took the opportunity to get out of there ourselves.

'Dyke,' Seán said as we trotted down the front steps of the hotel into the spring evening.

I grinned. 'I don't think so,' I said. 'At least that's not what I've heard about her. She's just not a fucking eejit like all the other women you meet.'

'Ha ha,' he said, lighting a cigarette as we got into our car and drove back to work.

*

Billy Hendrick's murder was, unsurprisingly, all over the media next day. So at our first conference, as well as assembled detectives and files and photographs and reports piled high on the long meeting table, there was a stack of newspapers. I rubbed my temples when I saw them – I hated high-profile cases. It was hard enough doing the job without having to do it under an unfriendly – and often inaccurate – microscope.

I started the meeting and after a couple of minutes we all began to forget the surrounding hoo-ha as routine took over.

Most of the people there were local and knew each other, but as expected there was a larger than usual contingent from Dublin. This was definitely a double-edged sword. On the one hand, these were experienced and able detectives who could greatly aid an investigation. On the other, there was Seán like a terrier defending his patch and the odd NBCI person inclined to throw his or her capital-city weight around.

The meeting started and I summarized the great big nothing we had so far.

'OK,' I said. 'This is what we have. Nobody living in the area saw or heard anything the night of the murder.'

I paused just in case somebody had something new. Seán stuck his pencil in his mouth and winked at me. I looked down at my notes.

'OK. We know that his wife spoke to him the night before he was killed and called him a number of times the night of the murder, leaving two messages on both his mobile and landline. Did we get a copy of her mobile bill to verify this?'

Amy O'Brien, a newly hatched detective with serious brown eyes and a slight lisp, slid the bill towards me.

'Thanks, Amy. All right. Now, we know he was in Finn's pub from three to six in the afternoon – drank quite a bit and watched a rugby match on TV. We know he left – half cut – just after six and then . . . we have no idea where he spent his time between then and the time of his death.'

I searched through my folder to find the forensic report I'd received just before the meeting. 'The only fingerprints in the car were those of the victim, his wife and his son. There was an earprint on the window, but that is now confirmed as also belonging to the victim. The bullet, re-covered at the scene, was a nine mill, probably from a Beretta but the jury's still out on that. Don't you have some other reports, Seán?'

Seán nodded. 'Yeah. OK, you probably know this but there was some evidence in the car of back-spatter from the shot, so whoever killed him has blood on their hands in every sense.'

Everybody smiled as Seán paused and sighed loudly. 'But that's not much good to us at the minute unless we find a potential shooter. Billy Hendrick was shot at close range – very close range – the gun being put to his temple before it was discharged. As a result there is a stellate tear and burned and unburned gunpowder tattooing around the entry point.' Seán sat back in his chair and folded his arms.

'That it?' I asked.

He nodded.

'OK. Johnny Quigley and Paul "Monkey" Hannon?' I asked Hugh Kelly, reviewing the list of tasks in front of me. According to my notes, Hugh'd had the job of interviewing two of our favourite pimps. Hugh sat up straight in his chair, his young face clean-shaven and bright. I remembered vaguely being like that during my two-year probationary period before I became a fully fledged detective. Rita'd been delighted when I'd been made a detective. I'd bet Hugh's young pregnant wife was just as delighted.

I rubbed my face to bring my attention back to the matter at hand.

'Well . . . OK, both Johnny and Monkey have alibis for Sunday night,' Hugh said.

'There's a surprise,' Seán said. Everybody laughed. Hugh looked slightly embarrassed.

'Go on, Hugh,' I said.

'They were together at an Eminem gig in Dublin,' he said, shuffling through the paper on the desk in front of him. 'They have the tickets.' He pulled two ticket stubs from a folder.

'Could belong to anybody,' Freddie Truby, an NBCI importee said. Freddie had never worked in Limerick before but I knew him from when I was stationed in Dublin. Freddie could be a bit of a pain but actually wasn't a bad guy underneath it all. His main problem was that he always wore a dark suit, which made him look more like an FBI agent than an Irish cop. That made it a little hard to fit in.

Hugh looked a bit flustered. 'Monkey said he bought them with his credit card, though. I checked. And he did.'

Freddie Truby shrugged and turned his palms upwards.

I could sense Seán's hackles rising and knew I'd better get in fast before he did.

'OK, good work, Hugh. Look, hang on to those tickets – we'll keep an eye on the two boyos for a while, I think.'

Hugh nodded, sitting back in his seat.

Denise Simmons from the Bureau went next. I introduced her again to the room, though some people already knew her. It was Denise's doubtful privilege to report back on Billy Hendrick's post mortem. Denise was small and blonde and wore a lot of make-up. Seán called her the Hairdresser behind her back. He wasn't wrong: she looked more like a hairdresser than a police officer who specialized in forensics. But maybe it was the same thing, when you thought about it. All that attention to detail. Whatever the case, Denise was a meticulous and careful crime-scene analyst and I was glad to have her there.

'William Hendrick. Well-nourished male, 1.87 metres in height. Weight 93.64 kilos. Forty-six years and two months old. Post mortem performed by John Murphy, assistant state pathologist at the Limerick Regional Hospital, yesterday, 4 April, at 3.00 p.m. . . .'

I tuned out momentarily as she read off the boring details of who was there and who assisted, etc. I'd heard it all once too often. Denise's report was long and detailed and I forced myself to concentrate as she began to describe Billy Hendrick's injuries.

Not that the report told us much that we could use.

'. . . the bullet entered the frontal lobe through his left temple, travelled across his brain exiting via his right frontal lobe and creating a bevelled exit wound approximately one centimetre in diameter,' Denise read from her notebook. 'The projectile therefore passed through both hemispheres of the brain, causing both extensive ventricular damage and massive haemorrhaging due to the rupture of both carotid arteries. This resulted – most likely – in his almost immediate death.'

Seán slid a note towards me. 'Cause of death: a bullet in the head.'

I crumpled the piece of paper and glared at him. He grinned.

Denise paused to flick through her notes and Seán leaned forward, smiling seductively at her.

'May I add to this?' he asked her as if he meant it. Denise

looked startled. 'Well, I was at the PM as well,' he continued, without waiting for an answer. Everybody looked at him and he smiled laconically. Seán had wanted to attend the post mortem, the gory bastard. I'd been happy to pass and also happy to have someone local there along with the Dublin people as well, if I'm honest.

He flicked through his notebook and cleared his throat. 'OK, hang on a minute – let's see, here it is. William Hendrick, aged forty-six . . . well-nourished – I think myself over-nourished – male . . .'

Somebody laughed I glared at them and him. We'd be there all day if Seán decided to perform.

He grinned at his audience. 'OK, OK. Denise told you all the details of the PM, the injury and all that boring stuff and there isn't really anything else except . . .' He paused again. I felt like thumping him. 'Except that the Doc says that in his opinion Mr Hendrick hadn't had sex just before he died.'

Everybody was suddenly paying attention. I looked at Denise, who was flustered by Seán's sudden hijacking of her report. Her Bureau companion, Jason Devlin, sat forward in his seat.

'That's true,' he said. 'Very little semen on his clothes, nothing else – no vaginal fluid, etc. No evidence that he'd ejaculated.'

I sat back in my seat. That was certainly news to me. The level of my surprise told me that I'd really been working on the premise that Billy Hendrick had had a bit of bad luck with a prostitute and her – or his – pimp. I was a bit thrown – not so much by the information as by my own lazy assumption. That wasn't like me. Or at least I didn't like to think it was like me. But my head was just so full of other stuff nowadays it was probably only a matter of time before it took over completely. Still, I hadn't realized I was so far off my game.

I recovered my composure and we discussed the jobs still to be done. Apart from Freddie Truby, the other three NBCI detectives in attendance had remained silent for most of the meeting. They were obviously judging the lie of the land and not just in relation to the case. I decided it was time to make use of their skills as we divvied up the work.

Janice Long – a willowy redhead with intelligent green eyes, with whom I'd worked a number of times in the past – readily agreed when I asked her and Freddie to interview half of the Hendrick brothers' extensive client list. Seán and I were going to take the other half.

Denise and Jason agreed to chase up all the forensic stuff.

The other two NBCI detectives, Tommy Hogan and Jim O'Reilly – both Dublin boys in their early thirties and both creating a stir in the station with their designer stubble and bachelorhood – I sent along with Hugh Kelly to canvass everybody they could find who knew Billy Hendrick. Especially if they'd seen him in the twenty-four hours before his death. Basically their brief was just to search for anything that might give us some small clue as to why Billy Hendrick had been murdered. And so on.

After everybody had been assigned work, I drew the meeting to a close. But even as I talked and laughed and divvied up the work, inside me was a new raw place born of my lack of real engagement with the case. Billy Hendrick might have been a bit of a prick but he was still a human being – and someone had murdered him. There was a time when that was motivation enough for me. Not any more, it seemed.

5. Tuesday 5 April

Hi Clint –

I'm back. I didn't get a chance to write any more yesterday. The last thing I was telling you was about all the worrying, wasn't it? Anyway, there I was, trying not to worry, but it was fucking impossible. Nat was worried as well, I could see that, but she's better than me at putting things out of her head.

I don't know about Kelly because Kelly said nothing about any of it. Just kind of haunted the place, smoking fags and not talking.

She has a phone, by the way – did I tell you that? I don't know where she got it but it's one of the things that makes me think she's up to something. I asked her where she got it and she said she bought it off a fella Sunday when she was out – before we found the dead guy.

Natalie went mad when she heard that and said, Oh great, now people know we're out of jail, blah blah blah – the usual. Kelly said nothing – also the usual. So now we have two phones – the one Tony gave us and Kelly's. Though maybe not. What's ours is hers and what's hers is her own.

Like Natalie's vodka. Another big fucking fight. She took Natalie's vodka. Never asked her or nothing – just took it and drank most of it. We never even noticed – it didn't seem to make her drunk or anything or we'd have noticed, wouldn't we? I only found out about it when I went looking for it myself.

You know me. I don't bother mostly but like I said

already, I couldn't get the picture of that dead guy out of my head again last night and I was worrying away about everything, no matter how hard I tried not to. So I decided to have a couple of drinks to see if it'd help. But when I went for the bottle of vodka it was almost empty.

Natalie went ape-shit. Said she'd only had a couple of mouthfuls so it had to be Kelly if it wasn't me – and it wasn't. Sometimes I think she just wants to go on about Kelly – any excuse will do – so I gave up talking to her and poured what was left of the vodka into a mug and drank it. It might as well have been water for all the good it did. I'd say I'd have needed at least a full bottle of vodka to make me feel any better.

I got into bed and turned on the radio to listen to the news. Did I tell you about the radio? Tony gave it to us on Friday when we were leaving the upstairs of his shop. At the time I didn't want to take it – it was just like another thing to drag with us if we had to run again. But Natalie acted all excited when she saw it and said it might come in handy when we were bored. Then she kissed Tony and said he was an angel as well as being a bit of a ride and that he looked like George Clooney and did he know that? It was really funny – you'd have burst your arse laughing at him, Clint. He blushed pure red – the gay old fart!

Anyway, there was nothing on the news about us all day yesterday or even last night and even though I'd been dreading it I was kind of disappointed, believe it or not. I know that's mad but the truth was I'd sort of got a thrill when I heard it on the radio on Friday night about our escape and all that. I'd called the others to hear it. Kelly roared laughing when it was over. Three twenty-one-year-old women, she said in the same voice as your woman on the news – Kelly's fabulous at imitating people. She was known for it in jail.

Anyway, there she is doing the posh radio voice and then

she starts walking up and down the warehouse in front of us like a model. Making posing faces and acting the fool and Natalie and me are at her to sit down and shut up but it was funny and we were laughing really. So then she starts on at us to get up with her and walk and we're all, Fuck off, Kelly, but she's on a bit of a roll and she pulls us up and then the three of us are walking up and down like mad models and Kelly's at it again.

Three twenty-one-year-old women escaped from the custody of their prison officers today, she said in the radio voice. *In a dramatic escape* – walk faster, Nat, that's it. *The three female prisoners, who were on their way back to prison from a beautician's course they were attending, managed to get away from the officers in charge.*

She linked arms with us and the three of us were walking faster and faster and swinging round and I was laughing so hard I couldn't breathe. It was like a ceilidh or a mad game at school or something – us walking faster and faster and faster in this circle until we just kinked with laughing and fell down on the ground, with Nat screaming 'cos she'd wet her knickers.

After a few minutes Kelly leans over towards me and shoves an invisible microphone in front of my face and asks me how it feels to be famous. I started laughing and saying we weren't famous yet 'cos they didn't even use our names. We were just young women. Female prisoners. Anybody. Nobody.

But I spoke too soon. Saturday morning on the eight o'clock news they gave out our names. I was sorry I'd said it then, imagining the Guards up at Ma's asking her questions and all that shit. Not like I thought the Guards needed to hear our names on the radio but me hearing them on the radio made it real or something – everything seems to be only half real to me at the moment, doesn't it?

40

Writing things down is funny. When you say stuff it disappears and you can't remember it but when you write it there it is and you can't forget it. And I can see that I keep saying something makes something else real like it wasn't already or something – ah, fuck it, you know what I mean.

Anyway, when I woke up at six o'clock this morning I forgot for one minute where I was. Did that ever happen to you? I bet it did. It's good, isn't it, for that few seconds and then it's shit when you remember all the stuff. I pulled my sleeping bag over my head and tried to go back to sleep for a while because it's a very long day when you're hanging around doing nothing. But I couldn't. The picture of Billy Hendrick's dead body was back and anyway the floor was too hard to get comfortable.

I heard Natalie getting up and looked out from the sleeping bag and asked her to stick on the kettle. She just started laughing, a fag in her gob as usual, and told me to fuck off – she was going to make a piss. Then she put on her shoes and her fleecy jacket and ran down the warehouse.

Did I tell you about the jacks in this place? Oh God, it stinks. You think after three days I'd be getting used to the smell but I don't think it's possible to get used to the smell of sewers – not for me anyway. It's hard to believe we've been here three days, do you know that? It feels more like three years.

Anyway, then Nat comes back from the jacks looking for a mirror – that yoke in our toilet is so old and spotty you can't see anything. She starts rooting in her make-up bag but of course she couldn't find one – she can't find shit in that disaster area.

So I gave her mine and I was glad then that I hadn't thrown it into the river like I'd wanted to when we were running away from the screws. You'd slag the arse off me,

Clint, if you saw my make-up bag, but I'm kind of proud of it.

On the course the instructors were always giving out because most people's make-up bags are a tip. Or like Glenn says about my bedroom – like a plane wreck. Not mine, though. I keep all my make-up in small coloured pouches. Green for eye make-up, blue for foundation, pink for lipsticks and lip glosses. All my brushes are in a see-through bag and the mirror is in a plastic pouch at the very bottom.

Looking at my make-up makes me feel calm. But maybe you wouldn't slag me – you always kept your paints pretty tidy, didn't you? Well, tidier than anything else.

Anyway, there we were. Kelly was up and she made the tea. Nat was squeezing a pimple on her forehead and I was snuggled down in my sleeping bag thinking maybe I'd be able to get back to sleep after I had a cup of tea. And then the phone Tony gave us rang.

It was lying on a cardboard box beside Kelly but she just looked at it. And then she looked at me and I looked at her and at Natalie and neither of them moved. And Natalie said, Who could be ringing us? I wanted to thump the heads off the two of them but instead I jumped out of my sleeping bag and ran over and grabbed the phone and said hello.

It was Tony, of course – who the fuck else could it be? The prison asking us to come back? Sometimes I really wish I'd stuck to my original plan and run by myself.

How are you all? Tony said, all sing-song as soon as I said hello, and I knew there was something wrong by the sound of his voice but I just said, We're grand.

Natalie was mouthing something at me like, Is it Tony? What does he want? but I looked away and pretended I hadn't seen her. Pity about her.

Then Tony starts on about how Mam is fine and he was

up at the house last night and Jimmy was there with his kids – the twins – and how they looked like me and did anyone ever say that before? And I said no and then he said, Well they were the dead dab, and when he said it last night above in the house everybody agreed.

I said nothing mostly – just let him talk because I knew full well he had something bad to tell me. So he went on and on and I let him, 'cos I was afraid to hear whatever it was he had to say, but then my hand that was holding the phone started shaking with nerves.

Sometimes, you know, I wish I smoked. If I was a smoker, I could have smoked a fag then and that might have calmed me down. I mean, I know it's bad for you and all but the way I'm going for the last while I'll be lucky to live long enough to die from the fags.

For a finish I couldn't take it any more, and you know Tony – he can avoid getting to the point like nobody else, so I said it straight out. Did you ring for a reason, Tony?

He didn't say anything for ages and I was just about to lose it when he started talking again, asking me if we'd heard the news yet and I said, No, we just woke up, and then he said he knew it was nothing but a frame-up but that the Guards are looking for us to help with their enquiries into the murder of Billy Hendrick.

What do you think of that? I fucking knew it.

If all the things they say are true then maybe you have some influence where you are, Clint. Who knows? If that's the case you'd better use it because we are really up shit creek this time.

Be good.

Love,
Gina xxx

6. Tuesday 5 April

Seán and I interviewed the first three people on our half of the Hendricks' client list on Tuesday afternoon.

Mary Considine, an up-and-coming drug dealer who lived in Meelick and managed to never spend any time in jail – always a sign of success.

Tom Galvin, a publican with a propensity for breaking the licensing laws.

And Thady Williams, a slick young accountant accused of date rape.

None of them was any help with the Hendrick case. Or, as Seán put it, 'I wouldn't invite any of those fuckers to my house but I don't think they shot poor old Billy.'

I said as much, but in different words, to our Superintendent in the course of the four calls she made to me that afternoon. Each time she rang I told her the same thing – nothing new, really, sorry about that, Superintendent, but there's nothing new. Each time she reminded me of the importance of the case. And each time the call finished with me promising to get on to her if anything new broke.

By the time the day was nearly over I was worn out but still reeling from my epiphany at the morning conference about how careless I'd become. So I was quite glad to be having a hard day. It was a way of punishing myself for turning into the type of callous bastard I'd always hated.

At five o'clock I was in my office, surrounded by bits of paper, going back over everything for the umpteenth time, when the door opened and Seán came in.

'Oh good, you've solved the case all by yourself.'

I rubbed my aching eyes. 'Will you look over this stuff with me before we go?'

He lit a cigarette as soon as he closed the office door.

'For God's sake, Seán! There'll be war if you're caught.'

'I haven't had a fag for hours and you know that I can't think if I don't smoke,' he complained, inhaling deeply a couple of times in a row before flicking his cigarette out of the open window. 'OK. Talk fast. I have about twenty minutes' worth of concentration with that amount of nicotine.'

'I only need you for a couple of minutes anyway. I want to get in to see Rita and then have an early night for once – I'm shagged.'

'So, we're not running tonight?'

I shook my head. 'I'm too tired. Tomorrow night?'

'Grand. I'll go to the gym tonight, so.'

I opened the Billy Hendrick file, skipping over the photographs of his dead body and concentrating on the typed pathology report.

Seán leafed through the rest of the pages on the desk. 'Nothing here, really, is there?' he said.

'Not really.'

'No sign of a match for the gun?'

I shook my head. 'There's no record of that gun ever having been used in a shooting.'

'Not that it made much difference to him what gun it came from – a bullet in the head is a bullet in the head is a –'

'Shut up, Seán. Concentrate.'

Seán sat on a chair and put his feet up on the desk. He yawned loudly. 'Do you think Caroline Hendrick is right about Kelly Moloney?' he said.

I put down the page I'd been reading. 'That she killed Hendrick?'

'Yeah.'

'I don't know. Maybe she is. Any progress on finding Kelly's mother, while we're on the subject?'

'Naw – I just asked Amy on my way in.'

I leaned towards my computer and scrolled down the screen on to a new page. 'Her last known address was somewhere on the North Circular,' I said.

Seán nodded. 'Saw that.'

'She seems to have sold that house and there's no other house registered in her name. That's odd, don't you think?'

'Yeah, it's odd all right, but it doesn't necessarily mean anything. Maybe she's moved to England or something. I think there's something much odder about Caroline Hendrick.'

'Like what?'

He yawned again. 'I don't know, but the stuff she's saying is a crock of shit. Did you read her file?'

'Kelly Moloney's? Yeah. Did you?'

'Of course, which is why I think it's a crock of shit. I read the other girls' files as well and they didn't even know him.'

'He had a history with Kelly, though. She was fostered by the Hendricks for a couple of years,' I said, yawning in sympathy with Seán. 'She also said Kelly called him after she legged it from prison. So maybe he met her.'

'Maybe he did. But it doesn't mean she killed him. She was in jail for prostitution – no history of violence. The other two are in for things like credit-card fraud and shop-lifting. Come on, Rob. It's a bit of a jump to murder.'

I nodded. 'Natalie O'Rourke has a drug problem.'

Seán shrugged. 'Even so.'

'I know – still, it's the closest to a lead that we have at

the moment. I'd love to talk to them.' I rubbed my forehead to ease the headache that had started up. 'Even if they weren't involved they might know something.'

'Don't think they'll be dropping in for a chat, Rob.'

All I wanted to do was put my head on the desk and go to sleep.

'We have to put a bit more energy into trying to find them,' I said. 'We urgently need to talk to their families and friends – see if anybody knows anything.'

'True. I've already started trying to contact the families. No luck so far. I keep getting side-tracked with other stuff.'

'So maybe we should assign somebody to that task alone. Would that be a good idea?'

Seán stood up and stretched towards the ceiling. 'That'd be an excellent idea. Hugh? Amy?'

'Tommy? Janice?'

He glared at me.

'They're here in Limerick, Seán – we may as well use them.'

He didn't answer.

'Or maybe you think we just let the NBCI people have a nice holiday in the mid-west while we do all the work?'

He still didn't speak; he just cracked his knuckles and looked at the wall over my shoulder.

'I'm going to use them, Seán. That's the point in having them. And the point in having a team. Otherwise it's like having a dog and barking yourself.'

Seán shrugged and nodded and bent over to stretch his hamstrings. 'Did you see the photograph of Kelly Moloney, by the way?' he said, looking up at me from under his eyebrows and winking.

I tutted and frowned at him. 'Dirty old man.' I opened my desk drawer and found paracetamol. If I could just nip this headache in the bud . . .

He stood up. 'Look, Rob, I'm off – OK? You're the boss, so do what you like and just let me know.'

I grinned. At last, co-operation, Seán style.

'Anyway, the nicotine's run out and I want to get to the gym. See you in the morning.'

I gave him half a wave as I swallowed the tablets with the dregs of my cold coffee. They stuck in my throat but I forced them past my gag reflex. It'd be worth it if I sidestepped a full-blown migraine.

I put away the files and my remaining guilt about Billy Hendrick and made my way to my car. At least now I had a plan. It wasn't much of a plan but it was better than nothing. If we could find the runaways we'd have witnesses at the very least – if not the perpetrator, as Caroline Hendrick alleged.

What I needed now was to decide who should take over that part of the investigation. Probably Janice. She was bright and clear-thinking but also pretty good with people, so she'd be good with the families. As I drove to the nursing home I decided to ask her first thing next morning. That was good. That was settled. Now if only the traffic wasn't bloody treacle . . .

By the time I arrived at Árd Aoibhinn my head felt like glass but the nausea that'd been hovering had backed off. That was something. I parked the car and walked up the wide steps past tubs of bruise-coloured pansies. Pushing open the heavy cream-painted Georgian door, I let myself in.

The inside of the tall-ceilinged hallway was warm and bustling. Somewhere in the building a loud clatter echoed, followed by the sound of cutlery cascading and a loud woman's laugh. Elsewhere TVs and radios and people chattered and sang. A fragile but erect old lady, in a pristine white dressing gown, walked towards me, inclining her head like a queen as we passed each other. I smiled at her.

I let myself into the last room on the right at the end of the long corridor. The blinds were closed, though it wasn't dark outside. Why did they do that? Even the nurses who seemed to understand best of all what I wanted for Rita seemed to forget sometimes.

I jerked the cream-coloured roller blind and it snapped up. The room was still quite dark in spite of the fact that it was technically daylight outside, so I turned on all the ceiling lights. Then I switched on the TV that was perched on a high shelf on the wall across from Rita's bed. The room suddenly filled with light and noise, like water plopping into an empty bucket.

'Hello, love,' I said then, as if somehow I couldn't speak until I'd made the room more normal. 'What a horrible evening! I'd say it'll rain. It's as dark as night out there and it's only half six.'

Rita was propped up on pillows, her hands palm upwards, the soft light from the lamp above her bed making her dark hair shimmer. I kissed her smooth cheek. Her eyes were closed and she didn't move, but her soft breathing filled the air. It sounded slightly wheezy to me. That hadn't been there last night. I hoped she wasn't getting sick. She really didn't need that.

I was just considering seeking someone out to have a chat about it when the door opened. Maureen Jennings, the nurse in charge, came in.

'Hello, Rob,' she said brightly. 'You're not still here, are you?'

I smiled and pushed down the defensive feelings rising inside me. 'Back. Just back. I was at work.'

She smiled as she gently lifted the bedclothes to check

Rita's tubes. 'We all have to earn a crust, I suppose.' She pulled a stethoscope out of the pocket of her navy cardigan and listened to Rita's chest.

'She's a small bit chesty,' she said, as she finished. 'Nothing much – everybody in the place is coughing and wheezing, myself included.'

'Is it serious?'

Maureen wound the stethoscope into a neat bundle and put it back in her pocket. 'No, not at all. The Doc had a look at her – she's fine. It's just a cold. But don't worry, we'll keep an eye on it.'

'That's great,' I said.

She tucked the bedclothes back in place and walked towards the door. I carried a chair close to the bed and sat down.

'Rob?'

I turned to look at her.

'Have you eaten?'

'As I leave here.'

She smiled and looked then as if she was going to say something else. I smiled back, willing her to leave and keep whatever it was to herself. I didn't want to hear it. I'd heard it all before.

Whatever it was, she must have thought better of it and instead she just smiled again and said, 'See you, Rob.'

And then she was gone. I was relieved.

I moved my chair closer to the bed, leaning forward to arrange Rita's already tidy hair. 'OK, now. So how are you, love? How was your day?'

I paused briefly as if we were having a real conversation and she might answer.

'I just want to have a quick look at the news,' I said, flicking through the channels. 'See what they're saying about my case and then I'll see if any of your programmes are on – OK?'

I laid my hand gently over hers and turned towards the telly. The more I relaxed, the more I realized that I was really, really shagged. I made myself focus on the TV screen but the news was half over, so I'd missed whatever they had to say about Billy Hendrick's murder. Which was probably just as well. I hadn't the energy for dealing with arseways reporting. It'd been a very long day one way or another.

I wished I had a normal job. One that finished at six o'clock – or even if that wasn't possible one I could put out of my head when I wasn't on duty. I wondered if I should start listening to my father's hints about taking the pub in Lisheen. He had been dropping obvious hints for years and I had been ignoring them for years. Rita and I used to joke about it and sometimes I thought that maybe she was serious. She wasn't too keen on her job as an accounts clerk with the HSE. I, on the other hand, used to love my job. Now, though, things were different and Lisheen was looking pretty attractive.

'Maybe I'm just too old for it,' I said out loud, leaning forward so that my elbows rested on the bed. The solemn woman newsreader had almost finished her litany of world tragedy and mayhem and had moved on to some inane story about a dog who could play the piano.

'For God's sake,' I complained, picking up the remote and switching the channel to *Home and Away*.

'There you go,' I said, as I picked up one of her splinted hands in mine and stroked the tips of her long, graceful fingers. 'Though how you can watch this rubbish is beyond me.'

Some highly dramatic love scene played out on the TV and Rita moaned softly in her sleep. Maybe she could hear it. How the hell could they know what she'd respond to first when she came back? I turned up the sound on the TV.

Her hand lay sleeping in mine. Relaxed and curled open. I laid it back down on the blanket and gently removed the splints. Then I sat up on the bed and with the lavender-fragranced oil that stood permanently on her locker began to massage her hands.

Every day – at least once – a nurse came and rubbed oil all over Rita's body to stop her skin from cracking and becoming sore. Then either that nurse or sometimes another one gently moved her limbs through a range of exercises to stop her muscles from wasting away as she lay in that bed.

I loved that they did that and even though they told me it was just routine and didn't mean anything, it still made me feel hopeful. More hopeful than the feeding tubes and catheter that were sustaining her life made me feel. There was something about the massage and exercise that seemed more personal. It was the kind of thing Rita'd like, all those oils and massages – we had a bathroom full of candles and aromatherapy oils at home. And no matter what they told me, it still seemed to me as if they were keeping her in good condition for when she woke up.

I had listened to all that the doctors had told me about her injuries and very little of it was good. They said, for example, that the longer she remained in a vegetative state, the less chance there was of recovery. They told me the statistics and I pretended to listen calmly. They said that even though she could open her eyes and make small noises it meant nothing. They said it was just an automatic response and told me to look into her eyes and notice that she wasn't there.

I did as they asked but they were wrong. I could see Rita when I looked into those green eyes, even if they couldn't.

I could hear her voice in those small moans and, no matter what they told me, I knew the tears she shed were real.

The latest development with Rita's doctor – a kind man named Jerry Tuohy, who was my age with a wife of his own and a houseful of kids – was that he needed to prepare me for the anniversary of the accident. Maureen had been with him when he had tried to talk to me about it.

'You already know that if the patient hasn't regained consciousness within the first year it's not a great thing, Rob.'

'Well, a year is a long time,' I said, trying to be upbeat and smile because being positive watered down what he was saying.

He shook his curly brown head and put his glasses into the pocket of his navy jacket. 'It's considered permanent after a year. A permanent vegetative state.'

'I hate that word,' I said. 'Vegetative.'

He nodded and smiled kindly. 'I know. So do I.'

Maureen smiled and wrinkled her nose at me to let me know she agreed. That was great: we all agreed, then. We didn't like calling my wife a vegetable.

'May the seventeenth is the first anniversary,' Jerry Tuohy said.

I nodded and then I couldn't smile because for a few seconds I was caught up in remembering.

'I have a specialist in mind. Catherine Yarborough is her name. She's visiting the Regional at the moment and she knows a lot about VS. I'd like her to take a look at Rita.'

I shrugged. 'Fine with me.'

He swallowed hard. 'Because – well, if she's still in the same condition next month, Rob, we'll have to talk about it.'

'People wake up after years of being in a vegetative state,' I said.

'Very few.'

'Still, some do.'

He shrugged and nodded and pulled at the collar of his checked shirt.

'Really very few,' Maureen said, putting her hand on my arm.

'Should we shoot her on the eighteenth of May, so?' I asked, anxious breaths rising in my chest as I faked a laugh. 'Is that the idea?'

Jerry shook his head and Maureen looked shocked.

'Rob,' she said.

'No, because I can, you know – I have a gun.'

'No, look Rob – we just need to talk,' he said.

I held up my hand and turned away. 'I don't want to talk about it – OK? Not now or ever. Get your specialist to see her and maybe she can help. But if she can't, that's OK too. I can wait as long as it takes for Rita to wake up.'

I turned, then, and walked away. And they let me go.

When she'd first been moved to the home after three months in hospital, I'd tried to do all Rita's massage and exercises myself. I was damned if I was going to pay any attention to the suggestion that there wasn't anything that could be done to help her. I knew there was a lot that could be done to lure her back to me.

The staff at the nursing home were great. They had offered to do the massage but I refused. I wanted to do it. It wasn't a chore; it was wonderful for me to feel Rita's skin under my palms again and smell her and talk to her.

Eventually, though, I had to admit that a ham-fisted policeman – no matter how motivated he is by love – was probably never going to be as good as the professionals. So I let them take over.

Out of the goodness of her heart, Maureen had taught

me how to massage Rita's hands. I did that every time I visited and it made me feel better – and probably didn't do Rita any harm either.

I had a whole routine surrounding the hand massage. And as *Home and Away* bleated behind me on the telly I began. First I held the oil under her nose so that she could smell it. Then I told her everything that had happened since I had last seen her. Everything except for the fact that officially all hope was set to evaporate on 17 May.

When I had finished the massage, I gently put her hands back in the splints and closed the blinds. I changed the channel on TV to *EastEnders* and kissed her cheek. It was wet, so I knew another tear had escaped, and my heart jumped with excitement and disappointment that I hadn't noticed exactly when it'd come.

Maybe when I'd told her about Dylan Hendrick. Maybe she'd responded to the sadness of a small boy whose dad had been murdered. If she had, it meant that she was definitely in there because that was exactly the type of thing that made her cry.

Rita really liked kids. Not in that vague way that some people do, but in a real way. They liked her back as well. Kids always know which side their bread is buttered on. She should probably have worked with children instead of going into accountancy but I suppose that's how things shake out sometimes. And anyway we'd been planning to have our own kids. Loads of them.

But it hadn't happened and we were just in the early stages of investigating fertility treatments when she had the accident. Still, I figured she was only thirty-three – there was plenty of time to be having babies when she was better.

The more I thought about it, the more I was sure it'd been hearing about Dylan that had made her cry. Typical

Rita. I was elated but I knew better than to tell anybody. They'd just try and explain it away.

Emmet was watching a movie in my sitting room when I got home. I could smell cigarette smoke.

'*They Shoot Horses, Don't They?* – that's the name of it,' he said in answer to the question I didn't ask. 'I found it here. Have you seen it?'

'A long time ago. It's Rita's. Does your mother know you're here?'

He nodded but kept his eyes on the TV screen.

'I'm making dinner. Do you want something?'

He nodded again and I went to the kitchen and threw four lamb chops into the pan. Emmet never turned down food these days. I tidied the kitchen while the chops cooked – not that there was much to tidy. Apart from forgotten ashtrays under the couch in the sitting room, Emmet didn't make much of a mess when he came round. Other than that there was only me.

The phone rang.

'Rob?'

'Maria. How are you?'

'OK. Is Emmet there?'

'Yeah, he was here when I got in. Probably came after school.'

'Or instead of school. I got a call at work. He hasn't been in school for over a week.'

'Oh shit.'

My sister sighed long and loud. 'Exactly what I thought. I don't know what I'm going to do with him. He's going to fail his exams and get kicked out of school like that eejit of a friend of his, Shane Harris.'

'I didn't know Shane Harris had been expelled.'

'He was caught selling drugs.'

'Great.'

'I know. He denies it, of course, saying they weren't his, but they expelled him anyway. I hate Emmet hanging around with him. I've told him but I might as well be talking to the wall. Anyway, look, send him home, Rob, will you?'

'I have food on for him.'

'OK, feed him and then send him home – if that's OK with you.'

'Fine.'

'Anyway, how are you? I never even asked you.'

'I'm OK. Just came from Árd Aoibhinn.'

'How's Rita?'

'Fine, she's fine. Got a bit of a cough but seemingly they all have it and they say she'll be fine.'

Maria was silent and I was afraid that we were about to take a trip down the you-need-to-be-getting-on-with-your-life road.

'Do you want me to talk to Emmet?' I said to change the subject back to topics I was willing to discuss with my sister.

Maria didn't answer straight away. 'No. Thanks, though. I'll try first.'

'What about Frank?'

'What about him?'

'Well, did you tell him about Emmet? Maybe he'd have a word.'

Maria tutted. 'Frank'd just use it as an excuse to go on at me. I don't know why I'm paying maintenance when that child is running wild – the usual.'

'Why would he say that? Does he want to have Emmet live with him?'

That made my sister laugh. 'That'd cramp Frank's lifestyle a bit, don't you think? Look, I'm going to have a go at talking sense into him tonight and if I don't have any luck – which is likely – maybe you'd try?'

'No problem,' I said and then we said our goodbyes and I hung up.

The chops were almost cooked. I opened a packet of frozen potato waffles and a tin of beans – they'd have to do us for vegetables. I put the food on plates and called my nephew. He sauntered into the kitchen.

'Well? Do you like it?' I said.

'Not bad for an old movie.'

As I handed him a plate of food I noticed that he was looking me in the eye. When had that happened? He was still standing holding his plate when I turned around with my own dinner. He grinned.

'OK. OK, bring it in – I don't care. Just bring your plate out when you've finished.'

'Thanks,' he said, grabbing cutlery and a glass of orange juice. I followed him into the sitting room and sat on the couch, eating my dinner and watching Emmet watching the movie.

'Who is your man?' he said, pointing at the screen with his fork.

I looked at the dismal dance marathon on the screen and shook my head.

'Is your woman Jane Fonda?'

I nodded. 'And that announcer – I think his name is Gig Young but I'm not sure. Ask Seán – he's the one who knows about movies.'

We ate our food and watched the film in silence and then I put my plate on the floor and drifted off to sleep. When I opened my eyes, the TV was off and Emmet was standing in front of me with his school bag in his hand.

'I'm heading away, so.'

I nodded. 'Do you need a lift?'

'No. I have to call in to Shane on the way.'

I looked at him then and remembered. 'By the way, your mother rang. She didn't know you were here.'

He shrugged his thin shoulders and made a face. 'I told her. She forgot.'

'You should go straight home.'

He raised a hand and waved. '*Hasta la vista*, Roberto.'

'Very funny, scut. See you.'

Emmet left then and my head ached so much I couldn't keep my eyes open, so I fell immediately back to sleep and dreamed of Rita and me being in a car with a man who'd been shot. The fright of it woke me up and I went straight upstairs and fell into bed, hoping that lying down might improve both my dreams and my headache.

7. Wednesday 6 April

Hey Clint,

How's it going?

Tony came himself for us today. He and Eric came in Eric's van. He said he was sure nobody'd ever look for us where we were, but still. Just to be on the safe side he said he was taking us to another warehouse.

This one is the same as the last one – it even has the yard with the small gate in the bigger gate. The good thing is, though, the toilets aren't as smelly and it has electricity. I was delighted when I saw that. Funny what'll make you happy, isn't it? This new one is a bit closer to town as well, so we can go to the shop and stuff – it's only on the start of the Dock Road, not like the other one. That was out in Mungret somewhere.

I never met Eric before, Tony's 'special friend' – that's what Glenn calls him. He's nice.

I had to laugh, though, 'cos the whole time he was with us he kept looking at Kelly and it's not like he fancies her or nothing when you think about it. It's just hard not to look at her. I always used to see the screws looking at her in jail. But then loads of them were actually spotting her no matter what they said.

Kelly was pure odd the whole time Eric and Tony were here. I think sometimes there might be something wrong with her, do you know that? I'm not joking. I'll give you an example.

Today. There we were, just driving in Eric's van to this new place, when out of the blue she says, *We can't stay in empty warehouses for ever.*

Just like that! I mean what the fuck was that about? I was raging with her. I mean Tony's my uncle but he doesn't know her or Nat from shit and still he never once complained about helping them. And there she was whingeing because she didn't like where he was hiding us.

Fucking cheek. I didn't say anything, though I wanted to tell her what to do with herself. But you know how Tony hates fights, so I said nothing.

The thing is, Tony wasn't a bit mad at her for saying that stuff. He was lovely to her – just took her hand and started talking to her in this real soft voice like she was a kid and just afraid instead of pure cheeky. And that's when he told us that he had a bit of a plan for us to get out of the country.

Jesus – we were made up! I was at him to tell me more but he said he couldn't 'cos he had things to sort out and he'd tell us as soon as he could. Do you know something? Kelly might be a pain in the arse but Tony is the best, isn't he, Clint? You always said it about him.

And then – like that wasn't enough good news – he goes and gives me a big fist of money. I started screaming when I saw it and going on like, Jesus, Tony! Did you rob a bank? and Tony started laughing and saying there wasn't much there but there'd be enough to keep us going while he worked things out. Me and Nat put our arms around his neck at the same time and hugged him and kissed him all over his face. Tony laughed and laughed and Eric started laughing again as well.

And all that happened just on the way to the new warehouse. What a fucking day! Anyway, we got here and were just bringing in our stuff and getting set up when Kelly's phone rings. Well, it didn't ring out loud – it just flashed, 'cos she has the ringer turned off – but she was holding it in her hand, so we all saw. She said nothing and just turned it off. So we said nothing as well. And then Tony started telling us about a fella at work who met Jude Law in a lift in London.

After a while, Eric went to McDonald's to buy us a load of food and Natalie talked him into driving by the off-licence and picking up a slab of Heineken. When Eric got back we had a kind of a picnic and it was a mad laugh, and when we were finished eating, Tony kissed all three of us on the cheek, starting with me. When he'd kissed Nat and Kelly he came back over to me and gave me a hug and I asked him the one question I couldn't get out of my head: Was it on the telly?

He didn't answer – just hugged me a bit more and looked at Eric.

Arragh Gina – what do they know? Eric said.

I looked back at Tony and he was smiling as usual and he said they're not saying we killed him or anything, just that they want us to help with their enquiries. I didn't say nothing. I couldn't. Just stood there imagining Mam having to watch that on telly and then have all the neighbours thinking her daughter was a killer.

And then out of the blue Kelly starts talking, saying, That was the same thing and everybody'd think we did it. Which was exactly what I was thinking. And Tony said, No, it wasn't and nobody'd think that. But I think he's wrong.

Anyway, I didn't have too much more time to think about it 'cos next thing Tony says to Kelly,

You know your man, Billy Hendrick?

And his voice was pure kind, like she was a small kid or something.

Do you mind me asking you, love – you know the way

you met him early on in the night? Did he say anything to you that time? I mean was he going anywhere or meeting anyone else or anything like that?

Kelly didn't say anything and we were all watching them like it was a play or something and I was starting to feel sorry for her, even though most of the time I'm half wondering if she shot your man herself. And then she just shrugs and says no, he said nothing to her, just told her to come back at two, that he'd have money for her then. And Tony says, Right, right, and just one more thing, love – I don't mean to be nosy (though we know he's a nosy old fart, so that was a lie), but was he your solicitor or something, this Hendrick man? Why would he help ye like that?

Fuck! We all wanted to know the answer to that, of course, but none of us ever asked her straight out like that. At first she didn't answer. Just looked down at the floor like she does. Then she looked at Tony and said, He was my foster father for a while.

Fucking hell! It was like you dropped a bomb, Clint! Natalie said Jesus about ten times and then put her hand over her mouth like she was trying to stop more words escaping. I said nothing. Eric looked a bit like he was embarrassed. And Kelly – well, she just kept looking at Tony and he walked over to her and gave her a hug and she didn't hug him back but she didn't stop him either.

My head was buzzing with questions like why and who and what and all that – and I couldn't help thinking again that maybe she'd had a reason to kill him, especially if she knew him and all. But I knew I wasn't going to find out anything else 'cos I also knew Kelly'd finished talking about it.

So did Tony. So he says then that he'll call us later and then he and Eric linked arms and were kissing and messing and stuff and they left.

When they were gone it was kind of embarrassing between us because Kelly'd never said anything before about being in care. Though I'd heard it from Annie Freeman, a girl I knew from jail who'd been in the residential home with her.

Nat and me started tidying up a space for us to live in. First Kelly didn't even help – just looked at the wall, and I felt bad for her because it dawned on me that maybe I was wrong to be suspecting her like that. Maybe Billy Hendrick was important to her and he wasn't just some dead guy to her like he was to me. I mean, it was bad enough for me seeing him dead like that – it had to be worse for her.

After a while, though, she started helping and then we started talking about what plans Tony might be making. And that was good 'cos it gave us something to say that wasn't about Kelly being fostered.

Anyway, there we are talking about Tony's plans and cleaning up, and Natalie starts going on about how if he was sending us to America then she was going to enter *American Pop Idol*. So me and Kelly start laughing at that, of course, and Natalie gets all insulted and goes off in a huff and when she comes back she starts on again about how she can sing and she doesn't care what we say.

That just made it worse and we laughed more and then after ages and ages I said it out to her about how maybe it mightn't be a great idea to be seen on American telly when you're on the run from the law.

First she was still pissed off but then she got it and started laughing herself as well at how stupid she was and all. So at least we weren't fighting any more.

We did more cleaning up and when we were sitting down drinking tea, the two of them smoking fags, Nat says, I wonder what plan your Uncle Tony is really cooking up for us?

And I say it could be anything 'cos Tony is mad and then Kelly says, He's nice, though.

Jesus, Clint, I was surprised because I don't think I ever heard her say anything good about anyone before, do you know that? But anyway, it's true.

The phone rang then. Kelly jumped about a foot in the air and me and Natalie started laughing – though I think the reason she's so jumpy is she thinks it's that phone of hers ringing.

Anyway, as usual they waited for me to answer. It was Tony ringing to say that he'd talked to Derek Greene – do you remember him? Fucking crook of the highest order, but he has houses in Spain and according to Tony he's willing to let us stay in one for a while. How cool is that?

I asked Tony why he'd let us stay but he wouldn't tell me. Just said not to worry about it – said Derek Greene bought four or five houses to get rid of his drug money when the euro came in a few years ago and he wouldn't notice one less. Tony definitely has something on him but I couldn't give a shit! Isn't it just brilliant?

Tony has it all worked out. He's already been on to Glenn about passports and he says he and Eric'll lend us the money for tickets and stuff.

I don't know what I'd do without Tony – do you know that, Clint? Not just now but when all the shit happened with you. We'd never have got through it without him. Anyway, he says we'll be tanning our arses in Spain before we know it.

There is one thing, though. He kind of shoved it in at the end of the conversation: told me he's going into hospital tomorrow. I was upset, of course, and he started laughing and said that's why he hadn't told me. He says it's just a bit of a lump on the family jewels, as he calls them, says it's not serious or anything but the doctor wants to remove it. He swears it's just routine. Do you think he's telling the truth? I think he is – I'd know by him if he was worried.

Anyway, he'll be out for the count tomorrow – which is why he told me – but home and everything by Friday. I hope he's OK. I was slagging him, of course, saying I hoped they took the right lump and stuff like that, and he was killing me for not being sympathetic, but I am really.

When I came off the phone Natalie was hopping up and down to know what he'd said and even Kelly was looking curious.

He said he's got us a house in Spain, I said straight away to put them out of their misery.

Natalie went mad when I said it, thumping me in the arm and going, No fucking way! No fucking way!

I thumped her back and I was all, Fucking way! and Kelly wanted to know where in Spain and I said I didn't care – as long as it's not a jail or a warehouse I couldn't give a fuck. And then she smiled – a real smile – and said I was right. And it was like a party. Natalie started dancing and singing bits of songs. And I was starving again – the McDonald's had well worn off – so I made us a load of sandwiches and Kelly made three cups of tea. We sat on empty crates around the gas heater to eat – these warehouses can be really freezing, you know.

When Kelly'd finished her sandwich she lit a cigarette and told us she was in a place in Spain called Javea with the Hendricks once. I said that was great but the furthest I'd ever been from Limerick was Kilkee and Nat said she was the same. Then Natalie started talking about us getting work once we're settled and she said maybe she could get gigs in the tourist pubs. Kelly and me started laughing again and Kelly said it was better than her *American Pop Idol* plan anyway and Nat was all, Shut up you! – but she was laughing. Kelly was laughing as well. It was easily the best mood we'd all been in for ages. Fair play to Tony, all the same.

I started getting into it then and said maybe I'd get a job drawing people's portraits on the beach. Do you remember Ricky Mitchell and Tracey O'Neill had theirs done when they were in Spain on holiday?

Natalie said I'd be great at it and I said I didn't know but I was delighted she was saying it all the same.

And then Kelly said, I saw your work in prison – it's really good.

And Nat said, I can't draw a straight line with a ruler. Even when I was a kid I hated drawing 'cos nothing ever came out the way I wanted it to.

And I said, me and Clint were forever drawing. And suddenly I was remembering you showing me how to draw horses. Do you remember that as well? It was September and we were just back at school and we were supposed to be doing our homework, but instead we were drawing – as usual. I was drawing fairies. I loved drawing fairies with their wings and tiny pointy faces. You were saying how dumb they were and you wanted me to draw horses instead. I said I couldn't and you showed me how. But your horses were still better than mine no matter what I did. And I remember at the time thinking you were secretly glad about that 'cos when we finished you started praising my fairy pictures after all the things you'd said about them.

It was like I was asleep or something because next thing I knew Natalie was shouting at me. I told her to shut up and do you know what she said? I called your name loads of times – you were away with the fairies.

I couldn't believe it and I started laughing of course, but I didn't say why. And that made Natalie peeved, probably 'cos she thought I was laughing at her, so I tried to make it up to her. Asking her real nicely what she wanted and stuff, and she said she'd been telling Kelly she could work as a model in Spain because you wouldn't need the language or anything. I said that was a great idea and Kelly was acting shy and stuff but I knew she was chuffed as well.

Then I went down to the jacks and when I came back Natalie was crying. Just like that! One minute she's all excited – going on about Spain – and the next there are tears running down her face. I can't keep up with her.

I asked her about a hundred times what the fuck was wrong and she just kept crying and then, for a finish, she said, she shouldn't have run.

I've been waiting for that to happen – do you know that, Clint?

I didn't ask you, I said, after ages of silence. Because that's true – I didn't ask them to come. I only said I was going.

She said then she never said I did and she was all shaking and crying and lighting one fag off another and then she says she only had six months left and she might have been out in less.

Kelly said then, So what? It was the same for all of us – she only had four months and I had seven. But that didn't make any difference to the crying and then Natalie says, Yeah, but you two don't have a kid.

That kind of stopped me, all right, Clint. I always forget, because Natalie is only my age, but she has a six-year-old son called Ryan who lives with her sister. I think he'd mostly lived with his aunt even before Natalie was caught shoplifting. She was only sixteen when he was born and into all sorts of shit. She loves him, though. Nothing but pictures of Ryan all over her cell. I think her sister isn't supposed to send them to her but she does anyway.

Nat got another can of beer and I felt like saying it to her that she was drinking a lot but I decided to shut up instead. None of us talked for a while, so I was just listening to the silence. This warehouse is a bit weird – do you know that? Even if it's better than the last one. It started raining outside when we were sitting around like that and the sound of the rain on the galvanized roof was like millions of birds pecking.

And then Natalie says, 'I can't go to Spain.'

Kelly was pissed off then and starts shouting and going on about how a few minutes before Natalie was talking about singing in pubs and clubs in Spain and now she's doing this. And I agreed, but I didn't think there was much point in killing her so I start going on about how it'll all work out and not to worry.

But Natalie just shook her head the whole time and drank more beer like she'd made up her mind, and when we shut up she said, I can't leave Ryan.

Kelly jumped up then and went over to where Natalie was standing.

I'd love you to see them, Clint. They're complete opposites. Kelly is so tall and skinny and dark and Natalie so short and blonde and all there.

Anyway, Kelly grabbed her by the arm and leaned in close like she was threatening her. And then she says it's all bullshit and Natalie has no choice – she has to come with us or we'll all be in danger.

Natalie pulled her arm away and I thought she was going to dig Kelly in the face. I got up as well then and went over to them and told them all to calm down, but neither of them even looked at me.

Fuck off, Kelly, Natalie says then, all bitter like.

I'm warning you: don't ever fucking touch me again or you'll know all about it.

I'm not afraid of a knacker like you, Kelly says.

You have no choice in the matter. Tony will fix it up and we'll all go to Spain. End of story.

And then Natalie goes, I'm fucking telling you I won't leave my son.

That's when Kelly said it.

Well, that'll be the first time, so.

Oh man! I couldn't believe the words were coming out of her mouth.

Natalie's face went all red and she asked Kelly what she meant and Kelly was smiling now like she was glad she'd hit Natalie a dig where it really hurt. And then she said, You know what it means, Natalie. Pity you didn't think about him when you were busy robbing and doing drugs and getting sent to jail.

Well, at least I'm not a whore, Natalie says then.

The words were hardly out of her mouth when Kelly grabs her by the neck of her jumper and Natalie headbutts her in the face. Oh Jesus! I thought there was going to be another murder.

But it's like the head in the face changed Kelly and even Natalie looked a bit like she was surprised or something, even though she's the one who did it. Kelly was just standing there, pumping, and her eyes were suddenly all full of tears. Not that she was crying or nothing – she stopped them coming. But I still saw them. Anyway, all she says is, Fuck you, Natalie. What do you know about anything?

And we all just stood there for ages and ages with nobody else saying anything and then Kelly went off down to the jacks to wash her face or something. In my head were loads of things that I could say to them, but I couldn't be bothered my arse.

The truth is, I don't really care if they do kill each other.

It isn't like they're really my friends anyway, is it? I mean, I never even saw Kelly Moloney before I met her in prison. And that Natalie's a total fucking alcoholic, no matter what she says.

I mean Natalie's fine in a way – she's not weird like Kelly. And I've known her for years – she was in my class at school, but she wasn't really my friend even back then. Just a girl I knew. I didn't need friends when I was at school. I had you.

The thing is I thought I'd always have you. Do you ever think about that? Sometimes, you know, Clint, I think you're the biggest bastard I ever met. If it wasn't for you I wouldn't have ended up in jail. I never did anything like that before in my life. Fucking eejit. Why didn't you tell me what was going on?

I'm going to sleep now, Clint. I'm sick of everything and I don't think I can stand being awake another minute, even though it's only six o'clock.

Fuck off, Clint. Sweet dreams, you bollocks.

Gina x

8. Wednesday 6 April

First thing Wednesday I called Janice into my office and asked her to take over looking for the runaway girls.

'I'd be delighted,' she said, sitting back in her chair.

'That's great. It's not that I'm dropping it – just that, well, it needs someone to really chase it at the moment. I mean, it's about all we have. I'd love to talk to those girls.'

Janice nodded her red head and fiddled unconsciously with a silver and turquoise necklace around her neck. 'Do you think Kelly Moloney killed him?'

I laughed. 'Everybody keeps asking me that. I don't know. Do you?'

She shrugged. 'I don't know either. But I do agree that we need to find her and probably the others as well.'

I nodded and smiled. 'Exactly. And I think if you dedicate yourself to that part of the investigation for a few days it might help. It's impossible to focus on everything at the same time. I'm afraid I'll overlook something.'

I paused. If only she knew how likely I was to fuck up, she'd be applying to have me removed. Meanwhile, act as if.

'As I said, I'd be delighted to do it. Can I get Amy to help me?'

I looked at her and raised my eyebrows.

'Someone local. Always good – they know the place better,' she said, grinning. We both knew, of course, that that was about Seán rather than Amy.

I grinned back at her. 'You're a genius. I knew I was right to ask you.'

She smiled, stood up and left with a wave.

The morning conference that day was pretty short. It looked as if the Hendrick case had stalled and I said as much. Nobody disagreed.

'OK, so,' I said, after stating that obvious fact. 'Janice and Amy are going to take over operation runaway – basically finding the girls. To be honest, I don't really like any of them for the murder but who knows? And anyway, right now they're the best lead we have. So anything you stumble over about Kelly, Gina and Natalie – feed it on to the ladies.'

Everybody nodded and Seán made silent kissing motions at Amy, who ignored him like the sensible detective I knew her to be.

'All right. Well, there's not much point in sitting here going over things we've already discussed when we could be doing work, so let's just divide up the rest of the jobs and get going.'

I shot off the list of jobs, everybody noted his or her task for that day and we broke up.

In the afternoon, Seán and I visited the family of Natalie O'Rourke – one of Kelly Moloney's runaway pals. He'd set up the appointment early that morning and it'd been a job of work, as he'd said himself.

Janice tactfully backed out of the interview, insisting that she and Amy would be better off getting hold of Gina Brennan's family. So Seán and I went alone. As we drove to the house he filled me in on the hassle he'd had convincing the O'Rourkes to talk with us.

'I'd say if we were calling to tell them she was dead, they'd be happier,' he said as we parked outside their house.

'That's a bit harsh.'

He shrugged. 'But true – you'll see.'

73

The O'Rourke house was situated in the heart of a middle-class housing estate. The woman who opened the door was more than a little relieved to see that we were in plain clothes and driving an unmarked car. She was young – twenty-four, twenty-five – and good-looking in a plumpish way with the soft skin of somebody who takes meticulous care of herself.

She introduced herself as Melanie O'Rourke and though she didn't say she was Natalie's sister she was enough like her sister's photographs to make that obvious. She led us into a freshly polished sitting room, instructing us to sit on a plastic-covered white flowery sofa while she went to get her mother and father.

'I'd turn to drugs myself if I grew up in this house,' Seán said as soon as Melanie O'Rourke left the room.

'You've already turned to drugs.'

'Yeah, but real drugs. If you farted in this house they'd probably throw you out.'

'You don't know that,' I said, standing up as the door opened and an elderly couple came in.

'Yes I do,' Seán muttered under his breath as he stepped forward, hand extended, to shake hands with Mr and Mrs O'Rourke.

Melanie followed her parents into the room and after the introductions we all sat there on the plastic covers in awkward silence for a few seconds. Mr O'Rourke had to be seventy if he was a day and he had the wiry hard body of a man who kept fit. Possibly even an ex-soldier. I imagined him digging the garden and painting the house and generally imposing order on everything around him.

His wife was softer- and younger-looking. But she was still at least in her early sixties. She looked like the type of woman who did as she was told. Even before we began to ask questions she was darting nervous looks at her husband every few seconds.

'Well, Mr and Mrs O'Rourke,' Seán said in his booming I'm-such-a-jolly-fellow voice. 'We're sorry to disturb you but as I told you on the phone – it was you I was speaking to, Mr O'Rourke, wasn't it?'

The elderly man gave a sharp nod of his head. 'That's correct.'

'Grand. OK. Well, you know that your daughter, Natalie, escaped from prison last Friday afternoon.'

The three O'Rourkes sat like waxworks, staring at Seán.

'And we are trying to locate her.'

Again no response.

Seán looked at me. I coughed.

'OK. Well, we were wondering if perhaps you could help us work out possible places Natalie might be,' I said. 'You see, the thing is, we need to speak to her. Not just about her prison break but also in connection to another crime about which she may have some information.'

A tiny sob broke out of Mrs O'Rourke but she suppressed it almost as soon as it escaped. She glanced quickly at her husband and then looked at the floor. Melanie looked pained and reached out a hand to rest on her mother's shoulder. Her father cleared his throat and barrelled out his chest.

'I'm afraid, Inspector, that we have no idea where Natalie might be. The truth is, we haven't seen her in almost six years and, much as it grieves me to say it, we never want to see her again.'

'You've had no contact with her at all?' Seán asked.

Her father shook his head. 'None. And we don't intend to have any.'

'None of the family has been in contact with Natalie for the past six years?' Seán said.

'Absolutely no one.' Mr O'Rourke sat bolt upright in his chair. 'I presume this interview is confidential?'

Seán and I both nodded.

'Of course,' I said.

'Natalie was never any good,' the old man said, tilting his head back so that his chin jutted forward, 'even as a child. Unruly. Disobedient. Wouldn't take correction. When she had the boy that was the last straw.'

'The boy?' I said.

'Ryan,' Mrs O'Rourke said, and we all started slightly at the sound of her voice. It was a thin, reedy voice that sounded as if she didn't use it much. 'She was only a child herself. Sixteen.' She covered her mouth with her fingertips.

'I pulled her out of that abortion clinic – may God forgive her,' her father continued, his nostrils flaring. 'When we found out . . . Oh look, we don't want to start all that again.'

He glanced at his wife, who was weeping silently, big tears splashing on to the backs of her hands knotted together in her lap. Mr O'Rourke coughed. Melanie's face was unreadable.

'Mary took the boy and she left,' he said.

'Mary?' Seán said.

'Our eldest daughter.'

'Your eldest daughter, Mary, took Natalie's baby and then Natalie left home?' Seán said, making notes.

All three O'Rourkes nodded slowly.

'Did you know that she was in prison?' I asked.

'Limerick is a small town,' Melanie said and her mouth twisted a little.

'And that she'd escaped?'

Mr O'Rourke shook his head. 'Not until we saw on the news about the man who was killed.'

'Natalie'd never hurt anyone,' her mother said all of a

sudden. Melanie tightened her grip on her mother's shoulder but this time it didn't work. She looked straight at me, obviously avoiding eye contact with her husband. 'You can't think she would. I know her and she might hurt herself but she'd never, never, never hurt somebody else.'

'We don't know that, Mother,' her husband said, crossly. 'I think that girl could do anything. Those druggies she runs around with could put her up to it.'

His wife shook her head slowly, still focusing on my face. 'Do you really think she murdered that man?'

'We don't know much yet,' I said, but her eyes were locked on to mine and I could almost feel the pain emanating from her chest.

That was another problem I'd been having since Rita's accident. I no longer had any way of keeping out other people's pain. I'd lost my armour or something I hadn't even known I had. Whatever I'd lost, now I was a man with no skin and I could feel all sorts of things I'd never been able to feel before. Considering my line of work, that was yet another huge issue.

'But do you think she killed him – shot him?' Mrs O'Rourke said to me.

Seán cleared his throat as if to speak but I got there first.

'No,' I said, looking straight into her eyes. 'No, we don't think Natalie killed him. But we can't be sure of anything just yet. We need to speak to her though, because we think she may have some information that would help us find out who did.'

Mrs O'Rourke smiled and, shooting her husband a half glance full of triumph, returned her gaze to the floor. Mr O'Rourke looked momentarily rattled himself but soon contained whatever emotions were hopping around inside him. He stood up.

'If there's nothing else, detectives . . .'

We took our cue and stood up as well.

'If you hear anything—' I began.

'Don't worry – I'll be on to you straight away. Do you have a card or something?'

I nodded and handed him my card with all my numbers. Then we shook hands all round and left.

There was something so depressing about Natalie O'Rourke's family that we didn't say much about it. As we were going back into the station, Seán paused in the doorway.

'Do you think they know where she is?'

I shook my head slowly.

'Or care?'

'Her mother, maybe, cares,' I said. 'But she doesn't know where she is and I'm not even sure she'd want to know.'

'I agree,' he said, holding open the big plate-glass front door for me to enter into the building. 'Another dead end, so.'

I nodded and we parted ways in the busy hallway.

As if Seán and I hadn't spent enough time together that day, we also went running straight after work that evening. He called me in the late afternoon and nagged me until I agreed to go.

'Now aren't you glad you came?' he said as we ran along the green verge of the Condell Road, trucks and cars trundling back and forth in both directions.

'Fucking nag.'

Seán trotted ahead of me. He looked back and grinned. 'This way at least we'll have had our run and I can be happy that your health is looked after.'

'Jesus, that's rich out of Smokey the Bandit. I think it's a miracle that you can breathe, let alone run, with all the fags you smoke.'

'Well, think what you want – I can outrun you any day.'

Seán took off then like the greyhound he resembled. I tried to catch up with him, running as fast as my legs and lungs would allow. But I couldn't catch up. I watched as he disappeared down the narrow gap into the bird sanctuary. I followed but there was no sign of him.

I stopped to get my breath. It was a damp, mild evening and, as usual, a kind of hush hung over the pond and marsh that created the bird sanctuary. All sorts of birds I couldn't identify swam by. And a leggy bird I was pretty sure was a heron flew low overhead.

Originally the bird sanctuary was almost in the country. Now it's bordered by busy roads and houses, and even so the air there is different to any place else near by. No matter what the weather, the atmosphere in that place is still and the traffic sounds – though being created literally a few metres away – are muted and distant. Sort of as if it takes itself seriously as a sanctuary. Seán suddenly appeared from behind a tree, zipping his fly.

'Oh Jesus,' I groaned. 'You are uncivilized.'

He winked and jogged on the spot. 'Let's get going.'

'No, I'm shagged. Let's walk for a while.'

Seán laughed and ran backwards out towards the main road. 'Come on – another few minutes and then we'll have a rest.'

I shook my head but began to run behind him. Five minutes later Seán ran off the main road again into a secluded park area. I followed him and sank gratefully on to a scuffed wooden bench. Seán lit up a cigarette. We sat there in silence for a few minutes, Seán smoking, me gasping for breath.

'You are really out of shape, man. They wouldn't let you into Croke Park now.'

I hung my head and tried to consciously slow down my heart. 'That was a long time ago.'

'Still.'

I sat up and leaned back. 'I was never that fast anyway. But you should have seen me with the hurley and ball. I was like Setanta – I could take the eye out of your head.'

'Conceited bastard.'

I laughed and closed my eyes. 'No sense in false modesty.'

We sat there again for another while and as my breathing normalized I began to feel quite good.

'Now aren't you glad you came?' he said after a while.

'I hate to say it but I feel better.'

'It's the endorphins – they kill the pain, all kinds of pain. You can't beat 'em.'

I nodded. 'I could do with that, I suppose.'

He laughed. 'Why the hell do you think I run? For the exercise?'

I leaned back against the hard rungs of the bench and closed my eyes.

'I have something to tell you,' Seán said all of a sudden. I looked at him.

He was looking at the ground, concentrating on stamping out his cigarette end. 'Mary Hayes is going to talk to you tomorrow anyway but I thought I'd tell you first.' He stopped for a moment and looked around him, looking at everything except me.

'What?' I said, trying to sound more patient than I felt.

He took a deep breath. 'They have a new witness to Rita's accident.'

9. Wednesday 6 April – Thursday 7 April

Hi Clint,

Sorry about the way I left things. I was upset. Anyway, listen to this. Yesterday when I wrote to you, I told you I was going to bed at six. I actually did that. I was all sort of depressed and shit so I wanted to just curl up in bed. I wasn't really planning to sleep – just wanted a lie down.

But I must have dozed off, 'cos next thing I know Natalie's shaking me and I'm telling her to stop and stuff but she won't. Eventually I open my eyes and look at my watch and see that it's after midnight and I'm raging because I didn't mean to fall asleep and now I know I'll be up for the night.

So anyway, I open my eyes and look at her. She looks really freaked out but even so I'm pissed off and then she starts going on about there being a noise and something about rats and shit like that. I was still half asleep and she wouldn't shut up, no matter what, even though I kept telling her that nothing was there and even if there was it was probably only a mouse and it wouldn't come near us.

But by then, right, she's totally fucking hysterical and babbling about not being able to sleep and she's going, Oh please, please, please, Gina, please help me. I can't bear rats. We have to find it. And she's nearly crying.

I needn't tell you I was withered with the whole fucking game of soldiers – like you used to say. And all I was thinking was, The sooner we get to Spain the better.

*

So Natalie's there, half-crying and pulling at her fingers like a fucking head-the-ball and then she starts shouting, Listen! Listen! There it is. I can hear it again.

I listened then, to keep her quiet. At first I thought I was right and it was just her imagination and then I heard it too. This weird noise, kind of scraping and snuffling. I got up and shoved my feet into my shoes and Natalie stood up as well and then we stood really, really still and really, really quiet. Just listening.

Kelly groaned in her sleep and Nat and I giggled, though it was more with nerves than anything else. Then we heard the noise again. She grabbed my arm, but we didn't say a word. This time as well as the scraping and snuffling there was a squealing sound. Natalie squeezed my arm and nearly climbed on to my back, and then we heard the squealing again. Jesus, to be honest, even I was getting the willies by then.

And then we heard it again. More scraping. And kind of loud this time and I figured it was coming from behind this pile of old busted-up cardboard boxes down in the part of the warehouse we don't use.

I wanted to run away but there was nobody else going to do anything about it, was there? So I start walking down to the boxes and Natalie's still holding on to my arm but now she's behind me, dragging me, and I try to shake her off but the bitch wouldn't let go.

When we got close to the boxes I couldn't pretend there was nothing there. There was definitely something in those boxes and the noises were getting louder and louder as we got near. Snuffles and scrapes and two tiny squeals. I was afraid of my shit! You know me, I hate rats as well – everybody does – but by then I was afraid of them getting into our food and stuff and I was hoping that maybe if we

82

could just pull off the boxes we'd scare the little fuckers and chase them out of the warehouse.

The cardboard was piled in this big torn lump but it was almost as tall as me and there was kind of a cave between it and the wall. I figured that that had to be where the little bastards were living. Natalie let go of my arm and I knew there wasn't much point in trying to get her to do anything. I'd have to do it myself.

As usual.

Why hadn't I just waited to make the break when I was by myself? Why had I even said anything to them that day when Reynolds was gone into the shop to buy her *Hello* magazine? I just had to be the big woman and tell them all they could come along if they wanted, didn't I?

Anyway, there we were and I could definitely hear something behind the boxes so I reached out and lifted off a big piece of cardboard. It was soggy and disgusting and sort of flopped when I pulled it. I heard another squeal and I jumped away. Then I saw a long piece of wood leaning up against the wall behind Natalie. I told her to grab it and that I'd pull off the boxes and she was to hit him with the plank and we'd try and chase him out of the door so that he wouldn't go up towards our food.

And she starts this whingeing noise. I just fucking knew she was going to freeze if the rat ran in her direction.

OK, then, I said, and I was sounding calm enough but I was fit to be tied. How about this? Give me that wood and you pull away the boxes and I'll chase him out the door.

She didn't say anything but at least she shut up whingeing and she handed me the piece of wood. I took it and tried to calm myself down. I really didn't want that rat running up and hiding in my sleeping bag or getting into the food.

I shouted at her to pull it back and she looked at me and

I wanted to hit her a belt of the plank, but that'd be a waste of time as well so instead I just said it again: Pull it back. Now.

Natalie grabbed hold of a load of boxes and yanked hard and the cardboard crumbled on to the floor behind her. She jumped back and I was ready with the plank. And nothing came running out.

Then I thought maybe we had the wrong place. The warehouse ceiling is very high, so it can be hard to tell exactly where noises are coming from.

I was really starting to get nervous now. If he wasn't in there behind the cardboard, then that meant the little bollocks could be anywhere. Now what were we going to do? How the hell would we find him?

I saw then that there was still this low wall of cardboard in front of where we thought we'd heard the noise. Maybe he was hiding in there after all.

So I said, real loud, like an order, Kick away the rest of the cardboard, Nat.

She looked at me like I was speaking Russian. Holy God, Clint, I thought I was going to kill her.

Do it, I said.

That kind of woke her up and she took a deep breath and lashed out with her foot. The cardboard wall went up into the air in one lump and then fell on to the floor and smashed into a million pieces that flew everywhere. There was a loud scream and we looked at each other.

A tiny baby was lying in the middle of the smashed cardboard, screaming like a banshee.

Oh my God! Natalie screamed.

And I said, Holy Jesus.

And then Kelly shouted, What the fuck is going on down there?

And I could hear her footsteps running towards us.

I bent down low over the baby. It was a boy, wrapped in loads of those cotton baby blankets but all covered in blood and goo like he'd just been born. Natalie pushed me away and picked him up. And she was still all, Oh my God, and wrapping the blankets around him and stuff, and he was whimpering still but at least he'd stopped the screaming.

Natalie jigged him up and down and walked away with him back up to the sleeping area. Kelly and I followed her without saying a word. Then Nat told us to turn on the gas and that the poor boy was frozen, and of course Kelly didn't move – just stood staring. So I turned it on and tried to get my head around it all.

A baby?

Jesus, Clint, a tiny, weenchy little baby. I mean, what kind of a person would leave a small baby all by himself like that in an empty warehouse? There could easily be rats or dogs or anything that'd eat him. Not to mention that he'd starve or freeze. I mean, we mightn't even have heard him, with all the boxes and palettes and shit in this place.

And he was in behind a big stack of them. So if it wasn't for it being the middle of the night and quiet and Natalie being awake and scared of mice and rats and stuff . . .

Jesus, I don't even want to think about it.

Well, at least it's not a rat, I said to them when the three bars were lighting, standing close to thaw out my hands, which were frozen. I bet Spain isn't cold like this in April, is it?

Kelly didn't look at me – just kept staring at Natalie and the baby. The baby had stopped crying altogether now and he seemed to be falling asleep in Natalie's arms.

The magic touch, Nat, I said then, slagging her. But she just shook her head, kind of sad like, and said he probably needed food and how long did I think he was there?

I said, How the fuck would I know? but she kept going on so I said, It must be at least since this morning and maybe last night, 'cos we got here today about two, didn't we?

And then I got what she was saying and I was all, Oh Jesus, that's long and where will we get him food?

And then Kelly the statue spoke.

We can't feed him, she said.

We just looked at her. Natalie had the baby up on her shoulder and her green jumper was wrapped all around him and she's all, Great idea, Kelly – will we let him starve?

Just bring him out and dump him somewhere else. Someone'll find him eventually, Kelly says then, pure cold.

Natalie looked like she was ready to blow her top and starts shouting at Kelly about the baby being dead of hunger before anyone found him – if the poor little bastard wasn't frozen to death. And that we had to feed him at least. And then Kelly is arguing back saying, Where the hell will we get baby food, and so on, and I jumped in then before things got out of hand and we ended up with Natalie sticking a head in Kelly again – or worse.

I'll go, I said to shut them up. There are a few of those all-night garages on the Dock Road.

They won't have baby's bottles, Kelly said, like she won the argument or something. So then Natalie says, Don't bother with those shops. There's an all-night chemist down near Dunnes. And Kelly says it's not open all night and Natalie says it is 'cos she robbed it a few times and I should get nappies as well if I'm going.

So I'm all, OK, OK, and I grab forty euros out of my make-up bag and head off, leaving the two bitches staring at each other in the light of the gas heater. I felt sorry for the poor little baby having to stay there with that pair.

Anyway, that's why I went out. I was nervous, but it was

after half twelve when I left the warehouse and I was pretty sure it was safe. But I was still a bit scared.

It was weird being suddenly out like that. I walked along trying to look like I was just on my way home from work or after meeting my boyfriend or something normal like that. The streets were empty and a cold wind was coming up off the river and that, and the nerves were making me shiver, even though I'd so many jumpers on I was like a barrel.

Every now and again a car'd pass by and I'd have to stop myself from running. When I came to Henry Street, I was really shitting but still trying to look casual. Jesus, I didn't ever remember the street being as long as that. Though I did remember the police station on Henry Street, 'cos that was where they'd brought me first when I was arrested.

Mam couldn't believe it when the Guards came to the house for me. Sorry, Sergeant, she kept saying. I'm very sorry now and I understand what you're saying but you must have the wrong girl. Sometimes people do things and give the wrong name – I've heard of that. Somebody must have given you Gina's name.

The Guard was lovely to Mam. Garda Tom Johnson. He was really young, not much older than you and me. He could see she was telling the truth. She knew nothing about what was happening.

Sorry, Mrs Brennan, he said over and over when he kept asking for me and she kept telling him about his mistake. And, It'll all be fine, Mrs Brennan. And, Don't worry, Mrs Brennan.

I was in the kitchen the whole time, listening, and I thought I could probably make a run for it. But I couldn't be arsed. In a way I was even sort of glad not to have to do the stuff any more.

It was the woman in Hanley's Jewellers who'd recognized me. She knew my face – that's what she told the police. She said nothing, though – just let me buy the watch I was buying, let me sign the credit card slip and all. Never pretended that she knew I wasn't someone called Geraldine Flanagan. But as soon as I left she called the Guards. I'd gone straight home that day; if I'd gone somewhere else I'd probably have got away.

Henry Street was busy enough tonight, considering the time. I passed the Garda station and looked straight ahead, though all the time I was thinking that with my luck the Guard who had arrested me would probably walk out just as I was going by. If that didn't happen, then I was probably all right. I don't know too many Guards and I don't think they know me.

I walked fast as I was passing because I wasn't able to walk slow. Nobody shouted my name or came running at me or nothing, and soon enough I was past the station and coming up by the side of the GPO. I calmed down then, 'cos I was nearly there.

Then this drunken eejit with his shirt hanging out and an unlit fag in his gob made a grab at me when I was passing Elvery's. I ducked and told him to fuck off and kept going. It started raining then – this light cold rain – and I wanted to run again, but I didn't.

After ages I got there – to the chemist, I mean. It was empty. Only me and this funny-looking woman with a wig who was working there. I know it was a wig because it was a little bit crooked and I could see her baldy head underneath. I bought three baby's bottles off her and a few boxes of food for newborns. I told her they were for my sister's baby.

The wig-woman asked me if I needed a sterilizer and said that if I did then she had just the one for me, 'cos there was a special offer on a very good steam sterilizer. I said, No thanks, it was grand, but was there some other way of sterilizing the bottles because my sister might need that and maybe she forgot to tell me? So I bought a big bottle of Milton and a packet of disposable nappies and said I'd come back tomorrow to buy the sterilizing unit.

I felt a lot calmer walking back with the stuff. I decided to walk up O'Connell Street this time so that I wouldn't have to be nervous about Henry Street Garda station all over again.

There were still loads of people around, even though it was a Thursday night and after one in the morning by then. Then I remembered: Thursday night, student night in town. Annoying little bastards mostly. Anyway there must have been something pretty big on – one of those rag week things or something –'cos there were loads of people and loads of cars.

I looked at the tall buildings and the Jesuit church and the statue of Daniel O'Connell. I don't know if I ever really looked at them before. Did you ever look at them? They're nice.

And then I was thinking about how it was ages since I'd walked along like that. Nearly two years. And how it'd be even longer before I did it again because I wouldn't be coming back from Spain any time soon. And then it happened.

Someone called my name. Oh holy Jesus, Clint – I'll never forget it!

I froze to the footpath holding on to the big brown paper bag your one in the chemist had given me, like it might make me invisible. But it didn't work because then I heard my name again and then as if that wasn't bad enough someone grabbed me by the arm.

Gina x

10. Wednesday 6 April

After Seán told me about the witness he shut up completely. As if it was all he had to say and now he was emptied out. I couldn't speak either. I tried really, really hard to understand what he'd said as I watched him grind his cigarette butt into the worn grass in front of the bench. My head was buzzing. A new witness? After eleven months, a new witness? Somebody had seen the bastard driving into Rita when she was on her way to work and they'd only come forward now?

There was a horrible taste in my mouth and my heart was thumping fast again. I knew it was only anger and that it'd pass if I could just hang on. I also knew that was why Seán was telling me now instead of having me disgrace myself as I had the day Mary Hayes told me they might never find the driver.

'You know it happens, Rob,' she'd said, as if that would make a difference to me.

'There must be something else,' I said to her. 'There has to be another line of enquiry you could follow.'

She shook her head. 'Not at the minute. It's such a quiet road and there were no eye witnesses. Regina Farrell came out of her house when she heard the commotion.' She paused and tried smiling at me. 'Rob, you have to understand, she's an old woman and she was shocked by what she'd seen and busy looking out for Rita.'

Mary paused again. A part of me that had separated out and was observing the conversation could tell this wasn't going as well as she'd hoped.

'Look, you never know – something else might turn up and if it does, then we'll be all over it like a rash, I promise you.'

'But you're at a dead end now?' I said.

Mary shrugged. And I bust the chair. Just like that – out of the blue. I lifted my foot and stamped down on a plastic bucket chair that was standing in front of Mary Hayes's desk and its legs folded under it. And then I turned and left without another word. Nobody ever said anything to me about it but I wasn't a fool – I knew they talked about it.

I never told Seán, for example, and yet I was positive that he knew what'd happened. And now, suddenly, there was another lead.

'Who is it?' I said.

Seán took a deep breath and sat back in the bench. 'A woman. She was in a cab on her way to the airport. She's been in Africa since then. She's a teacher, I think.'

'And she didn't think of using a phone?'

'Obviously not.'

'If she was in a cab, then there was a cab driver as well.'

Seán nodded.

'So? Why didn't he come forward? Mary ran ads looking for witnesses. And it was on *Crimeline*.'

'I know. Maybe he didn't see the ads or the TV programme.'

I looked at him.

'I know, Rob, I know. Bullshit. Anyway, they're looking for the cab driver. The car that knocked Rita down was a silver Honda Civic. The witness told Mary that much – said she was positive because her sister has the same car.'

'The year?'

'I don't think she noticed that but who knows – maybe the cab driver did. Talk to Mary about it yourself tomorrow.'

Seán jumped up from the bench and began jogging on the spot. 'Had a long enough rest now, Granny? Can we get going?'

I got up and before I could say anything he'd run off. I followed at a jogging pace, the rhythm of my footsteps creating a matching rhythm in my head.

A silver Honda Civic. A silver Honda Civic. The bastard that was driving that silver Honda Civic had not only run her down with it but then he'd driven away in his silver Honda Civic.

What kind of a person does something like that? Leaves a woman with a broken head lying in the middle of the road? I wanted him caught. I wanted him to pay. Even if the payment was inadequate it was still better than nothing.

Seán and I jogged back to the station and straight into the showers.

'Come to McDonald's with me and the girls,' he said, as we left the locker rooms.

I laughed. 'No – thanks all the same.'

'Ah, come on, Rob. They'd love to see you.'

'You just want me to act as a shield between you and Yvonne,' I said as we walked out of the station to our cars.

'And what's wrong with that? She likes you.'

I laughed.

'No, really, Rob – that woman is mad. I blame her solicitor. Things weren't half as bad before she started all this divorce stuff. I have my suspicions about that solicitor. I think he only wants to get into her knickers.'

I laughed again. 'Everybody isn't like you. Which reminds me – is it true about you and that new secretary? I can't remember her name.'

'Sarah Greene. Is what true?'

I looked at him and he grinned.

'You have the morals of a tom cat,' I said, unlocking my car. 'I'm going to see Rita before I go home. Have a nice time in McDonald's and I hope Yvonne gives you an earwigging first – it's the least you deserve.'

Seán waved as I drove off. As the solitude of the car folded over me I was half sorry I hadn't gone to McDonald's with Seán and his daughters. Rita'd loved those little girls. Always talking about them when we'd been over at Seán and Yvonne's. Fiona and Carrie this and Fiona and Carrie that. She envied the Ryans, but not in a mean way – just in a sad, wistful sort of way.

They're really great little girls, actually – I kind of like them myself. Funny and cute and happy. Like Yvonne and Seán themselves until Seán fucked it all up. I'm not as good a person as Rita, so sometimes I can't help resenting that he'd so casually thrown away what I'd give anything to have.

As I drove I found myself looking at every silver car that passed. Who had run over my wife? Was it that man? That woman? A silver car pulled into the line of traffic in front of me – but it was a Toyota. And another – this one a Renault.

As I stopped at traffic lights a silver Honda Civic passed in the opposite direction. My heart thumped. Should I follow it? Where was it going? It wasn't likely that it was the right person, but then again, who knew? Stranger things than that had happened in my life.

I managed to hold on to myself long enough for the car to disappear from view, decreasing my options. I'd just call Mary Hayes – that'd do me. I was sure I had a number for her somewhere at home. I could call her as soon as I got there – though I knew that Seán had probably told me most of what there was to know at this stage. Still.

Maybe there was a tiny pearl in the middle of the shit that would lead to something good or some relief. I reminded myself of Alan Hendrick when he was sitting in my office, desperate for some information about his brother's murder.

Like Mary Hayes I was running into dead ends all over the place with the Hendrick murder. In spite of all our efforts to find the runaways I wasn't at all convinced they'd had anything to do with the murder. The thing was, I kept coming back to the fact that he wasn't robbed – when we opened it we found almost five thousand euro in that briefcase sitting on the back seat of the car. Why? And if the runaway girls had killed him, why hadn't they taken the money? Surely they needed it?

Maybe he'd been planning to give that money to Kelly. Caroline said not. She said it was probably money he'd been supposed to deposit in the bank. She said that he was fond of Kelly but she didn't think he'd give her that kind of money – not without discussing it with her first.

I wasn't so sure. There could have been more to Billy and Kelly's relationship than Caroline knew – it happened all the time.

There were still some reports due back from the Bureau. Maybe when we had those it might open up some new avenues for us. I hoped so. I was a bit stumped and I didn't want to have to say that to the family. Because I knew what it was like to have to hear it. Which brought me full circle.

Mary Hayes's witness might have the information we needed to find the bastard who'd knocked down Rita. Suddenly the hope of finding the perpetrator mixed inside my head with the pain of all I'd lost and I decided I couldn't go and visit Rita yet as I'd planned. I'd go later. Maybe if I went home and had something to eat and tried to watch TV for a while I'd be less manic about this new witness – and everything else.

*

It was almost eight by the time I got home so I was surprised to see Emmet still there. He and his pal, Shane Harris. They seemed to be having a serious conversation of some sort.

'Evening, gentlemen,' I said, leaning against the door jamb. Shane looked embarrassed and I wondered what they were up to.

'Hey, Rob,' Emmet said, giving me a placatory smile. They were definitely up to something. I looked at the two empty pizza boxes on the hearth.

'I see you've already eaten,' I said. 'Nothing left, I suppose?'

'No, sorry about that,' Emmet said, standing up and checking the boxes. 'I was just telling Shane about Nana Maria.'

'Really?'

'Yeah – how old was she exactly when she died?'

'Eighty-six.'

'And she was your grandmother?' Shane asked Emmet.

Emmet shook his head. 'No, fool, I told you – she was my mother's grandmother, and Rob's.'

He paused and looked at me and I nodded.

'She married their grandfather – Gerry, wasn't it?' Emmet continued. 'He fought with Frank Ryan in the International Brigade during the Spanish Civil War. That's how they met.'

'Pretty cool,' Shane said, standing up and pulling on his jacket over his head.

'And don't we still have cousins in San Sebastián in Spain?' Emmet said, standing up as well and gathering his belongings into his school bag.

I nodded. 'Never met them myself, but your mother did when she was there years ago.'

'I might do something on Frank Ryan or even my great-grandfather, Gerry O'Connell, next year for my special topic in history,' Emmet said, slinging his bag over his shoulder.

'Good idea,' I said.

'Well, we'd better get going, so,' Emmet said.

'Right enough,' I said, stepping into the hallway. Emmet and Shane loped past me and with a nod of the head and a mumbled goodbye were gone. I went into the kitchen and made myself a ham sandwich and tried to figure out what Emmet was up to.

It had to be something pretty big if he was willing to engage me in family history conversation. I knew Emmet and I knew he ordinarily hated hearing about our Spanish ancestors and his great-grandfather's noble crusade in Spain in the 1930s. So why was he suddenly anxious to talk about it?

But my head was too full of Rita's assailant to figure out Emmet, so instead I brought my food into the sitting room and watched a programme about sharks. Then I dozed for a while and when I finally managed to wake myself up fully it was ten thirty. I jumped off the chair and went into the kitchen and drank a glass of water. Ten thirty and I hadn't seen Rita yet. Jesus. OK, it was OK. I just needed to wake up.

I drank another glass of water and tried to get my head to function. They wouldn't mind at Árd Aoibhinn – they'd just think I was working late, and it wasn't as if I was going to be really disturbing her or anything. I only wished that that was the case.

Once I'd woken up properly I pulled on my jacket and left immediately. As I drove to the nursing home I knew what Seán and my sister, Maria, would say if they knew. Go home, Rob. You're tired. Get some sleep. You can see her tomorrow – what difference will it make?

Months before I'd given up trying to explain to them how important it was that I visited Rita every day. The formula is simple. If you love somebody you want to be with them and I loved my wife. How hard was that to understand?

But it probably wasn't their fault. They didn't know what it felt like to be me. I'd probably have been just like them before Rita's accident. So nowadays I didn't tell them much. Didn't answer questions if I could help it. Never mentioned Rita's clothes hanging in the wardrobe. Her shoes lined up in rows beneath them. Didn't say a word about the make-up and the toiletries I kept in plain view as if she'd be in any minute to use them. There was no need. I knew what I knew and I didn't need anybody to agree with me.

The nursing home was in that semi-lit nightlight phase by the time I let myself in the front door. A statue of the Virgin Mary glowed in the light of small candles at the end of the corridor and the only sounds were those distant alive sounds of people sleeping. The night nurse had obviously been around before me and switched off the lights in Rita's room.

I stood in the doorway for a few seconds, letting the light from the corridor seep into the room. She looked so peaceful and so like herself that it made me feel calm for the first time that day. How come nobody understood how much I needed that?

At first when Rita was transferred to Árd Aoibhinn after the accident I hated the place. Hated the stillness in her room and what it meant that the hospital had said they couldn't help her any more. I cried a fucking ocean of tears on to her bedspread in that nursing home. Slept there at night on a chair beside her bed and staggered through my job most days, hoping Seán would catch the balls I was dropping. And he did. Never complained either.

Gradually though, I got used to it. It became part of my day to visit Rita. Tell her everything. Hold her hand. Look at her beautiful face. Occasionally all that made the loss of the real Rita worse but most days it was OK. I told myself it was only a temporary state and that someday it'd be all right and I'd tell her all about it.

Meanwhile I loved being with her in that room. The feeling I had when I was there reminded me of being in the bird sanctuary – only it was better.

I turned on a lamp and put our wedding video in the machine and as usual it leapt to life with the sound of Rita laughing. I played that tape every day because it contained all the voices she loved. All the sounds she needed to hear so that she'd remember why she should come back.

I pulled the fireside chair close to the bed and sat down and watched the video. Cratloe Church. Flowers. Seán and Yvonne when they still liked each other. Rita's face was so alive as she looked intently at the priest who married us. She seemed to be concentrating on his every word with such serious energy that it made my heart squeeze in my chest. It was as if she knew she should savour every second. I wished I'd known.

I looked down at her in the bed. She was still the same Rita lying there, her face bathed in the yellow light from the bedside lamp, her shiny mahogany hair brushed back from her forehead and spread on the white pillows like a dark halo. Her face was pale, but then it would be, wouldn't it? She'd not seen the light of day for nearly a year. I examined the contours of her face – the cheekbones and chin, eyebrows and small ears. The small mole asymmetrically placed at the hollow of her throat.

Her breathing was quiet and the room smelled of lavender. I was still tired, I realized, as I leaned forward and kissed the back of her hand. I really, really didn't want to fall asleep on the chair. I just wasn't able for it and there was a meeting at nine thirty in the morning and as we were staring at nothing but a dead end in terms of the Hendrick murder I knew I'd need all my resources.

I'd just stay a little while with Rita. Tell her about my day and especially tell her about the Honda Civic. My body began to relax and I found myself synchronizing my breathing with hers. I laid my head on the rough cotton coverlet. My Uncle Tom sang 'Spancil Hill' on the video and beside me Rita's hand was warm and still and being there felt a lot like everything was OK. I'd just close my eyes for one minute and pretend that was true. What was the harm in that?

Hey Clint,

Sorry, got interrupted by Natalie. She had to get dressed and she made me mind the baby. Hope it was a bit of a cliff-hanger for you – ha ha.

Anyway, where was I?

Oh, yeah, there I was on O'Connell Street when someone grabbed me. Fuck it! I nearly shit myself. I turned around. Real slow, like, thinking I could just throw the bag at them and run for it. And who do I see behind me? Glenn!

Jesus, the relief! He was laughing – the bollocks. Knew full well he'd frightened the shit out of me. I thumped the arm off him and he was still laughing and going on about why was I walking along on O'Connell Street when the Guards were looking for me? So I told him about finding the baby and he thought that was hilarious altogether.

I was all, It's not funny, and I was getting madder, and that only made him laugh more and go, It is, Gina, it's fucking hilarious. A fucking baby? What are ye going to do with him?

And then without any warning he gave me a hug – this real long, tight hug like he meant it.

It made me want to cry – but I didn't. He looks more like you as he gets older, actually – do you know that? He looked upset as well but he didn't say anything – just started telling me that he had the passport thing started and that he'd be up to the warehouse soon to take our pictures.

He said Tony had paid Jimmy Kiely for two birth certs

and as soon as they could get their hands on a third he'd go to Cork and sort us out. So I said that was great and I couldn't wait and stuff and he said yeah but I'd better get back to my baby and that made him laugh all over again. He was always annoying, wasn't he? Never knows when to stop and he thinks he's so funny.

Anyway, I said grand and he said he had to go as well or the mother'd be worrying. And when he said that, I swear it really nearly killed me. I had to work real hard not to start bawling.

How is she? I said to Glenn then, like it might stop me crying. And he said she was grand. Worried about me. And that was even worse to hear. And I must have looked it, 'cos he was all nice to me and told me Tony'd told her he'd sent me to England to stay with a friend of his and that that made her feel a bit better.

The bag of baby food was like a bag of stones and I just had to ask the question, so I said, She doesn't think . . . you know . . .

That you shot your man the solicitor? Glenn said, 'cos he knew straight away what I was saying. So he said I was mad to be thinking that – she'd never think I'd do something like that, and I was a bit relieved, 'cos, well, you never know, do you? And then he said that the Guards were up in the house about it yesterday. Just looking for me in case I knew anything.

Can you imagine that, Clint? And Mam is so – I don't know what to call it – innocent. She might tell them stuff by accident. But Glenn said, How would she do that when she doesn't know anything, and that's true. So I asked him if he was there and he said he was and I said did he think the Guards really thought we did it and he said no and then he said maybe and then he said he didn't know. Fucking eejit! I was laughing at him – but then he said, There was something on the news about the good-looking one. Fucking nerve! Like me and Nat were dogs! He said, They said Kelly had a history with your man and I said, So? She didn't kill him.

And I was losing my patience with him but I don't know why, really, when I half wonder the same thing myself. So I told him about Billy Hendrick being Kelly's foster father and about what happened that night and how he was dead when we went back so I know Kelly didn't do it. And he said yeah, unless she did it earlier on and just brought me along in case she was caught so I'd say, No, she was with me.

I told him he was stupid but his words kind of landed inside me, matching up with what part of me already thought. I said, Why would she kill him when we needed the money and anyway what kind of a witness would I make? And he said, OK, OK, calm down, and that he had to go 'cos the mother'd be waiting up for him – she always waits up for him these days. Then he headed off and I stayed watching until he disappeared around a corner.

I started thinking then about how maybe Glenn and Mam can come and live with me in Spain when I'm settled in. The rain was getting heavier so I started to trot up O'Connell Avenue. It'd be great if they came, wouldn't it? A real new start for all of us.

Nothing has been right since you died, Clint. Mam was destroyed by it and even Glenn was knocked sideways. I nearly went fucking totally mad. I'll never forget it. The pain filling up inside me like poison water. And the anger. I was furious with you for not telling me and with Mam for not watching you and with everyone for not knowing and with myself most of all. If there was anybody who knew you better than you knew yourself, it was me.

That was what all the credit card thing was about. I never used even one thing that I bought. I kept a few rings and things in a box under my bed and the rest were presents for Tony and Glenn. I'd wanted to buy Mam presents as well but she kept telling me she didn't want anything.

Tony copped on after a while – I think it was the designer suit I bought him. He told me it was lovely but I knew by his face that he didn't believe I'd picked it up in Oxfam.

But even though I knew I was going to be caught sooner or later, I couldn't stop. I wanted to fill up my head with copying the signature on the back of the stolen credit cards and then fill up the rest of me with the buzz of getting away with it. It was mad, but it was what kept me going after you were gone, you bastard.

It wasn't until I was in jail and the case was over and I was looking at two and a half years in prison that I slowed down. I can't remember if I ever told you this but I started crying two weeks after I was convicted. Two weeks to the day – it was a Thursday. I started crying then and I didn't stop for three days. I wasn't bawling or shouting or screaming. Just crying like all the things that had happened were overflowing out my eyes.

They gave me Valium and sent a shrink in to talk to me but I just kept crying and I couldn't be arsed talking. They thought it was because I was locked up. They didn't know I was already so fucking locked up inside myself it made no difference. One screw guessed, though. She's a bitter bitch from somewhere in Kilkenny but she knows somebody who knows our family. I'm not sure who exactly because I never asked her. I wouldn't give her the satisfaction of talking to her.

That was a shame about your brother, she said to me one day. I got such a fright I stopped crying for a minute. They never found out why, did they?

I looked at her and she folded her fat arms across her huge tits and I didn't say anything. I didn't want anything from any of them. I just couldn't stop crying, that was all. Until I started writing to you.

Did I tell you about the man I heard on the radio a few weeks ago? He does the same kind of thing but he writes to his wife, who died. The interviewer on the programme asked him why he didn't get someone to talk to about his feelings and he said he tried but it was no good. These were things he could only say to her. He said it was useless to say them to anybody else and he couldn't stop them piling up inside him, so that was why he wrote her letters every day. It's funny when you hear things like that, isn't it? Funny the way we're all kind of the same.

Anyway, enough about that. I still haven't finished telling you everything that happened last night. OK – where was I? Oh yeah, with Glenn. So he goes home and I head on back to the warehouse. By the time I got back, Kelly was lying on top of her sleeping bag, smoking, and Natalie was walking around singing to the baby.

Did you go to China for the fucking bottle? Natalie said the minute I came in and then she handed me the baby and went to fill the kettle.

The baby is really cute, Clint. You'd be mad about him. He's such a small little thing and he was so cute when I was holding him – all curled up in a sort of bundle making this snoring noise. It's hard to credit that someone left him behind the boxes like that. So small and raw with blood still in the little bit of hair he has.

I said he seemed all right and Natalie said no, he wasn't and that when Ryan was born there was a girl in the hospital and her baby was always sleeping. She used to want to leave her sleep but the nurses said that was no good for her and that sometimes babies could die because they slept all the time and didn't eat.

What do you think about that? I was shocked. He's too small to think about him dying. How small is a baby's coffin?

Natalie made his bottle and then it was too hot so she had to cool it down in a bowl of water and test it every few seconds on her wrist.

Kelly was just sitting there, smoking, the whole time we were talking about the baby and then suddenly she says,

His mother wanted him to die.

I made faces at her, trying to get her to shut up, and I covered the baby's head in case he could hear her, but she didn't give a shit and just said, It's the truth.

Natalie said she couldn't know that and to shut up. Then she took the baby from me and the bottle must have been ready then, 'cos she gave it to him and he started drinking it and Nat was tickling the soles of his feet to keep him awake and we were delighted he was taking the bottle.

Kelly said nothing. Just sat there looking at Natalie and the baby the whole time. When the baby finished drinking, Natalie put a nappy on him. Then she covered him in her jumper again and put him up on her shoulder to wind him. And all the time she was singing to him.

I couldn't stop looking at her and it seemed like Kelly couldn't either, even though she had a sour face on her the whole time.

The baby gave a big loud burp and me and Nat roared laughing. I said then what would we do for a cot and Nat said he could sleep with her and that she was going to bed. And all the time Kelly was looking at us – well, not really us, more Natalie and the baby. Fucking weirdo.

And then we went to bed. Natalie said she was wrecked and the baby was asleep and I wanted to write to you again before I went to sleep. Kelly went to bed as well but she didn't go to sleep – just kept lying there. Kept smoking.

She's really withering the shit out of me. I'd like to slap her but I'm going to ignore her instead. I'm too wrecked to be fighting – dodging Guards is hard work.

I keep trying to think of a plan for the baby but nothing is coming to me and anyway I want to get this written to you. I know I'll sleep better if I do.

The thing is, I keep wondering why Kelly is so quiet and so cross. I know she's not exactly a laugh a minute at the best of times but this baby seems to be really getting under her skin. While I've been writing this I kept peeking at her. Nat and the baby are asleep now but I can see Kelly's awake because I can see her smoking. Chain-smoking, more like. But I can't work it out. Not that I really want to. I'm just curious – that's all.

But as I keep saying to you, the minute I get to Spain it'll be bye-bye girlies. Talk to you tomorrow.

xxx

12. Thursday 7 April

It was almost eleven thirty by the time our Thursday morning conference was finished. Seán reported on our meeting with the O'Rourkes and Jason broke the bad news about the tabloids getting hold of the story about Billy Hendrick's state of undress. A low whistling sound of mock upset went around the room. I was finding it hard to concentrate.

'It was bound to happen,' I said crankily, and the whistling and messing stopped. 'Next item.'

I forced myself to listen to the bits and pieces that were still straggling in from the Technical Bureau and various detectives.

'How are we doing with the interviewing of everybody on his client list?' I asked, pretending I wasn't hurrying through the agenda. Pretending my head wasn't full of Honda Civic drivers instead of Billy Hendrick.

'Nearly there,' Seán said.

'And have we had a word with his neighbours? There might be something there.'

'Well, only one seems to have seen him,' Hugh said. 'His next-door neighbour, Mary Harris, saw him in the morning. You spoke to her, didn't you, Jim?'

Jim O'Reilly, a thin, young newly hatched NBCI detective with a shaved head and a spattering of black stubble, nodded. 'You have my report,' he said. 'She didn't have much to say. He bought a newspaper in the morning – we spoke to the shop keeper. Apart from that, the victim went to watch the rugby match, leaving at teatime, and that's about it. All that's left is the couple who found him and they're coming in again this afternoon.'

'What about the money?' I said, looking around the room. Most of the faces looked almost as tired as I felt.

Seán shrugged and chewed a pencil. You didn't need to be Sigmund Freud to see he wished it was a cigarette. 'We still have no idea where he got it,' he said. 'His bank doesn't know anything about it. Neither does his office. And before you ask, no, they never take cash payments and forget to put them through the system.'

'It's very odd. It says here that fingerprints were found on the briefcase. Billy Hendrick's and some other prints. No match, though.' I looked at my watch. 'OK, I suppose that's about it, so, for this morning,' I said, unable to take another minute of the meeting. If we went on for much longer I knew Mary Hayes would be gone. She said she had court at two and that she was taking an early lunch break at about twelve. 'That's great. Thanks everyone. That's it, so, I think. See you all in the morning.'

I stood up and pushed back my chair with my calves. The people sitting around the long table looked at me but I didn't care. We'd spent long enough talking about Billy Hendrick. There was nothing really new. Nothing to go on. More phone calls from his brother, who was getting increasingly irate and more and more pompous with every passing day. A few forensic bits and pieces. That was it.

With a quick wave and a minimum of eye contact I left the room. I knew I wasn't able to wait until evening to see Mary Hayes. It was just too long. Anyway, Seán would deal with anything I'd missed. I took the stairs up to Mary's office two at a time. She was still there – I could see her shape through the glass block walls as I approached. I knocked and let myself in to her small office without waiting for an answer.

Mary was about the same age as me and had graduated from Templemore in the same year. She was a tall, good-looking woman with cropped black hair and a loud laugh. She got married about a year before Rita and I did. We'd been at her wedding.

Mary had married Frankie Deegan, another one from our graduation class. Frankie was tall and blond and all the girls loved him. Unfortunately, he turned out to be a bit of a bastard and ran off with a publican's wife from outside Cappamore. Frankie and the publican's wife had run off to England – probably to avoid her furious husband – leaving Mary with two small children and a huge mortgage.

'Seán told you,' she said as soon as I walked into her office. I pulled out a chair and sat down. Mary was looking into a mirror that lay flat on her desk. She opened her mouth to a small 'o' shape as she put mascara on her eyelashes. When she had finished she sat back and looked at me.

'I want to look nice for Judge Sheehan,' she said, grinning. I smiled back – everybody knew Thomas Sheehan was almost blind.

'So?' I said, not able to wait any longer.

Mary sighed. 'I'm sure Seán told you everything. We have a witness, Fidelma O'Hagan. She's been in Africa since the accident but something made her get in touch when she got back.'

'Guilty conscience?'

'Probably.'

'Seán said that she was in a cab.'

Mary nodded. 'Mark Phelan is at the cab company as we speak. It's hard to locate a specific cab driver almost a year later. She doesn't remember much about him other than the fact that he was a man.'

Mary smiled then and looked at me and I could see that she was trying to assess my mental state. I forced myself to sit back in my chair and tried to look relaxed. I could think of a dozen ways to try to find out who had been driving that cab – but then again so probably could Mary.

'It's definitely a Honda Civic, so?' I said, as if it was all academic.

'Looks like it. The only thing is, it can be hard to be accurate about the exact model of a car under circumstances like those.'

'Yes,' I said, 'I know. Any idea why the cab driver kept going when he saw what happened?'

'He stopped for a minute, according to Fidelma O'Hagan, and she said she thought he was going to get out of the cab and go back. They were up the road past the accident. She didn't actually see the accident happen – only saw it out of the back window when the cab driver stopped. She thinks he saw it in his rear-view mirror, though.'

I nodded and forced myself to take long, deep breaths. If I freaked out again she'd never tell me another thing.

'The witness saw Rita lying on the road and she could see that the driver of the Honda was a young man. She says he got out of the car and went over to Rita. She said she thought he was going to help her. I don't know why the cab driver didn't go back to her, though. It's unusual.'

'Yeah, it is.'

Mary shrugged. 'Whatever the reason, he didn't. He opened the door, stepped out for a minute, looked back and then sat in the cab, telling Fidelma that they'd better get going or she'd miss her plane.'

I struggled to force away the picture of Rita lying, bleeding, on the road.

'Miss O'Hagan says she reassured him that she didn't mind missing her plane. I think that's a bit of a lie. At the time I'd say she was totally worried about missing her flight and delighted that he said they should get going.'

'Probably.'

'Which supports your guilty conscience theory.'

Mary reached on to the floor and plopped her handbag between us on the desk. She pulled out a tube of lipstick and tumbled it between her fingers.

'You want to get ready for lunch,' I said.

She smiled.

I stood up. 'Will you let me know what happens?'

'Of course.'

'Thanks.'

There was a pause for a few seconds.

'So? How are you, anyway, Rob?'

'Not bad.'

'And Rita?'

'Good. Good. The same.'

Mary nodded and fiddled with the lipstick again.

'I'll talk to you later. Have a nice lunch.'

'Thanks, Rob.'

I left her office and hurried down the corridor. The building was suffocating me and I just wanted to be outside, where I could breathe. All the usual shit that surrounded the accident swirled around inside me. But more than anything I wanted to know why it was possible that some bastard had broken my beautiful wife's head and that he was still walking around as if he'd done nothing.

As I cantered down the concrete stairs I knew I was

feeling the typical feelings of the victim of crime, but somehow knowing that wasn't making a blind bit of difference. I let myself out of the back door and went into the car park. It was a sunny day – first real bit of heat in the sun so far. I walked out of the station gates and along the footpath.

Sarsfield station is a reasonably sized, purpose-built station set on the outskirts of Limerick. When the site was originally acquired, it was a fairly quiet, traffic-free area. By the time all the arsing around was over and the station was actually built – we'd only finally moved in less than a year earlier – the quiet suburb had turned into a busy thoroughfare. Cars and buses passed back and forth. People, alone and in groups, strolled past. Hundreds of individuals lived on that street alone. Hundreds and thousands of seconds of existence. It was all too much.

I started into a slow run so that maybe the thump of my feet on the footpath would help me come back into the world. I could take the rest of the day off if I wanted – but for what? To go home and think about all the shit that was going on in my life? Anyway, I had to go to Billy Hendrick's funeral at two. O'Toole had called specially to make sure I was going and not sending someone else.

Seán was coming to the funeral with me – and so was Janice. Seán didn't know she was coming yet, but I was sure he wouldn't like that. I didn't care.

I sort of liked Janice – I'd worked with her on a murder case a couple of years earlier – so I was glad when I heard that she was one of the NBCI detectives sent to work on the Hendrick case. I turned around and walked back towards the station.

Just as I was going in the gates, the same Janice Long appeared. She was tall and skinny with long, curly red hair that she usually kept tied back. She had a piece of paper in her hand.

'Rob. They found an address for Agnes Moloney.'

'Who?'

'Kelly Moloney's mother.'

I nodded. 'Yeah, sure, sorry. That's great. You should probably go see her today.'

Janice nodded. 'I think you should come along – if you're around, I mean.'

More sad relatives.

I nodded. 'Sure. Where does she live?'

'It's an apartment in town. They traced her through a mobile phone bill.'

'OK, OK,' I said, gradually coming back into the world. I'd be as well off to be interviewing Agnes Moloney. 'Maybe we'll drop in and visit her after the funeral.'

Janice smiled. 'I'm sure she'll be thrilled.'

'What's happening with the Brennans?' I said.

Janice crossed her eyes and sighed loudly. 'Amy and I have just come back from Gina Brennan's house. Hugh had visited them the other day but I thought maybe if we called we might have a bit more success.'

'And?'

'Nothing. I hate this stuff. The mother is this really soft-spoken woman. A nice woman, actually. She's a bit dazed by all the shit that's going down.'

'Does she know anything about Gina?'

Janice shook her head. 'Said she didn't and I believe her. There's a brother – Glenn, I think, is his name. Hugh talked to him. Same story – knows nothing. The only other thing is that there's an uncle as well. I'd like to have a chat with him but he's in the hospital for minor surgery. He and Gina are very close – or so her mother says.'

'Father?'

'No sign of him since 1985. Lives in England as far as the mother knows.'

'Anybody else?'

'That's it. She had another brother but he died about three years ago.'

'OK, well maybe something'll turn up.'

Janice smiled. 'Yeah, maybe. Listen, do you want to grab a bite of lunch before we go to the funeral?'

I smiled back at her. 'Sounds good. A pub or the canteen?'

'You're the local. You choose.'

'Well, it's Thursday and so I think it might be lasagne day. Molly, our cook, does a mean lasagne.'

Janice smiled. 'Lead the way.'

We headed back into the station. I was glad to be going to lunch with Janice. It'd be a distraction for me and that was good. Then I had to go to Billy Hendrick's funeral immediately afterwards and straight on to Kelly Moloney's mother. A full dance card. Which was good. As long as I could stop seeing silver Honda Civics everywhere I looked I might actually make it through the day.

13. Thursday 7 April

Hi Clint,

Me again.

The baby is great, do you know that? I really like him. The only problem is Natalie and Kelly. If things were bad between them before, it's totally cat now.

Kelly really seems to hate that baby. She just sits there smoking and sort of glaring at him and she's driving Natalie mad, and between the two of them they're driving me mad.

Kelly went for a walk earlier this evening and all the time she was gone Natalie just read the arse off her saying she had no nature and, how could you not love him, really, 'cos he's a bit of a puddin', isn't he – which is true. I think he's really cute and he has this skin that's so soft it's like it's not even there and this way of looking at you like he already knows you even though he's only a couple of days old. He's pure crabbid – a real old man.

I didn't say anything when Natalie was reading Kelly because OK I know it's ridiculous to be so uptight about one small baby, especially as we have nothing better to do for the next few days, but I just don't want to get pulled into their shit. And anyway there's something about her – Kelly, I mean – something in her face, and I can't help feeling sorry for her even though I don't know why I bother, 'cos she's acting like such a bitch.

I told you about Tony's operation, didn't I? I still haven't heard from him – hope he's not too sore. I was getting a bit freaked out waiting for him to call but Nat said he's probably forgotten to bring his charger to the hospital or something like that. Though he's supposed to be home today. I think I'll give him a ring in a while if I still haven't heard from him.

I can't wait to go to Spain. Being on the run is a lot more boring than you'd imagine. It's worse than jail. I mean, you'd think it would be kind of exciting – ducking the Guards and that – and at the start I was a bit pumped all right, but since then it's just loads of sitting around waiting.

Finding the baby makes it a good bit better, actually. There are always things to do for him – make bottles and change nappies and try to warm up some water to wash him. Natalie does a lot of it – she knows what to do. I just help. But it's still good 'cos at least it's something to pass the time.

We keep the radio on low all the time just in case there's anything new about us or Billy Hendrick. But there isn't. We're old news.

Natalie and me started to make a bed for the baby a while ago. It was Nat's idea. She handed him to me and was making him a bed out of cardboard and smoking a fag at the same time. She always gives him to me so she can go and smoke a fag 'cos she doesn't like smoking too close to him.

I like holding him. It makes me feel relaxed and warm or something, especially when he's changed and fed and falling asleep.

So Nat was smoking and dragging cardboard and I was holding the baby and then Kelly started. Out of the blue she clears her throat and coughs and stuff like she's going to give the sermon at Mass.

We need to get somebody to take that little bastard away, she says in this real weird voice.

Me and Nat just looked at her, 'cos we haven't heard her voice at all nearly since we found the baby. She wasn't looking at us, though – just still lying on her bed, looking up at the galvanized roof over our heads.

First it was a surprise to hear her talk, but then I could see that Natalie was getting mad with her – as usual. She rolled her eyes at me and lit another fag and said that there wasn't anything we could do anyway until Tony was better. Kelly kind of laughed then – if you could call it a laugh – and said that was the most ridiculous thing she ever heard in her life.

That fucking drove Natalie over the edge, of course, and she squared up – all chest out again and that fighting look in her eyes – and she went to stand over Kelly, who was lying on her bed.

I beg your pardon? says Natalie, looking down at her like she was a piece of shit on the floor. I cuddled the baby, who was asleep and making a funny snoring noise, and my heart sank. They were off again.

Kelly didn't bother her arse moving – just looked up at Natalie, and Nat puts a hand on her hip and takes a long drag from her cigarette and then puts her head back and blows smoke up in the air. Kelly still didn't say a word or move – just kept looking at her.

If you know so much, then maybe you'd like to enlighten us and tell us what we can do with the baby? Natalie says then.

Kelly didn't say anything for a few seconds – just put her hands behind her head. And then she says, Well, I already told you that we should have let the little bastard die like his mother intended.

Natalie made this loud tutting noise and then blew out her breath in an angry way and said that was a shitty thing to say and Kelly didn't know what his mother wanted. But you could see she was kind of shocked as well, for all her tough woman carry-on. I don't blame her – so was I.

Kelly was totally calm. You should have seen her, Clint. She got up out of her bed, real slow, talking real quiet, saying it had to be what his mother wanted 'cos she left him in a deserted warehouse.

Natalie was starting to pant and I was waiting for the go to start and though I didn't want the two of them fighting, Clint, to be honest I thought Kelly deserved a hiding for saying something like that. Even if I secretly think she's probably right. There are still things that shouldn't be said, aren't there?

Anyway, there they were like two bitches. Nat stepped on her fag and put her hands on her hips, and Kelly folded her arms and looked like she was finding the whole thing a great laugh. If it wasn't so fucking tragic it might have been actually funny.

Natalie starts on then, trying to get her to take back what she said – which is dumb when you think about it. How can you take something back? When it's said, it's said. Anyway, that's what she wanted but Kelly wouldn't. She said it was obvious what the woman was thinking and Nat said, Well, how about the fact that we found him, so? And Kelly said, That was just a fluke.

And it was. She's right. His mother couldn't have known we'd be there. But maybe she hoped someone else would.

Natalie's eyes filled up with tears and I could see she was really struggling hard to keep them all in. I don't give a shit. We found him and that's all that matters, she says then.

Kelly gave this big, loud sigh and bent down to root in her handbag for her fags. She found a pack and slowly lit one. Natalie never moved. Then Kelly started to walk around as she smoked. She stopped every now and then to take a pull off her fag and then walked around another bit.

The baby woke up and wriggled on my lap and I pulled him close to me. I wonder if he knows how shitty his life is already? Kelly stopped walking after a while and looked at me and the baby. And then she said she wasn't looking for a fight – just trying to talk sense, and that we should dump 'it' somewhere. A church or somewhere like that.

Nat went mad and said he wasn't an 'it', he was a real person, and Kelly didn't look at her – just kept looking at me, the mad bitch. Then she said we should go out tonight and leave him somewhere. That it was madness to keep him and what would we do if his mother changed her mind and told someone where she'd left him?

And I started laughing then and said I thought she was sure the mother wanted him dead, 'cos she can't have it every way, can she?

Kelly smiled this awful smile she has and shook her head and Natalie was nearly crying and saying she wasn't leaving a tiny baby nowhere by himself. I said then we should all calm down and wait for Tony to get better, 'cos he'd know what to do.

Natalie said that was true and Kelly said it was risky and we should just get rid of him tonight but she's mad about Tony so I knew she wouldn't say much.

Then I said I wanted to keep him for a while, 'cos he's a bit of entertainment when you don't have a telly.

Natalie smiled at that but Kelly still looked cross and said, I don't see how he's so entertaining. Shitting and pissing and crying and eating and sleeping – that's all he ever does.

I had a boyfriend like that once, Natalie said then. And we all laughed at that – even Kelly – because in fairness it was funny. Which was good, 'cos it was like the fight was over again for a while.

Love,
Gina xxx

14. Thursday 7 April

As I'd predicted, Seán was peeved when he heard Janice was coming to the funeral. But there was nothing he could do about it except bitch to me on the way to the church. I don't know why he was so peeved. Seán and Janice and I were only a small part of the police presence at Billy Hendrick's funeral. The place was full of cops: our whole team; Sharon O'Toole and her minions; and men and women in all shapes and sizes – plain clothes, uniformed, armed, unarmed. Just another thing to gripe about for Seán, I supposed. A token whinge in case I thought he was going soft and welcoming the NBCI people.

Funerals are interesting. You can learn a lot about any person by having a look around you at their funeral. Having said that, Billy Hendrick's funeral was unremarkable. There was a good showing of solicitors, of course – that was to be expected. Six politicians – five local, one national. A number of people who looked as if they might be acquaintances. And then, of course, there was his family.

At the cemetery, the family formed a semi-circle around the open grave. At one end of the crescent-shaped group was Alan – Billy's only sibling – in an expensive-looking charcoal suit with a pristine white shirt and sombre black tie. A cold wind shuffled through the crowd all through the graveside service and in spite of the warmth in the sun, I found I was shivering for most of the time.

Alan never moved once. In spite of the fact that he wasn't wearing an overcoat and that his broad chest was taking the brunt of the wind, he stood solidly beside the grave like a six-foot-three effigy. Janice murmured something to me about how handsome he looked and I had a quick survey. She was right.

I imagined that the Hendricks had probably been handsome, athletic little boys and then tall, broad, rugby-playing teenagers. By the time he was shot, though, Billy was a hefty six three but his bulk was probably largely due to too much alcohol and food rather than genetics and sport. Alan, on the other hand, looked like a man who still took care of himself – broad, healthy-looking, flat-stomached and – now that I looked for it – handsome in a chiselled Action Man way.

Throughout the entire graveside service, Alan kept his arm firmly around the shoulders of an old lady in a blue coat. This woman was very elderly-looking, fragile and almost translucent, with wispy white hair and a placid expression on her criss-cross lined face. It stood to reason that she was Helen Hendrick, their mother. She looked so unperturbed by the proceedings that it was obvious she'd mentally checked out of this vale of tears long ago.

Next in the family arc was a dark-haired woman in an olive-green coat and a teenage girl and boy. They had to be Alan's wife, Grace, and their children Henry and Lucy. I'd read all about them.

Slightly in front of this group stood the grieving widow, Caroline. She wore a voluminous black coat that fell almost the whole way to the muddy earth and a black hat that shaded her eyes from the world. I wasn't any great judge of fashion but even I could see that she looked as if she was modelling funeral wear.

Dylan stood as motionlessly as his Uncle Alan beside his mother, the expression on his face resigned, as if he was waiting out his father's funeral. His mother clung to his hand with both her hands even though she never spoke to him – never even looked down at him. Completing the family group was Billy's coffin, resting on a green baize-covered board surrounded by flowers and wreaths, waiting to be lowered into the grave.

The priest prayed and the crowd muttered responses. Alan Hendrick's wife and daughter cried openly. His mother looked around her as if she was lost and I was sort of glad for her – no matter what – that she wasn't following the proceedings. Two women at the back of the crowd talked the entire time and Caroline Hendrick never moved her eyes from the hole in the ground waiting to take her husband's body. Just as Alan Hendrick never took his eyes from her.

'I met a woman at the church,' Seán said as we drove back to the station together after the funeral. Janice had decided to take her own car and I didn't blame her. Seán was a bit of a pain in the arse when the chip on his shoulder was running him.

I pulled out into the traffic and wondered aloud if we should have gone to the after-funeral reception in Power's Hotel. I thought we probably should go along or at least arrange for somebody to go. There was the Agnes Moloney interview this afternoon but I'd see if there was someone available to go to the rest of the funeral when we got back to the station.

'Did you hear what I said?' Seán said, opening the window and lighting a cigarette.

'What? You met a woman. Jeez, Seán, not exactly a rare occurrence.'

'Very funny. This woman is a solicitor – Cora Hourigan.'

'Still not rare. I know her. I never knew you slept with her,' I said.

'I didn't say I slept with her, Roberto. Do you want to hear what she said?'

'Obviously.'

'Well, she told me a very interesting thing. She said that before Caroline and Billy got married, the merry widow and Alan were an item. In fact, that's how she met Billy – through Alan.'

'But Alan Hendrick must have been married himself before that.'

I looked at Seán and he looked at me and raised an eyebrow.

'Oh,' I said.

'Cora says everybody knew. Caroline was the ultimate trophy mistress and they were together for ages – years. The speculation was that he'd never leave the missus for her, though – wouldn't like to be parted from her money. Then, next thing anybody knew, she was married to Billy.'

'That is very odd,' I said, pulling into the station car park, 'but it doesn't really shape up to a motive for murder, does it?'

Seán shook his head. 'Unless there's stuff we don't know.'

'There's always stuff we don't know,' I said as we headed indoors.

'Yeah,' Seán said, 'like the fact that I did sleep with Cora Hourigan.'

'No, not like that – I already knew that.'

Janice was waiting in my office when we arrived. As soon as he saw her, Seán's face seemed to close.

'I forgot to tell you – Janice is sitting in on the interview with Agnes Moloney,' I said, silently cursing myself for forgetting to tell him and cursing Seán for being so bloody hard-headed that it made a difference.

Janice smiled and raised her eyebrows.

Seán smiled a tight smile. 'Great. Great. Do you know what, Rob? I think I'll go along to that funeral thing in Power's Hotel after all. Two of you will be plenty to do that interview.'

I looked at him and he shrugged. 'You can learn a lot at stuff like that.'

'If you mingle,' I said.

Seán grinned in spite of himself.

'Give my regards to Cora,' I said as he disappeared out of the door.

Janice sat on the windowsill and watched as Seán left the room. I pulled the Hendrick folder towards me and tried to get in the mood for the interview ahead. My head was full of the funeral – especially Dylan's patient face – and I wondered if he was right: maybe it was possible to just wait this stuff out.

'Do you have that address?' I muttered, as I flicked through the pages of my folder. 'Did you give it to me?'

'Apartment 1, Whitethorn Hall,' Janice read from a slip of paper. 'Do you know where that is?'

'I certainly do. Shall we go?'

Janice and I travelled together in my car the short distance to Whitethorn Hall. It was a tall, modern glass apartment building set in its own grounds on the banks of the River Shannon.

'Agnes Moloney obviously has plenty of money,' was all Janice said as we parked the Avensis and walked through the carefully planned wild garden edged by the abundant whitethorn hedges from which the name was obviously derived. And she was right. She obviously did have plenty of money – or at least whoever was paying the rental on the apartment had a few bob. I was betting that was likely to be somebody other than Agnes Moloney.

We had deliberately not called ahead as we were hoping to catch Agnes off guard. But an up-market private apartment building is a little hard to access without notice. Though we managed to make our way through the revolving door without issue, the security man at the desk was not too happy when I insisted he not ring ahead to announce our arrival. He gave us a disgruntled agreement but I would have bet my life savings that as soon as the lift doors closed he was on the phone to Ms Moloney.

The door to Apartment 1 opened on the first ring. Standing there was a tall and handsome middle-aged woman dressed in an expensive-looking purple tracksuit. Her dark hair was pulled back into a short ponytail and her make-up-free face was as pale as a corpse.

'Yes?'

'Agnes Moloney?' I asked.

'Yes?'

'My name is Detective Inspector O'Connell and this is Detective Sergeant Long. We were hoping we might have a word with you.'

The woman in the doorway looked so surprised that it confirmed my suspicions about the security man. Nobody with a daughter who'd been in jail could be that surprised by a visit from the police.

'But why would you want to speak to me?' she said, and Janice shot me a quick sideways glance.

'It's in connection with your daughter, Kelly,' Janice said.

Agnes's face was still a picture of bewilderment.

'She recently escaped from prison,' Janice continued.

Agnes Moloney covered the lower part of her face with one manicured hand and her dark eyes filled with tears. 'Have you found my baby girl? Is she all right? Come in. Come in.'

We followed her into the large living room of the

penthouse apartment of Whitethorn Hall, with its glass wall and cream carpets. We refused when she offered us coffee but accepted her invitation to be seated on a gigantic cream leather sofa in the centre of the room. Janice and I sat side by side as Agnes perched on the edge of a matching armchair opposite.

'Is she OK?' she asked in a shaking voice, as soon as we sat down. 'I've been so worried about her. I heard it on the news and . . . and . . . I haven't slept a wink since.'

'I'm afraid we haven't managed to locate your daughter, Ms Moloney. That's why we're here. We were hoping you might be able to help us find her, actually.'

Agnes Moloney picked up a pack of cigarettes from the glass coffee table between us and lit one with shaking hands. She took a few deep drags and then exhaled with force as though she was expelling something solid from her body. She leaned forward then, elbows on knees, chin on hands, smoke curling up the side of her head.

'I have no idea where Kelly is.' She paused briefly to inhale and exhale smoke. 'And I have to tell you, Detective, that I am very, very worried. Why would she do such a thing? She only had four months left in her sentence. Four months before she could come home to me.'

She took another long hard drag from her cigarette and then without warning jumped up from her armchair and ran from the room. Janice looked at me and grimaced. I shrugged in reply, but we needn't have worried. Within a few seconds she was back, carrying a leather-bound photograph album. She opened it on the coffee table and pivoted it towards us.

'There she is – my Kelly. See here.' She looked up at me and held me with her dark gaze. 'She was just three months old. Have you ever seen a more beautiful baby?'

She paused, waiting for her answer. A clock ticked loudly

somewhere in the room and in the distance the traffic hummed.

'No,' I said when I realized she wasn't moving on without a reply. And anyway it was true. I hadn't. The baby in the photographs with her enormous black eyes and dark hair was prettier than any baby I'd ever seen either in real life or in ads. With her regular features and open expression she was like an idealized baby.

'She was very beautiful,' Janice said.

Agnes nodded, pleased now that we were all singing from the same hymn sheet. She began to turn over pages. Photo after photo passed by, plotting the trajectory of a small girl's growth between zero and five. Kelly on beaches. Kelly on Santa's knee in 1985. Kelly in the bath, in the garden, at all her birthday parties, blowing out candles. And again on Santa's knee – 1986, '87, '88. Nothing was undocumented in those first five years. It was a hefty album and there were a lot of photographs. As Agnes herself was only in a couple of the pictures she'd clearly been the devoted photographer.

'Have you any children, Detective?' she asked me, leaning slightly forward so that the view of her cleavage under the zipped top of her tracksuit was maximized.

'Unfortunately not.'

She shook her head sadly. 'And are you married?'

I smiled. 'Indeed I am.'

'Well, some day – some day I hope you'll be blessed with children.'

I continued to smile but her dark eyes and the subject matter were unnerving me.

'I have a daughter,' Janice interrupted.

Agnes sat back in her chair and looked at her with a slightly surprised expression, as though she'd momentarily forgotten she was in the room.

'Children are the most precious thing in the world,' Agnes said, looking back at me as she stubbed out her cigarette and immediately lit a second. 'Kelly was everything to me and they took her away. I mean, how can it be good for a small girl to be away from her mother? It's not good for her. It's not good for Mummy . . .' Her voice trailed off as tears began to slide down her face. Janice silently closed the leather-bound album and the three of us sat there without speaking as Agnes wept. When she had finished she blew her nose and took a long, deep drag on the cigarette that'd been burning between her fingers.

'We were hoping you might know where Kelly is,' I said quietly. 'We'd really just like to talk to her.'

Agnes shook her head and leaned forward towards me again. I looked into her eyes and noticed that one was very, very slightly turned.

'I wish I knew,' she said. 'If you find out anything – anything at all – please, please, Detective, will you promise to let me know?' She grabbed my hand and rubbed the back of it gently with the tips of her soft manicured fingers.

'I promise,' I said, gently releasing my hand. 'Thank you for your time, Ms Moloney . . .'

'Agnes.'

I nodded. 'Thanks again for your time. If we hear anything we'll let you know and maybe you'd do the same?'

She stood up and so did Janice and I. 'I'll call you straight away, Detective, if I hear anything. Do you have a card?'

I fished one out of my pocket and handed it to her. She made a show of reading it and then placed it on the coffee table beside the photographic record of Kelly's babyhood.

We all shook hands and said goodbye, making promise after promise to keep each other filled in.

*

'Do you believe her?' I asked Janice as we glided silently to the ground floor in the lift.

She didn't answer for a few seconds. 'I felt sorry for her, for some reason.'

'OK, but did you believe her?'

'No, not really. Did you?'

'No, but I'm not sure if that's to do with all the stuff about baby Kelly or if she was hiding something fresh.'

'We should probably pay her another visit in a few days,' Janice said, leading the way through the lobby, past the security man, who became deeply engrossed in his newspaper as soon as he saw us.

'Agreed.'

It had started to spatter rain, so we ran to the car.

Janice looked at her watch as we crawled through the rush-hour traffic back to the station. She leaned back in her seat and stretched.

'Knocking-off time,' she said.

'So it is.'

'How about a drink?'

'Don't mind if I do,' I said, pulling into a long line of traffic.

A drink was a very attractive option – a lot more attractive than the idea of sitting at home trying not to obsess about the bastard who'd run over my wife. There'd be plenty of time to do that later as I lay awake staring at my bedroom ceiling.

I parked the Avensis in the station car park and Janice and I walked to the nearest pub, O'Malley's. There was no point in driving anywhere – all we needed was something to take the edge off the day. I texted Seán to tell him where we were just in case he'd like to join us – though I knew well he wouldn't. Which was stupid, really. I knew that he and

Janice would probably get on if he gave her half a chance.

O'Malley's was packed with people — mostly men — having a quick drink before going home. It's a dark, cavernous pub that hasn't seen a coat of paint since about 1978 but I like it. It's always full of Guards doing the same thing we were doing — postponing going home — and as everybody has the same idea nobody bothers much with anybody else.

As we made our way through the throng, I saluted at least three detectives from the station. One — Derek Reynolds — was a little the worse for wear and he looked as if he might be going to come and talk to me.

The gossip about him was that his wife had left him. I felt very sorry for him but I wasn't sure I had anything to give him right at that moment. So I was relieved that he seemed to change his mind when he saw Janice.

The TV news blared at full volume as I found us a small booth near the back. I asked Janice what she'd have but she could barely hear me, so I had to almost shout into her ear. As I shouted I was distracted by the smell of her neck. It reminded me of Rita and hurt some place in the pit of my stomach that I hadn't realized existed.

As I stood at the bar waiting for Hoppy the deaf barman to get us two pints of lager, I couldn't help but wonder how she could smell like Rita. Not a perfume or any fragrance but a soft body smell — kind of like the smell newborn babies have. Somehow the fact that I noticed it made me feel a bit guilty.

Janice was sending a text message as I returned to the booth with our drinks.

'My daughter,' she said. 'She hates it when I'm away, so I let her text me all the time. That way she's happy.'

'What age is she?' I asked as I sat beside her on the sticky red leatherette seat.

'Ten.'

'You look too young to have a ten-year-old daughter.'

Janice laughed and her pale face flushed a little. 'That's the right thing to say. She was a bit of a surprise, I admit, but now – as they say – I wouldn't be without her.'

She took a long drink from her glass before returning it to the table. Then she looked straight at me. That was the thing I liked about Janice: she was straight in every way – except for her curly hair. Straight backed. Straight talking. Straight up. It made her very easy to be around.

'I was twenty-two. Got pregnant at a party – the usual story: nurses and Guards, hard drinking, wild parties.'

'The father?'

'I'm ashamed to say I don't really know for sure. But I decided to keep her and, well . . . it was the right decision.'

'What's her name?'

'Emma.'

'That's a nice name.'

She smiled at me. 'I think so, anyway.'

'So where is she while you're away?'

'With my parents. They love her and she loves them, so it's all grand, really. We only live down the road from them.'

She smiled and I could see that we'd finished with that topic. And that was fine with me. There were plenty of topics I was anxious to avoid myself.

I'm not quite sure how our one drink turned into two and then three or how exactly I started to tell her about Rita – and even about the new witness.

The relief in saying it all to someone who wasn't trying to tell me anything or advise me – for my own good – was enormous. Janice just sat there and listened to it all: comas and vegetative states and nursing homes and doctors and friends. She just sipped her lager as I spoke and I felt better than I had in ages.

15. Thursday 7 April

Hi Clint,

The baby must have been bored with us 'cos he went back to sleep, so I put him down on my bed and covered him with a jumper. And then Nat and me got back to making his bed like we'd been doing before the last fight. We made this really cool bed out of cardboard and jumpers and stuff and then Nat said we should give him a name.

I said that was a great idea but Kelly was all, For fucksake, and went off to the jacks. We just ignored her and Natalie said, What about Brad – like Brad Pitt, 'cos he's blond as well. And I said that I knew Brad Pitt was a ride but Brad's a shit name and Nat said I should think of a name if I was so fucking smart – and I did. Peter. It just kind of came into my head and Nat said OK, maybe, and then the two of us stood there looking down at him while he was asleep.

You should have seen him. He was lying on his back and his head was turned to the side and one of his little fists was under his chin kind of like he was thinking or something.

And Natalie says then, Jesus, he's very cute.

So I says, We can't call him Jesus.

And she thumps me and says he does kind of look like a Peter and so that was decided, and anyway whatever we called him it'd be better than calling the poor little bastard 'the baby' all the time.

So then me and Nat went back to finishing Peter's bed while he snored away. By the time we were finished, Peter was awake and Nat had to change his shitty arse. She told me to make him another bottle, 'cos he was starving, and I said he just ate and she said, Shut up you fool, he's been asleep for nearly three hours, 'cos it's past nine. I looked at my watch. She was right – it was twenty past nine. For once I hadn't felt the time pass. Then Kelly suggested we have a Chinese for dinner – which was good thinking out of her 'cos we hadn't had any dinner and we'd eaten almost all the food that Tony'd brought us. I went to my bag and took out some of the money he'd given us and handed it to Kelly and told her I'd have a sweet and sour chicken with fried rice and a couple of spring rolls.

Then she's all, Who said I was going? but she was grinning. So I said it was her turn 'cos I went out to get the bottle and food and nappies and stuff for Peter. Then of course Kelly starts rolling her eyes and saying 'Peter' like it was something stupid, and I was waiting for another round of fighting to start but for once Nat ignored her. She just stared at her for a few seconds and then said would she get her chicken chow mein and a two-litre bottle of Coke and to get some bread and milk as well while she was out.

Kelly made a face but she took the money off me and put on her denim jacket, and just as she was going Natalie called her name. Kelly stopped and looked at her.

And Nat says, her face all serious, What do you have against babies, anyway?

Kelly said nothing. Just looked at her.

I mean, I know he's not ours, but if you'd ever had one maybe you'd feel different, that's all I'm saying. It like opens up something inside of you – even if you fuck it up, Nat says.

I was very surprised with that, Clint – it's not like Natalie to be all philosophical and shit but she really meant it, I could see that. Kelly was still standing there with her jacket half buttoned when she said it.

That's shit.

No it isn't, Natalie says back to her.

Then why didn't it open something up in me, if it's such a special thing? Kelly says and that was that. We just looked at her with our mouths open and she just turned around and left. What the hell was that supposed to mean?

Natalie and me played a game of Lifes while Kelly was gone. Neither of us said nothing about what she'd said. I don't know why Nat didn't say anything – especially as she's such a mouth almighty. I didn't say anything because I knew that there was something about what Kelly had said that was connected to the sad thing I can always see in her. Stupid, isn't it? But it takes one to know one, as Mam always says.

My head was busting from the whole lot of them, so I was glad just to be playing cards and then even happier when I won the game. I always win Lifes – remember?

It wasn't long, anyway, before Kelly was back with a bag full of food. And no one said nothing about what'd been said earlier. Tony'd brought us paper plates and I found us three and we put food out of the foil containers on to them. Then we sat around the gas heater and ate our Chinese without talking much, 'cos it tasted so good and we were all so starving we hadn't any interest in talk. When we were finished Nat made us all a cup of tea and then the two of them smoked fags and baby Peter blew bubbles and moved his legs and arms like he was that clockwork bunny in the ad. I said that and it made everybody laugh, even Kelly again – another good sign – and then I started writing this . . .

Oh Jesus, Clint, just when I was writing that part above the phone rang. I looked at the screen and saw Tony's name and I was delighted because even though I was telling myself not to worry I was still worried. The girls were drinking tea and listening to the radio and Natalie was amusing herself letting baby Peter grab her finger and let it go over and over. I answered the phone as usual.

Hey, Tony, how's it hanging? I said straightaway. How are you feeling?

First the person at the other end said nothing and then it was, Hi, Gina, it's me – Glenn.

So I says, Glenn? Are you ever going to come and take those photographs? We're going to be stuck in this bloody place for ever if you don't make us passports.

And he took this loud, rattly breath and then he said, Gina, look, I don't know how to tell you this except to just say it out – Tony's dead.

I wrote those words there, Clint, and then I sat and looked at them for ages and ages and I couldn't write any more. I think I should stop for a while, OK? Talk to you later.

Love,
Gina xxx

16. Friday 8 April

Waking up beside Janice was terrifying. I woke up suddenly and fully aware but with no idea where I was, and I was absolutely shit scared that I was in my own bed. I stared at the ceiling, because ceilings are all the same and I could be anywhere if I just looked up at the white plasterboard.

Sweat poured down my face and into my mouth and my heart thumped so loudly I thought it might wake Janice. Because I didn't need to turn my head to know it was Janice. I remembered that.

The smell and the heat of her body. Her long, narrow, white-skinned back, curving under my hands. The almost painful relief of the feeling of another person touching my skin. The sex and then sleep and then more sex at some stage during the night when we woke with our limbs entangled. I remembered all that – I just couldn't remember where we were.

Janice must have heard my heart thumping because she moved close to me and rested her hand on my chest. I prayed she wouldn't talk because I didn't know what I'd say or how to get away. I didn't move and barely breathed. Gradually, Janice's hand slackened and fell away from me. She turned on her side, facing away from me, and I listened until I was pretty sure her regular breathing meant she was asleep again.

Then I made myself turn my head and was almost sick with relief as I saw that I was in a strange room. White texturized wallpaper, generic pencil sketches of Limerick, heavy drapes and glass-topped bedside lockers. A TV high on a wall bracket.

Some hotel.

Thank you, God.

I slid out of the bed and found my clothes on the floor and silently dressed, trying to ignore the smell of sex that was everywhere. At least it hadn't happened in my bedroom. That was something.

At least I hadn't fucked some woman in Rita's bed. I looked at my watch. Six o'clock. They'd let me in to see her.

I was afraid to shower in case I woke Janice, so I'd have to go home and get cleaned up before work, but it wouldn't matter if I was late. Seán'd take the meeting at ten.

The night porter gave me a knowing look as he let me out of the glass doors at the front of the hotel into the grey dawn. I wished I could tell him I wasn't the sad bastard he thought I was – but I couldn't, because I was. I didn't want to think about it, so I made a plan for the morning instead.

Go and see Rita first. Call Seán then. Ask him to start the morning conference for me. Tell him something. Anything. A lie. Bad night. Bad flu. Whatever. It didn't matter. I had to see her and that was all about it. My stomach turned over as I realized that Janice would be at that meeting but I couldn't even make myself think about that yet. First I'd see Rita and then maybe I'd know what to do.

The nursing home was waking up by the time I arrived and slipped quietly into Rita's room. The nurses had obviously already been in there before me, as someone had opened the curtains. The light in the room was dull and weak, but I liked it because I was too ashamed to want to see clearly.

Rita lay there like a marble effigy and the minute I saw

her, my heart seemed to slow down and the terrible agitation that'd occupied my whole body since I'd woken drained away. I kissed her lips and felt the lightness of her breath on my cheek and it smelled so pure – like a baby's breath.

I pulled my usual chair close to the bed and sat down and took her right hand. I held it for a few seconds and its warm, limp weight pressed on my palm. I saw that they'd put splints on her hands again and gently unfastened them before reaching for the lavender oil.

'Dark old day out today,' I said as I smoothed oil into her fingers. The words hurt my throat. 'Bad traffic too, considering it's so early in the morning.' The words inside me were drying up and for the first time ever I couldn't think of even one thing to say to her.

I furiously massaged the hand I was working on and then began the other. Too late I realized that I hadn't showered and so the touch of Janice was probably still on my hands.

How could I have had sex with Janice? I wanted to be sick. As soon as I finished oiling Rita's hands, I replaced the splints, and because I couldn't say another word I laid my head on the green cotton coverlet and closed my eyes.

The next thing I knew my phone was ringing. I jerked awake, pulling Rita's hand slightly as I sat up. I rearranged her hand on the bed and dragged my phone from my pocket. Seán.

'You OK?' he said.

I struggled to focus on the face of my watch. Fuck it. Ten o'clock. Fuck, fuck, fuck. 'Seán, I'm in Árd Aoibhinn.'

'Is something wrong?'

'No, no – I just had a bad night. Fell asleep here.'

'As usual.'

I pretended to laugh. 'As usual. Will you take the meeting?'

'No problem. I'll get it going for you.'

'Maybe take it altogether, if you could? I need to go home and have a shower and a shave before I go in to work.'

'Don't worry about it. I'll enjoy making these NBCI bastards give an account of themselves.'

'Don't torture them, Seán. They can't help it that they're from Dublin.'

'Talk to you later,' he said and hung up.

I stroked the back of Rita's hand and suddenly I remembered something I could tell her. 'Do you remember I told you they'd found a witness, love?'

She breathed.

'Well, Mary spoke to her. It's a woman. She'd been in Africa but now she's back. She saw the whole thing and there was a cab driver as well. They're trying to find him and find out why he didn't do anything about what happened.'

I fixed a stray strand of hair behind her translucent ear and kissed her, gently.

'I'm sorry I missed last night.'

A picture of Janice's face as she moaned with pleasure shot in front of me and I felt like beating my head against the wall to erase it.

'I'll see you tonight, love.'

I kissed Rita again and then left. For the first time ever I was glad she hadn't opened her eyes once during my visit.

It was almost twelve by the time I got to the station. Seán was in my office, sitting on the desk reading a newspaper.

'Hard at work, I see,' I said as I came in.

'That's nice talk out of someone who didn't bother his arse to come into work until midday.'

'How was the meeting?'

He folded his newspaper and stood up. 'Fine. Nothing new really. Janice reported on your interview yesterday.

Conn Holmes had a bit of information about the money: seemingly one of the junior secretaries in Hendrick's office saw him with the briefcase on Friday. She was sent into him with papers and she said he was looking in the briefcase and he closed it as soon as she came in, but she thought she saw money in it.'

I looked at him. 'On Friday?'

Seán nodded.

'Two days before he was killed. So if he had it on Friday he should have been able to go to the bank and deposit it.'

'Well, maybe not. It was late Friday – she was working back.'

'Night safe?' I said.

'Yeah. Well, might have been other money, for all we know. There is something else, though.'

'What?' I said, sitting down. My body felt like lead and residual memories of the night before floated into my consciousness like pieces of a shipwreck.

Seán walked over and looked out of the window. 'I met Cora Hourigan again yesterday at the yoke after the funeral.'

'And?'

'And she was pissed – Jesus, those solicitors know how to drink. Anyway, she fucking hates Caroline Hendrick. If we were to listen to her, we should have arrested the grieving widow the day of the murder. Cora is completely convinced she killed Billy.'

'But she was away.'

'I know. I told her that but she went on and on and on. Apart from being pissed, Cora's a bit heartbroken about Billy.'

'Why?'

'Because she and he were a couple as well, for years.

That's how she knows so much about Caroline and Alan. Cora was part of the family, as it were.'

'So why did Billy marry Caroline?'

'Well, Cora says Alan made him. All she knows for sure is that he broke up with her and three months later was married to Caroline. She's pretty good on the information before she and Billy broke up – a bit sketchy after that, though. A lot of speculation.'

'A woman scorned?'

Seán nodded. 'She thinks Alan got Caroline pregnant with Dylan and made Billy marry her.'

'Sounds a bit far fetched.'

'Cora says Alan Hendrick is a bastard – much more dangerous than all of the scumbags he represents put together. She thinks he and Caroline continued their relationship after Billy and she were married.'

'Jesus, people really make a pig's arse of their lives, don't they?' I said, thinking of myself and Janice Long rolling around in that hotel bed. Christ, how was I going to work with her? What the hell was I going to say? Was sorry the kind of thing you said under the circumstances, or was it an insulting thing to say?

'Tell me about it,' Seán said. 'I have to go out and smoke a fag. Do you want to come with me?'

I nodded and followed Seán through the busy building, half on the lookout for Janice. No sign, thank God. Spared for a while. We walked out of the gates on to the public footpath and as soon as we were outside he lit a cigarette.

'As people clean the streets for a living, is the public street technically a workplace and therefore is it against the law to smoke there?' I asked.

'Shut up,' Seán said, inhaling with satisfaction.

'Did you share this information you got from Cora Hourigan at the meeting this morning?' I asked, sidestepping a teenage girl with a blonde ponytail who was pushing a baby in a buggy and speaking excitedly into a mobile phone.

Seán shook his head. 'It's too vague. Thought I'd run it by you first.'

'I don't know what we can do about it. I mean, it's all very interesting and probably mostly true, but it still doesn't amount to much of a motive for murder, does it?'

'No. But it is very suspicious, all the same.'

'But not against the law.'

Seán sighed wistfully. 'No. Not like smoking.'

I laughed and a soft misty rain began to fall. We turned back towards the station and my phone rang.

'Rob?' a woman's voice I didn't recognize said, quietly.

'Hello,' I said guardedly.

'Hi, it's me – Janice.'

'Hello, Janice,' I said, so loudly that Seán turned his head to look at me. I looked away. 'How are you? Sorry to have missed the meeting this morning – something came up. You know how it is.'

'Don't worry about it,' she said and I felt lousy because I knew we were really talking about my screw-and-disappear act. Maybe I should tell Seán. He had legions of experience at this sort of stuff – he had to know how to deal with it.

'There's a woman looking for you. She keeps ringing the office. Says she's your sister and that she has to get in contact with you.'

'My sister has my mobile number,' I said.

'I figured. Anyway maybe if you call your sister – just in case.'

'I'll do that. Thanks, Janice. See you later.'

I pressed the hang-up button and scrolled down through

my address book until I found Maria's mobile number. No answer. I tried her home number. The phone rang and rang and I was just about to disconnect when she answered.

'Hi, Maria – it's Rob. Were you looking for me?'

'Oh Jesus, thank God.'

'What's wrong?' I said, freezing to the spot.

'Oh Rob, I lost my phone and I couldn't find your mobile number and I had to get in touch with you . . .'

'Maria – what is it?'

'Oh Jesus, Rob, you have to do something. Emmet and Shane have been arrested.'

17. Tuesday 12 April

Hi Clint,

Sorry I haven't written for a few days. I just couldn't after Tony and all. Anyway, they buried him today. Heart attack after the surgery, they said. Just one of those things – that's what the doctors said, according to Glenn. I hate that.

After you died a doctor with grey wings in his black hair said the same thing when we were trying to find out what had happened. He talked about the drugs in your blood and called it a lethal concoction.

Were you depressed? he wanted to know. Had you ever attempted suicide before? It was a fucking nightmare – worse than finding you in the sitting room, even.

Mam covered her mouth with her hand and her eyes looked at him all the time he was talking and tears just ran down her face. She kept asking him why and he talked more and talked faster and Mam listened but he wasn't answering what we wanted to know. So she asked it again.

But why, Doctor? Why would Clint do that?

I could see that the doctor wanted us gone. He never even looked at Mam. He looked at the floor and then at me and then he smiled, but his eyes were empty. Closed.

I'm afraid it's just one of those things, he said for a finish, like that was an answer.

I wanted to punch his mouth and make blood flow out on to his tanned face and then tell him it was just one of those things and that I knew he'd understand. But I knew Mam'd go mad and she was upset enough.

In the cab on the way home she asked me if I knew about the drugs and I said no because I did, but it was like I didn't, because I didn't think it was serious. I was wrong, though, Clint, wasn't I?

Glenn just rang. He said Mam cried and cried and cried at Tony's funeral. I can easily believe it. He was only forty-three – he wasn't supposed to die yet. Mind you, that's shit, isn't it? You were nineteen.

Mam'll be lost without Tony, though. He was her best friend in the world as well as being her brother. She said to me once that she didn't know how she'd have managed without him after Dad left. I'd say he gave her money and everything when we were growing up. What'll she do now?

Fuck it, Clint. I can't believe Tony is dead. When you're dead do you meet people that you know? Have you met Tony yet or is there some kind of a waiting period before you meet up? I'd say he'll be delighted to see you.

Glenn was in a pub after the funeral when he rang and he was pissed and crying and I warned him not to tell anyone where I was, no matter how pissed he got and then he got mad and said did I think he was a fucking eejit altogether? I said, No, just be careful, that's all, and he got mad again and was saying stuff and some of it was about you and I wanted to hang up – but I didn't. After that stopped I told him to tell me all about the funeral. So he did.

He said it was great. That the sun was shining and that all Tony's friends were there and everyone was shocked and saying what a great man he was. Glenn said he remembered being a kid and someone at school slagging him and saying that Tony was a big poof and not a real man and how he punched the shit out of the kid and said he was wrong. Tony was so a real man.

He'd never told me that before but I was glad because it was true. You know as well as I do that Tony was more of a man than loads of other men. He was definitely more of a man than Dad. I said that to Glenn and that made him cry again.

I was sorry I'd said it then and tried to get him to promise that he'd tell that story to his girlfriend Amy. He said he would and then I said he was to come up and see me. He said he'd do that as well and anyway he had to get the photographs or we'd never get passports and we'd have to be in that fucking warehouse for ever. Tomorrow, he said then – I'll come up tomorrow. I said OK and he hung up.

There I was, Clint, sitting on an empty barrel out the back in the small yard while I was on the phone to Glenn. I could hear radio music from inside the warehouse and my heart felt like it was going to burst open inside me. And all of a sudden it really hit me: Tony is dead.

It just makes no sense to me at all. I mean, fuck it, the world is oxter deep in bastards who should be dead, evil fuckers we'd all be better off without, and they aren't dead but Tony is. And you. I couldn't cry – even though I wouldn't have minded a good bawl, 'cos maybe it'd have made the pressure in my chest a bit better. My eyes were hot and burning but no tears came out of them. I must have been out there for ages.

Kelly even brought me out a cup of tea. I can't figure her out. She's very deep. Very hard to know what's going on there. I knew she was very upset when I told her Tony'd died but she never said a word. I heard her crying when she thought we were asleep but I didn't say anything because she didn't. Even that time when she brought me out tea she didn't say a thing – just gave me a smile like she meant it and was sorry for me and went back inside.

I held on to that cup of tea and it was lovely and warm in my hands but I couldn't face drinking it. I just stayed sitting there while it was getting dark and I could hear traffic in the street outside the high walls of the yard and Peter shouted and Nat said something to him in a soft voice and he was quiet again.

And then everything started piling in on top of me. Now what are we going to do? No Tony any more to help us. No Tony to help Peter. No Tony to help me. My heart thumped and felt like it was swelling and swelling in my chest, but still no tears.

My tea went cold and I poured it down a drain and went back inside and told the others I was tired and wanted to have a sleep. Nat was holding Peter as usual and Kelly was actually cleaning up the place for once.

Nat smiled at me and said I should have a rest and then she started off into this big speech about how I shouldn't be trying to keep it inside and I figured she meant all the stuff about Tony and I said I knew but I was tired so I just wanted to go to sleep.

So I got into my bed and pulled the damp covers up over my head and looked at the wall and I didn't have any intention of falling asleep – just wanted to get away – but that's exactly what happened.

When I woke up Kelly was holding the phone in front of me. I couldn't make out what was going on and everything was the same as always and then I suddenly remembered about Tony being dead and it all fell on me like rocks.

I just looked at her until she said, It's Eric. And even that didn't make any sense to me and she seemed to know that, 'cos she said, Tony's Eric.

And I just couldn't bear to talk to him, so I asked her to tell him I'd call him back and he said no, it was OK, he had to go someplace and was it all right for him to call back later and talk to me then and I said grand, that'll be grand.

I couldn't face talking to him then. I wanted to write to you first, 'cos I haven't written in days and everything is all jammed inside of me and I thought maybe if I wrote I'd feel a bit better and be able for talking.

And I do sort of.

xxx

18. Friday 8 April – Tuesday 12 April

I did as Maria asked and went to find out why Emmet and Shane had been arrested on Friday, and then I ran away. Not physically far away up a mountain or into the wilderness somewhere – though I'd have loved to do that. Just away inside my head.

The only person I had any intention of seeing after I'd heard what had happened was Rita. That way I'd not only be happy but if anybody was trying to find me I wouldn't be home. And I was fairly certain they wouldn't come to the nursing home. Rita didn't get too many visitors any more. Both her parents were dead and she was an only child, so that meant the only real family she had was mine.

My family had always adored her and had visited all the time straight after the accident. But once she'd been moved to the nursing home things always seemed to come up to prevent their visits. Too far for my parents to travel. Too hard for Maria and that bollocks of an ex-husband.

Sure they still came the odd time. Christmas and stuff. But when they visited they brought flowers and talked to me as if Rita was no longer in the room. I didn't mind. I understood. Sometimes I thought maybe if I understood less I might be better off.

I'd always been aware that Emmet had never been to the nursing home at all. I'd understood that as well. I knew that he'd been completely devastated by Rita's accident and I'd sort of figured he was just doing that teenage thing and trying to avoid anything that made him feel unhappy.

Now I wasn't so sure that the explanation was as simple as that.

'They were picked up just outside Parteen,' Mary Hayes had said to me when I asked why Emmet and Shane had been arrested. 'The car was stolen. I've been getting the lads to send me up descriptions of everyone they pull in for joyriding now that we have a witness. It's not foolproof but you know yourself: these young fellas tend to keep right on stealing cars until they're caught.'

She paused and looked at me. I nodded as if everything was fine and, to be honest, right at that moment I didn't feel too bad because I was sort of frozen.

'How do you know that the car that ran into Rita was stolen?' Seán said.

'We don't, but it's a fair bet, don't you think?'

Seán and I both nodded.

'Did you find the cab driver?' I said.

Mary rubbed her lips together and made a small sighing noise. 'Not yet, but Willie O'Neill is on it now and he's like a terrier – he won't stop till he finds him. I'd safely say he's already interviewed almost every cab driver within a ten-mile radius.'

'But no luck?' I said.

'No. There are a few drivers who are away on holiday and another two or three who've changed job since the accident, so he has to talk to those guys and we'll see then.'

'That's good,' I said in my calm voice.

'But your woman – what's her name?' Seán interrupted.

'Fidelma O'Hagan.'

'OK. O'Hagan said Emmet was driving the car?'

The words actually felt as if they hurt my ears as Seán spoke them. Mary's face became softer and she looked at me. 'That's what she said. She's not a great witness, though

– full of herself and trying to salve her conscience for not coming forward sooner.'

I nodded and my heart beat hard inside my chest and my head began to race. Emmet's name swirled around and around, and Rita's face, and I wondered what fucking cruel twist of fate could have made it true that the person who destroyed my beautiful wife was my own sixteen-year-old nephew whom she adored. I swallowed hard.

'But you're not charging them with Rita's hit-and-run, are you?' Seán asked.

'No, not yet – we haven't enough evidence, but I'm afraid Emmet fits the description all right.'

Seán paced back and forth. 'Come on, Mary – for God's sake. What's the description? Lanky young fella with dark hair?'

Mary nodded. She was still looking at me. 'Longish dark hair.'

'So fucking what, Mary?' he said, and I noticed that Seán was matching my progressive detachment with his own progressively building agitation. 'I could go into town right this minute and pick up at least five or six teenage boys who fit that description.'

Mary turned her attention to Seán. 'They're not all riding around in stolen cars.'

He tutted. 'Just because he was in this one car – he wasn't even driving, was he?'

Mary took a deep breath. 'No, Seán, he wasn't, but I'm afraid this isn't the only stolen car he's been in.'

'How do you know that?' I asked.

'We matched his prints to prints that we've recovered from two other stolen vehicles.'

Seán muttered something to himself and shifted around. 'Still doesn't mean he was in that car.'

'I know, but he does fit the description,' Mary said.

'Full circle,' I said and they both looked at me, but I was too far inside myself to explain what I meant.

'You're not keeping them, are you?' he asked.

Mary shook her head. 'All the parents have been contacted. I'm expecting them along any minute now.'

'No need to stay, so, is there?' Seán said to me. I frowned and stared at him.

'Maria'll be along in a few minutes. What else can you do here, Rob?'

I smiled a brittle smile. He was right. There wasn't a fucking thing I could do and I didn't want to see Emmet – I didn't even want to see Maria – and Seán knew that. So I left and went home, turning down Seán's offer of company for the evening. I needed to be alone.

It was almost six o'clock by the time I let myself in home. I closed the door and sealed myself into the silent house; then I stood in the hallway, staring at the small red and black mosaic tiles Rita'd picked out when we'd moved in. What was I going to do now?

For the first time I consciously realized that two things had kept me going since 17 May: the picture I had in my head of when Rita would open her eyes and say my name and the day I could eyeball the bastard who'd hurt my wife. And now it turned out that it was Emmet? That was just insane.

I moved into my small sitting room and sat there on the only straight-backed chair, thinking and trying not to feel. Maybe Seán was right. Maybe it wasn't Emmet. Maybe it was all a big mistake. He'd said it – loads of young fellas looked like Emmet.

It began to get dark outside but I didn't move to switch

on the light – just stared out through the open curtains as the sky turned from cloudy pale blue to a kind of royal blue with pink candy-floss streaks until finally it was all just ink. The streetlights came on, pale at first and then more and more orange against the darkening sky. The telephone rang and I noticed that it made a tinny noise in my empty hallway, but I didn't answer it, and then my mobile rang as well in my jacket pocket. I didn't move.

Eventually I must have dozed off on the chair because I woke up with a start and the telephone was ringing again. I walked into the hallway and looked at the small screen on the phone and read the name I expected. Maria. I imagined her anxious face all scrunched up with worry and I thought I should really pick up but instead I bent down and unplugged the phone from its socket. Then I went to my car and drove to the nursing home and spent the rest of the night staring at Rita's face.

Morning came and the nursing home erupted with the sounds of radios and telephones and voices talking and calling and laughing. The breakfast trolley trundled by the bedroom door but nobody came in – there was no need. Rita lived on whatever it was that was fed to her through that long clear tube they'd inserted into her stomach.

The smell of toast or whatever the patients were having for breakfast made me feel hungry. I thought of going out and cajoling a cup of tea and some food from the nurses, but then I remembered the Emmet stuff all over again and felt nauseated.

At around eleven, two chatting, blonde teenage nurses came into the room, pushing a trolley laden with fresh bed linen. They looked at me and gave me smiles tight with embarrassment.

'I'd better get going,' I said.

They just nodded and made more fake smiles, so I left. Once I'd stayed and watched as Rita's bed was changed, and the sheer floppiness of her was unbearable. Anyway, I hadn't slept a wink all night and really needed to get to bed. And then there was the fact that I was beginning to find it hard to think of things to say to Rita as I collected more and more that I didn't want her to hear.

First Janice. Now Emmet.

It'd been OK to sit there during the night in silence, but now that it was daytime I felt she should be hearing conversation and be moved and massaged and generally stimulated, and I wasn't up to any of it. I felt like shit. My throat was sore and getting sorer by the minute. It felt as if there was a briar stuck halfway down.

I drove home and planned maybe to take some of the sleeping tablets the doctor had insisted I have after the accident. I needed a good sleep and though I knew it would solve shag all at least it'd be a short reprieve from my head, and that was fine with me. But somebody up there definitely hates me.

Emmet was in my house when I got home.

I'd forgotten he had a key.

He ran to the hallway as soon as he heard me open the front door. His baggy clothes hung so loosely on him it was as if there was no one inside. His blue eyes were red-rimmed and his breath sounded loud. I looked at him and then looked away.

'It wasn't me,' he said.

I walked past him into the kitchen and filled a glass of water, but I couldn't drink it because the briar was growing up along my throat. I sipped enough water to wet the inside of my mouth and stared out of the window. It was raining and windy and the apple trees in the back garden were flinging their pink and white blossom around in a petal carpet.

'It wasn't me,' Emmet said again from behind me. I didn't turn around – just sipped more water and tried to swallow. A magpie landed on the stone wall at the end of the garden.

'You have to believe me, Rob. I wouldn't do something like that. Not to Rita. Not to anybody.'

I still didn't answer, but now it was partly because my throat was closing and something was busily hammering a hole in the left side of my head. The magpie chattered and looked around as if he was searching for something specific and he didn't seem to care about the rain that was showering down on his sleek black and white body.

'I never drove a car in my life,' Emmet said.

I swallowed and coughed. 'They found your prints in stolen cars,' I said and my voice sounded mean and rasping.

Emmet didn't answer and I leaned against the sink and my neck began to feel too weak to hold my head. 'A number of stolen cars,' I said.

I turned around. Emmet was staring at the black and white floor tiles. 'I never drove, though.'

'Big fucking deal,' I said, walking past him and up the stairs to bed. I fell into my bed fully clothed and didn't even bother to take off my shoes – just rolled myself into the duvet. The last thing I remember was wondering where I'd put those sleeping tablets.

19. Tuesday 12 April

Hi Clint,

When Eric rang back I was waiting for the call, so I answered it myself. After we said hello neither of us said anything for a few seconds. And then he said, I know it's a horrible shock. Tony was . . .

But I didn't want to hear that so I said, Yeah, before he could finish.

Eric's voice was all wobbly but he kept talking about Tony. Telling me what they'd said at the hospital – just died peacefully in his sleep. Didn't suffer.

And all I said was, Yeah, because that was all I could think of to say. My eyes burned like there was shampoo in them. And Eric said then the hospital also told him they thought the growth might have been cancer and so maybe he had been spared.

I said nothing to that first and then I said, Well, they can treat cancer, can't they? and Eric said I was right. And I said Tony'd told me it was nothing. Just routine. And Eric said he didn't want to worry me 'cos Tony was the softest bastard he ever knew. Then Eric stopped talking for a few seconds and I just listened because I sort of liked the sound of his crying. I heard him blow his nose at the end of it all.

And then he said Glenn would be up to take the pictures maybe tomorrow and I wasn't to worry about anything 'cos he was going to make sure we got away to Spain and all that. And he wouldn't let me thank him – just said Tony'd already made most of the arrangements and he just wanted me to know everything would be all right.

Then he said to be sure to call him if I need anything and I said OK. He's a really nice man, Clint. I swear. Saying he'd still help us even though Tony's gone. I can't get over it. I know it should have made me feel a bit better that we weren't up shit creek but you know yourself there are times when nothing makes you feel better.

After Eric hung up I got out of bed. Peter was asleep and even though he was supposed to be in his own bed now he was snuggled up beside Natalie and she was falling asleep as well.

You OK? she said in this heavy, sleepy voice when I got up and started moving around.

So I said I was fine, that Eric said he'll help us like Tony'd have done.

Natalie said that was great and she looked like she thought maybe she should get up and talk to me, but I didn't want her to do that. I wanted to be by myself and not have to talk to anybody at all, so I told her to stay where she was and that I was going to make a cup of tea and then go sit in the yard and get some air.

She looked at me for a minute and I could nearly hear her head working and then she smiled and said, Don't get cold out there. And I said I wouldn't and boiled the kettle.

I looked at Kelly while I was waiting for the kettle, but she looked like she'd gone to sleep. That was good because even though she wasn't like Nat and trying to help me and talk to me and stuff she might have changed and decided I should talk to her and I just didn't have the energy.

Anyway, what's the point in talking? What can I say? There's nothing to say, not a fucking thing. I kept thinking what I'd really have liked then would be to paint but it was late and I didn't have paints anyway so it was a stupid idea.

It used to drive me mad when you did that. Painting for hours and hours. Especially if I wanted you for something. I'd go in your room and you'd look at me and say that annoying thing about not letting the door hit me on the way out. Bastard. But maybe now that I want to do it as well I'm starting to feel the way you must have felt. If that's the case I'm sorry for not knowing and stuff.

Since Tony died especially I keep thinking about you even more than usual. We never found out what exactly made you feel so bad but I'm starting to think it's no wonder you topped yourself if you were going around feeling like I feel at the moment. It's kind of like there's a fire lighting inside you that's burning your guts and you can't get at it, isn't it? That's the way I feel, anyway.

There's only one thing about that, Clint, when you did that – you know, decided to quench the fire inside you by eating a fistful of pills: did you know you were setting fire to our insides? I can't believe you'd have done it if you knew. Not to Mam, anyway.

I tell myself you couldn't help it. That whatever was going on for you, you didn't know what you were leaving behind. I hope it's true because I couldn't bear it if you knew and didn't care less.

Anyway, I was thinking about you and that shit – as usual – while I waited for the kettle. When it boiled I made tea and walked away from Natalie and Kelly and Peter. The warehouse was as dark as the inside of the coalhole at home but the tea was hot and someone had bought fresh milk, so it tasted good. I went outside and sat on my barrel. It was half twelve in the night and it was cold out and it'd been raining, but the air tasted clean and I liked it.

It reminded me of the night me and Kelly found the dead

guy. The sky was black and full of stars and it wasn't too windy because of the high walls around the yard and I wondered what it's going to be like when we are in Spain. If we ever get there.

For all I know we're going to end up back in jail, and do you know something? I don't really give a shit now. My head started thinking again when I was sitting there in the yard and I couldn't stand it, so I left my cup on the barrel and got up and ran around the small yard until my chest hurt and then I lay down on my back on the freezing concrete and looked at the stars. I thought about you again and knew if I had any drugs there and then that'd make the pain inside me go away I'd have fucking taken them without hesitating for a second.

And that reminded me of Ray Walters. Did you know I was always a bit in love with him? You probably did, you bastard. Ray was a fucking ride with that black hair and those brown eyes with the thick, curly black lashes. I never saw anyone else in Limerick with skin that colour – always like he was tanned.

I think you were jealous of him when ye were kids – the way the girls would follow him round and phone him and put notes through his letterbox. You were always slagging him about it but I think you were just raging it wasn't you. Even Jenny Wilson was always on about Ray. It drove me mad, 'cos she never shut her trap about him and she even told him loads of times. He'd just laugh and pretend he thought she was joking.

Sometimes I was sure you knew that I had a thing for him and for a while I used to be afraid you'd say something – start slagging or whatever – but then I realized you wouldn't, 'cos it'd have ruined everything between the three of us.

Anyway, it didn't matter and after a while Ray started

going out with Melissa Devine and you used to slag him about her name – do you remember? I didn't say much about her but once all right I said she was an idiot – because she was. She was small and blonde with big tits and she used to giggle all the time, which drove me mad. Jesus, Melissa. I wonder where she is now? I bet she wasn't stupid enough to end up in jail. Ha ha, Melissa, you can have the last laugh on me.

Do you remember how Ray used to tell me and you about her and how she was as thick as two short planks but a great ride? We used to laugh, but I always felt a bit sick inside me and couldn't help wishing it was me even if he was a big bastard who talked afterwards.

You don't know this but the first time I ever had sex was with a fucking eejit I met at a party. I can't even remember his name now. I was sixteen and out of my head and it just happened and it was pretty shit really and I made a promise to myself that that'd never happen again.

All the girls I knew were always on about how great their sex lives were and I used to feel a bit of a freak, but after that night I knew they were full of shit and that it was all big woman talk. I decided after that that I'd never do it again until I met somebody I had a real relationship with and I didn't give a fuck if that was old-fashioned. At least maybe it'd be true and that'd do me.

But I didn't keep that promise either. The night of your funeral I fucked Ray Walters in our front room. We did it on the floor and I could hear Mam crying through the floorboards from her bedroom and my heart was pounding like a train and it was really, really good sex and I could see then what all the fuss is about. Afterwards Ray was crying about you and then so was I and we fell asleep on the carpet and when I woke up he was gone.

I rang his house a few days later when I didn't hear from him and his mother said he'd left for England and didn't I know Ray had a job with his brother in Coventry and it'd be a great start for him after all that had happened. I said nothing and after a minute she said, How's your mother?

And I said, Not too bad, thanks.

Then the silence again until she said, I'm so sorry, you know I am, Gina. I was very fond of Clint.

So I said I did know that and thanks, Mrs Walters, thanks and goodbye. Afterwards I felt bad because I'd broken a promise to myself. Except now I think that maybe I didn't completely break it because I did love him in a way.

Sitting in the yard tonight thinking about Ray made me tired and that was good because I thought if I was tired then maybe I'd sleep, so I went back inside. It was after two and everyone was asleep but as soon as I went back inside I woke up and I really didn't feel like going to bed, but what choice did I have? So I did.

I lay there and listened to the small baby sounds Peter was making in his sleep. Babies are gas, aren't they? Gurgling and squeaking. Between him and Natalie and her snoring I thought I was awake for the night, but I was wrong – I did fall asleep.

The thing is, I dreamed about Ray Walters. I often used to dream about him, but last night was the first time I let myself think about him in years, so that's probably why. It was a good dream. I don't think I'll tell you what it was about, though I know a nosy bastard like you'd love to know. Just be happy for me that it was a good dream, will you?

Love,
Gina xxx

20. Friday 8 April – Tuesday 12 April

Once I fell asleep I was plagued by dreams – Emmet at the door of my bedroom and Maria asking me to drink water and a blonde woman in a tight black polo-neck sweater who smelled of apricots and asked me if the light hurt my eyes. And some of them were about a tall tower that stood in the middle of the ocean where an evil witch was holding Rita prisoner. I was on the shore and I couldn't swim, and anyway I was tied to a concrete post with a rope strung around my neck and most of the beach was quicksand. And far away I could hear Rita's voice calling my name over and over.

When I woke up there was dusky daylight filtering through the closed bedroom curtains and Maria was sitting on my bed reading a magazine by the light of my bedside lamp. She smiled when I opened my eyes.

'How are you feeling?'

I tried to swallow. It was sore but I could manage it. 'Not too bad.' I smiled at her and her eyes filled with tears and I remembered.

'It wasn't him,' she said, her voice brittle.

I felt my body sink into the bed as all that had happened and all that it meant came flooding in as if it was new. I swallowed a couple of more times until my throat felt as if it might work. 'I want to believe that too but they must have told you about the other cars as well and that witness identified him.'

Maria nodded and sighed. I saw that her almost black hair was speckled with grey. 'It's a mistake. I know him and he might be a bit of a fool and I know he's mixing with a bad crowd, but surely to God, Rob, you don't believe Emmet is capable of not only running Rita down with a car but leaving her there in the middle of the street? He'd never do something like that, especially not to Rita – he loves her.'

I looked at my sister's worried face and felt sorry for her suddenly. Her life was almost as full of shit as mine. I rubbed my head and my skull hurt. 'Have I been asleep for long?'

Maria rolled a corner of her magazine page into a small cylinder. 'Yes. You were very sick. I called the doctor and she said you'd probably sleep it off.'

'She was right. Did she smell of apricots?'

Maria shook her head and laughed. 'I don't remember. Why?'

'Doesn't matter. What time is it?'

'Six o'clock.'

'I've been asleep for hours.'

'Told you.'

And then I remembered the length of my dreams. 'It's not Saturday, is it?'

Maria shook her head. 'Sunday.'

I lifted my legs and they felt pinned down. My throat hurt. 'I feel like shit.'

Maria beckoned to me to sit up and then handed me two green and red capsules and a glass of water. I took them and she watched me. The water tasted great and made my throat feel free for a couple of seconds.

'It's not him,' she said. I looked up at her. She'd folded her arms across the pale blue short-sleeved T-shirt that clung to the heave of her breasts. Maria was nearly forty and still quite beautiful in a dark-skinned Mediterranean way. I seemed to have inherited all the Irish genes. She, on the other hand, would have fitted in without a squeak in any

163

Spanish town. How had she managed to end up with that loser Gerry Burke?

I cursed as I moved my head and it banged with pain. Maria blinked her brown eyes to move the tears collecting there. One escaped and ran down the side of her face and she pretended to rearrange her hair so that she could brush it away. 'Would you like something to eat?'

'No thanks.'

I tried to smile but my face was stiff and all I wanted to do was close my eyes again. I thought I should probably talk to her for a while, but my throat was closing up again and my eyes were grainy and heavy and impossible to keep open. So I gave in.

In the distance I heard the door close as Maria left the room and I heard voices, but by then I was more than halfway asleep and seeing pictures of Billy Hendrick's corpse in his car – except that instead of blood all over the driver's door window there was yellow paint and Seán was eating a Big Mac and telling me he'd slept with Janice and I was jealous.

By the time I woke up properly it was Tuesday morning and whatever had been boiling my brain was gone. I had a shower and a shave and even managed to eat a slice of toast.

The telephone rang. Seán's mobile.

'Hello?'

'Hey, Rob – you sound better.'

'Not too bad. How did you know I was sick?'

'Maria.'

'Oh.'

'So you're better?'

'Nearly. I think I'll come in to work tomorrow.'

'Take your time.'

'Yeah,' I said, but I knew I'd have to go to work if I was conscious. I couldn't bear more sitting around thinking. 'How's the Hendrick case?'

'Not much happening. One small thing, all right: one of the cases Billy Hendrick was working on before he was killed has a connection to Gerry O'Hare.'

'Do I know him?'

'Jesus, that bug has cooked your brain, Rob. Bunny O'Hare? He and his pal Ollie Richardson had a falling out over a girl and Bunny cooked Ollie's goose, so to speak.'

I laughed. 'I remember now, but you're some bastard.'

'I'm only telling you what they say.'

'Ollie was shot in the back of the head, wasn't he?'

'In his car as well, coincidentally enough. And that case isn't up yet, so Bunny's still around,' Seán said.

'But was Billy representing him? How come that never came up before? When we looked at the cases he was working on they were all compensation and traffic offences. Nothing significant.'

'He wasn't, but it appears that he did represent Bunny's mother in a compensation case – she slipped in a restaurant jacks and hurt her leg.'

'Sounds just like most of his cases.'

'Yeah, but this one he lost.'

'You're kidding.'

'No. Seems she set it up herself – poured something on the floor and then did a Jurgen Klinsman on it.'

'Took a dive?'

'Exactly. Unfortunately for Mammy O'Hare the cubicles were too small, so she did her little act in front of the sinks, which are just inside the door. Unbeknownst to her, however, just outside the door is a security camera and as the door wasn't closed properly . . .'

'The camera picked her up.'

'And she almost got done for fraud.'

'And you think Bunny might have had an axe to grind with Billy because of that?' I asked.

'I think this might be called grasping at straws, but we have nothing new. None of it is making great sense.'

I leaned against the wall, tired from the simple exertion of standing and talking. 'Have you had a chance to have a word with O'Hare?'

'Not yet. Thought I'd wait till you came back to work.'

'Maybe we'll have a word tomorrow. He's out, isn't he?'

'Yeah. Bail. I'll try and set it up.'

'Great stuff. Look, thanks for calling, Seán. I'll see you tomorrow.'

'*Adios*, boy. Who knows – this O'Hare thing might be the key to the whole case and we'll be able to wrap it up and move on.'

'*Lo mismo que yo.*'

'Show off,' Seán said and rang off.

I felt a bit better after I'd spoken to him. More normal. That was Seán for you – there was nothing he couldn't normalize except maybe his own life. My legs ached and I was seriously considering returning to my bed when the doorbell rang. My first instinct was to ignore it, but as I was just standing there I opened it. It was Emmet and Shane and they looked as if they'd run all the way to my house.

'Can we come in?' Emmet said, wiping the perspiration back from his forehead into his hair.

I shrugged and walked into the house. I was too tired to argue. I'd just let them in and go upstairs to bed. It'd be the easiest option. The front door slammed.

'Wait,' Emmet said as I lifted my foot to climb the stairs.

I turned towards him but didn't look. I didn't need to

166

look at him to know what he looked like. Tall, gangly Emmet, chin-length black hair parted in the middle emphasizing the length of his thin white face, big dark-lashed blue eyes. I looked at the denim of his jeans legs and the tear on the side of his sneakers – all the particulars of his shape – but not the details of his face.

I'd looked at that face for his whole life and probably knew it better than my own. The scar on his right cheek where he'd fallen out of a tree when he was little. The pale pink acne trail underlying every new crop of spots and the beginnings of stubble along his cheeks and neck.

He was panting slightly. 'Wait. Please.' He paused. 'Please just give me and Shane a couple of minutes. We have something important to tell you.'

21. Wednesday 13 April

Hi Clint,

Glenn came yesterday with his new digital camera. Eric brought him and the minute they came in the warehouse Glenn looked for me. The hug he gave me nearly broke my spine. I hugged him back and he smelled like Cool Water aftershave and beer. I know that he's shit scared that something is going to happen to me as well.

Eric looks like a different man since the last time I saw him, laughing and joking with Tony. His face is collapsed and old-looking now and his eyes are black. But I suppose that's just it. You can't have someone like Tony in your life and then not have him any more and just get over it like it was only a small thing. Someone like Tony leaves a huge fucking hole when he's gone.

I hugged Eric and he held on tightly as well and all the hugging made me think of Mam and I'd have given anything to have had her there at that minute. But there was nothing I could do except ask about her. So I did. They both looked even sadder and said she was devastated after Tony and I know that's true.

I imagined her face and the fat around her chin and that made me remember how I used to be kind of embarrassed by her when I was a kid. I don't think you were but I was. I don't know about Glenn, I never asked him. Maybe it was to do with being a girl.

It was just that she was always sort of fat and she wore

glasses and her cheeks were a bit red and she looked like an awful bogger. She never bothered dyeing her hair when it went grey and she always wore the same kind of clothes. Do you remember them? Those navy or black or brown skirts that went to just below her knee and the turtle-necked jumpers in different colours. And plain, flat shoes like nun's shoes. I was mortified because all the other mothers wore make-up and high heels and had their ears pierced, and in the summer when it was hot they wore shorts and halter-neck tops while Mam wore these short-sleeved blouses that always had big flowers all over them and the skin on her upper arms was white and jiggled. Thinking about her while I was standing there with Eric and Glenn was taking my breath away, so I thought maybe if I said something it might improve.

But, Poor Mam, was all I could think of saying.

Glenn nodded his head and Eric put his hands in the pockets of his pants and kind of rocked backwards and forwards on his heels. Glenn started putting batteries into his camera then, like he didn't want to be looking at me, and I looked at the top of his blond head and it reminded me of you and of himself at the same time and my heart hurt like something that'd been shot to shit.

And then, all of a sudden, Peter gave an unmerciful roar. Natalie went over to her bed to get him and he was wriggling and making these wet, annoyed noises. And she said he was starving and gave him to me as usual. He was cross all right 'cos he was whingeing and wriggling and arching his back and kicking me with his skinny little legs which were cocking out the end of Natalie's yellow T-shirt she'd put on him.

She said we couldn't keep him just wrapped up all the time or he'd grow up to be a cripple from not being allowed to move. I caught hold of one of his small little feet in my hand and it wasn't the size of my palm and he kicked like mad and scrunched up his face and that made me laugh. And then Eric says – all calm like – 'Where did that little guy come from?'

Me and Nat didn't say anything for a second 'cos we were surprised – just thought he knew, but then again how could he know? Glenn probably forgot to say, what with Tony and all.

But we should have said something straight away, 'cos when we didn't it let Kelly get her spoke in.

His mother left him thrown down there, she says, all prim like.

We looked at her. She was half lying on her bed and her long legs were crossed in front of her and she was smoking and smiling up at Glenn like they were at a party. Glenn couldn't take his eyes off her.

She held her packet of fags towards him but he shook his head. None of us ever smoked. I suppose that's something. We drank and robbed and took drugs but we'd no time for the fags.

Fucked him away like rubbish in a load of wet cardboard boxes, Kelly said then, singing her favourite song.

Natalie told her to shut up and took Peter off me to give him his bottle and he started sucking like a calf then and we all just looked at the two of them – except for Glenn, who was still looking at Kelly.

Eric asked then if Tony knew about the baby and I said no, 'cos we'd only found Peter after we'd got here and Tony was on his way into hospital and I thought I'd tell him about the baby after he was better and that he'd know what to do and stuff.

Eric smiled at that and said, Yeah, Tony always knows how to fix things. And I was going to say something about how now it was *knew* not *know*, but the words stuck in my throat and it felt like it was closing and the words I was saying were bits of rocks that were making a huge lump I could feel there. And for the first time since he died I started to cry because, well, there's no Tony now any more, is there? Nobody to fix things for Peter or me or Glenn or Mam or anyone. I just felt so lonely after him at that minute that I could taste the pain in my mouth like sherbet.

I was embarrassed to be crying then with everyone there looking at me and feeling sorry for me, but I didn't want to stop either 'cos I was fucking sick and tired of the hard hot feeling inside me and shite and all as crying is, it's way better than that. Glenn put his arms around me and I bawled and then blew my nose and then bawled again and nobody said anything about it.

I could hear everything going on outside me. I could hear Eric's voice and I knew he was talking to Natalie. And I could hear Peter, who had finished his bottle and was making those happy full noises. Glenn was holding me tight and that was good 'cos otherwise I knew that my body would fall apart. He was minding me and he was sad for me and even so I knew he was probably still looking at Kelly. It really is hard not to look at her.

After ages I stopped crying. The feeling inside me was telling me that it was the start of the crying, not the end. But that's just the way of it and anyway I didn't care because at least I felt better for that moment. Glenn kissed my cheek and hugged me hard again. He was great, Clint, really – he's so grown up now.

Then he ruined it by saying my nose was red and I was going to look like Rudolf in my passport pictures. I punched him hard and he was laughing at me, but it was good all the same to have him there. Normal or something.

Kelly'd made tea while I was busy crying and when Glenn

and me stopped hugging she gave us two cups. I saw she was all sheep's eyes with Glenn and I kind of wanted to tell her to get away from my brother but decided that'd be a bad idea and just start another fight, and anyway what did it matter? We were going to Spain. Glenn was safe.

You should have seen it, though. Glenn was killed thanking her for the tea and it was Kelly this and Kelly that and showing her his camera, while she pretended to be interested even though I knew it was all an act. Kelly could hardly work the hairdryer on our course and I didn't think she could make head or tail of what Glenn was saying about his digital camera. But I just watched and drank my tea and said nothing.

After a while, Eric took Peter from Nat and the three of us started to do our make-up. For a finish we did each other and it was a mad laugh and great to be doing something normal together for a change. Kelly did my hair – sprayed it with lacquer and tied it up in a bun with long straggly bits at the front – and it looked really nice. Even if I say so myself.

While we were doing the make-up Glenn took out a white sheet he'd brought with him and pinned it on to a stack of boxes. Then he turned on all the strip lights and was going on and on about the quality of the light and all that shit while he was making another seat out of boxes in front of the white sheet.

Peter was in great form and Eric was mad about him and said he wished he could take him himself, and that he'd really love a child but he'd never be able to mind him because of the truck driving and being away a lot. He didn't say anything about how Tony would probably have wanted them to keep him as well but I knew he was thinking it and I knew it was true and it nearly made me start crying again when I thought how lucky Peter would have been if he had had Tony minding him.

But I didn't cry because it'd wreck my eye make-up and Natalie'd spent ten full minutes on the eye shadow alone and I knew she'd go mad, and anyway there was no point. Tony's dead and now he's never going to be anybody's father, is he?

Glenn took the pictures and while I was having mine taken I could hear Natalie talking to Eric about Peter. She was saying we'd have to find a nice home for him and that she knows his mother left him but maybe she was only a kid or something and didn't mean anything to happen to him. I knew Kelly'd heard her as well but she said nothing.

I thought it was a pity Eric couldn't keep him, really, 'cos he was looking a whole lot better since he'd started to hold the baby.

Eric and Glenn left not long after that because Glenn had to meet a fella who had another birth cert. He looked bad before he left – Glenn, I mean. All sad again and sort of fragile like a very thin piece of glass, but he said he was grand when I asked him and that he'd do the passports straight away 'cos he'd taken the rest of the week off work after Tony's funeral.

Kelly asked them when they thought we'd be able to go to Spain and Eric said he'd buy the flights soon and that he'd sort out all the stuff about the house and the keys and that.

Kelly asked Eric where exactly we were going and he said it was to a place near Alicante and that was all he could remember but he'd find out the exact information from your man who owned it.

Natalie asked Eric if maybe your man'd change his mind now that Tony was dead and he said no that was grand 'cos luckily enough he knew the same stuff about your man as Tony. I asked him again about the tickets and he said he'd been afraid to buy them too soon in case something went wrong with the passports and Glenn said, I beg your pardon, are you saying there'll be something wrong with my work? And that started us laughing again and I even felt excited thinking about Spain and kind of forgot everything else for a few seconds and it was great.

Then the lads left. Eric kissed and hugged Peter and kept saying how cute he was and promised to drop in some baby clothes. After they left, the place felt sort of empty again. And sad. But I turned on the radio and had a lie-down on my bed listening to the charts. I even had a bit of a cry, though I made sure no one saw me. It seems as if the tears inside me aren't blocked up any more.

I often wonder what it's like being dead. I mean, where are you, exactly, Clint? Can you see stuff like I can see? Like this evening when I was getting the pizza for dinner and there were kids everywhere. Playing on the streets – skipping and skateboarding and kicking footballs. It's nice the way the fine weather brings out the kids, isn't it? Like swallows or something. I hope you can see it.

Anyway, watching the kids while I was walking back with the pizzas made me remember being hot and dusty from running and playing with you and Ray Walters. And drinking from the Walters' outside tap and laughing when you squirted me and Ray and then us squirting you back. I remembered it so clearly that I could nearly smell the water and dust on my hot skin.

And I was enjoying it nearly. But it didn't last. As soon as I got inside the door with the pizzas Natalie was waiting for me, all freaked out because Peter is sick. I calmed her down but she's getting upset again because he doesn't seem to be any better, so I'd better go and see what's happening.

Talk to you later.

xxx

22. Wednesday 13 April

After Emmet and Shane left I walked the floors of my empty house for hours, and in every room I could see Rita and hear her and smell her in a way I hadn't been able to do since her accident. And now almost a year after the fact I finally knew who'd knocked her down – Jimmy Boy Lane.

Knocked down. What kind of a stupid expression was that for what had happened? It sounded like what happens when your sleeve catches on a vase and accidentally knocks it on to the floor. Not like ploughing into an innocent woman in your speeding car and leaving her in the road to die.

Where was she now, my beautiful wife? I mean where was she really? Not just her body – I knew where that was – but the real thing about her that was Rita. I sat down on the side of our bed suddenly as all the energy left me. Her clothes were still hanging in the wardrobe, her toiletries and make-up still ranged along the shelves in the bathroom. Everything was there, waiting for her to take up where she'd left off. And suddenly I was tired of not knowing when that might be. Worn out from convincing myself and everybody else that any day now, any time now, any hour now, Rita'd be back in our lives.

Since the accident I'd tried to keep this picture of Rita in my head as if she was just outside the door, waiting to come in, but it was slipping. I wasn't sure she was as close as that – no matter what I said to the doctors. I wasn't sure I knew where she was. I thumped the bed with balled-up fists. Bastard! Fucking bastard!

Wherever Rita was I now knew that she'd been put there by Jimmy Boy Lane. The fucking Lanes. Everybody hated them. They had more money than I'd ever see in my whole lifetime and no charge against them ever stuck because they'd beat seven kinds of shit out of any potential witness. Teflon criminals.

Well, this charge'd stick – I'd fucking make damn sure of that. Jimmy Boy Lane was a savage. I wanted to thump Shane for being stupid enough to get involved with them, but I also could see why he'd been scared to come forward.

I was awake all Tuesday night and fairly strung out by the time I got into work next morning. The first thing I did was to go to Mary Hayes's office and tell her what Shane and Emmet had told me. She listened to everything I had to say without interrupting once. When I finished we sat across from each other in her small, bright office with leafy, green pot plants all along the narrow windowsill. Neither of us spoke for a few seconds. Eventually Mary broke the silence.

'Do you think he's telling the truth?'

I nodded. 'Definitely.'

'He wouldn't just be saying this so that Emmet can get out of trouble?'

I laughed and rubbed a hand over my face, discovering that I'd forgotten to shave.

'Well, unless Shane is the dumbest kid in Limerick he wouldn't make up stories about Jimmy Boy Lane.'

Mary nodded but her face was unreadable. 'I suppose.'

'Jesus Christ, Mary, come on – that bastard'd kill him if he thought he'd ratted him out.'

'How do they even know Jimmy Boy Lane?'

I shrugged. 'I don't know for sure, but I think Shane was setting up his dealing business, so he may have started running around with the Lanes, who were obviously his suppliers.'

Mary nodded. 'So why is he telling us now?'

I shrugged. 'I suppose that's for Emmet all right. He's his best friend but the kid is shit scared.'

'And it was Jimmy Boy's own car?'

'Yeah. They were coming home from a party. It was eight in the morning. Rita was on her way to work. They'd been there all night and were probably still stoned. Shane said he was half asleep in the front seat and next thing he knew there was a bump and he woke up. He said Jimmy Boy got out and had a look and that he was shouting. But then he just got back into the car and drove away.'

'Did Shane know it was Rita?'

'He says he didn't but I don't know if I believe that – he is Emmet's friend so he'd know about Rita. I think he probably did. At least afterwards.'

'Was there anybody else in the car?'

'No,' I said. 'Well, Shane says no, anyway, but he might be lying about that as well.'

Mary tipped back her chair and chewed on her bottom lip. 'We need to have a look at Jimmy Boy's car.'

'Shane thinks he sold it.'

Mary sighed. 'Figures. We won't get much out of it anyway at this stage. Still, we'll try to find it and have a look anyway.'

I nodded.

Mary stared at me and then gave another loud sigh. 'Shane won't be a great witness.'

'Why?'

'He's a scut – we've picked him up a few times.'

'I bet the cab driver could identify Jimmy Boy,' I said.

She nodded. 'If we could find the cab driver. And there's

also the fact that if Jimmy Boy Lane finds out Shane is saying this . . .'

'I know. Look, I know I shouldn't have, but I sort of promised Shane we wouldn't say he'd said anything unless we had no choice.'

'Jesus, Rob – why?'

'Well, he was scared – for God's sake, I'd say that cab driver was scared as well and that's why he drove away.'

A tiny dot of blood appeared on Mary's lip where she'd been chewing it. 'Probably. I wish we could find him, though.'

'I wonder – did Jimmy Boy notice that the cab driver witnessed the accident?' I asked. 'Maybe that's why you can't find him.'

'Shit,' she said, biting her lip again.

'Will you bring Jimmy Boy in?'

'Mmm. Don't worry, we won't say anything about Shane, but the thing is, if he's telling the truth Jimmy Boy'll know it was him. Where is he now?'

'At Maria's.'

'I think I'll send someone around to talk to Shane first and then we'll see where we can go from there.'

I stood up. 'Let me know how you get on.'

'Will do. Thanks, Rob.'

I left Mary's office and went straight to mine, picking up a cup of coffee *en route*. It tasted like shit but it was strong and hot. As soon as I swallowed the first mouthful I could imagine my heart speeding up and I began to wake up. As usual Seán was in my office and as usual he had the window open and was blowing smoke into the rainy outdoors.

'Stop smoking in my office.'

'Good morning, Roberto. You should be in bed – you look like shit.'

'Thanks. I keep telling you: smoking in a workplace is against the law.'

'There's no one working here.'

'Shut up, Seán. Is the morning conference arranged?'

Seán flicked his cigarette butt out of the window. 'Ten o'clock.'

'Good.' I sat down at my desk and my body ached with tiredness. 'Shane Harris came with Emmet last night. He says Jimmy Boy Lane was driving the car that hit Rita.'

Seán's eyes widened and he whistled loudly. 'Holy fuck. No wonder nobody came forward. Did you tell Mary?'

I nodded.

'It'll be hard to make that stick,' Seán said. 'You know that, don't you? Any sign of that cab driver?'

'No, but they're still looking.'

'Good. Fuck it, I don't believe it.'

Seán sat down in the chair opposite me and put his feet up on my desk. The sole of his right shoe had a small hole in it. 'I can see how Jimmy Boy looks like Emmet. Same dark, lanky look.'

'Maria wouldn't like to hear you saying her son looks like that scumbag.'

'I'd say she'd be happy to hear it under the circumstances.'

'Maybe. Anyway, there's nothing I can do about that. Anything new on the Hendrick case? What's happening with Bunny O'Hare?'

Seán crossed his ankles and put his hands into the pockets of his cord trousers. 'Janice is meeting him tomorrow morning at eleven. But listen to this: we turned up a new lead yesterday.'

'At last.'

'Don't get too excited – just let me tell you. This woman came in. Saw it on the news. She works for a temp agency and was working in Hendrick's practice on the Friday before Billy was shot. She says Alan and Billy had a huge fight early in the morning. A screaming match.'

'About what?'

'Well, she wasn't sure. This one is great, though. She's pretty old – sixty if she's a day – and good and gossipy.'

'Thank God for that,' I said, grinning at Seán as I started to feel normal for the first time in nearly a week.

'Exactly my own sentiments,' Seán said, dropping his chair legs back on to the floor. He jigged his chair close to the desk and propped his head on his hands.

'What did she say?'

'Oh, she hummed and hawed but said she overheard Alan shouting at Billy and saying something like he didn't care whether or not Billy liked it, he'd do what he was told and if he didn't he could F-off – her words not mine. And then Billy said Alan could go FHS.' Seán stopped and grinned. 'FHS,' he repeated. 'Those were her exact words.'

'What does it mean?'

'Fuck Him Self. Good, isn't it?'

'No, it's stupid. What age are you? Did she say anything else?'

Seán shrugged and shook his head.

I tutted. 'Not exactly great evidence, Seánie. Two brothers having an argument – big deal. Billy could have been talking about anything – the affair with Caroline, anything.'

Seán smiled. 'I said she was a great gossip, not a potential witness. But she is a fucking world-class gossip and I'd say she has shit-hot radar and she said she knew by the way Alan stormed off that there was a lot of bad blood between the brothers. She wasn't a bit surprised when she heard Billy was dead.'

I laughed. 'Is she saying Alan killed him?'

Seán shrugged. 'Not in as many words.'

'So what is she saying?'

'It doesn't matter, Rob. She said there was an argument and I think that gives us good reason to pay Alan a visit. You know, it might be no harm to visit the grieving widow as well while we're at it.'

'That's a good idea. When?'

'Today some time? We'll just arrive along unannounced. I love paying surprise visits. What do you think?'

'Good idea.' I looked at my watch. 'Is that it, so?'

'Pretty much. Come on, it's almost ten – we have a meeting to go to.'

23. Wednesday night

Clint –

I was telling you how when I came back Nat was demented about Peter. I looked at him. He was lying on her bedclothes and he still had her big yellow T-shirt on and he was fast asleep all right but that was all I could see and I said that to her but it didn't make any difference.

She shook her head and did this nervous fiddling thing she does with the three silver rings on her right hand and then suddenly she pulled me until my hand was on Peter's forehead and he did feel hot right enough. Not sweaty but just hot like a stone in the sun. I asked her what she thought we should do, 'cos I always think she'll know what to do with Peter, and she said she didn't know and just sat down beside him, stroking his small head very gently. Peter didn't move. Just made small wheezy noises with his super-fast breathing.

I was trying to be cheerful then and started saying that babies are always getting sick, aren't they, and they get better just as fast, but she knew it was shite 'cos I know nothing about babies. Then Nat says he needed to see a doctor and I thought she was probably right but where the fuck were we going to get him a doctor? Natalie got up then to smoke a fag and I just stayed there and stroked his head because it was sort of like somebody should be touching him all the time when he was so small and so sick.

Kelly didn't say anything – just ate her pizza like nothing

was going on. And then Natalie had an idea and she asked me to ring Eric, 'cos he might be able to help. I said, Yeah straight away, 'cos it was a good idea, but then I realized I forgot to get his number so I said I'd have to try Tony's and see if he answered that.

So I did it – rang Tony's number, I mean. While I was doing it I was trying to get Natalie to eat her pizza – she hadn't touched a bit of it – but it was a waste of time: she just kept saying, I can't, I can't. So I just kept going on about ordinary things, thinking that might calm her down, and the phone rang on and on in my ear with no answer. Natalie lit another fag and I was slagging her then about the healthy dinner she was having and then the phone stopped ringing and this voice said, 'Hi, it's Tony. Sorry I missed you. Leave a message.'

I swear to God, Clint, my heart actually stopped for a couple of seconds and when it started again it felt like there was a knife in my chest and hot tears rushed up against my eyeballs. I hung up but it was too late.

Why the fuck hadn't I expected to hear Tony's message on Tony's phone? That was stupid, wasn't it? I should have remembered from when you died. I mean, I know it and all, but somehow I just forgot the way people leave pieces of themselves all over the place even after they're dead.

Natalie'd put out her fag by then and gone back over to Peter and she was talking to him and trying to wake him up so she didn't see my face, but Kelly did. She came over to me and asked me if I was all right.

I looked at her. Her face was like a mask it was so perfect and I saw that there was a tiny sprinkle of pale brown freckles across the bridge of her nose. Like Lucy Liu. I'd never noticed that before.

I nodded because the words dried up in my mouth. And

then Natalie asked me if he'd answered and I said no because I didn't want to tell her. Then – like God sent him – we heard the metal door opening and Eric appeared with loads of Mothercare bags. He stopped walking when he saw my face and looked like he was going to say something but Natalie ran up to him before he could open his mouth.

Oh Eric! Oh Jesus! I'm delighted to see you. Peter is sick.

Eric walked past me with Natalie to see Peter and Kelly went back to sit on her bed. I was glad of the few minutes to get myself together. When I turned around to look at them, Natalie had Peter in her arms and she was talking a mile a minute and Eric was concentrating hard on her face. When she finished he said Peter would have to go to a doctor and Nat said, 'How?' and her voice was all raggy and full of tears. I felt lousy for her.

Eric hugged her like he knew and said he'd pretend to be her husband if she'd have him and that nearly made her smile but not quite. Then he said he had a phone book in the van and that he'd start ringing doctors and everything'd be grand.

Eric ran up the warehouse then and we watched him but none of us said a word. Peter wheezed loudly and Natalie hugged him tight and was muttering into the side of his hot little head, and when she looked at me I said, Now it'll all be fine. Eric'll sort it out.

She didn't answer – just jiggled Peter as if he was crying, but he wasn't making any noise except for that horrible wheezing, which was starting to sound like he had a Tayto bag in his throat. Eric came running back in with the phone book and started ringing doctors until he got one who was there. He said he and his wife were on holiday up from Cork and their week-old baby was sick. We stared into his face while he was on to the doctor and when he hung up he said she'd see him if they came straight away. Nat started walking to the door and Kelly said, Stop – you can't go. And Natalie was mad at her, saying she was a heartless bitch. But Kelly was rooting in the bags Eric had brought and she said if they brought the child dressed in a big T-shirt then the doctor's definitely going to get suspicious. And she was right of course. So Eric told her she was a gem and then they put a Babygro on Peter and left.

I was a bit freaked out watching them, Clint, because though I didn't say anything I could see that Peter was pure floppy and he never woke up even once in spite of all the pulling and dragging. Even I knew that wasn't normal, so I was glad they were going to the doctor.

Then they were gone and everything was suddenly quiet. Me and Kelly tidied up and I tried not to think about there being something seriously wrong with Peter. Kelly swept the floor around where we live in the corner of the warehouse and I piled up the dirty cups and took them down to the jacks to wash them.

When I got back Kelly'd already made my bed and she was just finishing off Natalie's and she'd folded up Peter's yellow T-shirt that Nat'd pulled off him before they left and put it all neatly on top of Natalie's sleeping bag. And even though it wasn't much I thought tidying Nat's bed was dead sound out of Kelly considering that the two of them never stop fighting, especially since Peter came along.

When we finished tidying up neither of us had the energy to talk. I told Kelly I was going for a sleep and she said she was going to do the same. I got into my sleeping bag and tried to drop off because that way at least I wouldn't be worrying about what was happening at the doctor's.

But I couldn't get Peter out of my head and that made me think about his mother. About who she was and how she fell pregnant in the first place. Was she young? Was she scared? Did she think her baby had died in the warehouse? I really wanted to fall asleep but instead I kept picturing this terrified kid having a baby all by herself and leaving him in an empty warehouse like Natalie said.

But maybe that's not true, Clint. Maybe she's some kind of bitch who couldn't wait to be rid of the little fucker. Maybe she doesn't give a shit if he lives or dies as long as she doesn't have to look at him. Anyway, you look at it though there's nothing good about it.

I must have half dozed then because all of a sudden my phone was ringing like it always seems to do when I fall asleep. I didn't recognize the number but it was Eric.

I was scared and relieved to hear his voice at the same time and when I asked him what was wrong with Peter he said he was very sick. He said the doctor thinks he has a thing called bronchiolitis and he needs to be in hospital 'cos he's so small and all. And he said she gave them a letter for the Regional to have him X-rayed and looked at and that's where they were going now.

First I said, Oh shit, oh shit, and then I said, Don't worry, it'll all be OK, and Eric said he had to go so I was all, Everything'll be fine and stuff. But I didn't mean a word of it. Not one single word.

Talk to you later.

Gina xxx

24. Wednesday 13 April

Seán and I arrived at the morning conference and the room was full of chatter. I called everyone to attention immediately, not because I was so efficient but because I didn't want to have to speak to Janice alone. We sat down and began, and even though I avoided eye contact with her I was acutely aware of her presence. Jesus, what she must think of me? It couldn't be much worse than what I thought of myself.

Two minutes into the meeting Sharon O'Toole arrived unannounced. I was one happy man. Sharon was an attention vortex – she just sucked everything in a room into her space and there was no resisting the pull. It suited me in a number of ways. Before she sat down, Sharon shook hands with me and Seán and Janice and most of the detectives near the top of the table.

'Just ignore me,' she said with a big smile and we all knew that she knew full well that that was impossible. But she smiled again and carried on her pretence, sitting back in her chair as if she was paying us a social call. 'Act as if I'm not here – I'll just be a fly on the wall so that I can get up to speed with the case.'

I looked at Seán and he winked and I was positive she'd seen us – but I didn't really care. Anything was better than having to look Janice in the eye. And so we began.

Everybody gave their reports.

'We have the DNA results from the cigarette butts found near the car, but we've nothing to compare them to, so that doesn't make much difference, I'm afraid,' Jason Devlin said. His Bureau colleague, Denise the Hairdresser, kept her eyes on the report in front of her on the desk. She still hadn't completely recovered from being upstaged by Seán. However, the surreptitious glances she was shooting at him were telling me that he was probably busy flirting with her as well as undermining her. I felt sorry for her – she had to be confused by him. I certainly was.

The reports continued. Straggly bits and pieces of information, one even more of a dead end than the next. As she listened our Superintendent remained silent but she shredded a sheet of paper until a small mound of confetti had grown in front of her on the table.

Seán's report about Gwen Goulding – the temp from Hendrick's office – was definitely a bit of light relief.

'And I think that Mr Alan Hendrick and Mr William Hendrick were not at all cordial in their relationship,' Seán said, imitating Miss Goulding's droll country accent. Everybody laughed, including Sharon O'Toole.

'No really, Detective, I heard them argue and when Mr William Hendrick told his brother to go FHS . . .'

The room erupted in laughter as everybody – obviously all smarter than me – got the joke.

As soon as everything had calmed back down, Freddie Truby sat forward in his chair. 'I think we should pay Alan Hendrick a visit,' he said. 'I mean, I know he's been interviewed, but how closely have we really looked at him? I think it's time we started to pay a little more attention to Mr Hendrick.' He sat back and folded his arms, a sudden look of self-satisfaction on his face.

'Jeez, thank God they sent you down from Dublin to tell us that,' Seán said before I could intervene. 'Did the FBI teach you those detective skills?'

Freddie's face flushed and his lip curled. 'I'm just saying . . .'

'Well, don't bother saying – we've already arranged an interview with Hendrick . . .'

'OK, enough,' I interrupted. 'O'Hare? Any news on him?'

Janice winked at Amy O'Brien, who'd been working on O'Hare with her. She gave her the nod and Amy cleared her throat.

'No, nothing new. We already know that Billy Hendrick was defending him in the Ollie Richardson murder – that's it. We couldn't find out anything else.'

She looked at Janice. Janice smiled and nodded. 'And the rest of the list?' she prompted.

'Yes, yes,' Amy eagerly agreed. 'We had a look over the final people on the client list and there's nothing we can find there either. Most of them are scumbags and crooks, but again we all knew that as well, didn't we?'

'Do the Hendricks represent the Lanes?' I asked, all of a sudden, as the thought struck me.

Janice looked at me. 'They're not in the files if they do.'

Seán coughed. 'No – I think the Lanes use David Kelliher, Rob.'

'Why?' Sharon O'Toole asked.

I shrugged.

'Just checking to make sure we hadn't missed them,' Seán said.

Sharon frowned and I shuffled the papers on the table in front of me. 'OK. That's great, so,' I said, trying not to sound as full of haste as I felt. 'Let's divide up the jobs. There aren't that many, unfortunately, unless something new comes in, and I'll see you all tomorrow.'

I called out the list of tasks and assigned workers to each and then drew the meeting to a close. As chairs were scraped back from the table and chatter broke out all over the room, I pretended to read so as not to look at Janice.

Sharon O'Toole turned her matronly form in her chair until she was facing me. 'A word, Rob?'

'Sure.' I looked up as she moved closer. She was smiling widely as if she was telling me a joke, but I could tell by the strain at the corner of her mouth that she wasn't all that amused.

'We need to make faster progress,' she said, in a low voice.

'There's not much more we can do,' I said, feeling suddenly defensive of my team, who were working their butts off in spite of their lack of a break.

She shrugged. 'Well, there are a lot of rumbles coming from Dublin. They want the NBCI to take over the case altogether.'

'Alan Hendrick.'

'He's very well connected and he's saying we're not working hard enough to find his brother's killer. He's suggesting that the local Gardai have a history with him and that's having a bearing on the investigation.'

I made a face. 'Aw, poor Alan. He thinks we don't like him. He's right.'

Sharon's face froze into a mask of mild horror. 'But that's not impeding the progress of the investigation, I hope?'

'Oh, for God's sake, Sharon – what do you think?'

She looked at me and didn't answer. In truth I didn't care what she thought. I sat back in my chair, suddenly exhausted. 'Let them have it. There's nothing they could do that isn't being done. Let them try.'

I turned to look at her. Her blue eyes were hard and flat and her smile had turned into a determined line. 'No way. They can't have it. I won't allow it. There's another press conference due – I'm trying to stall it.' She stood up. 'Try and come up with something for me to tell the press.'

'I'll do my best,' I said with a grimace and then she was gone in a flurry of handshakes and politician talk.

I stared at the typed pages on the desk in front of me. It was all too much effort, really. And I had no idea where we should go next. But maybe I was wrong. Maybe there was stuff we could be doing that I wasn't seeing because I was so preoccupied. Surely Seán or Janice or someone would see it if that was the case? I tried to focus by making myself think of questions Seán and I could ask Alan Hendrick later that day.

'Rob?'

I looked up. 'Jesus! Janice! How are you?' My heart thumped in my chest as I struggled to stand up, the heavy wooden chair catching me in the backs of the knees. I stumbled to my feet. 'How are things with you? I've been sick – some kind of a bug. Jesus H. Christ, it was unbeliev-able – I was out of it for days and . . .'

'I know. Seán told me.'

'Oh.' I tapped the sheaf of papers I was still holding against the desk.

'It's OK, Rob.'

I looked at her. Her face was clear and open and framed by long red curls that had escaped the huge tortoiseshell clip on the back of her head. She was wearing a blue and white striped blouse and was holding a bundle of folders tightly against her chest. She smiled. Behind her I could see Seán watching us and as soon as he caught my eye he winked. I turned towards Janice.

'I'm sorry,' I said, looking into her pale blue eyes.

'I mean it,' she said, touching my wrist lightly. 'It really is all right.'

'But I am sorry,' I said again.

Janice gave a small laugh. 'Was it that bad?'

'That's not what I meant.' Heat and redness climbed up my neck as flashes of Janice's naked body flickered inside my head. I dropped the papers on the desk and rubbed a hand over my lower face.

Janice grinned. 'I know that.'

I blew out my breath and laughed. 'Sorry Janice . . . I'm making an arse of it but you know what I mean.'

'Yeah. Anyway, Rob, it's all fine – that's all I want to say.'

'Thanks.'

She stopped, looking earnest and worried at the same time, which made me hate myself even more. 'Anyway,' she said, pausing to take a deep breath, 'what happened between us happened and we can't pretend otherwise, but I'd hate us to be awkward.'

'Me too.'

'So can we be friends?'

I looked at her thin face and suddenly, tired and confused as I was, I appreciated how hard this had to be for her. 'I'd like that.'

'OK – that's great.' She brushed invisible dust off her jacket and I could see that she was as relieved as I felt. 'Maybe we can have another drink some time?'

'That'd be nice,' I said.

'OK,' she said again. 'That's that. Now, have you a few minutes to spare?'

'For a drink?'

Janice laughed and shook her head. 'No, no, sorry. I mean here – now, for work.'

'Sure,' I said, embarrassed.

'It's just that I had a call there as the meeting finished to tell me that Gina Brennan's mother is here. I met her last week. Just thought you might like to have a word yourself as she's here.'

'That'd be good. Hold on a minute and let me have a word with Seán – he should come along as well.'

I looked around the room but there was no sign of him. I looked back at Janice. 'Well, he seems to have vanished. We'll walk out and if I pick him up on the way, well and good.'

She grinned and walked ahead of me out of the conference room. I made myself look away from the curve of her back.

We didn't get a chance to look for Seán as Amy was already on her way into the room to find Janice.

'She's very nervous,' she said, as soon as she clapped eyes on her colleague.

'Mrs Brennan?'

Amy nodded anxiously. 'I think you should talk to her straight away – she's already been here for about fifteen minutes, it seems, and I think she's going to leave. She's in Interview Room 4.'

'OK, Amy. Thanks,' Janice said, squeezing her arm.

We hurried to the interview room. Amy'd been right. Inside, a short, over-weight woman with silver-rimmed glasses, permed grey hair and flat black shoes was buttoning a shapeless brown woollen coat and looking as if she was about to leave.

'Mrs Brennan,' Janice said immediately, reaching out to shake her hand. 'How are you? Nice to see you.'

The woman stopped buttoning and returned the handshake.

'This is Detective Inspector O'Connell,' Janice said.

Mrs Brennan and I shook hands. Her handshake was limp and empty as if she wasn't there. She probably wasn't.

'How have you been?' Janice said.

'Not too bad, thanks,' Mrs Brennan answered in a quiet voice. She tried a smile but she couldn't quite pull it off.

Janice chattered for a few seconds as she manoeuvred the nervous woman back into a chair.

'Is everything all right?' Janice asked then as soon as we were all seated.

Mrs Brennan sat back in her chair and began to open her coat buttons. Her fingers were ringless, short and red-skinned with nails bitten down to the quick.

'I was wondering if you'd found my daughter,' she said, quietly, a slight shake in her voice.

'No, I'm afraid not,' Janice said. 'Have you heard from Gina yourself?'

Mrs Brennan shook her head and her eyes filled with tears. She fumbled in her handbag for a tissue.

'Mrs Brennan,' Janice said quietly, leaning across the table to take hold of the woman's hand. 'Do you have any idea where Gina might be hiding?'

She blew her nose before looking up at Janice. 'No. But you have to find her for me. I'm afraid something will happen to her.'

'Like what?' Janice asked.

Mrs Brennan shook her head slowly and sadly, biting her lower lip with her eyes fixed to the table as if she could see horrible scenarios unfolding in the wood veneer beneath her eyes.

'In today's paper it says that one of the girls she was with might be involved in that murder you were talking about and . . . and . . . I'm worried about her.'

The tears started again, which was just as well as it gave Janice and me a chance to exchange looks. What papers? Whose job was it to look through the papers? I couldn't remember. And with Sharon O'Toole at the meeting I hadn't even noticed the absence of a media report. Shit. Shit. Shit. I stood up.

'Excuse me for just one second, Mrs Brennan.'

As I opened the door of Interview Room 4 a tiny, dark-haired secretary with an armful of folders was passing. I grabbed her by the arm.

'Now. Go now and buy all today's papers,' I said to her startled face.

She didn't move. 'Now,' I repeated, handing her fifty euros. 'Go. Good girl.'

She nodded and ran off.

I closed the door and returned to my seat. Mrs Brennan was still weeping.

'Do you have any of those papers with you, Mrs Brennan?' I asked.

She looked at me and nodded, and then unfastened her handbag and handed me a folded sheet of tabloid newsprint. I opened it. My heart sank. As well as photographs of the runaway girls and Billy Hendrick laughing outside the Four Courts, there was a big black headline that read 'IS ONE OF THESE GIRLS WANTED FOR MURDER?'

As I scanned down through the article underneath, I felt like choking the journalist. Who the fuck had given him this information? As always the reportage managed to keep just on the legal side of truth.

According to the article, we were looking for the girls to help in our enquiries. Everybody knew that – we'd released that bit of information ourselves. It then described the three girls and their own criminal careers – a matter of public record. Finally it described in sensational detail their prison break. None of that bothered me. What I wanted to know was, who the fuck had told the journalist that one of the girls

– unnamed – was suspected of murdering Billy Hendrick?

'I know Gina didn't hurt anybody – she wouldn't – but if that's true and one of those other girls shot that man and if Gina was there maybe she might . . . she might . . .'

'This is just gutter journalism,' I said. 'It isn't necessarily true.'

She looked at me. 'So nobody thinks one of those girls with my Gina is a murderer?'

Fuck. 'We just want to talk to the girls in case they can tell us anything that'd help us find whoever is responsible.'

She looked at me and I knew she could see my lie in the air. She blew her nose again and then replaced her tissue in her handbag.

'My son is dead,' she said then, in a quiet voice. 'I didn't know he was in trouble and so I didn't do anything about it. And he died. I've just buried my brother and now, today, when I open the papers I see Gina might be in danger as well.' She paused and took a deep breath. Janice and I didn't move. I found it almost impossible to take my eyes off that pale, open face. 'You have to find my daughter because I can't bear it if she dies as well.'

Nobody said anything for a couple of seconds after she spoke. Then Janice cleared her throat. 'We don't know where to find her.'

Mrs Brennan didn't move. 'My brother was supposed to send her to England. Send her somewhere safe.'

'I thought you told us you didn't know anything about where Gina might be?' Janice said quietly.

The shapeless woman shrugged. 'Tony would have made sure she was safe.'

'But he died?' I asked.

Mrs Brennan nodded slowly. 'Suddenly.' Her eyes filled with tears.

'So now?' I said.

'So now Gina has nobody, wherever she is, and this' – she tapped the sheet of newsprint between us on the table – 'this says she might get killed. You have to find her.'

'You have to help us,' Janice said.

Mrs Brennan nodded again. 'I will. I don't care if she goes back to jail. I don't care about anything, as long as she doesn't die. Just that.' She began to button her coat again and stood up. Janice and I stood as well.

'Is there anything else you can tell us that might help us to find Gina?' I asked.

'No. But my son, Glenn – I'll talk to him when he wakes up. He's asleep – he's on evenings. Glenn might know something he isn't telling me, thinking it's for the best not to worry me. But he hasn't seen this. I'll show it to him and I'll talk to him.'

'Maybe we should have another word with Glenn as well?' Janice said.

Glenn's mother nodded. 'I'll tell him to expect you. Now I better go. I have work.'

Janice walked Mrs Brennan to the front door and I back towards my office. There'd be major ass-kicking when Sharon found out about the newspapers. Especially as we'd missed them. But then so had she and her people, which was even more remarkable, as the media was everything to her.

Seán was in my office, reading the papers, when I arrived.

'Fucking Nora,' he said, waving the paper Mrs Brennan'd shown me.

'I know. Where did they get that information?'

Seán opened a broadsheet and rapidly flicked through it. 'Page six – look.'

I groaned. Same pictures. Same story. Less sensational headlines. 'How the hell did they get that?'

'Either someone on the team or one of the Hendricks. There isn't any place else to get that information.'

'Shit! You're right. The bloody Hendricks.'

'Alan doesn't trust us, you know that.'

'Yeah, but this is ridiculous.'

Seán shrugged. 'He probably thinks it a good strategy.'

I sat down. My bones ached and a headache was hovering and it was still only eleven o'clock in the morning.

'They must really believe Kelly Moloney killed him, though,' I said.

Seán nodded. 'We can ask them about it. Are you ready to go pay them a visit?'

I groaned and stood up. Everything really, really hurt. 'Yeah. Let's get it over with. I just want to grab a cup of coffee on the way – see if it'll wake me up.'

'Grand. Listen – one more thing before we go.'

'What?'

'What's going on with you and Nicole Kidman?'

I looked at him, genuinely puzzled this time.

'Janice.'

I shook my head. 'Nothing.'

'I saw her talking to you at the end of the meeting.'

'About Gina Brennan's mother.'

'Don't play the innocent with me, Roberto O'Connell, you Spanish harlot.'

'Look, Seán, get over yourself. We need to get going if we're going to visit both Hendricks before quitting time.'

'Don't try to fob me off, boy. What's the score? She must have asked about you a hundred times when you were out sick.'

'Concern for my health.'

'Yeah, right.'

I pulled on my jacket and smiled at Seán. There was

something satisfying about his manic curiosity. 'You look like a dog with a flea on his arse that he can't quite reach.'

'You're a fucking poet, Rob,' Seán said with an exasperated wheeze.

'Let's go see Caroline Hendrick.'

'OK. Maybe she'll answer my questions.'

'Maybe she will – come on.'

25. Wednesday night

Clint,

It's me. Back again after all the shit.

Well, a lot has happened since I was last talking to you. For starters it was one o'clock in the morning when Natalie and Eric got back from the hospital. Me and Kelly didn't talk much while they were gone. There was nothing to say, I suppose.

I fooled around with the radio and found the news and some music and then listened to half a play about an old woman and her parrot. Kelly flicked through magazines and basically chain-smoked the whole night. This place is really starting to smell like an ashtray – it's disgusting. But it wasn't the time to complain about it, so I just let it go.

When I finally did hear the metal gate open I nearly jumped out of my skin. Suddenly – after all the waiting – there they were. I started shaking the minute I saw them and asking if Peter was all right and what did the doctors say and stuff. Natalie didn't say anything – just sighed and pulled hard on her cigarette like it was oxygen and she was going to die without it.

She sat down on her bed, smoking and staring at the smoke she was making all around her, and I was starting to feel afraid, though I wasn't sure why. I thought maybe there was something wrong with Peter and they didn't want to say, so I asked if he was all right and Eric said yeah and Natalie just looked at me for a few seconds and then it was like somebody switched her on.

She jumped up and started going on about how the doctor they went to was so freaked out about Peter and how she nearly puked when she said they had to bring him to the hospital – though Natalie knew she was right.

Then she lights a second cigarette off her first one and she's talking to me like I'm the only one in the room. Telling me how Eric went in to the hospital by himself first and she stayed out in the van. But she couldn't stick it and she went in after them even though she was afraid someone'd see her. I said nothing – just kept looking at her and nodding – and she kept talking.

She said she was glad she went in 'cos she was losing her mind in the van and anyway Peter was calmer when she was there – wasn't he, Eric? – and Eric said it was true, he was calmer. And it was worth it 'cos she didn't meet anyone – at least if she did she didn't see them.

She told me how they X-rayed the baby and said he was very sick all right but they thought he had bronchitis and that isn't as serious as that bronchiolitis yoke. Then she showed me the antibiotic they gave her and this one tablet in a foil wrapper that she was to give him if he couldn't breathe.

Nat was looking at that tablet like it was the Holy Ghost or something and telling me they said as well that she was to boil the kettle and steam him to help his breathing. And then she stopped as suddenly as she'd started and nobody said anything for a while. We just sat there drinking our tea that I'd made.

And after ages Natalie started talking again. She said she and Eric were talking and that she needed to talk to the two of us – me and Kelly, like, now. And then she went over to Kelly and asked her to get up but she just said no, she could talk to her there, so Natalie said all right.

And that's when she started on about how the warehouse

was no place for a sick baby. I said it'd only be a few more days and anyway we had to find a proper home for Peter, but she said no, no, it was too long.

And Kelly said nothing.

Then Eric said we could all go stay at his brother's place – 'cos he's away – until Glenn sorts out our passports. That was the first I heard of him even having a brother, let alone one who'd let us hide in his place. He swore it wasn't risky but I was a bit freaked out. Worried that they'd tie Tony to him and then him to me and all that. But Eric said he doubted it.

I tried to be calm but inside me was a bit churned up. I mean, I felt bad for poor Pete – I love the little guy – but I couldn't face going back to jail. I didn't say anything, though. Just tried to think it out in my head.

I mustn't have been the only one thinking, 'cos nobody said a word. The only noise in the place was that faraway squealing noise the strip lights made and the quiet wheezing of Peter's breathing.

After about a minute, Eric finished his tea and put the mug on the concrete floor and started talking about how he thought it was a good idea and I said, Well, what about your brother, though? And he just said what Finbar (that's his brother) doesn't know can't worry him.

And then I was sort of coming round – but not Kelly of course. Never Kelly. She sat up and said it was too risky and she didn't think we should go. And then Nat was all freaked out and said fine – you two stay and I'll go by myself with Peter. But Eric kept saying to Kelly he didn't think it was risky and I was getting to like the idea. 'Cos he's right – I mean, why would they find us there and not here?

So I asked Eric if Finbar has a telly and he started laughing and said if he hadn't he'd get us one and then I was all, Oh, does it have a proper toilet and a kitchen and real beds? And Eric and Natalie laughed at that but Kelly didn't move or make a sound. I looked at her and she was like a ghost with her sleeping bag pulled up around her shoulders.

So I said it to her then. Fuck it, Kelly, everything is risky.

And she said no, she thought it was worse in the flat, so I said she could stay and she said no, she hadn't said she wouldn't go – just that it was very risky. She'd wear the patience of a saint, that one. Anyway, then Eric says tonight might be a good time to move and he just has to pop out and if we're ready when he gets back he'll bring us to the apartment.

I said it sounded like a plan and that we should start packing and Kelly looked like she might say something else, but then she must have changed her mind because she unzipped her sleeping bag and stretched her long legs out in front of her and then she stuck her feet in her runners.

Then we started collecting up our bits and pieces and Eric headed off for a while. Halfway through the pack-up, Peter woke up and drank a bottle. Nat was thrilled and said it was an excellent sign that he was hungry again and that the antibiotics must be working.

Nat and me talked while we were packing and Kelly kept quiet – but really we're used to that carry-on out of her by now, so it didn't make much difference. And then when we were really sure she wasn't going to say a word, she asked the question that's been in the back of my head the whole night:

Why didn't you leave him in the hospital?

Kelly's face was white but you could see she was kind of worked up inside. She started saying then how we're always going on about wanting to make sure he's safe and all that and wasn't the hospital the perfect place to leave him? They'd look after him – get him a home and all.

I didn't want to be having that conversation, even though I was thinking it too, but Nat looked so small and kind of battered I couldn't bear it. So I said, Shut up Kelly, she couldn't leave him when he was sick, for God's sake.

But Natalie said, No, Gina, no, Kelly's right for once. And then she said she could have done it and Peter might be safe and he might even be happy but she couldn't make herself do it. When she was in the van and Eric and Peter were inside in the hospital she said she tried to imagine what it'd be like to be without him – and it was horrible.

'I want to take him to Spain,' she says then and she folded her arms across her chest like she was holding herself together and I could see she was shaking.

Fuck it, I should have known, Clint, shouldn't I?

Kelly went ape-shit and I was all, Look, we'll talk about it later, 'cos I was hoping that Natalie'd change her mind once she had some sleep.

But she shook her head and said no – she knew he wasn't her baby and all that but she feels like he is. His mother doesn't want him but she does.

Kelly was smoking a cigarette and just said, No way, fuck off Natalie, we can't bring him.

And even I said, Jesus, Nat, what are you thinking?

Then Kelly laughed this weird cold laugh and said Natalie must have lost her mind and that it was bad enough risking everything moving so Precious Peter won't have to be in the damp warehouse but Spain? I tried to shut her up but she was hopping and wouldn't stop. And she started on at me then, saying I'd been on Natalie's side since we'd found that runt – as she called him – and now she'd really lost it and didn't I know if they caught us they'd throw away the key?

And all the time Nat was pure calm and when Kelly was

finished saying all that Natalie just says will we listen to her for one more minute? Then she tells us this plan where we pretend to be three sisters going on holiday with a baby. She said she'd talked to Eric about it and even he thought it was a good idea and would we just think about it?

Nobody said anything for a few seconds and I started to see Natalie's plan. I knew she was saying it because she wants to bring Pete but that doesn't mean she's wrong, does it? Then I had an idea as well and said that if we dyed our hair and cut it and stuff that might help and then with the baby it'd be a great cover, wouldn't it?

Kelly looked at me like I was losing my mind as well, but the more I thought about it, the more I was getting excited. Kelly was still raging. But I was on a roll by then and started going on about how sisters often look different and how me and her are tall and me and Nat have the same colouring so maybe you could take us for sisters. And by the end I could tell even Kelly was beginning to calm down and see that maybe this might not be such a bad idea after all.

Natalie was all into it of course and saying we could bleach Kelly's hair and maybe cut it and nobody'd recognize us, especially if she dyed her own hair black and what did I think? Would I like black hair too?

I said I'd call Glenn and get him to take more pictures and get him to make Peter a passport and stuff. My head was racing, making plans.

Kelly had finished her fag and was just standing there watching me and Nat and then she smiles and she's all sweet-looking and she calls Natalie's name and Nat says, What, Kelly? And Kelly says, Why do you want a baby, Natalie? You already have a child.

Fuck it, Clint – it was worse than if she'd punched her in the face. Natalie's eyes went big and round and filled up with tears and her lips were shaking and I wanted to thump the head off Kelly.

Natalie took loads of deep breaths but she said nothing and Kelly was still smiling. You should have seen her – you couldn't credit the meanness of it. And then she says,

I was just wondering what you're going to say to – what's his name? Ryan, is it? How will he feel when you take that baby with you and leave him here?

Ah fuck it, Clint, that was well out of order, so I told her to shut up and leave Nat alone then, but she didn't even look at me. Natalie didn't say nothing for ages and then she started talking and I was telling her to shut up and that Kelly had no right to be asking her questions like that.

But she didn't seem to hear me – just kept talking in this real quiet voice. Saying how she'd been thinking about Ryan too but Mary was his mother – he calls her Mam and everything – and she couldn't take him away from his mother.

I lost it then, Clint, and told Kelly she wasn't a fucking social worker, but she just smiled at me and packed her bag. Poor Nat – Jesus she was like a kid – still explaining herself to that wagon. Telling her how she's been clean for ages – even in jail – and how all the trouble she was in with the law was for robbing and shoplifting to keep her habit going.

And after all that Kelly just shrugs and says she hopes she's right but she wouldn't bet on it. And then this weird thing happened.

Natalie changed. She walked over to Kelly and looked straight at her. She looked really different – taller even, like something inside her had made her stretch.

I know I won't ever use again if I take Peter with me, she says to her. 'Cos I'll have a reason not to. I haven't even been drinking since we found him. He needs someone to mind him and I need someone to mind.

I was good and impressed with Nat and even Kelly couldn't answer that and then we got lucky and Peter woke up and Nat went running to him. I said I had to go down to the jacks, which I didn't really but I had to get away.

I couldn't bear to look at Kelly after seeing that cruel smile on her face. I know she's beautiful. Really she is, Clint – you'd be mad about her. But she looked ugly to me right then. I couldn't stick being in the same room as her. So I fucked off.

Anyway, Eric is here. Talk to you later.

xxx

26. Wednesday 13 April

The home of Caroline and the late Billy Hendrick was a huge double-fronted red-brick Georgian house with wide bay windows and a long gravel driveway. It was set in at least an acre of manicured gardens and as it was about fifteen minutes' walk from the centre of town I couldn't even hazard a guess at how much it might be worth.

We parked our unmarked car near the front steps and rang the doorbell. I was exhausted and would gladly have laid down and slept beside one of the perfectly round standard bay trees that flanked the white front door. My body felt heavy and achy as if I had flu again and as we waited for the door to open I promised myself I'd go straight to bed as soon as I got home.

'Fucking hell,' Seán said as we waited on the steps. 'Look at the gravel – it's like one of those Zen gardens. They must have a Japanese gardener who rakes it every day – there isn't a stone out of place.'

I laughed. He was right. The door opened behind us. To my surprise, Caroline herself opened it.

'Mrs Hendrick, how are you? Sorry to disturb you. We were wondering if we might have a quick word?' I said.

'Is there something wrong?'

'No, no. Not at all – just passing and we thought we'd drop in and see how you are.'

She looked as if she might be about to call my line of bullshit but instead she stepped into her vast hallway and beckoned to us to come inside. The last time I'd seen

Caroline Hendrick was over a week before at her husband's funeral and the only time I'd spoken to her for any length of time was that day when she told me she was sure Kelly Moloney had murdered her husband. Other than that she rang the station at intervals to find out if we'd found Kelly Moloney and I'd fielded a couple of those calls. The whole team thought it was odd that she never asked any other question about the murder investigation, but as it wasn't illegal there wasn't much we could do about it.

'Any news about Kelly Moloney?' she asked as she led us through a huge stripped pine door into a small sitting room. Seán grinned and winked at me.

'No, no. We've talked to just about everybody we can think of and to be honest we're still no nearer to locating the girls,' I said.

She motioned us to take a seat on an overstuffed red velvet sofa. It looked sumptuous and soft but was actually as hard as a rock when you sat on it. She stood in front of the fireplace and looked at us.

'Do you mind if I ask you a question, Mrs Hendrick?' Seán said, giving her his broadest, more sincere-looking smile.

She shrugged and folded her arms across the chest of her well-cut white linen blouse. 'Of course not.'

'You seem to be totally convinced that Kelly Moloney shot your husband . . .'

'Yes. Absolutely.'

'OK. Well, I can see how she's a suspect, but I was wondering if we're missing something here. I mean, why exactly are you so certain that she's the one? She has no history of violent crime and she is only twenty-one years of age, after all.'

Caroline shrugged again. 'So what? I'm aware of her age.'

Seán nodded and settled back into the sofa as if he was a social caller. 'That's right – she lived with you, didn't she? Was it here in this house?'

'Yes.'

'Until she was sixteen? Seventeen?'

'Fifteen.'

'Sorry, fifteen. I remember now. And why exactly did she leave at that time, if you don't mind me asking?'

Her face blanked for a moment and then she smiled as broadly and as falsely as Seán. 'Kelly was impossible. We did our best with her. I suppose if we'd known more we might have been better able to help her. But what can you do when you're young and inexperienced?'

Seán nodded sympathetically. 'And you say your husband was always very fond of Kelly?'

Not a flicker. 'That's true. I've told Detective Inspector O'Connell already that I spoke to Billy the night before he died and he told me she'd called him after she'd broken out of prison.'

'They obviously were very close if she called him when she was in trouble,' Seán said.

Caroline's face was impassive. 'I told you that.'

'So you think that Kelly Moloney was probably as fond of your husband as he was of her?'

She shrugged. 'I don't know. All I do know is that she called him and that in all likelihood he met her that night. I understand that somebody saw a girl fitting Kelly's description in the vicinity the night of the murder.'

'That's right,' I said.

She nodded but continued to look at Seán. 'I just know that that girl killed him.'

Seán looked thoughtful. 'There's only one question I have about that, Caroline – may I call you Caroline?'

She nodded again and smiled.

'Did you tell the newspapers that?'

Caroline Hendrick looked taken aback. 'I'm sorry? What do you mean?'

'Have you seen today's paper?' I asked.

She shook her neat head.

'All the papers are carrying a story about the three runaway girls and the suggestion that one of them may have killed your husband.'

She shrugged. 'Are they? I haven't seen the papers today.'

'So who told them about Kelly?'

She laughed. 'That she was a suspect? It wasn't me. Why would I go to the papers about something like that? Though I can't say I'm unhappy about it – it might help to find her if people are on the lookout. Maybe you should have thought of going to them yourselves.'

I raised my eyebrows. 'So you think it's a good thing, this story?'

She shook her head. 'Of course not – I hate those papers and the way they report stories.'

'Which papers?' I said.

She paused, momentarily rattled. I could almost see her collecting her thoughts. 'All of them. I hate all of them.'

'But you didn't read the articles?'

'No matter – I know what they're like.' She smiled. Subject closed.

'You really are convinced Kelly killed him?' Seán said.

'Yes.'

Seán mmmed and looked into space for a few minutes. He looked so like Columbo that I wanted to laugh.

'Well, my only problem with that is that you keep saying he was very fond of her,' he said after he'd finished making thinking noises.

'That's true.'

Seán raised his eyebrows. 'I'm sure it's true, but if it is, it begs a question, doesn't it? Why would she kill him? Do you know of some motive she might have had? Maybe something we don't know about.'

She shook her head slowly. 'No. Sorry.'

Seán scratched his chin. 'Well, that sort of leaves us stumped, doesn't it? I mean, there could always be a reason you know nothing about but you're so convinced . . . See, the thing is, bad as the world is nowadays, I find that it's still the case that most people don't shoot the people they're genuinely closest to without some very compelling reason.'

Her mouth twitched at one corner and she tugged at her ankle-length black skirt as if it was twisted. Then she recovered and the smile was back in place. 'That's a good point. But still, you have a witness who saw her and Billy is dead and she is a criminal . . .'

'Of sorts,' Seán said.

'If Kelly Moloney didn't kill Billy, then who did?' Caroline looked at me then and I had a chance to examine her face, which was a perfectly symmetrical, beautifully made-up mask. Maybe if you were a model they taught you how to actually hide behind your own face.

'We're not ruling her out just yet, but we are casting our net a little wider – that's all,' I said.

She nodded. 'So, how can I help you today?'

Seán coughed and leaned forward. 'Well, maybe you could tell us a little bit more about Kelly as we're here now and talking about her.'

She shrugged. 'I'll tell you anything you want to know.'

'Just a little on her background, if you could,' Seán said, flicking a notebook from the pocket of his tweed sports coat. 'All we know about her is that she has no visible father and an alcoholic mother who seems to have a history of mixing with bad boys who like to thump kids.'

Seán paused. Caroline was as still as a rock.

'As a result Kelly was a ward of the state and served her time on the Children's Ward before she was taken into care. After that it seems she just bounced back and forth between the children's home and various foster homes until she left at sixteen.'

She listened as if she was examining his words for inaccuracies. When he stopped she nodded. 'All of that is true,' she said. 'She was hard to place, I'd imagine. Kelly was a difficult child. Wilful.'

'How long exactly was she with you?' I said.

'Two years. She was thirteen when she came and fifteen when she left.'

'And exactly why did you decide to foster at that time – if you don't mind me asking.'

Caroline turned around and picked up a small carriage clock from the mantelpiece and began to wind it. 'I met Kelly at a charity do – a modelling fund-raiser for the children's home. I was just married and had finished modelling and to be honest I was maybe a bit bored. When the home started a big sister/big brother scheme it seemed really, really worthwhile, so I got involved in that as well.'

'And you became Kelly's big sister?' I asked.

Caroline nodded.

'And that entailed?' Seán said.

'Oh, just visiting and taking her out and stuff. It was easy and a lot of fun. She was only a kid at the time and I suppose you could say that I became sort of attached to her, so I applied to foster her.'

'And she came to live here?' Seán said.

She nodded again and then turned her back and replaced the clock.

'What did your husband think?' I said.

When she turned around, her mask was completely back in place and she gave me a Princess Grace smile. 'Billy was behind me all the way with the idea of fostering. He used to say we were so fortunate and that we should share our good fortune.'

'That's a very generous attitude,' Seán said.

Caroline smiled. 'He was right.'

'So what went wrong?' I asked.

She gave a deep sigh. 'At first it was great. I loved having Kelly here, but then as she got older I suppose her hormones intervened.'

'In what way?'

'Oh, you know how it is – she was out all the time. Became cheeky. Took up with a very unsuitable crowd. Managed to get herself involved with a total loser of a boyfriend.'

'So you sent her away?' Seán asked.

Caroline turned back to the mantelpiece, picked up the carriage clock again and went to wind it until she remembered she had just done so and replaced it. 'Yes,' she said. 'Yes, we did. We didn't have a choice.'

'Who was her boyfriend?' Seán said. 'If you can remember.'

'Oh, I remember all right. His name was Mike O'Neill.'

Seán wrote the name in capitals on a blank page of his notebook.

'And why was he unsuitable?' he said.

'He was a criminal. Always being picked up by the police. Billy knew his family and he said every single one of them was in trouble with the law one way or another.'

'That must have been upsetting for you,' I said. 'Sending Kelly back to the home, I mean.'

She looked at me and allowed a single tear to openly trickle down her face. 'I loved Kelly. It broke my heart.'

We sat in silence for a few seconds as Caroline went to a box of tissues that was sitting on a glass coffee table. She pulled out a single tissue and quietly patted her eyes and blew her nose. 'Is that it, so?'

'Pretty much,' Seán said. 'We're sorry to have to upset you at a time like this.'

'I understand,' she said. 'You have to do your job.'

'Just one more thing,' I said.

She looked at me.

'Do you know anything about the case your husband was working on before he died?'

'No. Billy never discussed his work.'

'Have you ever heard of a man called Gerry O'Hare?' Seán said.

She shook her head. 'No. Sorry. Was he one of Billy's clients?'

I nodded and stood up. Seán followed suit. 'Well, thank you for your time,' I said, reaching out and shaking her narrow hand.

'No problem.'

She and Seán shook hands as well and she saw us to her giant door. As I drove down the Hendricks' gravelled driveway Seán took out his notebook.

'Mikey O'Neill,' he said.

'Yeah. Do you believe her?'

'About what?'

'I mean in general,' I said, scrutinizing the oncoming traffic outside the Hendricks' tall wrought-iron gates. 'Do you think she's telling the truth?'

'Not really, though some of what she says is probably true.'

'I think I know Mike O'Neill,' I said, waving thanks at a woman in a yellow Punto who let me out.

'So do I. I'd say there isn't a Guard in town who hasn't picked that little fucker up at one time or another.'

'I haven't seen him in a while, though. I was thinking he might have straightened out.'

'Well, funnily enough I saw him last Friday. He's working in that Texaco garage on the Cork road.'

'Should we pay him a little visit?'

'Well, as we're out and about in the vicinity and in the business of paying social calls today I'd hate to leave Mikey out,' Seán said with a grin. 'Turn left here and we might just swing by and see if our boy is at work.'

We drove the short distance to the Texaco garage and I pulled the car to a stop behind the carwash. A chubby young man with shoulder-length blond hair and a short-sleeved bowling shirt was chatting to a middle-aged woman in the forecourt.

'Is that him?' I asked, squinting through the windscreen.

'Yes indeed. He's piled on the weight a bit. I wouldn't recognize him except that I was talking to him on Friday.'

'I remember him as a skinny little runt who was always breaking windows and shoplifting.'

'The running away from the police must have kept him in shape. He's on the straight and narrow now. Or so he told me.'

The woman sat in her car, waved at Mikey and pulled out of the garage. Seán and I got out of the car and walked towards him. He was bending down, picking up a lump of oil-stained paper towel, when we reached him.

'Mikey! How's it going? Jesus, we haven't seen each other in years and then we meet twice in less than a week.'

Mikey straightened up. He brushed a floppy blond fringe back from his eyes and stuffed the paper towel in his hand into a tall, black metal bin.

'Hello,' he said, and he looked at me. I could see the skinny, good-looking kid I'd known sort of surrounded by the jowls of this older Mikey. He was still good-looking in a kind of overblown ex-boy-band way.

'How are you, Mike?' I said.

'I'm good,' he said. 'Really good.'

'That's great,' I said.

'Could we ask you a few questions?' Seán said.

Mikey looked scared. 'I don't ever do any of that shit any more,' he said.

'That's great,' I said.

'No. Seriously. I'm not just saying it. I work here and I have a girlfriend and a baby and I'm strictly legal now.'

'A baby?' Seán said. 'Jesus, that's great. Girl or boy?'

'Girl. Triona.'

'Congratulations,' Seán said. 'What age is Triona?'

'Nearly two.' Mikey shifted from foot to foot and looked as if his natural nervousness with being around cops was struggling with his need to boast about his daughter. 'You should hear her talk. Jesus, she'd buy and sell you.'

'That's good,' I said. 'Kids are great.'

'Mikey, speaking of kids – do you ever remember a girl called Kelly Moloney?' Seán said.

Mikey's jaw actually dropped. I thought it was just as well that this young fella had decided to give up his life of crime – he wasn't a great man to hide his feelings.

'Do you?' Seán said.

'Sure,' Mikey said. 'It was a long time ago, though – ages.'

'And she and you were – seeing each other?' I said.

He nodded and pushed his hair behind both ears. 'For a while.'

'How long is a while?' Seán said.

He shrugged. 'Maybe six months? I'm not too sure, but something like that.'

'And why did you finish with her?' I said.

'We never finished properly. She was sent away and we kind of lost touch after that.'

'But she was only sent back to the home. Couldn't you have stayed in contact when she was in the children's home?' Seán said. 'You weren't much of a boyfriend if you couldn't even manage that.'

Mikey looked at each of us in turn and then he stared at the sky over my head as if there was something important there. 'They wouldn't let me near her. I tried but they went mad and wouldn't tell me where she'd gone or anything. I was broken up about it at the time. I was mad about her, you know.'

'What do you mean, wouldn't tell you where she'd gone?' I said.

'Just what I said,' he said, becoming more and more agitated as he spoke. 'I went up there, to the children's home place, and knocked on the door and everything. I was really shitting myself with that bitch of a nun but she just kept saying I had a nerve and I was lucky the Guards weren't after me. I hadn't a fucking clue what she was talking about and then she started saying stuff about statutory rape and that I was eighteen and they could have me up in a minute if they wanted.'

Mikey paused and I saw that a fine sheen of sweat was covering his face.

'What did you do?' Seán said.

'I asked her what she meant. I said, "Look, I don't have

a clue what you're talking about, Sister. I only want to see Kelly."'

'And?' I said.

'And she said hadn't I done enough damage getting Kelly pregnant when she was only a child herself and not to darken their door and that kind of shite.'

'She was pregnant?' I said.

He nodded.

'So they sent Kelly away to have the baby?' Seán said.

Mikey shrugged. 'Looked like it.'

'And you never heard from her again?' I said.

'No.'

'That's rough. It was your baby as well,' Seán said.

'But that's just the thing,' Mikey said. 'It wasn't. Kelly was only a kid and I really, really liked her and we messed around a bit but we never had sex, so if she was pregnant I don't know who the father was. But it wasn't me.'

27. Thursday 14 April

Hi Clint,

By the time we got to Finbar's flat it was almost four this morning. It's not a bad gaff at all, Clint, I have to say. It's in this real nice quiet old building near the park – not a million miles away from where me and Kelly found dead Billy Hendrick. It's one of those tall red-brick houses but it's been all done up, so it looks bright and not old and shabby.

The flat is at the top of the house. It's not very big but it does actually have two bedrooms and a kitchen and a bathroom and a sitting room. And these lovely high ceilings as well – I really like that about it. But do you know the thing I like the best about it? It has beds. In one bedroom there's a double bed and there's two singles in the other.

I said Natalie should take the double so she could mind Peter and that me and Kelly'd take the single beds in the other room. Kelly is still in a bake so she said she didn't care when I asked her if that was all right with her.

As soon as Eric left, we went straight to bed and I swear to God, Clint, when I got into that bed it was fucking brilliant. I know you always think you'll appreciate things but really I will always appreciate beds for the rest of my life after sleeping on those warehouse floors.

Just before I dropped off I heard Peter crying and Kelly tutting to herself. But I was so warm and comfortable I didn't really give a shit about any of it, so I turned over and fell asleep and had another dream about Ray Walters.

I dreamed me and Ray were getting married. I was wearing a long white dress in the dream and just before the ceremony started I put on the white shoes I'd bought for my wedding, but I couldn't wear them 'cos they made my dress too short. Then everything went mad in the dream and I was flying around trying to find a pair of flat sandals so I could wear those instead. Eventually I put on a pair of red and black sandals covered in sequins and I thought everything was all right. Then I put my hand up to my head and discovered that the thing I thought was a veil all along was really a big huge lampshade and it was hurting my head.

When I woke up I was full of panic and I thought it'd all been real but then I remembered where I was – and best of all I remembered the shower. Two weeks of washing yourself with cold water in a warehouse is nearly enough to make you give yourself up. And I wasn't disappointed.

The shower was nearly as good as sleeping in a bed. I found towels in the hot press on the landing and even shampoo and shower gel in the bathroom. I stuck my head around Natalie's door before I got going. She was sitting on the bed giving Peter his bottle and she said he was much better and cool and eating and everything. I was glad about that.

As soon as I got under the water I felt hot and clean and good for the first time in ages. I stayed in the shower for at least a half an hour and while I was there had a bit of a cry about Tony and then a longer cry about you, you bastard. Then I remembered my dream about Ray Walters and the lampshade and that made me laugh.

When I came out of the bathroom, Kelly was waiting outside the door to go in. I still couldn't look at her after the stuff she'd said to Natalie but I didn't say nothing.

Eric and Natalie were drinking tea and eating toast in the kitchen. Eric was holding Peter, who was awake and wheezing but happy as a pig in shit, hanging over Eric's arm and looking all around him. I started slagging them, saying they were like the Waltons, and then Nat said she'd been telling Eric all about the plan to dye our hair and stuff and that he thought it was a great idea.

I made myself toast and tea and I said I thought so too now that I'd slept on it and that I'd better ring Glenn to tell him about the changes. But then they said they'd already done it and Natalie had said it to him about getting a passport for Peter and all. So that was good.

My tea and toast tasted great – in a proper kitchen, that's why – and while I was eating Eric was talking and wondering where Glenn would get a birth cert for Peter. That made me laugh and I said, Go way, Eric – you really don't want to know. And then Nat started on at me as well and I was all, Oh definitely Natalie, you don't want to know. But nothing would do them, so I told them.

Natalie was fucking gobsmacked and saying it after me, like, He'll buy it off a guy who reads death notices. And I said, Yeah, that's what he'll do. And she said that wasn't so bad. So I said, I suppose not if you think stealing the identity of dead people is OK. And she was all shocked and stuff and I was laughing. Nat's not the sharpest knife in the drawer if you know what I mean.

But Eric is. And he said, Do these people get the name and the parents' names and the dead person's date of birth from the death notices and buy new birth certs? I said, Bingo, and he said, Jesus.

Even Natalie got it then. She wanted to know how I knew what these guys did and I told her you and Ray did it for a while to make money.

Sorry, Clint – I hate speaking ill of the dead – but it's true: ye did do it. They were upset, though. Eric looked shocked and you could see he wanted to say something about it but didn't want to be saying bad stuff about my dead brother.

So I said it for him: It's a shit thing to do. He just nodded, 'cos it is. I told him then how I used to kill ye for it and that ye didn't do it for too long. Do you remember those fights, Clint? Not that any of it did any good.

Then Nat says that we can't complain really 'cos now we're glad to be getting birth certs and passports, aren't we? And I said yeah and then she said that the dead people won't mind helping us and I told her that's what you used to say and she started laughing.

Eric went away, then came back about four this afternoon with the bag of hair products we asked him for. He also had yesterday's newspaper with him and there were pictures of us and Billy Hendrick in it – all over it – and headlines about us being wanted for murder or something like that. I wanted to get sick when I saw them. But Eric said not to worry – we'd be gone soon and anyway weren't we changing how we looked? And that's true.

So we did the dyeing and cutting and stuff. It was a really good idea, wasn't it, now that our faces are plastered all over the papers?

You should see us now. We all look so fucking weird! Natalie cut Kelly's hair tight into her head and she looks fantastic. Like Sinead O'Connor, Eric said, and he's right. Even after we bleached it, she still looks like her.

And Natalie's hair which was so blonde is pure black now and all tied up and I look a good bit like Victoria Beckham with my dark kind of mahogany bob. I really like it. Maybe it's about more than how we look, Clint. Maybe I like it because if we look so different it might mean everything will be different as well. Stupid, I suppose.

223

Anyway, by teatime we were all looking like different people – you should see us. Glenn arrived then with his camera and a Chinese takeaway and he couldn't get over the difference. He took the pictures and he even took some of Peter. And I asked him if Mam had seen the papers.

First he didn't answer and then he said yeah, she had and she was afraid I was going to get killed, 'cos there was a story about one of us being involved in killing Billy Hendrick. I was nearly crying when he was talking 'cos I feel so bad for her but I warned him not to tell her anything and he promised he wouldn't.

After that, Glenn said he'd go straight home and do the passports and Eric left as well and the rest of us settled down to watch telly for the whole evening. Kelly and Natalie were in better form since doing the hair but what Kelly'd said about Ryan was still between them and I was too shagged to try to do anything about it.

About ten Kelly said she was going for a walk. She said she couldn't stand being cooped up all the time. Me and Nat said nothing – just kept watching *Friends*. Peter woke up when she closed the front door and I gave him his bottle and he was much better and more like himself, and me and Nat talked about Spain and what we'd do and stuff, like wasn't it funny to think that Peter'd be able to speak Spanish better than English?

When Kelly came back she was with Glenn and he had the passport forms with him and he had a funny look on his face and only stayed a few minutes. Just long enough to check that everything was all right. That's what he said.

We looked at them and saw that he'd called us all Ryan because according to the birth cert he'd bought, Peter was now called Jake Ryan and all the other birth certs were in the name of Ryan, 'cos Glenn said that around here it's easy to find Ryans living and dead and all he'd ever have to change would be the date of birth. I wanted him just to shut up. I didn't want to think about any of it. I made myself put the idea of the real Jake Ryan out of my head and cribbed about my picture to take my mind off the dead baby.

Glenn just listened and said yeah, yeah, yeah. He was weird but I thought it might be something to do with Tony, so I asked him was he all right and he said he was and then I let it go. Then he said he'd better get going – he had work in the morning.

Peter fell asleep just after Glenn left. Nat put him into bed and then came in to watch a documentary about rabbits on telly with me, and Kelly went into the bedroom and I thought I heard her talking on her phone.

There was nothing really on the telly so me and Nat just went in to our lovely beds. I was inside in my bed and Kelly was in the shower when my phone rang. I looked at the screen and it was Glenn.

Can you talk? was the first thing he said as soon as he heard my voice.

So I said, Yeah, what the fuck? And he said then, Are you alone? And I said, Who the fuck are you? James Bond? Then he says if he tells me something will I promise not to lose my knickers?

My heart kind of froze because I was afraid but I said, I promise. Go on.

So he starts off about being on his way back to us and he met Kelly and she got in the car and said she wanted to go for a drive so he did. Then next thing he's all, Oh, Gina, she's very good-looking, I couldn't help it, she really came on to me – I mean, what do you expect? Anybody'd do the same in my place.

You screwed her, I said because it was so obvious and

I'd known in my heart that she was sort of focusing in on Glenn all the time anyway. And I knew he'd never be able to resist her – you wouldn't have.

And of course I was right. Anyway, he was upset about it and going on and on and saying he loved Amy and that shit. Amy's his girlfriend. Did you ever meet her? I can't remember. She's sound.

Anyway, I couldn't follow half what he was saying, so I asked him if that was why he rang – to tell me he fucked Kelly Moloney. And he said yeah and no and stuff and started off again. So I said, Calm down, I won't tell Amy if that's what's worrying you. And he said, No, it wasn't that.

And then he calmed down and told me that afterwards they stopped in this garage and he went into the shop to pay for petrol and she got out of the car 'cos she said she had to make a phone call and there's something about his car and phone coverage. Anyway, when he came out of the shop he went to look for her and she was talking to this woman. A fucking fine woman as well, according to Glenn – old, though, he said. And they got a bit of a fright when he came around the corner and your woman just kind of waved like she knew him and then she left.

Isn't that weird? I asked him if he knew who she was and he said no and that Kelly said she was just someone she used to work with. So I said that was grand, so, 'cos I'd say most of the people Kelly worked with wouldn't talk to the cops. And he said he didn't know nothing about that but that when he was coming around the corner he could hear them talking and he didn't know what they were saying exactly but it was definitely something about going to America.

He said the woman said something like once she had the ticket for Boston and the money she'd do it then. Of course

I said, Do what? But he didn't know. Just said there was something about her and the way Kelly was talking to her and stuff.

He sounded so sort of sorry and ashamed it made me laugh, even though there was nothing really funny going on, and I told him he was a total fucking slapper and he said yeah, yeah, he was. But he knew Kelly was up to something so we should look out, that's all. Watch our backs. Then he hung up and I was as tired as I'd ever been in my whole life. I can't believe it.

So that's it, Clint. What the fuck do you make of that? I have to turn off the light now: Kelly is after coming back into the room and she's in bed and I need to stop writing. But you know if you're really there and listening to this stuff and know anything about what's going on, maybe you'd appear to me in a dream or something? Have a chat with the boss and see what you can manage.

Love,
Gina xxx

28. Thursday 14 April – Friday 15 April

It took us almost a full twenty-four hours to find Mikey's nun. Seán rang the station while we were driving to Alan Hendrick's office and got one of his female admirers to dig in the files and find a name for us to contact at St Brendan's Children's Home. Then he tried that but everybody was at a childcare seminar in Cork and wouldn't be back until the next day.

'Fuck it,' Seán said, hanging up. 'Now what?'

'Well, we'll find someone tomorrow and meanwhile we might ask Alan if he knows anything about Kelly having a baby while we're visiting him.'

'Good idea,' Seán said. 'Surely he must know something – especially if he was sleeping with the lovely Caroline all that time.'

'Exactly,' I said, pulling into a miraculously empty parking space in front of Hendrick's office. The Hendrick brothers had a very nice suite of offices in a restored Georgian building in the Crescent. The building had wide steps, complete with restored bootscraper by the big red-painted door and minimalistic décor in the glass and cream reception.

'Can you imagine Froggy Plunkett with his greasy head in here?' Seán said, laughing, as we walked up to the steel and glass-block reception desk and asked for Alan Hendrick.

A pale-skinned woman in her mid-twenties with the hacked blonde hair and undernourished good looks of a supermodel shook her head sadly at our request. 'I'm afraid Mr Hendrick was called away.'

'But he's expecting us,' Seán said, with his woman-melting smile. 'Detectives O'Connell and Ryan.'

The young woman looked at us in her unfocused way. 'Hold on – I think he said something about you.' She fiddled with a Post-it note and read aloud something scrawled across its yellow face. 'That's right – tell the detectives he had to go and if there's anything important to call him tomorrow.' She looked up at us again, and then back at the note and once more at us. 'Sorry.'

'We'll call him later,' I said before Seán started in on her. 'Thanks.'

Seán glared at me and then at the receptionist before swivelling away and stalking out to the car in front of me.

'Fucking bastard,' he said, fastening his seatbelt as I started the engine. 'Who does he think he is?'

I looked at my watch. Four o'clock and I was getting more and more tired by the second and finding it hard to give a shit about Alan or even Billy Hendrick. Exhaustion that felt like a concrete block on my chest seemed to press me against the driver's seat. I'd really have to get some sleep. Take time off. A course of vitamins. Something. Anything. I knew for sure that I couldn't keep going like this.

The town traffic was almost gridlocked and it took us ages to get back to the station. I was so tired I could hardly speak and just went up to my office as a matter of form and half-heartedly filled out some reports. Seán headed off to see if he could find out more about the nun in the children's home.

I sat at my desk and tried to make myself think about Billy Hendrick's murder instead of Jimmy Boy Lane running over my wife. But I was finding it increasingly difficult to concentrate on anything else. I read through the notes on my desk. Nothing major. Ten phone calls with sightings of the girls. Those newspaper pictures were rapidly becoming a pain in the ass.

I scanned through the list. Three for Kelly Moloney – Tesco, Dunnes and Colbert train station. Gina Brennan was today's winner with five sightings. According to the phone calls, she'd been seen in a hairdresser's in the Crescent shopping centre, on O'Connell Street, in Pizza Hut, checking in for Frankfurt at Shannon airport and at a Shell garage on the dock road. Poor old Natalie O'Rourke had only been seen twice – in Tesco as well as her friend and in the Regional Hospital A&E.

I wrote a note to myself to have one of the lads call back all the callers first thing in the morning – you never know. But I wasn't hopeful that any of them were going to lead to anything. Truthfully, I also just wasn't hopeful in general.

At half five I struggled to my car and into my evening routine. I'd just visit Árd Aoibhinn for a little while and then home to bed. The bloody flu was really taking its toll.

Rita's eyes were open when I went into the room and *Neighbours* was on the TV. I didn't sit down – just turned on the video of our wedding and let the tinny amateur soundtrack fill up her room. I stood and stared at her for a few seconds and then picked up the bottle of oil. No hand splint today, which was good; her hands must have been relaxing. Inside my head I struggled to think of things to say.

'Bad old weather today, love,' I said eventually, as I smoothed oil around a cuticle. My Uncle Dan, who made the video for us, was shouting at Rita to look at the camera and I could hear her laughing and a child crying in the background. I knew that was the part where she was on her way into the church. While that was happening I was inside waiting at the altar, momentarily terrified she had changed her mind.

'Desperate weather for the time of year,' I said out loud. I was so strung out I felt as if my whole body had been sanded and I'd have liked to bawl like a baby. My voice faded away and I busied myself with the massage. I couldn't think of a thing to say. It was just exhaustion, I told myself. I still wasn't fully recovered from the flu. Whatever the reason, the words inside me were gone for the moment.

When I had finished the oiling and massage I listened to her breathing, which was still a bit wheezy, and then I kissed her lips gently and held my face close to hers so that I could look into her open eyes.

It was a strange phenomenon, this eye-open state. I remembered when it first happened, about a month after the accident. I remembered most of all my elation and the crushing despair that followed when they delivered the news that it meant nothing. How could it mean nothing?

I examined her eyes. They were so beautiful – and so clear. Green irises with tiny yellow flecks. Like a crumpled leaf. As I looked she stared back at me and all of a sudden and for the very first time I saw the emptiness the doctors described. My heart thumped with fear. I kissed her again and let her soft breath rub my cheek so that my skin could remember who she was.

'I love you,' I said, tracing the shape of her lips with my index finger. 'I really do love you a lot, Rita. Please don't be gone away.'

I felt her breath on my finger as I rested it on her lips and a wave of despair flowed like water through me. How was my life supposed to continue in this way? Her eyes closed gently and I instinctively moved my finger away so as not to disturb her sleep.

I especially didn't think I could keep going as a cop without a soft place to fall. I hadn't realized it consciously before but that'd always been the unspoken deal with the universe. I could do all the shit work and see all the sadness and maybe even help some people some of the time, if at home there was Rita. But now what?

I stared down at her. Now how long could I survive my world? Her chest moved up and down gently with her breaths and I heard a slight wheeze again. Leaning forward I shook her gently by the shoulders to see if her breathing would clear and it did.

'You've a bit of a cold there, love,' I said, gently removing one of the pillows from under her head so that she could sleep more comfortably.

I thought of the doctor and the deadline and it made me feel sick. Then I thought of seconds earlier when I'd looked into her eyes and seen nothing and that made me feel sicker. I couldn't afford to become like the doctors and stop seeing her, no matter what else happened. In spite of everything they said, I just knew that buried as she might be underneath damaged brain tissue there was a tiny part of Rita still around.

What the hell would happen if I gave up on her? Would she give up as well? If it was hard to be me it had to be hell being Rita, locked inside her own body. I had to believe in her; it was as simple as that. Fuck the doctors and their magical calendars, anyway. How could they believe her brain was following a time span in its healing? That was just illogical for people of science. I knew it was an organic process and that it'd just take as long as it took for Rita to get well and come back.

Anyway, what else did I have to do except wait for her? Nothing except my job, and I was seriously beginning to think I'd have to give that up. Maybe I'd never really been cut out to be a policeman. For most of my life I'd seen people as correctable. Fixable. Basically good. In spite of all the crap around me and what looked like evidence to the contrary. That's why I did my job in the first place. Why I decided to be a Guard when I was eighteen. Seán, on the other hand, was the original believer in original sin.

But I was beginning to slide in my belief in people, especially since the accident. Surely the longer I stayed with my nose pressed up against the shit side of life, the harder it was going to be to maintain my way of thinking? And I wasn't so sure I wanted to spend my life with Seán's view of the world. Maybe it really was time to go and run the pub for my parents so that they could retire to the seaside.

I kissed Rita again and left for home, buying myself a pizza on the way. I ate half my dinner out of its cardboard box in front of the TV as I watched the news, and as soon as I had finished eating I staggered up to bed and fell asleep.

I probably had dreams but I don't remember them. All I remember was taking off my clothes and then next thing it was morning and my alarm was going off and I could hear rain tapping against the bedroom window like fingernails.

Seán met me on my way into the station and we walked up the back stairs together. I'd probably have taken the lift if I was alone but I knew Seán'd nag about me getting out of shape.

'Yvonne rang last night,' he said, pounding his feet hard on the steps.

'I hope you weren't entertaining.'

'Ha ha. She's getting married.'

'Oh.'

We pounded up together in silence for a few steps. As we hit the first landing Seán stopped and looked at me. 'That geek she's with – fucksake, Rob, have you seen him?'

I shook my head.

'Fucking weed. He's after getting some big job, though, and she wants to move with him.'

'Where?'

'Germany.'

'What about Fiona and Carrie?'

Seán gave an unamused laugh and started off up the stairs again. I followed.

'That's what I said to her, but she wouldn't talk about it on the phone. Wants to meet and discuss it properly.' Seán said the last part in a high-pitched falsetto, which was supposed to be an imitation of his ex-wife.

'When is it to happen?'

'August.' His breath caught in his throat then, and I watched his broad back heave slightly under his navy sports coat and knew it wasn't the stair climbing.

'You'll work something out,' I said.

'Mmm.'

More silent climbing.

'Did you lose your temper with her?'

Seán laughed then. 'What do you think?'

'What did you say?'

'The usual – who did she think she was and I didn't have kids so that she could fuck off to some foreign country with another man. That sort of thing.'

'Great.' Now I was beginning to laugh as well. 'You probably should have thought of that before you screwed around on her, Seánie.'

'Which is more or less what she said. Anyway, fuck it! I don't want to think about it. I found the nun, by the way,' he said, not even slightly out of breath as we mounted the concrete steps.

'What?'

'The nun Mikey told us about. Well, I don't know if it's the same nun, but I have found a Sister Therese who remembers Kelly Moloney.'

'Excellent.'

He turned his head to look at me. 'By the way, you look like shit, Rob. Did you sleep?'

'Thanks. I slept. Have you spoken to this nun?'

'After you left yesterday. We're meeting her at twelve.'

'In St Brendan's?' I said, trying to conceal my slight breathlessness.

'Yes. I asked Janice to go and have a word with Bunny – see if she can find any reason he might have wanted to kill his own solicitor.'

'Good thinking,' I said.

Seán smiled. 'I knew you'd want to see the nun. Janice isn't the worst of them, anyway – I mean any friend of yours . . .'

He turned his head to look back at me and I grinned. 'Tell me about our nun.'

'Secretive bastard. OK, she's old by the sound of her but seems to be firing on all cylinders. She said she'd meet us in the parlour at twelve.'

'Jesus, it's a while since I've been in a nuns' parlour,' I said, opening the fire door at the top of the stairwell and stepping out into the bright corridor.

'I've never been in a nuns' parlour,' Seán said. 'Though I have to admit I've had a few fantasies set there.'

I laughed and we collected our morning coffee at the communal coffee station before going to my office. Seán settled down in a red upholstered armchair with his coffee.

'Don't even think about lighting up,' I said.

Seán gave me a false smile and took a long drink from his mug. 'What did you think about that fucker blowing us off yesterday?'

'I don't know. Putting us in our place? I'm not sure. Maybe he was called away urgently.'

'I doubt it. I think you should call him and invite him down here for a chat. Why should we run around making his life easy?'

'Police stations are almost like home for Alan Hendrick.'

'Still, it's the principle.'

'I agree,' I said. 'I'll call him in a minute.'

We settled back and drank our coffee in silence. I didn't know what I was going to decide about my work, but I was feeling quite a lot better about everything now that I'd had some sleep. I'd ring Mary Hayes as soon as I got a minute and see what the word was with Jimmy Boy Lane. There was no point in fixating on it – it wasn't my case and there was nothing I could do about it. On the other hand, Billy Hendrick's murder was my case and I should put my energy into that.

I looked around the office at the pale green walls and metal filing cabinet and it struck me that it could have belonged to anybody. I'd moved into that office a few months after Rita's accident, but somehow, though I brought my stuff, I'd never managed to fully inhabit it. No wonder Seán didn't feel he was trespassing – my office was as impersonal as a canteen.

Seán had his own office – well, that was what it was called. He never used it though. He said there was no privacy – which meant he couldn't smoke – as it was just a partitioned section of a huge work area. It was still more obviously personal for all that. The desk was littered with old newspapers and *Q* magazines and there was a photograph of Seán and his little girls visiting Santa last year propped in the middle of the desk.

Seán was slumped back in his chair with his long legs stretched out in front of him and his mug cradled in his hands against his stomach, like a man who'd dozed off in front of TV. His body was in great condition and I could see the muscles under his shirt as his torso rose and fell with his relaxed breathing. No wonder the ladies loved him.

His eyes were closed and it looked as if he was asleep, but I knew he was actually more wide awake than I'd ever manage to be. That was his nature. Seán was like a cat. Even when he was asleep the tiniest sound would wake him. He usually said it was his sensitive nature and once – when he'd been pissed out of his head after his marriage broke up – he'd said that when he was a kid he'd learned to sleep with one eye open so that he could hear his old man coming in at night. He didn't say why he needed to hear him and I didn't ask. I already knew his father was a drunken bastard who beat the living daylights out of every one of his kids until he dropped down dead when Seán was sixteen. I wasn't sure I wanted to know any more.

Seán's light sleeping used to drive his ex-wife bonkers. I never said anything to her when she complained about it, but I thought it was unfair. I felt she should have been grateful, as it meant that Seán was the one who looked after the girls in the middle of the night when they were babies. But it was hard to make her happy.

Rita used to say that I should have more sympathy for Yvonne. She'd say it was just her way of getting back at him for all the bed-hopping. Then I'd say, 'Well, maybe they might all be happier if Yvonne came out with whatever the fuck it was that was upsetting her.' Rita'd laugh at that and say, 'Sure, yeah, easy for you to say – everything is so easy for you, Rob. Life is straightforward. The good guys and the bad guys and nothing in between.' Mostly those conversations would finish when I'd grab her and kiss her neck and slide my hands under her T-shirt.

I flicked open my desk phonebook, found Alan Hendrick's office number and dialled. The phone rang a couple of times before it was answered by the young woman we'd met the day before.

'Good morning, Veronica. Detective Inspector O'Connell here. Could you put me through to Alan Hendrick, please?' I said in answer to her generic 'Good-morning-Hendrick's-Solicitors-Veronica-speaking-how-can-I-help-you?'

'I'll see if Mr Hendrick is available to take your call,' Veronica said.

'Oh, right. Look, if he's busy you might pass on a message for me. Tell him we'll expect him at the station in my office at three. Is that OK?'

'Great. Please hold.'

In less than thirty seconds Alan Hendrick was on the line. 'Good morning, Detective. Sorry to have missed you yesterday.'

'No problem, Alan. I was hoping you might drop in to my office this afternoon – threeish – if you're available.'

'Oh. Has something new come up?'

'Well, nothing too exciting – a couple of new witnesses. We'd like to have a chat, that's all.'

'What time?'

'Three.'

'No can do.'

'Really?' I said, struggling to keep my patience.

'How about four thirty?' Alan Hendrick said.

'No. Sorry. Four thirty is no good for me – I have another

appointment then. Three it is or we'll have to reschedule.'

There was a short pause.

'OK. Look,' Alan Hendrick said, 'three o'clock in your office. I won't be able to stay for long.'

'No problem. See you later,' I said and hung up.

Seán drained his coffee mug and grinned at me. 'What's all this about an appointment at four thirty? Am I going too?'

'Come on, we've a meeting to go to.' I grabbed my folder and a pen as I stood up. 'Are you coming?'

'I love it when you're masterful,' Seán said, standing up slowly and having a stretch. 'You're my role model, Rob – d'you know that?'

'Shut the fuck up and come on,' I said, leading the way out of the office. Seán followed still laughing.

29. Friday 15 April

Hi Clint,

How are you? Apart from being dead, I mean. I know, I know – I'm a howl. Things are really weird around here at the moment. I said nothing about what Glenn had told me because I thought maybe Kelly'd say it herself and that'd be way better. But she didn't say a word about calling anybody or America or any of that shit and the more the day went on the less I knew what to do, to be honest.

I mean, if I said it to her, then she'd know Glenn'd told me. And as well as that I knew Natalie'd go mad when she found out – and I wouldn't blame her.

Do you know what I realized this morning? I realized that it's more than two weeks since we legged it on the way back from the beautician's course. It feels like another lifetime.

The other thing I realized is that I really miss Tony. I know that's obvious but I do. It's the usual thing with people when they die – the longer it goes on the more you miss them. I mean, when you think about it, I still miss you, you bollocks, and you're dead years.

The thing about Tony, though, especially at the moment, is that if he was around I could call him and ask him what to do about the stuff Glenn overheard Kelly saying. If he's there with you, maybe you'd ask him, 'cos I'm completely fucking stumped.

In other ways, though, even with Tony dying and all, we've actually been very lucky: he left us Eric. Thanks for that, Tone.

Eric rang us early yesterday morning to tell us he'd bought us Ryanair tickets for a place called Girona near Barcelona. We're supposed to be flying out of Dublin on Tuesday morning. I told the girls. Natalie jumped up and down with excitement – she's a gas woman, the way she gets all worked up and everything. Like a kid.

Kelly said something like oh that's good, but she didn't even crack a smile. All the time Nat was screaming and dancing around the place singing I watched Kelly to see if anything at all about whatever she's hatching showed in her face – but not a thing.

For a finish I couldn't take it any more and I went over and sat down on the couch beside her. She hardly looked at me – just kept flicking the channels on the telly. Peter started crying down in the bedroom and Nat went to get him, so that was kind of my opportunity, wasn't it?

So I asked her what did she think about Spain and stuff. She didn't even look at me – just flicked over to *Oprah* and said it sounded fine to her. So I said, Are you sure? and then she looked at me all right. Stared at me for ages like she was thinking something. Then she gave me another one of her half smiles and said, Why wouldn't it be fine with me?

Fuck it, Clint, I could feel the stuff Glenn had told me rising up inside me like vomit but I still couldn't say it out.

Then Nat came in the room with Peter in her arms and she's going on about buying sunscreen for Jake before we go and I'm all, Who the fuck is Jake? And Natalie thinks that's a howl, 'cos of course it's Peter's new name and she tricked me.

She held Peter up in the air and he burped and we were laughing and I said I'd have to write our new names on my hand or I'd forget them and Nat said half the people she knew were called something different to the name on their birth cert. And Kelly's not talking, of course – still watching *Oprah* – and I ask her does she think she'll remember our new names and she just says, yeah, why wouldn't she?

Natalie then was going on about how long would we be able to stay in Derek Greene's house in Spain and I said as long as we like 'cos Tony and Eric definitely have some shit on him. And Nat's all delighted and wondering if it has a pool and stuff and saying we can teach Peter to swim.

I told her then about this programme I saw once on the telly about newborn babies swimming and how they said all newborns could swim and Nat says if that was true why couldn't she swim, so. I swear that girl is as thick as a plank sometimes.

I told her I'd teach her and I told her about how I'm well able to swim because of how me and you – and Ray a lot of the time – used to spend all our summers swimming up in Enda's. I even told her about the time we nearly got arrested for swimming in Ardnacrusha. Do you remember that?

I didn't say anything to you at the time 'cos I didn't want to look like a fool, but I was afraid of my shit when those sirens on the turbines started going off and then the cops came along. It was a laugh as well, though, wasn't it? We had some good laughs together, me and you.

It'll be a new life, Natalie said then, all dramatic like.

Kelly – the bitch – rolled her eyes and tutted real loud.

So I ask her then if she can swim and she says, Like a fish. And all the time she's looking at the telly, where a skinny man with grey hair and a thick black moustache is bending forward, crying.

I felt sorry for him, thinking how mortified he must be to be crying in front of millions of people. Oprah put her arms around him and the writing on the screen said his name was Billy. That's a bit of a coincidence, isn't it – Billy? Like Billy Hendrick, the dead guy. I didn't want to start thinking about him all over again so I started on at Kelly again. You were in Spain before, weren't you? I said to her.

She just nodded and Natalie asked her what it was like and she said it was just like anyplace else only hot. And Natalie said it'd be better than here, anyway, and I said nothing, 'cos I think I might miss Limerick when I'm gone. Instead I started talking about getting work in Spain and how Glenn'd get us RSI numbers and stuff and Natalie said, How? And I didn't even answer her and she got it then and said, Is it the dead people? And I said yeah, and she was upset.

I told her not to think about it and that we didn't really have a choice, and she agreed and said I was right and she'd not think about it, and then all of a sudden Kelly joined in. She started going on about how there's always loads of work that doesn't need any papers and Natalie said she didn't want none of that shit. She wanted everything straight from the beginning for Peter.

Kelly smiled at her as if to say yeah, right, Natalie, best of luck – you'll never get that in your life. Natalie opened her mouth like she was going to say something else, but then she took a deep breath instead and just left the room. I was fuming. Kelly's some bitch. She could just have left Nat alone. So what if it all falls apart on her? At least she's trying.

I keep thinking about what Glenn said and how Kelly might be plotting to go to America instead of Spain and I'm beginning to hope that it's true because I'm sick of her. I don't like her. I'd never really liked her but that wasn't a problem – you can't like everyone. Now, though, I don't trust her and I'm not sure what the fuck I'm going to do about that.

She hasn't said anything about America and I've left it so long at this stage that I'm afraid to bring it up. For all I know maybe Glenn got the wrong end of the stick and she's going to turn us over to the cops.

Or – and I know I thought this before and put it out of my head – maybe she is the one who shot Billy Hendrick. Maybe she shot him and hid the money and that's what she's using to go to America. Anything is possible with Kelly. But I said nothing and just watched the rest of *Oprah* with her like nothing was going on inside us.

Gina x

30. Friday 15 April

That morning the conference ran very smoothly. Seán reported on our interviews with Caroline Hendrick and Mikey O'Neill and our proposed meeting with Alan Hendrick and our nun at St Brendan's Children's Home. Janice had an interesting bit of news in that one of her people had turned up another address for Agnes Moloney – a house this time, and one that was registered in her name. It was new, and just registered in the Land Registry office, which was why we hadn't turned it up the first time we looked.

Apart from that, various people reported back bits and pieces of information – all trivial. The thing with all investigations is that it's like being on a gigantic pebbly beach where you just turn over stone after stone after stone until eventually – if you're lucky – one of the stones happens to be covering the answer to your puzzle. As a result you never know what's important until afterwards, so we all listened intently to the list of trivia.

Towards the end of the meeting, Janice gave another report, this time on the fruitless interviews she'd had with the three Hendrick clients who'd been on holiday when we began and her intention to meet the last two clients on the list, as requested by Seán.

'OK, that's it for today,' I said, closing my folder. 'Unless there's some other business?'

Everybody shook their heads and then Margie, one of the secretaries, came in and said she had a message for me from Alan Hendrick. He'd said to tell me that he couldn't keep our appointment after all and he'd call me later.

'Arrogant prick,' Seán said to a murmur of agreement as soon as Margie had left.

'I'll call him again,' I said.

'Why don't I?' Janice offered. 'Aren't you off to see the nun?'

I thanked her and ended the meeting, and the room erupted into chat and the noise of shifting chairs. Seán was still seated and still doodling.

'It's half eleven, Seán,' I said. 'We need to get to St Brendan's.'

Seán nodded and stood up. We left the conference room and headed straight to our car. Seán drove and we were almost at the Children's Home before either of us spoke.

'I have to ask you something, Rob. It's driving me mad.'

I looked at his profile but he never took his eyes off the road. 'What?'

'Janice – something happened, I know it did.'

'It's none of your business, Seán.'

He still didn't look at me. 'No, it is Rob, it is my business. I know you and I know what you're like and you've had a shit year and I'd be glad if something happened with you and her. You can't live the rest of your life like . . . like this.'

'You don't understand what it's like.'

'I know,' he said in a soft voice. 'But even so . . .'

I sighed long and hard and tried to feel annoyed with him but I knew he meant well. 'All right, Seán. Something did happen between me and Janet, but we were drunk and I feel like shit about it and nothing like that is ever going to happen again.'

A smile spread across Seán's face, but he still kept his eyes fixed forward. 'She's a good-looking woman, right enough –

even if she is from Dublin. You could do worse than be involved with her, I suppose.'

'I'm not involved with anybody, Seán.'

'It's not a crime, Rob.'

'I know that, but I'm still married.'

Seán pulled the car in through the tall gates of St Brendan's and parked in the nuns' tarmac-covered car park in front of the convent. 'Just one question,' he said, looking at me for the first time as he switched off the engine.

I shook my head and opened my mouth to object but he had no intention of waiting.

'Was she any good in bed? Those skinny birds are often useless.' I laughed in spite of myself and got out of the car.

The children's home – not much used now, seemingly – was a long building obviously built in the 1960s with big windows and oblong blue painted decorative panels at intervals of twelve or fifteen feet. The convent, on the other hand, was a much older building. It reminded me of Billy and Caroline Hendrick's house with its double-fronted bay-windowed shape and carved quoin stones along the edges.

I knew the convent was probably bigger than the Hendricks' house but it honestly didn't look like that. It certainly had smaller gardens, as most of the surrounding land, which had no doubt once belonged to the order, was populated by houses and offices. It had probably been sold off to raise revenue for the elderly nuns still living there.

A young woman wearing a black ponytail and a red tracksuit opened the door.

'Sister Therese is expecting you,' she said, leading us into the wide hallway before we even spoke. 'You are the detectives, aren't you?'

'We are,' Seán said with his best smile. The young woman

blushed and led us down a long corridor that smelled of baking bread and furniture polish. I wondered if postulants nowadays wore red tracksuits and ponytails.

The high-ceilinged corridor had a number of small alcoves along its length, each of which housed a statue of a saint and a small red glass bowl with a burning votive candle. The floor was intricately tiled in randomly laid cream and brown and terracotta-coloured tiles, giving an overall effect of being speckled. The woman in front of us opened a tall, white painted door and ushered us into the nuns' parlour.

When I was a kid my mother had an aunt who was a nun in Crosshaven and maybe twice a year she'd force Maria and Dad and me to get dressed up and go visit Sister Gertrude. I hated it because the nuns' parlour was always as neat as a museum and not completely silent but sort of buzzing with hushed noise as if everything was alive and listening.

We'd all walk in, as stiff as puppets, and sit on the hard, high-back dark wood chairs. Sister Gertrude would give us weak orange squash and soft Marietta biscuits and ask us about school, and we had to tell her our teachers' names and what we'd done that week. Then she would tell us to work hard at our books and spend the rest of the time talking to Mam about this dead aunt and that dead cousin.

Dad smiled a lot in the nuns' parlour, but we could tell that he was as anxious to get out as we were. Every single time when that convent door closed behind us he lit a cigarette and said the same thing: 'Never again.'

But he didn't mean it because a few months later there we would be again, taller, older, but still drinking weak squash and trying to swallow those biscuits, which stuck to the roof of your mouth like Holy Communion. The only person who didn't dread visiting the nun was Maria. Even our mother – though she didn't say anything – would be as cross as a wasp all the way to Crosshaven in the car. But not Maria.

I couldn't figure it out. When I asked her about it she said she liked it because it was quiet and clean and smelled good. That didn't explain it to me, but it was all she ever said. Maria's love of the convent was such a remarkable thing that my mother told me years later she was sure she was going to become a nun. That was until she married Gerry Burke three weeks after meeting him.

All this came rushing back as we walked across the square parlour to shake hands with a soft-looking woman with neatly cut white hair, bright blue, intelligent-looking eyes and a tidy grey round-necked cardigan that displayed just an edge of white nun's collar. She smiled but didn't stand as we reached her. Seán and I shook hands with her and introduced ourselves in turn.

'The knees are bad,' she said, as she made hearty handshake contact. 'So you won't mind if I don't stand.'

'Stay where you are, Sister,' Seán said, sitting on a fireside chair covered in green knobbly fabric. I sat on a matching chair. It was nice and comfortable.

'Would you bring us a tray, Helen, please?' Sister Therese said looking at me. 'Tea? Coffee?'

'I don't mind – whatever you're having yourself,' I said.

She looked at Seán.

'Likewise,' he said.

'Bring us a pot of coffee and a few biscuits, dear,' the nun said to the woman we now knew was called Helen. The woman nodded and Sister Therese looked back at me. 'I love the odd cup of coffee. The doctor says I should stay away from stimulants but God knows at my age if it wasn't for the odd stimulant I'd hardly tick over at all.'

I smiled at her and tried to guess her age, but it wasn't

possible, and I could see that behind her broad, friendly smile and casual air was a mind that was busy assessing everything about us.

'So, gentlemen, how can I be of assistance?'

I spoke first. 'Well, Sister, we're trying to find Kelly Moloney and having a fair bit of difficulty. We thought as you knew her you might be able to tell us something that could help.'

Sister Therese looked at me, her face a picture of guilelessness. 'Did she do something wrong?'

Seán cleared his throat. 'I'm sorry to tell you Sister, but she was in prison and she and her friends broke out – but that isn't why we're looking for her.'

Sister Therese turned her innocent face towards Seán and I could see that she had no intention of answering anything until she was good and ready.

'Kelly may be able to help us with a murder investigation,' he continued.

The big white door opened and Helen came across the room with a laden silver tray. She placed it on a mahogany coffee table situated close to Sister Therese's bad knees and poured the thick, fragrant coffee into three large, paper-thin porcelain cups. She handed one to each of us with an accompanying side plate of assorted biscuits. Finally, she did the honours with the sugar and milk before leaving us with a nod and a smile.

We concentrated on our very good coffee and for a few seconds the only sound was the clink of porcelain against porcelain. For the first time I sensed that familiar Crosshaven convent parlour hush, where the furniture and walls and drapes seemed to be listening. It seemed that the chairs could be softer and the room brighter, but still a nuns' parlour was a nuns' parlour. Maria'd have loved it.

'I haven't seen Kelly in years,' Sister Therese said, breaking the silence.

'How many years?' I asked.

She looked at me. 'Hard to remember off hand – old age doesn't make for the best memory.'

I smiled and finished my coffee. 'What do you remember about Kelly when she was living at St Brendan's?'

'That was a long time ago.'

'I know, but you never know what'll prove to be helpful in a police investigation.'

'All right. Kelly first came here when she was almost six – but I'm sure you have a file on her, so you probably know that. She was a cute little thing and bright as a button. She was very easy to place with a family at first because she was so pretty. You'd hate to say it but the more attractive children are always easier to place.' Sister Therese paused to sip her coffee. Seán and I waited. 'Anyway, she wasn't here long before she went to a family. I can't remember who took her that first time but I'm sure that's in your file as well. In fact I probably wrote it up myself. I was still in charge at the time.'

'Did she stay with this family for long?' Seán asked.

Sister Therese shook her head. 'No. Nor with the next one or even the one after that. It was her mother – well, I'm not really supposed to say this, am I? But I always felt it was true. That woman turned up like a bad penny at every single foster home Kelly was ever in. And once the mother appeared that was the end of it.'

'What do you mean?'

The elderly nun's plump face sagged with the weight of unhappy memory. 'Kelly'd become impossible. Bold wasn't the word for it. She'd act like a child possessed, it's the only way to describe it: breaking things, screaming and roaring, fighting with the other children. She even killed a kitten once when she was told to do her homework.'

'So what would happen then?' Seán asked.

'Well, the family would find it impossible to keep her, so she'd come back here for a while. Then a few months later another couple would fall in love with her and take her home with them and it'd be fine for a while until she started up her usual carry-on.'

'Fall in love with her?' Seán echoed. 'That's an unusual thing to say about a child, Sister.'

'I know,' Sister Therese said, 'but I've been thinking about that time since you rang and I promise you, Detective, it's the right phrase. Kelly wasn't only beautiful: there was something else about her that was like a magnet. Even the families she destroyed with her tantrums and destruction cried bitter tears as they handed her back to us. That mother of hers has a lot to answer for.'

'Why?'

'I don't know what that woman did to Kelly but whatever it was, the minute she appeared on the scene you could guarantee that Kelly'd soon be demented. Have you spoken to her?'

'The mother?' I said.

She nodded.

'Yes.'

'And she doesn't know anything?'

'Apparently not.'

'Well, it might be no harm having a closer look at that woman. I never knew her tell the truth in the past. I doubt that she's started lately.'

'OK,' Seán said as he scribbled a reminder note. 'And you? How did you get on with Kelly, Sister?'

The nun didn't answer for a few seconds – just smiled

vacantly at Seán. 'I loved her too. It was hard not to love her.' She refilled her cup and offered us more coffee. Seán and I both refused.

'The murder we're investigating is that of a man called Billy Hendrick. He was one of Kelly's foster parents,' I said.

Sister Therese looked at me and I could see that she already knew.

'But you probably heard that on the radio or TV,' I said. 'Or indeed saw it in the papers – it's been all over them for the past few days.'

She smiled. 'Kelly stayed with the Hendricks longer than any place else. Two years, as far as I recall. For Kelly that was a record, unfortunately.'

'We spoke to a young man a couple of days ago who says that he came here looking for Kelly after she was sent away by the Hendricks,' I said.

Sister Therese looked at me enquiringly.

'He says he spoke to a nun who told him that Kelly was no longer here.'

Sister Therese nodded, still listening intently.

'He also said she spoke very angrily to him and accused him of getting Kelly pregnant.'

The nun closed her eyes. 'I don't think that was me. At least I don't remember a young man coming here – though if he did speak to me I'd probably have been angry with him. The pregnancy was most unfortunate. She was only a child – barely fifteen – and she was very upset about it.' The clever blue eyes opened.

'So she was sent away?' Seán asked.

'She asked to go. She went to our home in Cork. And was this young man who came looking for Kelly her boyfriend?'

'So he says,' I said, 'but that isn't the issue really. The thing is he says he wasn't the father of her baby.'

'What?' Sister Therese sat forward in her seat and her hand flew up to her soft cheek like a character in a melodrama. 'But he must have been.'

'He's adamant,' Seán said, 'and to be honest I believe him.'

The nun slumped a bit in her chair and looked into the empty firegrate.

'Did she ever say who the father was?' I asked.

Sister Therese shook her head. 'Not to me. Kelly was quite wild, you understand. It was easy to believe her foster parents when they said she was running around with boys. Especially as she ended up pregnant.'

'And that's what they said?' Seán asked.

'Yes. Almost word for word. And what could we say? She didn't exactly have a sterling history. This looked like an accident waiting to happen. They said that as well.'

'Who?' I said. 'Who said that? Caroline Hendrick?'

'No. Her brother-in-law.'

'Alan Hendrick?' Seán asked, shooting me a look.

She nodded. 'He actually arranged the adoption. At the time it seemed a good solution – you know, good family, plenty of money and that. Kelly didn't object. In fact when I think of her at that time I remember her as almost totally silent. A completely changed little girl.'

'And when she came back after having the baby? How was she then?' I said.

'She never came back here,' Sister Therese said. 'Kelly turned sixteen a couple of weeks after her baby was born, so she was no longer a ward of the state.'

'You never saw her again?' Seán said.

Sister Therese shook her head sadly. 'I never even heard of her until I accidentally heard her name on the news last week.'

'How did you know it was the same Kelly Moloney?' I said.

Sister Therese laughed softly. 'That too was waiting to happen. Kelly was never the most temperate of creatures. A bit like Achilles, she was always given to terrible temper outbursts, so she was bound to get into trouble with the law sooner or later.'

'And what happened to her baby?' I said.

Sister Therese looked at me with a slightly confused expression. 'Well, I presume he's still with the Hendricks.'

31. Saturday 16 April

Hi Clint,

Fuck it – things are really going mad now. I told you about trying to get Kelly to say if she was planning something yesterday and how she was cool out and all. After that we were just hanging around and Peter was a bit cross and Natalie was worried about him but he looked fine to me, not sick or anything – probably just a bellyache.

So we had pizza again for dinner and then watched a couple of old films and hardly talked at all. Eric rang but he was just checking that we were all right. I told him we were fine and that Peter wasn't too bad at all and he said he'd call over the next evening if he could.

Me and Nat talked from time to time but it was hard to talk to her because she was always doing something with Peter and you just knew she was only half listening. Anyway, she headed off to bed around ten with Pete, leaving me with Kelly. Which was a dead loss. All she ever seems to do is watch telly and smoke fags. I was so bored I wanted to scream or punch something. Instead I went to bed myself at eleven.

I flicked through some magazines in bed but I must have been wrecked from doing nothing because I fell asleep after a few minutes. At ten to four I woke up to go to the loo. When I turned on the light I saw that Kelly's bed was empty and neat like nobody'd been in it. I figured she must have fallen asleep in front of the telly. I decided to go and wake her up after-I'd been to the loo – I mean, even if she's a bitch I couldn't let her freeze on the sofa.

I don't know who was more surprised, Kelly or me, when I went in to the sitting room. There she was, sitting on the couch, and laughing and talking with this woman I'd never seen before. Kelly jumped up like I'd caught her doing something she wasn't supposed to be doing – and I had, really, I suppose. She said my name and the woman turned around to look at me. She didn't jump up, though. Just stayed where she was and looked at me as if I was the one who wasn't supposed to be there.

Gina, did we wake you up? Sorry about that. I didn't think we were making much noise. I hope we haven't woken the others, Kelly says then and it was more than she usually says in a full day.

I didn't say a word. Just stood there in my T-shirt and knickers and kept looking at the woman. She was a good bit older than us. Forty maybe. And good-looking in a kind of melted way – like she'd done something to herself to make her good looks go away but you could still see where they'd been. She was wearing a satiny black dress. It was nice and she had a great figure in it. She was sort of glamorous-looking and classy, even though the dress was up to her arse and a Wonderbra pushed up her tits to her chin. It suited her. Her hair was black as well and cut a bit like my new haircut – all bobbed around her face.

She smiled at me and crossed her long legs, which were tanned and silky-looking, and I could see she was wearing these great sandals. Black patent with really high heels and a delicate-looking ankle strap. When I had a good look I could see that all of her was pretty tanned-looking actually. Probably sunbeds.

Still, she looked good, if she didn't mind the cancer she was giving herself. But then she was smoking as well, so if the sunbeds didn't kill her she was probably relying on the fags to finish her off. While I was thinking all that, your woman was looking at me and Kelly was hopping from one foot to the other. I'd never seen her like that before and then she says: Gina, this is my mother – Agnes Moloney.

I must have looked surprised then because you know me, I'm not all that good at hiding what I'm feeling and I was definitely feeling good and fucking surprised. I hadn't even known she had a mother. Do they put you in care if you have a mother?

But I couldn't say that, could I? So I just said, Hello and nice to meet you. The woman smiled at me but her mouth was crooked and I could see that her red lipstick was leaking a bit at the corners. Which somehow was how I knew she was drunk.

Nice to meet you, Gina, she said, standing up and walking over to me to shake hands. I believe you're the genius who planned the jail-break?

Fag ash was dripping off her cigarette and you could tell that she was trying her best to look sober. Not that she was falling around or anything – just doing that super-careful drunk walk. I shook hands with her and the fag ash fell on to her foot and was on top of her sandal strap but she didn't notice – just walked back over to sit on the couch.

There was nothing to say then, so I just said goodnight and went into the kitchen to make myself a cup of tea. While the kettle was boiling I heard the voices again and then the front door closing. Just when I was making tea Kelly came in.

I asked her if she wanted some but she shook her head. Her face was white and her freckles were like tiny painted-on dots of brown. She lit a fag and said she could explain. I said nothing – just squeezed my teabag with a spoon.

Then she says her mother likes to see her and when I

didn't say anything she said it again and I said how did she know where we were and she said wasn't that obvious and I said yeah, it was. And then Kelly started laughing, asking me was I saying she was a security risk and that was funny when you consider me and Natalie wanted to bring the rug-rat to Spain.

I was pure mad with her then and I said, though I'm not sure I believe it a hundred per cent, it isn't a risk to take Peter. I thought we'd agreed on that.

But Kelly was ranting, so she wasn't even listening, and she said me and Natalie agreed – as usual. And I said she should have told us if she was getting in touch with her mother and she got all snotty then and said it was her own business what she did with her mother. And was I saying her mother'd rat us out?

I said I wasn't. But still. That I was just surprised. I mean, Clint, anyone'd be surprised if they got up at four o'clock in the morning to make a piss and found a stranger in the sitting room, wouldn't they?

So I said that to her and Kelly shrugged and threw her fag butt into the sink. It made a sizzling noise when it hit some water and she stood there looking at it for ages. So I said I didn't even know she had a family. That I thought she grew up in care, 'cos that's what she'd said to Tony.

She said she did grow up in care, but that didn't mean she didn't have a mother. She told me how her mother was only seventeen when she was born and she had a bit of bother looking after her – not abuse or nothing, just bother. Whatever that is. Then she stopped talking for ages and looked into space like she was thinking or remembering.

So eventually I said, 'Why did they put you in care, so?'

And she said, I don't know why they took me, to be honest. She wasn't doing it the way they say you're supposed to do it or something like that – so some interfering biddy told the social workers and bam! That was it – I was washing in a bathroom with twenty sinks and saying yes sister no sister three bags full sister to a load of nuns.

Jesus, I said then, because that really took the wind out of my sails. What age were you?

Kelly made a face and said, Five.

I said that was lousy and she said yeah, but fuck it, and that her mother does her best for her and I needn't worry – she wouldn't tell anybody where we were 'cos the one thing she knows for sure is her mother'd never do anything to hurt her.

I said I wouldn't tell Natalie if she wanted and she said it made no difference. Her mother just came to say goodbye. And I remembered Glenn and the stuff about America and I said, So you told her we were going to Spain? and she said yeah, she had, and what about it? And I said, Nothing – just wondering.

Then I said I was freezing and going back to bed and she said she was too and we turned out the lights and went down to bed. We didn't really talk any more after that – only to say goodnight and stuff.

I couldn't get to sleep for ages, thinking about Kelly and her mother. Maybe that's who she was talking to in the garage. What do you think? Now I half wish I'd asked her while the subject was kind of being discussed but I didn't want to say Glenn had said anything.

Maybe she was talking to her mother and maybe Glenn hadn't understood and they were talking about somebody else going to America. Or her mother was going to America. Or else Kelly wasn't telling me the whole truth and she was actually a bit afraid her mother'd blab so she was telling her we were going to America in case she let something slip.

When that idea came into my head I started to relax and fall asleep. Everybody is weak when it comes to their family – who knows that better than me? I figured there was no point in telling Nat because that'd just cause another fight, and anyway we only have a few more days to put down before we leave and hopefully nothing else will happen.

Once I'd worked all that out I started dozing off to sleep. And instead of being angry or worried about Kelly and what she was doing, I started feeling really sorry for her. A picture of that small girl with long dark hair and big eyes in front of the rows of sinks stayed in my head the whole time while I was falling asleep.

xxx

32. Saturday 16 April – Sunday 17 April

I was sitting beside Rita's bed on Saturday night when I got the phone call. I pulled my phone out of my pocket and would just have switched it off except that I saw Seán's name.

'Rob?'

'Yeah, Seán, what is it?'

'Where are you?'

'With Rita. She's a bit under the weather – a chest infection. They say she'll be OK, though.'

'I'm sorry to hear that.'

'No, no, it's grand. She'll be fine. What's up?'

'I had a call from Caroline Hendrick. She wants to know if we can go over to her house.'

'Where did she get your number?'

Seán laughed. 'I gave it to her one day when she rang to find out if we'd made any progress.'

'Bit of a mistake giving her your mobile number.'

He laughed again. 'I know, I know – I suppose it's just a habit with me. I can't resist giving women my number.'

'Does she want us to come tonight?'

'Yeah. That's what she said.'

'Why?'

'She wouldn't say on the phone. I said I'd call you and see if you were available. Don't worry about it – if Rita's not well, I'll call her back and tell her she'll have to wait.'

'Do that,' I said. 'If you don't mind. I want to stay here tonight.'

'No problem. I have the girls here for the weekend, anyway. I'd have to get a babysitter and I'm not even sure if I'd get one at this short notice. Look, I'll call you back after I've talked to her, OK?'

'Great. Thanks, Seán.'

I put my phone down on to the bedspread after Seán hung up. Bloody Caroline Hendrick. Why was it that people never seemed to know that people like me and Seán have lives of our own? We were like traffic lights or automatic level crossings – just something that existed to make people's lives safe.

Rita's breathing was rapid and there were two round pink spots on her cheeks. She looked lovely, in fact. Healthy. But I knew she wasn't. Jerry Tuohy, her doctor, had said they weren't worried but they'd put her on intravenous antibiotics just to be on the safe side. He said you couldn't be too careful about chest infections in patients like . . . like – then he'd paused – like Rita, he said, finally.

I told him she was hardy and told him she could shake off flu like no one I'd ever seen. She was amazing like that. Healthy as a trout. Jerry didn't say anything for a few seconds; then he smiled and said that was good to hear. And we agreed that she'd be fine. This bug was obviously a bit harder to shake, though, than other bugs she'd had in her life. Her real life.

I fixed her pillows around her hot head and smoothed her hair off her face. 'You'll have to be better for that specialist woman. She'll be in to see you on Tuesday,' I said, tracing the side of her face with my index finger. 'We can't have her getting a bad impression of you.'

I laughed then at the absurdity of what I'd said and kissed her hot, dry cheek just as my phone rang again.

'She's insisting on seeing somebody,' Seán said.

'For Christ's sake.'

'She says it's important and can't wait and that she can't talk about it over the phone.'

I groaned.

'Don't worry about it,' he said. 'My neighbour, Kitty, will stay with the girls and I'll go over. I'll call you when I get back to let you know what all the fucking mystery is about.'

'Are you sure, Seán? It's just that I hate leaving her when she's sick . . .'

'Look, stop it. Why does Caroline Hendrick need to see both of us? She's lucky to be getting anybody on a Saturday night. Talk to you later.'

'Bye, Seán.'

The door opened and a nurse whose name I couldn't remember came in with her trolley to get Rita ready for the night.

'Rob,' she said with her pleasant smile.

I smiled back and stood up so that she could get close to the bed. She took Rita's temperature with an electronic ear thermometer and then checked her blood pressure and all her tubes and lines. Finally she fiddled with the bedclothes, folding back the crisp white top sheet and gently placing Rita's splinted hands on the bed covers. I had begun to watch a re-run of *Only Fools and Horses* as she worked. I liked the way she handled Rita as if she was disturbing her. Liked how she chatted quietly to her all the time. The programme was funny and began to take my attention until she called my name. Elaine – that was her name. I swivelled round.

'You're officially sleeping here tonight?' she said.

I nodded. 'Pauline – the girl in the kitchen – gave me the fold-up bed and some blankets. Is that OK?'

Elaine nodded. 'That's fine. Just that she isn't very sick – you could go home if you wanted.'

'I know. But I'd be awake all night. This way at least I'll get some sleep.'

She didn't say anything for a minute – just rearranged pillboxes on her trolley and then fixed her short blonde hair as if it'd been tossed. 'I noticed that Catherine Yarborough is seeing Rita on Tuesday.'

I nodded.

'She's very good,' she said, and then she stopped as if she wasn't sure about the rest of what she wanted to say.

'So Jerry says,' I said.

She hefted her trolley and began to move towards the door. She turned to smile at me. 'She'll only be examining her, though, Rob. Assessing her because the year is nearly up.'

'I know.'

She shrugged. 'Don't get your hopes up.'

'I don't care what she says – I know what I know.' I looked at her and then we both looked at Rita.

Elaine looked away first. 'Call me if you need anything, and if you want a cuppa during the night just go into the kitchen and help yourself.'

'Thanks, Elaine,' I said to her back as she disappeared through the doorway. After she had left I was suddenly exhausted. What was it with this bloody assessment? I'd meant what I said. I didn't care what Catherine Yarborough concluded; still, somehow, it was as if I had to protect Rita from what she and all the rest of them might decide about her. Stupid really. Nothing was going to change on Tuesday just because some new doctor was coming in to poke and prod.

I turned off the TV and made up the collapsible bed. What was going on with Caroline Hendrick? I checked my phone in case I'd missed a call or a message but there was no word from Seán. The legs of the flimsy bed creaked as I lay down and my head went into overdrive. Where the hell was that cab driver? Who the fuck was he? And why hadn't he come forward?

Afraid of Jimmy Boy, probably. Bastard. I knew him of old. Scrawny little fucker. Only about five four but with that hard, tough body you get from working out in expensive gyms. He was young. Maybe twenty-two. And dealing drugs since he was thirteen or fourteen. Never been in jail, though everybody knew what he did. But his father was rolling in money, drug money as well – the family business. It annoyed the life out of me and seemed like another excellent reason to retire and run a pub.

There was nothing I could do about Jimmy Boy Lane, at least until Mary found something on him. I just had to put it out of my head. Think about other things. Emmet, for example. I turned over in the bed and it moaned dangerously but stayed standing.

Somewhere along the corridor a telephone rang and I heard a woman's muffled voice. Emmet was mad at me now for not believing him. I could see why he'd be mad but he'd just have to understand really. He wasn't a child. I needed to talk to him. Talk it out with him. Cab drivers, Jimmy Boy, Billy Hendrick, phones, machines, voices, Emmet, doctors. My head buzzed like a colony of bees but my body was exhausted so I fell asleep mid-think.

Next thing I was aware of was Elaine, back in the room and doing her morning check. Bright yellow sunlight leaked into the room around the edges of the curtains. I turned on to my back, my body aching.

'So?' I said.

She started and looked at me. 'She's fine. The same.'

'Can I go home and have a shower, do you think?'

'As I say to my husband, in the interest of the well-being of the rest of us it's the least you can do.'

Elaine took off with a wave to complete her rounds and once I'd satisfied myself that she'd been telling the truth and Rita really was the same, I left for home. The sooner I left, the sooner I'd be back, I reasoned as I drove through a blindingly sunny morning.

Early Mass goers trickled along the bright streets and I bought some Sunday papers and planned my breakfast. Maybe I'd call Emmet before I went back to Árd Aoibhinn.

I hit the shower and was halfway through a shave when the phone rang. By the time I reached it, it'd stopped. I went back to the bathroom and finished shaving and then went in search of the number that'd called. I couldn't afford to leave it – it could be something about Rita. I didn't recognize the number but pressed the call return button anyway. The phone barely rang before a woman's voice answered.

'Hello?' I said. 'Rob O'Connell here. I think you just called me.'

'Hi, Rob. This is Yvonne Daly.'

I didn't answer for a second.

'Yvonne? Seán's wife . . . ex-wife?'

'Oh Jesus, Yvonne! Sorry about that – I'm a bit wrecked. How are you? How are the girls?'

'We're fine, thanks. Listen, Rob, I'm sorry to disturb you but it's about Seán.' She paused. 'I don't suppose you know where he is?'

'He's at home, Yvonne. I was talking to him last night. He told me he had the girls.'

She gave a small, bitter laugh. 'Oh, he has the girls all right – or should I say his neighbour, Kitty, has them. She rang me a while ago, all worried about Seán. Says he went out last night and was only supposed to be gone an hour but he never came back.'

My heart thumped in my chest. 'He was working, Yvonne. He called me about a case. Somebody wanted to talk to us and I couldn't go – Rita's not well.'

'Jesus, Rob, I'm sorry – I never even asked about Rita. How is she?'

'She's fine – just a bit of a chest cold. Seán said he'd go by himself. Are you sure he's not home?'

'Positive. I just told you – his neighbour rang.'

'That's odd.'

Yvonne laughed that same laugh again. 'It's not that odd for Seán not to come home, Rob. I thought you might know where he is, that's all.'

I didn't want to hear any more about Seán. 'OK, I'll have a look for him. What about the girls?'

'That's the thing – my car is out of action. Seán was supposed to bring them home and now I can't collect them . . .'

'No problem. I'll collect them and drop them out.'

'Thanks a million, Rob.'

'Don't worry about it. See you later.'

I tried Seán's phone but there was no answer, so I grabbed a slice of toast and half a cup of tea and set off for his apartment. Since he and Yvonne had split up, he'd lived in the centre of town in an up-market apartment in a converted flourmill. Rented, of course, but Seán loved appearances. 'Women love all the beams and exposed stone and shit,' he'd told me with a grin when he moved in.

Seán's neighbour, Kitty, opened the door of the apartment almost as soon as I rang the bell. She was a plain woman in her late twenties with a straight waist, thick ankles, wiry black hair and a notion of Seán. He'd never admitted it to me but I'd always suspected that he wasn't above a roll in the hay with the devoted Kitty when there were no better prospects on the horizon. She didn't recognize me.

'Hi. Kitty, isn't it? Rob O'Connell. Seán's friend.'

Kitty stepped back from the doorway and held the door open wide. 'Oh, hi. Come in.' I followed her along a narrow corridor into a kitchen/dining room where Fiona and Carrie were lying on the floor watching TV. They'd really grown since I'd last seen them. Rita'd be amazed if she saw how tall they'd grown – *when* she saw how tall they'd grown.

'Hey girls,' I said and kissed both of them on the top of their dark, silky heads. They looked up and smiled at me and then continued to watch some beautiful black girls singing and dancing.

'Do you think he's OK?' an anxious Kitty blurted out as I moved away from the girls.

'Sure – he's fine. Look, I was speaking to Yvonne and I said I'd drop the girls out home. Thanks very much for staying with them. I'll take over from here.'

Kitty looked crestfallen, as if I'd given her bad news. 'Oh,' was all she said for a few seconds. She picked at the skin around her thumbnail and I willed her to just take her stuff and go. The sooner I got the girls out home the sooner I'd be able to get back to Rita.

'Your Mom's car is off the road. I said I'd drop you home. Are you ready to go?'

Twelve-year-old Carrie rolled on to her back. Her shoulder-length dark hair spread across the red Persian-style mat and she hooked a finger into the waistband of her jeans just above her concave belly. She looked at me with Seán's brown eyes. 'Where's Dad?'

'He was working last night,' I said.

'Yeah,' Fiona said, sitting up and pushing her fringe out

269

of her eyes. What age was Fiona now? Eight? Nine? Something like that. 'Why didn't Dad come home last night? Kitty had to sleep here in Daddy's bed.'

I looked behind me at Kitty, who had the grace to blush. Turning back, I smiled at the girls, who were standing up. 'I told you, Fi – work. Now come on, get your stuff together. Mom is waiting.'

When I looked around again, Kitty was on her way out of the front door. I called thanks after her and sat on the sofa, flicking through the TV channels, as Carrie and Fiona went into their bedroom to collect their bits and pieces. Inside me was the beginning of a worry about Seán, but I dismissed it. He was always disappearing overnight.

Still, he had been called out by Caroline Hendrick last night. As soon as I'd dropped the girls home I was going to give her a call. I continued to flick from channel to channel but the worry was starting to get legs. Sunday morning TV isn't exactly gripping and even the highlights of a premiership match from the day before didn't succeed in distracting me.

Maybe Kitty was right to be concerned. Maybe we were all putting Seán's absence down to his usual bad behaviour – but what if something had happened? Billy Hendrick had been murdered, after all.

33. Sunday 17 April

Hi Clint,

It's me. By the time I woke up this morning it was ten and Kelly was already up. I could hear voices and got the sounds and smells of frying from the kitchen. Kelly and Natalie were both there when I came in, Natalie standing in front of a pan full of sausages and Kelly sitting at the table in front of an overflowing ashtray.

Kelly just told me about her mother, Natalie says to me as soon as I came in. I filled myself a glass of water at the sink. She said you got a terrible fright in the middle of the night.

I just said yeah and drank the water. Kelly looked at me and smiled.

I wish my family gave a fuck about me, Natalie said, cracking eggs into the pan.

I'm sure they do, I said.

But I didn't mean it really. I know Natalie's family. They care a lot about what people think. Nobody ever even visited Nat when she was inside.

Anyway, there I am, half awake, and Natalie hands me a plate of food and she's all cheerful like, even though she's saying nobody cares about her. There wasn't anything I could say to that so I took the plate of food from her and said thanks and asked them if they'd eaten and they said yeah, they had. So I sat down at the kitchen table and started in on my fry. It tasted pretty good after all the takeaways we'd eaten.

I asked where Peter was and Kelly said he was asleep in the bedroom. I was surprised she answered but I said nothing – just asked how he was and Nat said his chest was really clearing up. And then the weirdest thing happened: Kelly said, Isn't that great?

I nearly choked on the bit of fried egg I was eating. I looked at her to see if she was being sarcastic. But no. She was smiling at Natalie, who was smiling back. I kept eating but my head was buzzing, trying to work out what was going on.

Then they were talking about maybe he was just a chesty baby and Natalie was saying Ryan had been a bit chesty. I said nothing. I couldn't, I was so gobsmacked.

Then Kelly says, The climate in Spain will be much better for him, so.

Well, Clint, that was it. When she said that I laughed out loud and they both looked at me and were all, What's so funny and stuff, and Kelly was like she was daring me to say something. I looked at her unreadable face and I was thinking that she was figuring I wouldn't say anything because she must know by now that I hate fighting and stuff. But of course the thing is she doesn't know I broke my arm twice on account of dares.

I suppose it's just you, I said.

Kelly shook her head, all surprised and innocent, and I started laughing and said I couldn't believe she was suddenly so concerned about Peter. And she gets all huffy – if you can believe that – and says, Thanks a lot, Gina. I'm not a complete bitch, you know. Which isn't true. She is a complete bitch.

And then as if that wasn't weird enough Natalie has to have her tuppence ha'pennyworth as well and she says, Give her a break.

Give her a break? For fuck's sake, the two of them have

done nothing but fight since we ran away from the screws. They beat the shit out of each other and Kelly said Peter should have been left to die and now Natalie wants me to give her a break?

I couldn't believe it, Clint. But I didn't say anything. Just put milk and sugar in my tea and had a think. I figured Kelly had been working on Natalie while I was asleep and I was good and sorry that I hadn't told Nat about what Glenn had overheard.

But I just couldn't pretend like none of the other stuff had happened. I had to say something, so I asked her why she had had a sudden change of heart, and when she didn't answer I asked Natalie if she thought it was strange that Kelly was suddenly mad about Peter and all concerned for him and shit.

Oh, for Christ's sake, Gina, Kelly said after ages and ages and the nerve of the bitch but she was cross and half laughing at me at the same time. I've come round. You were the one who said Peter might be a good cover for us and I was telling my mother about him and she said the same thing as you. No big mystery.

I was starting to lose my temper then and I didn't want to, so I drank my entire cup of tea in one go and filled my cup again. Natalie was washing the dishes, so I asked her again if she didn't think it was funny Kelly changing her tune. And she just kept washing up and said all this shit about people changing and how that was good. And I said I thought it was weird and then she said I should just be happy 'cos now everyone was happy Peter was coming to Spain. I didn't answer. She turned around and looked at me, and her face looked so much like a kid's face, I couldn't keep going.

My phone rang then, which was good because it sort of

broke the tension in the kitchen. It was Eric to see how Peter was doing. I gave Natalie the phone so she could tell him all the details and then I washed my plate and cup. Kelly never moved in her chair. Just sat there, smoking and drinking tea like she hadn't a care in the world. I wasn't a bit convinced, though.

I'm not a fool. I know Nat wants to believe people can change because, well, that's her own stuff, isn't it? And it isn't that I really believe they can't. I've changed in my life. Changed for the worse as it happens but still changed. But there's a smell off the stuff with Kelly and I don't know what to do about it.

Anyway, there wasn't much I could do after the Happy Families scene in the kitchen so I went for a shower and when I was dressed Natalie was in the sitting room changing Peter's nappy and singing to him. He smiled when I cooed at him and I was delighted, though Natalie says he's too young to recognize me and that it was just gas.

I switched on the telly – and before you start there's nothing else to do around here. Anyway, then I asked Nat where Kelly was gone and she said she'd gone to town to meet her mother. I couldn't believe my ears – just sat there staring at Nat as she picked up Peter's legs by the ankles and wiped his arse with a baby wipe.

I started giving out then – I mean, our pictures were in the paper and everything but Natalie thinks Kelly can do no wrong now and she's all, Calm down, her hair is different nobody'll recognize her. But I don't know. It's hard not to remember Kelly no matter what colour her hair is.

I looked at the telly for a few minutes to calm me down. The news was on and there was nothing about runaway girls or dead solicitors. Then it was the weather forecast. It was going to rain – now that was a surprise.

Then Natalie sat beside me on the sofa and gave Peter a bottle. He must have been starving because he was gulping like mad and she asked me what Kelly's mother is like. And is she good-looking like Kelly and all that.

I said yeah and good-looking and good and drunk. Then I said I didn't trust her and Natalie said she was from a well-to-do family and I said, So what? I still don't trust her.

The front door opened just at that second and Kelly came in with Eric. For a mad minute I wondered if she'd been riding him as well but then I remembered that he probably wasn't as taken away with her as Glenn, all things considered.

Anyway, Kelly is waving these printout yokes and shouting about how Eric bought us our tickets and she's using this girly, excited voice that's more like Natalie than her. And I was just about to ask to see the tickets when from behind Eric I saw a tall woman in a short black skirt and a white blouse that was opened enough to show plenty of cleavage. Her make-up was perfect and there wasn't a hair out of place.

Agnes Moloney, she says, walking over to the sofa. You must be Natalie. Lovely to meet you.

She shook hands with Nat and then looked at me.

We met last night, I said to her. I'm Gina.

Agnes Moloney smiled at me. I remember. How are you today, Gina?

I stood up. Not too bad. Would you like some tea or something?

She shook her head and smiled and underneath the smell of perfume I'd have sworn that I could smell booze but she didn't look at all drunk.

Then she's all chatting about the baby and saying she can only stay for a few minutes 'cos she has an appointment at two and stuff and you should have seen Kelly: her face was different, kind of flushed, and her eyes were all glittery and bright. I'm telling you, Clint, I hope to fuck Kelly isn't doing drugs because I can hardly stick her in her senses as it is.

Kelly is nodding and smiling like she was actually happy for once and then Agnes took a deep breath and claps her hands together like a PE teacher. OK! So! Has anybody got any sun cream? she says in her posh voice. I have very fair skin and I know I'm going to need it when I go to Spain with you.

Fuck it, Clint – you know when they say you could have knocked me down with a feather? Well, that's exactly how I felt. I couldn't believe my ears but that's exactly what happened.

Talk to you later.

xxx

34. Sunday 17 April

Just as I was really getting into worrying mode and had definitely decided to swing by Caroline Hendrick's on my way back from Árd Aoibhinn, the front door opened. Seán.

I stood up, angry with relief. 'Where the fuck have you been?'

He stood in the doorway of his living room, the very picture of a man who'd been out all night, complete with stubble and crumpled clothes.

'Rob! What are you doing here? Is everything OK? Where are the girls?'

Carrie and Fiona came running at the sound of their father's voice and he kissed and hugged and tickled them. I watched the three of them lost in being together again. I was envious and I couldn't pretend I wasn't. At least if we had had kids I wouldn't be going home to that echoing house every night. I hated myself for thinking it but I couldn't help it. Seán didn't deserve his kids. He loved them but he didn't deserve them. I hated feeling jealous, so I looked away.

'Do we have to go home now?' Carrie said, pulling back, her arms looped around his waist as she leaned back to look up into her father's face.

He shook his head. 'Do you want to go home early? I thought we were going to go swimming this afternoon?'

'I wanna go swimming, I wanna go swimming,' Fiona said, doing a mock tantrum dance, and her father and sister laughed.

'Yvonne asked me to drop the girls out,' I said.

Seán grimaced. 'I'll call Mom. Don't worry, she won't mind.'

'Where were you, Daddy?' Fiona said, staring intently into his face.

'Working, baby,' he said, stroking her head. 'Did Kitty stay?'

'She had to sleep in your bed,' Carrie said.

Seán looked at me and crossed his eyes and I looked away to hide the grin on my face.

'You guys go play on the computer in my bedroom for a while, OK? I need to talk to Rob about work for a few minutes.'

'But Mom –' Carrie began, her face serious again.

Seán shhshhed her. 'I'll call her. Don't worry about it. There are a couple of new PC games down there – now go.'

Fiona and Carrie ran off. I sat back on the sofa, watching as Seán lit a cigarette and then filled the coffee maker. 'Want some?'

I nodded. 'I didn't have much breakfast.'

He grinned and rubbed his stubbly chin as he leaned back against the worktop. 'Sorry.'

'Where were you? Even I was starting to get worried.'

'I'm sorry. But look, you know there's never any reason to worry about me. I can look after myself.'

'Answer my question.'

The coffee maker bubbled and steamed and Seán took two mugs out of an overhead cupboard. 'I met somebody.'

'You bastard.'

'No, no listen, really. I went to see Caroline Hendrick – Jesus, I'll tell you all about that in a minute. Anyway, by the time I was finished with her it was eleven and I knew the girls'd be asleep, so I went into Devanney's for one drink. I couldn't face coming back here and having to talk to Kitty.'

I grinned.

Seán rolled his eyes. 'Anyway, I met a woman in Devanney's.'

'Surprise, surprise.'

'I know I deserve that but this was different.'

'With you it's always different,' I said, with a long exaggerated sigh. 'I don't know if you're the biggest cynic or the biggest romantic on the planet.'

Seán made a face. 'We went back to her place and talked for hours. She's something else.'

'Talked?'

'Well, OK, we didn't only talk and the sex was something else as well, but that wasn't what it was about, I swear.'

'So you stayed the night?'

Seán poured two mugs of coffee and handed one to me. 'That was unintentional. I fell asleep.'

'Good job Kitty was here.'

Seán put milk and sugar in his coffee and drank half the mug in one long gulp. He groaned with pleasure. 'I'm sorry Yvonne rang you.'

I shook my head. 'I don't mind. It was nice to see the girls. I haven't seen them in ages. What's happening with you two now, anyway?'

'The usual – bitter arguments all the time. I don't think I can stop her taking the girls to Germany, Rob.'

A darkness momentarily flitted across his face as he disappeared inside himself. Then he looked at me and grinned. 'I'll still see them all the time – sure Ryanair are flying into Frankfurt from Shannon.'

'That's true,' I said.

'And I have a plan,' he took a slug of coffee. 'If she goes

to Germany I'm going to see can I get sent to Quantico on one of those courses.'

'You're joking.'

'No – deadly serious. I'm bored with the work, Rob, and it might be good. Who knows what the FBI can teach me?'

I laughed.

He raised his eyebrows. 'Not to mention that I might get to meet some of those hot FBI agents. I bet they could definitely teach me a thing or two.'

'I should have guessed,' I said. 'You've finally slept with every woman on this island so now you have to go the whole way to Virginia to find a woman who doesn't know about you.'

Seán lit a cigarette and shrugged.

'Anyway, Romeo, forget Quantico. Tell me about Caroline Hendrick.'

Seán laughed. 'Jesus, that was weird! It was a pity you couldn't come. How's Rita, by the way?'

'The same. Go on.'

'OK. When I got there it was after nine and they were waiting for me.'

'They?'

Seán nodded and finished off his coffee. 'Caroline and Alan Hendrick. They were sitting in her big posh room like a couple in *Hello* magazine.'

'But what did they want on a Saturday night?'

'To tell me that they were an item.'

I laughed and walked up to stand beside Seán in the kitchen area of his living room. 'But we know that already.'

He nodded. 'Yes, but now it's official. As far as I can figure, Alan's wife found out about them and they've decided they can't continue the charade any longer – Alan's words not mine.'

'Jesus,' I said.

Seán smiled. 'They said they were going to wait a while but the wife finding out sort of precipitated events. Caroline said she was glad and Alan seemed a bit less enthusiastic but still basically singing from the same hymn sheet.'

'But why did they want to tell us?'

Seán refilled the coffee machine. 'My guess is Alan wanted to tell us. They told me all about their relationship – nothing we didn't know. But now they've decided to come out of the closet, as it were, and Alan knows full well that makes them look very suspicious in terms of Billy's murder.'

'Maybe it's just a double blind. Maybe they really did kill him and think that by being upfront about their affair we'll eliminate them as suspects.'

'That's what I thought.'

'But you didn't say that, I hope.'

'I may be stupid but I'm not that bad.' He picked up the container of percolated coffee and raised his eyebrows enquiringly at me. I shook my head, so he refilled his own mug. 'So? What do you make of them eggs, Holmes?'

I shook my head again. 'No idea. You?'

'I'm not sure. My gut tells me they probably didn't kill him, for all that the situation is a bit bizarre. But then again it also tells me those runaway girls didn't kill him either – which leaves us with fuck all in the way of suspects.'

'I know. Anyway, look – I'm heading back to Árd Aoibhinn. What time are the girls going home?'

'Sixish. Why?'

'Do you want to meet for dinner?'

Seán looked down into his coffee. 'Can't. Sorry. I'm meeting Laura.'

'Who?'

'The woman I met last night.'

I laughed. 'Jesus, Seánie, it must be love. It's not like you to see someone two nights in a row.'

He didn't answer.

I thumped him in the arm. 'I'm off. Look, I'll see you in the morning.'

'Thanks for picking up the slack, Rob.'

I shrugged. 'No problem. What goes round comes round. See you later.'

By the time I had emerged from Seán's building the sun had warmed up the morning to a summertime level. It was almost lunchtime and as I was nearly passing, I decided to call by Maria's. See how she was doing. See Emmet. The front door of her red-brick terraced townhouse opened before I was halfway up the short garden path. Emmet stood framed in the doorway, bright sunlight shining from behind him. His face was mobile with emotion as I approached.

'Emmet,' I said, looking at my watch. 'You're up and it's only eleven thirty – I'm impressed. You did go to bed, I presume? I mean, you're not on your way in from someplace.'

Emmet gave a grudging smile. 'I'm studying. I have exams soon, you know.'

I walked past him in the doorway and into the tiled hallway. 'Now I'm even more impressed. Is Maria around?'

He shook his head. 'She's gone to see Nana and Granddad.'

'Oh right, I think she told me. Any chance of a cup of tea?'

Emmet nodded and I followed him into the sunlit kitchen. School books and pens and empty mugs littered the table. He pushed a geography book over an ashtray before filling the kettle. I watched him and wondered what it was like to be him. Sixteen and struggling with the world. I couldn't even remember that far back myself.

All the time the kettle was boiling, he kept his back to me, busying himself with spoons and teabags and milk and sugar. I sat down at the table. As soon as the kettle boiled he handed me a steaming mug.

'Thanks.'

He nodded and stood, leaning against the draining board, both hands behind him like levers.

'I really called to see you, anyway,' I said, pausing to take a mouthful of tea.

He didn't answer.

'I'm on my way to see Rita.' I had another mouthful. He continued to look at me, so I kept going. 'Do you want to come over with me for a while? I'll drop you home in an hour or so, if you like.'

His face paled and his body was as stiff as a six-foot-two pole. I wanted to say stuff, like 'You haven't even seen her, Emmet, and she loves you and it's still just Rita in that bed. Not a monster or anything.' But I drank tea instead as he struggled with whatever was going on inside him.

'OK,' he said then with effort.

I finished off my tea and it made me feel mildly nauseated. 'Great. Let's go, if you're ready.'

Emmet's eyes widened but he nodded and I stood up. I led the way out of the house to the car and we drove to Árd Aoibhinn in silence. On the way he fidgeted with a string hanging from the hood of his navy sweatshirt and I turned on the radio. I kept thinking there was probably some way to make this easier on him but I didn't have a clue what that might be. Rita would have known what to do but that wasn't worth shit to me under the circumstances.

The nursing home was wide awake when we arrived.

Visitors and nurses – walking, talking and laughing in the corridors. Two little girls with blonde pigtails chased past us. Radio and TV noises poured out of rooms and the window facing us at the end of the corridor was like a gold panel filled with sunshine. Emmet and I still didn't speak as we made our way purposefully to Rita's room.

When I opened the door the silence from inside it flooded towards me as usual. I walked over immediately and switched on the TV and an American woman's voice filled the room. When I turned around from the TV I saw that Emmet was still standing in the doorway.

'Come in, come in,' I half shouted, like a demented party host.

He stepped into the room and the door swung closed behind him. He stood with his back almost touching it. I pulled out a chair and plonked it close to the bed.

'There you go,' I said to him, motioning towards the chair. I sat on the bed beside Rita and touched her face. Still pretty hot. 'Emmet's here to see you love. Say hi, Emmet.'

I looked at him. He was sitting completely upright in the chair I'd pulled over. He made a mumbling noise and nodded in salute.

I picked up Rita's hand and touched each fingertip. 'I saw Carrie and Fiona this morning. Jesus, you won't believe it when you see how tall they are. Carrie is the image of Seán and Fiona just the dead dab of Yvonne. But you know that about them. You're the one who was always saying it – wasn't she, Emmet?'

I paused and looked at him and he nodded.

'You'll never believe what I caught this young fella doing this morning, Rita. Studying. I'll bet you can't believe that, can you? All the times you sat him down and tried to talk to him about studying, hah. Remember the Junior Cert?

Remember how you stayed up until four o'clock doing maths with this boyo? Do you remember that, Emmet?'

His head nodded slowly up and down but he never looked at me. He was looking intently at Rita, his eyes still wide and now shiny as well.

'You always said Emmet'd be as good at maths as you if he applied himself, didn't you, Rita?'

Emmet continued to stare at her and two huge tears rolled, unnoticed, down his cheeks. I looked away and opened the right-hand splint and her hand began to immediately turn in on itself. I started to massage some oil into her skin.

'Seán was on the missing list last night as well – typical bloody Seán. He's grand, though. Met a woman, you won't be surprised to hear.'

I finished the right hand and stood up to move around the bed to begin on her left hand, sneaking a look at Emmet as I passed. The tears had stopped but he still looked very shaken and pale. The manic words inside me dried up and I massaged her second hand in silence, listening to the soundtrack of an episode of *Hart to Hart*.

When I had finished and replaced her splints and laid her hands back on the bed covers I looked properly at Emmet for the first time. His face had changed and he was now concentrating on Rita's face. I watched his profile and tried not to feel the deluge inside me. More for myself than him, I offered to take him home.

He looked up at me and shrugged. 'OK.'

I kissed Rita goodbye and switched on the wedding video, avoiding Emmet's eyes as he recognized it, and we left her room.

We were driving out of Árd Aoibhinn car park before he asked the first question.

'Do you think she knew I was there?'

I didn't look at him, just concentrated on the traffic at the busy roundabout straight across the road. 'Sure she did.'

I drove on to the roundabout, complaining about the shopping centre and Sunday shopping and why couldn't people stay home from the shops even one day a week? Emmet didn't answer. More silence. I switched on the radio and the car filled with *Whiskey in the Jar*.

'Will she get better?' he said.

'Of course,' I said, immediately.

'Definitely?'

'They're not sure. See, it's nearly a year now and that's considered permanent, but I think she's still in there no matter what they say.'

I looked sideways at him and he seemed to be considering my words. Then he turned his head to look at me.

'So do I,' he said.

My hands tightened on the steering wheel and tears sprung into my eyes and I wanted to laugh and cry and scream and say, 'Fuck you and your experts – even Emmet can see that she's still here.' But I didn't say a word – just drove the rest of the way to his house. He thanked me and got out of the car when I pulled up outside. Just as he was about to turn away he leaned back into the car.

'Can I go with you to see her again?'

I smiled. 'Any time.'

Emmet waved and walked into his house. I drove away, trying to work out the mish-mash in my head. Emmet and Rita and work and Seán. I bought myself a sandwich in a garage and drove back to the nursing home. I ate my lunch in the car and then settled down to have a bit of a snooze before going back in to Rita.

Just as I drifted off my phone rang, but I let it ring out. I was just too fucked to talk to anyone.

35. Sunday 17 April

Clint –

If things were bad with us before Agnes said she was coming to Spain they've gone fucking straight downhill since then. The thing about it as well is that me and Nat used to be on the same side before that but since Agnes came on the scene it's sort of like Natalie and Kelly have ganged up against me.

I don't like Agnes. I mean, I don't say anything but I can't hide it. I don't trust her and Natalie's still fooling herself that Kelly and Agnes are on her side and I just have a shit feeling about the whole thing.

All day Agnes comes in and out of the apartment like she owns it. Keeps arriving with suitcases and clothes for herself and even for us. I just say, Thanks but no thanks, I'll get clothes in Spain.

I don't want nothin' from that woman. Though I can see she's right about one thing: I do need a suitcase, so I won't look suspicious. But I'll get Glenn to get me something.

When I said that to them, I caught Kelly making a face behind my back at Nat and I was hurt, but I didn't say anything. Fuck them. The sooner we get to Spain, the sooner I can get away from the whole fucking lot of them.

Glenn brought the passports. I look shit in mine but I don't care – at least we have them now. He was so nervous around Kelly that it was nearly funny. Staying a million miles away from her like she was going to jump him. He'd be so lucky.

I asked him about Mam – you know, just how is she and stuff – and I think he might have told her where we are and what we're doing.

Fuck it, I'll kill him if I find out that he did, the little bollocks. He swore a hole through a pot that he didn't but I have a feeling he's lying. You know him – he's an awful Mammy's boy.

I suppose it doesn't really matter, though, if he did tell her, does it? She's Mam. All she wants is the best for me, isn't it? She'll hardly go to the Guards or anything.

I was in bed this morning and I was thinking about everything and do you know what I'm the most sick of? More than hiding or fighting or putting up with shit from those bitches.

Waiting. I'm sick to fucking death of waiting.

All I ever seem to do since I got out of jail is wait. I swear to God, when I get to Spain I'm never even standing in a queue.

Talk to you later.

Gina xxx

36. Sunday 17 April

The ringing of my phone woke me up. That and the cramp in my legs from sleeping in the car.

'Rob? Mary Hayes here.'

'Hi Mary – what's up? Any sign of the mystery cab driver?'

'No, but it mightn't matter much now. Just had a phone call from Tom Gavin. Jimmy Boy Lane has been arrested for murder.'

As soon as Mary Hayes had hung up I rang Seán and told him about Jimmy Boy Lane. He didn't say anything for a while. I could hear tinny swimming pool noise and children screaming with excitement.

Eventually he gave a long sigh and said, 'Fuck.' And then we were silent again for ages.

Seán coughed. 'Which O'Riordan did he shoot?' he said.

'John.'

'Drugs?'

'Something about money John O'Riordan owed him but yeah, drug-related all right – you know yourself.'

'Fuck,' Seán said again. 'They might hold over the hit-and-run. See what happens with this. They haven't found the cab driver yet, have they?'

'No, but you know as well as I do that they'll stop looking now. Mary's dance card will fill up with live cases and unless he comes in and introduces himself they'll probably never find him.'

Seán didn't reply.

'Anyway, look, I have to get back to Rita. I'll talk to you later.'

'OK. How is she, by the way?'

'Not too bad. See you, Seán.'

I hung up and drove straight back to Árd Aoibhinn. Rita looked exactly as she had when Emmet and I had left, and it made me feel angry. I'd have given anything to see her curled in the sheet or wide-eyed and laughing. Anything but this fucking alabaster-statue look. I was sick of it.

And now that bastard was going to get away with it. Mary had said the evidence against Jimmy Boy for the murder was sound and they were pretty confident he wouldn't be able to wriggle or intimidate his way out of a conviction. She'd said it as if she was offering me a consolation prize of some sort. But it was no consolation.

I sat by the bed, listening to the sound of *All Creatures Great and Small* as they reran it for the millionth time on TV, and I was so filled with anger I could have lifted a truck. Sure I was glad that bastard was going to be locked up – it'd be a definite benefit to society to have that scumbag off the streets. But it still felt as if he was getting away with what he did to Rita.

I wanted him to feel some kind of pain for what he'd done. He'd run her down and then driven off, for fuck's sake. Left her in the middle of that quiet road where there were buds on the trees and daffodils in the neat gardens with her head split open and only an arthritic old woman to try to save her. He didn't care if she lived or died.

Neither did the cab driver, for that matter. Or that Fidelma O'Hagan woman he'd been driving around. They'd fucked off as well. What was their excuse? They needed to catch a plane. Maybe if they'd gone back and tried to help she'd be home by now and I wouldn't have to listen to the shit I had to listen to from doctors.

That bloody woman was in such a hurry to get to Africa to help theoretical people she couldn't be bothered helping an actual person. And I was as sure as anything that the fucker driving the cab had recognized Jimmy Boy and was afraid, and that was why he'd scarpered. Fucking coward.

I stood up and walked around the room. Touching the end of the bed and the windowsill. Running my finger across the glossy wall. My skin itched with frustration and I wanted to scream or thump somebody. I knew it wasn't my case. I knew exactly what I'd say to someone in my position. And more than anything I knew it was probably over. There was never going to be any justice for Rita.

I took out my phone and recalled Mary's number.

'Hi, Mary? Rob O'Connell here. Sorry to bother you on a Sunday evening.'

'No problem at all. What can I do for you?'

'I was just wondering about a few of the details with Jimmy Boy – if you don't mind me asking.'

'Go right ahead.'

'Well, before the latest development what was the progress with the search for the cab driver?'

'Nothing definite, but we had narrowed it down to two guys, both of whom used to be cab drivers and have changed to truck driving and who both happen also to have been away on long-haul jobs for the past few weeks. Hang on a minute, Rob, and let me get my notebook. I have names somewhere.'

I found a pen in my jacket pocket but couldn't find any paper. In desperation I tore the bottom off a blank page at the back of Rita's chart hanging on the end of the bed.

'Rob?'

'Yeah, I'm here.'

'OK, they both live in the county. Kenny Gleeson lives in Foynes and . . . OK, here it is, James Foley – he lives in Clarina.'

'And they're both taxi drivers turned hauliers?'

'Seemingly. Mark hasn't talked to them yet, though I think they're just about back home. He can have a word with them during the week – it won't do any harm. Is that all you wanted to know?'

'Yeah. Just curious, that's all. Oh yes, one thing: you know the woman in the cab?'

'Fidelma O'Hagan?'

'Yeah, that's her name – I'd forgotten it. Has she gone back to Africa or did I misunderstand what you said about her?'

'No, no. She was in Africa but she's back home now for good. She lives near you, actually. 11 Meadow Gardens – here it is, looking at me in my notebook.'

'Great. Look, Mary, thanks for everything.'

'OK. Look after yourself, Rob.'

I punched the hang-up button on my phone and stood motionless for a few seconds. Inside me the agitation and frustration whirled wildly. Rita was asleep. She wasn't better but she wasn't any worse and they were sure she was going to be OK, so I was really wasting my time in Árd Aoibhinn. I wasn't clear what else I should be doing, but I knew I wasn't able for sitting by the bed at that minute. Deciding that I was going, I walked over to the bed.

'I'm off, sweetheart. Meeting Seán for dinner. See you tomorrow.'

Her rapid breath brushed my face and I kissed her once more and left.

*

As I drove through the quiet Sunday evening town, squinting into the sunset, my mind began to calm down. I'd drive by Fidelma O'Hagan's house. Just pass it, that was all. I wanted to see where the heartless bitch lived.

A light mist began to fall as I turned at the traffic lights that led to Meadow Gardens. It was almost dark and there was nobody around the estate, which comprised row after row of white bungalows. If I ran over somebody here, chances were that there probably wouldn't even be a distressed old lady to run out and help.

I pulled up outside number eleven. The curtains in the front room were still open and I could see the blue TV flicker lighting up the room. I wasn't sure why I was there and I wasn't really willing to think about it.

Before I could talk myself out of it, I was ringing the doorbell. A tiny woman with short, wispy black hair and slanted dark eyes opened the door. She was barefoot and wearing black tracksuit bottoms and a red short-sleeved T-shirt. She still had the remains of her African tan on her arms and chest, though her face had reverted to its Irish white.

'Yes?'

'Detective Inspector Rob O'Connell. I wonder if I could have a word?'

She stepped back into the hallway, gesturing towards the front room with her hand. I walked where she'd instructed and she followed, switching on the light and closing the curtains as soon as we stepped inside. She picked up a remote control and turned off the TV.

'Please, Detective, have a seat.'

I sat on a red velvet sofa and she sat opposite me on a matching armchair. Beside her on the floor was a huge ebony giraffe.

'He's great,' I said, pointing.

She reached out and rubbed the wooden animal's head with her tiny fingers. 'Isn't he just? He was a present when I was leaving Africa. Anyway, how can I help?'

I looked at her open, earnest face. She smiled at me and I wondered what age she was. Thirty? Thirty-five? Somewhere around that mark. She seemed to live alone but maybe she had a partner and children and they had all gone to the movies or something. I looked around the sitting room and figured that whatever about a man there definitely weren't children living in this house. A fuzzy plan was beginning to form in my head.

'I'd like you to come and take a look at someone,' I said. She nodded. 'OK. Who?'

'I'd prefer not to say.' My head whirled with the effort of plausibility. 'I don't want to prejudice you.'

'Ohhh,' she said, and she nodded and bit her bottom lip. 'I've already looked at some people for Detective Hayes – you know that, don't you?'

I nodded. 'I know.'

'But then she said they didn't think the boy I'd picked out was involved.' Fidelma O'Hagan stopped speaking and her face creased with passing annoyance. She took a breath. 'She said they'd received new information. Is that why you want me to come now?'

'Just to have a quick look at some photographs. I know it's Sunday – but if you wouldn't mind?'

'No problem – I'm happy to help. I'll just get changed, if that's all right.'

'Take your time.' I looked at my watch. 'I don't need you this minute – I think in about an hour or so, but maybe a little longer, if that would be all right with you? I don't want to put you out.'

294

She shook her head vehemently. 'No. Look, anything I can do. I'm just happy that I can be of assistance.'

I stood up, swallowing the 'Too little too late' that was fizzing on my tongue like sherbet. We walked in silence into her hallway. As I drove away I could see that she was standing at the door, hugging herself against the evening chill and watching my car drive away.

I drove through suburban streets struggling to control the impulses that were straining my skin. I needed to calm down if the vague plan growing inside me was to become clear.

I pulled into a brightly lit Shell garage, stopping away from the pumps in the shade of a high stone wall. Then I went into the shop and bought myself a tall paper cup of coffee with a lid. That might focus me. I turned my car heater up high because I was freezing and then fished the crumpled piece of paper from my jacket pocket.

Kenny Gleeson – Foynes
James Foley – Clarina

I punched up the numbers list in my phone until I found the one I wanted and then sat sipping the scalding coffee as the phone rang in my ear.

'Hello?' a woman's voice said.

'Hi Terry? Rob O'Connell here.'

'Hey Rob! Long time no see. How're you doing?'

'Not bad and yourself? How's retirement treating you?'

'A bit boring but I'm getting used to it. I've taken up golf and I'm enjoying that.'

I laughed. 'I can't imagine you with a golf club, Ter.'

'We all get old. I can't be expected to be running after criminals all my life.'

A picture of Terry's girlish shape, hands on hips with a look in those pale blue eyes that'd freeze your insides, jumped into my head. She was the Sergeant in the small County Limerick station where Seán and I had started out together after we left Templemore all those years ago. I figured Terry Hanly might be the only person Seán was ever truly afraid of.

'You never had to do all that much running anyway,' I said. 'One roar was enough.'

'How's that reprobate friend of yours, by the way?'

'Oh, you know yourself – Seán is Seán.'

Terry laughed. 'Anyway, Rob, what can I do for you?'

'Do you still live out Clarina way?'

'I do indeed.'

'You don't happen to know how I'd find a man called James Foley? He lives in Clarina – used to drive a cab and now he's a haulier.'

'There's more than one James Foley around here.' She paused for a few seconds. 'Now you won't believe this but I think I happen to know the very man you're looking for – his mother plays golf with me. I know that Mary's Jimmy drives trucks and I'm nearly positive he used to drive a cab. I don't have a number for him or anything. He's not in trouble, I hope?'

'No, no – just want to ask him a few questions about something he might have accidentally witnessed.'

Terry didn't say anything for a few seconds. 'Do you mind me asking why you'd need to talk to him on a Sunday night?'

I swallowed hard. Terry was no fool, so I knew I had to play this one carefully. 'No, no, I'm not going to talk to him tonight – just trying to get a head start for the morning. Stuff is piling up – you know how it is. Thought if I could

296

find him tonight I could send someone out to have a word tomorrow.'

'Oh.'

'Yeah, Seán and I are working on the Hendrick murder and we're going nowhere fast. Trying to turn up something and you know yourself the longer it takes, the colder the trail.'

'I do indeed.' Terry's voice had reverted to normal and my chest softened with relief. 'I read about that murder. He was shot, wasn't he?'

'Yeah.'

'And no idea who did it?'

'Not really. It's a bollocks of a case – all dead ends.'

Terry laughed. 'Ah well, rather you than me. I'll be thinking about you tomorrow, up to your eyes while I'm strolling around the golf course.'

I made myself laugh along with her. 'It's well for some.'

'That young fella isn't married long. He lives in a small cottage – cute little place, all stone. It's immediately on your right after the roundabout.'

'Terry, you're a star.'

'Don't mention it. If you're ever in Clarina, you know where I am.'

'I'll get Seán and a bottle of wine and a big cheesecake and we'll come knocking on your door some day soon, I promise.'

I dumped the remnants of my coffee out of the window as soon as Terry had hung up and drove immediately towards Clarina. James Foley might not be the man I wanted but it was a start. Anyway, I could just continue on out to Foynes if the Clarina lead was a dead end – it was in the same direction.

I felt good for the first time in ages. My head was as clear as it'd ever been. I was no longer being confused by what ifs and whys. I knew what I had to do and that made me feel light and sort of free.

37. Sunday 17 April

Hi Clint,

Still here. Still putting up with shit. I'm really fed up of the whole lot of them and I must be looking it 'cos Eric called in a while ago and he kept asking me if I was OK. I said I was fine but he kept looking at me and asking and asking.

Then, out of the blue, he asked me if I wanted to go and visit Tony's grave. When he said it first it was like a belt in the face and my heart felt like it was shrinking inside my chest, but then when that passed I knew it was a good idea. I asked him if he thought anybody'd see us up there but he pointed out that I look completely different with the haircut and the dark hair so even if anyone I knew was there they'd never recognize me.

So I agreed, 'cos once he'd brought it up like that it made me really think about it. I hadn't thought about Tony's grave at all to be honest and then I realized it was probably going to be my only chance, 'cos of going to Spain and all, and I said that to Eric. He didn't answer – just gave me this real sad smile like he knew all along.

Then of course I wanted to go that minute once I decided. You know me, Clint, no patience, but Eric said, no, we'd go in the morning and I said OK.

The two of us were by ourselves in the kitchen, drinking a cup of tea, and Natalie and Kelly were off somewhere being each other's new best friend. And I don't care. They can fuck off, the two of them.

Then Eric said, out of the blue, I met Tony just a week after your brother Clint died, you know.

He was staring into thin air and there was a smile on his face. He looked at me and said, He was very cut up about Clint.

So I said I knew that and he said that Tony loved him – and me and Glenn as well. Loved us like we were his own kids and I said I know again but as I listened to him my heart hurt like a cut.

We didn't talk for a good few minutes and then he said, Can I ask you a question?

I looked at him and nodded.

Was it you that found Clint? he said then.

I just nodded. Remembering. Suddenly seeing it all like it'd just happened. You lying on the floor of the sitting room like you were asleep and me pushing you with my bare toe telling you to get up and stepping over you to switch off the telly that was on loud. Then back again. Poking you with my foot again.

And then – all of a shot – a feeling like ice water pouring over me. And I bent down and pushed you with my hand. You rolled on to your back and your face was calm and not twisted or anything, but I knew you were dead. Knew it as well as if there was a sign on your forehead telling me.

Could you see me then, Clint? Like those TV programmes where people say they died and were floating above everything, watching? Did you see me rubbing your cheek with my fingers and touching your mouth? You couldn't know what was going on inside me, though, could you?

It was the strangest thing. Instead of being freaked out or afraid or angry or any of the things I've been since then, all I was thinking about at that moment when I realized you were dead was that I loved you. I mean, I always knew I loved you – I just didn't go around thinking it much. But right then I knew it in a new way like it was solid inside me – made of concrete or something instead of just a feeling.

I knelt there on the floor beside you and thought of our Dad and him naming me and you after Clint Eastwood and Gina Lollobrigida and Glenn after Glenn Campbell. Stupid useless mad thing to think when your brother is dead, I know that, but it is what I thought.

Glenn came in the room then and he could see straight away what was wrong and he went and got Mam and they got the ambulance and the Guards and it was all too late: you were well dead. Drug overdose. Accidental? They said it like it was a question. Mam was upset when they said that.

Hardly on fucking purpose, I said to the policewoman who asked, and she gave me a mock smile and looked away.

Your brother had a drug habit? she asked in a Dublin accent.

Mam looked at me and grabbed my arm and I wished I could say no but then they'd definitely think you'd topped yourself and that wouldn't be any better for her, would it?

So I said, I didn't think it was really a problem.

They both looked at me like I was mad. Well, you know, he did do a lot of drugs, I said then. But that was just kind of Clint – he was always looking for a rush of some kind.

Mam and the Ban Garda didn't get it the way I was explaining it and I could see that when you said it out like that it didn't seem as harmless as I'd kind of thought it was. Mam started crying and I put my arm around her and asked if we could be finished for now. The Ban Garda nodded and said no problem – she needed to be off anyway. Me and Mam didn't talk about it.

I fried a few rashers after everybody had left and Mam pretended to eat them and then straight after that she said she was tired and that she'd go up to bed. That was the first time I heard the Hail Marys through the walls and the floors.

Glenn came in after that and I fed him as well and asked him if he thought you were doing a lot of drugs and he said no. Or at least no more than usual. He thought the same as me – that was just you. Glenn went back out then. Said he was meeting somebody, but I knew well he was off to get drunk and I didn't blame him one bit. So I was by myself again with only the soft sound of Mam's prayers.

I rang up Ray Walters. I didn't even know what time of the day or night it was and I don't know what I'd have done if his mother had answered the phone. But she didn't. When I heard his voice on the phone it reminded me so much of you that I could hardly say hello. Ray really does have a nice voice. Soft for a man. Kind of like a pigeon cooing or something. I know you were always slagging him about it but I really like his voice.

I was going to ask Ray about the drugs. That was my plan. But instead I said, Do you think he topped himself? Ray didn't answer for ages and then he said, Yeah. I started to cry and we stayed there on the phone without either of us talking for a long time. I had about a million questions inside my head but they were all knotted together, so I tried to find just one to ask.

Why?

I don't know, was Ray's answer.

So I told him what had happened and what the Guards had said and how they'd asked us if you were depressed. He didn't say a word, so I asked him the question, Was Clint depressed?

Ray made a sighing noise and said, I don't know. What's depressed, Gina?

So I got mad and said, For fuck's sake, Ray, you were his

best friend. I never saw him moping around and crying and shit but maybe you did.

And he said, No.

And I said, So maybe he didn't kill himself. Maybe it was just a few too many drugs and it was an accident. Jimi Hendrix.

Maybe, Ray said, but I could hear in his voice that he didn't mean it and was only saying it to keep me happy.

I was mad at him then, like it was his fault, and maybe in a way it was – he could have told me if you were depressed, couldn't he? You could have told me.

He didn't say anything for ages and I was getting more and more mad at him.

He stopped painting about a month ago, he said eventually.

And I said I never noticed and Ray said he'd tried to ask you about it but it was no good. You wouldn't say anything except it was a waste of time. And then Ray's voice went all weird and wobbly when I asked him if you meant painting and he said, Yeah and everything else.

So of course I'm all, Why? And he said he didn't know, but he remembered another time when the two of you were on the beach in Kilkee and you said you wished you cared. He said when he asked you what that meant you said it meant nothing – you were just messing. But there was something about the way you said it that made him remember it.

And I thought that he was right, there must have been something, but he was so upset then I just said, Don't worry, don't worry, and tried to get off the phone. Because even though I'd called him now I couldn't bear to listen to how sad he was.

After I'd finished talking to Ray I went straight upstairs

to your room and it struck me for the first time that it was tidy. I mean, everybody knows that your room was never tidy. You were a fucking legend of messiness. Mam was always giving out about you. But that night I saw that it was spotless – even your brushes and paints and stuff were tidy. Your bed was made. No clothes on the floor.

I started searching your room then, thinking maybe I'd find something that'd explain it all to us. I knew that Ray was searching in his head for answers just like I was searching in your room. It was dumb really. Like an answer would make the pain of it less.

But there were no clues in your room except for the tidiness. That was weird, all right – and when I thought about it I decided it was probably the way you'd like to leave some place when you were finished with it. I lay down in your bed then and wrapped myself in the quilt and smelled a faint smell of you, and every part of me ached. It made me think about all the stuff you read about twins suffering each other's pain and knowing things about each other. Pity it's a crock of shit. If it was true I'd have known, wouldn't I?

Gina xxx

38. Sunday 17 April

James Foley's house was easy to find. Terry was right: it was a cute stone cottage. I parked on the road outside and walked directly up the narrow path, past a red Fiesta parked on gravel. I knocked and a young man with cropped black hair and the beginnings of a goatee opened the front door. He was young-looking – younger than I'd expected, boyish – though I knew he was probably in his late twenties.

'James Foley?'

He nodded.

'Detective Inspector O'Connell. I wonder if I could have a word?'

His eyebrows knitted together in a sudden frown. 'About what?'

'Could I come in?'

He stared at me for a second and then nodded before leading the way into a small sitting room. The TV was on and there was a fire burning in the grate. It was all very cosy.

'Sorry to disturb you,' I said.

He shook his head and shrugged. 'What's this about?'

'Almost a year ago – the seventeenth of May to be exact – there was a hit-and-run accident in which a woman was seriously injured. We have reason to believe that you may have witnessed this accident.'

James Foley took a sharp, shuddering breath in through his nose and I knew immediately I'd hit the mother lode. His face went through a range of expressions and I knew he was trying to decide whether or not to tell me the truth.

'We've already spoken to Fidelma O'Hagan, your fare that day.'

He looked away from me at the fire and when he looked back his face was a bit different. It was hard to tell, but if I'd been forced to say what I thought I'd have guessed that he looked relieved.

'I was afraid to say anything,' he said. 'My aunt had one of the Lanes drive into her in William Street – smashed her driver's door. It was his fault completely. Said he'd fix her up. Gave her his number. Like a fool she rang him and he asked for her address and then all this stuff started happening.'

'Stuff?'

'Yeah. Her front window was broken. Her dog went missing. Her tyres were punctured. All the time when she'd ring your man of the Lanes he'd be lovely to her. Tell her he'd fix her up soon. Just waiting for a few bob from a job. But then more stuff'd happen.'

'Did she report it?'

James Foley nodded. 'No good. The Guards said there wasn't a thing they could do about it. No evidence linking what was happening to the Lanes. The Guard she talked to said he knew well she was right but there wasn't a snowball's chance in hell of catching them.' He paused and rubbed his goatee. 'Then her car mysteriously went on fire one night when they were all in their beds. They could have been killed if it had exploded in the driveway and blown up the house, only one of the neighbours spotted it on his way in home. My uncle said enough was enough and it was only a fucking car door after all. He wanted her to ring up the fella of the Lanes and say her car was grand.'

'And did she?'

He nodded. 'And they all lived happily ever after. Those bastards are animals.'

'So that's why you drove away?'

'I felt bad about it, but then I saw this old woman coming out of a house and I figured she'd call an ambulance.'

'And the woman lying in the road?'

'I know, but fuck it – the Lanes? What did you expect me to do?'

'Make a statement.'

He laughed. 'That's easy for you to say. It'd be no skin off your nose.'

'And now?'

'I'd still be afraid.'

'What if I told you Jimmy Boy Lane had been arrested for murder?'

He threw his hands up in the air and stepped backwards. 'I wouldn't be surprised.'

'And would you make a statement?'

'About a bastard who might murder me? I don't think so – I mean, what'd be the point?'

'Well, he might have to pay for driving into that woman and almost killing her.'

He laughed. 'He won't. You're a Guard, you know about the Lanes. He'll just kill me as well – or have one of his savage brothers finish me off.'

I nodded and looked around the room. The walls were painted white and there was a huge print of Van Gogh's *Sunflowers* over the fireplace. Inside me I was actually feeling fine – or, I suppose, more accurately not feeling anything.

'Would you come to the station with me and have a look at some evidence relating to the case?'

James Foley shook his head. 'My wife is just gone out to pick up a Chinese for us – she'll be back in a minute. Maybe tomorrow. I'll think about it.'

'It won't take long, I promise. Half an hour at the most.

We'll run in to Henry Street and I'll show you the pictures and then I'll drop you back home.'

He looked uncertain.

'You don't even have to give a statement,' I said. 'When we get back you can talk to your wife about it and see what you want to do. How about that?'

He rubbed the goatee again with his index finger as if he was checking it was still there. 'What do you want me to look at?'

'Photographs.'

'All right, if I only have to have a look at those photographs. Man, I feel bad about the whole thing, but when you think about it it won't help that woman if I get killed as well.'

I made myself smile and led the way out of the room.

As we drove back towards town, James's phone rang. He pulled it out of his pocket. 'Hi, love? Are you home already? Jesus, I must just have missed you. I had to go out for a few minutes. I know. Look, I'm sorry, I can't explain on the phone. What? OK. I know. Stick it into the oven and I'll be back before you know it.'

He made a face at me as he hung up.

'I take it she's not too delighted,' I said.

He smirked. 'She'll get over it.'

I turned on the radio. I couldn't bear to have to make conversation with him. Luckily he wasn't too chatty, just looked out of the window at the dark streetscape. I turned into Meadow Gardens and stopped outside Fidelma O'Hagan's house.

'Two seconds,' I said and got out of the car before he could answer. She answered the door as soon as I rang the bell. She was already wearing a jacket as if she'd been waiting for me. She followed me out to the car and, spotting my other passenger, got in the back seat.

'Fidelma O'Hagan, meet James Foley – your cab driver,' I said as I pulled away from the footpath outside her house.

'Oh my goodness, they found you. That's great.' She reached a small-boned hand into the front seat and they awkwardly shook hands. I could feel James Foley staring at me but I kept my eyes fixed to the road. Within five minutes we'd navigated the almost traffic-free streets and I was parking in the half-empty car park of Árd Aoibhinn. I cut the engine and looked at my passengers.

'This isn't Henry Street Garda station,' James said.

I nodded. 'But there's something in here I need you two to see. It won't take a minute.'

'I don't want to,' he said, turning in his seat to face me. 'I don't have to. It's the woman, isn't it? The woman Jimmy Boy Lane ran over.'

I didn't answer.

He shook his head. 'No way.'

Fidelma O'Hagan didn't make a sound.

'I want you to come with me to see my wife,' I said, quietly. 'It won't take long – five minutes. But I think it's important that you see her.'

'No,' James said, his hand on the handle of the door. 'You lied to me. I'm not going anywhere with you.'

I grabbed him by the arm. 'I'm not asking you, James, I'm telling you. I'm a detective and I'm armed. You'll do as I ask.'

'You can't do that,' he said, but I noticed his arm had stopped struggling.

'Watch me.'

'But it must be against the rules.'

'Make an official complaint. I'll give you the telephone number before you go home.'

I looked over my shoulder at Fidelma. Her shoulders

were hunched up to her ears and her face was almost luminous in the dark car.

'You just want us to see her?' she said in a thin voice as we made eye contact.

I nodded and she nodded as well.

'OK,' she said in a small voice.

I looked at James. He was looking straight ahead.

'Well?' I said.

'Do I have a choice?' he said.

'No. Come on.'

We got out of the car and to my amazement my two passengers walked in front of me towards the front door. I'd been pretty sure Fidelma was going to co-operate but I hadn't been so sure about James. But it looked as if I'd lucked out and he'd decided to humour me.

I didn't give a shit what his reasons were. He was coming to Rita's room with me whether he liked it or not and he could complain about me to the Garda Commissioner for all I cared. I'd be happy to have my decision about my future made for me.

I looked at my watch as we walked through the quiet corridor. It was ten fifteen. All the visitors were safely home and most of the patients were asleep for the night. That is, those who weren't permanently asleep. I opened the door to Rita's room. It was quiet in there. The TV had been turned off and the lamp over her bed cast a weak light on to her face.

I switched on the main light and the fluorescent strips flickered to life. I ushered my captives into the room. They stood close together at the end of the bed, both of them unable to look away from her stillness.

'I brought you a couple of visitors, love,' I said, loudly, kissing her cheek. 'Now, you never saw them before but they've seen you, haven't you, folks?'

I looked at them but neither said anything.

I laughed and fetched two grey plastic chairs from the six or so chairs stacked in the corner in case there was ever a sudden influx of visitors. I plonked one in front of each and motioned them to sit down. They did as I was suggesting.

I folded my arms and leaned against the end of Rita's bed and just looked at them both for a few seconds. They stared back at me. Eventually James began to regain some composure.

'Why are we here?' he said defiantly.

I smiled. 'I wanted you to see.'

He looked uncertain. 'Why?'

'I don't know. I just did. Now, hold on a minute – this is only half of what I wanted to show you.'

I walked over and ejected the video in the player just to check the label. Once I was sure it was the one I wanted I switched everything on. The doorway of Cratloe Church appeared on the TV and then a shot of clear blue sky and then a black car. A willowy woman in a white dress stepped forward and pushed her veil out of her face. Her eyes were bright and her face was beautiful. As she stood up and was joined by a plump grey-haired man she called Seán's name and laughed. It was Rita, of course.

I'd watched the tape maybe five or six times in the first eight years of our marriage and close to a hundred times in the first three months after Rita'd been brought to Árd Aoibhinn. I had to stop then because it was becoming unbearable and decided it was a much better idea to bring it to the nursing home instead to play for Rita to remind her of her life.

Nobody in the room spoke as we watched Rita's progress up through the church past row after row of delighted faces. My parents. Rita's aunts. Maria. Emmet. Yvonne – looking younger than I ever remembered her being. We watched edited highlights of the wedding Mass and then the explosion of people afterwards. All talking, laughing, kissing me, kissing Rita.

Then the hotel and people drinking and eating and making speeches. There was a full scene where my Aunt Joan and Uncle Declan – pissed out of their heads – sang 'Islands in the Stream' and a last long scene of us dancing through people's arched arms. Rita was laughing so hard she was crying and she had her dress hitched up high in her left arm. She was holding my hand with her right hand and I could still feel that sensation of my hand in hers.

I looked at my own face in the video and I could see that I was happy – any fool could see that. The thing was, I was also smug or something. I couldn't quite place the look. As if I was happy and knew I was lucky but also was sure that it was my right and that it'd always be mine. What would I have done differently if I'd known what was going to happen? I didn't know. The tape finished with my father singing 'The Cliffs of Dooneen' and Emmet and Seán laughing loudly in the background.

When it was over we stared at the blue screen in a heavy silence that was eventually broken by the sound of Fidelma gently blowing her nose. I switched off the TV and the main light and held the door open. They looked at each other and walked out. I followed them to the car and we were pulling out of the car park before anybody spoke. It was Fidelma.

'Why did you want us to come here?'

I didn't answer for a few seconds. Then I shrugged. 'You kept going that day. Were you afraid you'd miss your plane? Was that it?'

'No . . . Well, yes, but then James said it was OK . . .'

'I explained,' he said. 'And I told you I was sorry – and I

really am sorry about your wife. But what difference would it have made if I'd gone back?'

I stopped at a red light. The car hummed quietly and the heater demisted the windows.

'Maybe none,' I said. 'Who knows? Maybe if the ambulance had come faster it might have made a difference. That old woman had to run out when she heard the screeching brakes and then she had to run back inside and call for help. All that took time.'

The lights turned green and I pulled away.

'But you don't know if it'd have made a difference, do you? She might have been exactly the same,' James said.

'That's true,' I said, not looking at him. 'But you don't know that it wouldn't have, do you?'

There was no more speaking for the remainder of the journey, but it was an almost companionable silence. I pulled up outside Fidelma's house first.

'You can make your complaint about me first thing in the morning. If you call Henry Street they'll tell you what to do. My full name is Roberto Carlos O'Connell. There's only one of me – they'll know who I am.'

She looked at me with her big dark eyes and then just got out of the car. I drove away without even waiting to see that she made it indoors safely. Five minutes later I pulled up in the road outside James's house. He didn't move for a few seconds.

'Same advice to you about the complaint as I had for Fidelma – Henry Street.'

He didn't look at me – just let himself out. I drove off immediately again, thinking that his Chinese was surely dried to a crisp by now in the oven and his young wife was probably really pissed off.

A feeling of total calm seemed to wrap itself around me

as I made my way home. I knew I should have been upset. I was in deep shit but I didn't care. I knew that as soon as Sharon O'Toole found out what I'd done and had to field twenty or thirty calls from the press about police brutality and corruption I was finished. It didn't matter. I wasn't able for it any more. Too much pain and too many ugly things to look at.

Rita'd be upset when she came round and I told her but she'd understand. Anyway, even if they put me in jail for kidnapping it'd be worth it. Jimmy Boy Lane had done the damage and maybe I might try to grab him when he eventually got out on bail and force him to look at his handiwork. But I knew that'd be a waste of time.

There weren't that many Jimmy Boy Lanes in the world, but there were loads of Fidelmas and Jameses. Thousands and thousands of people who don't bother to act because they're afraid or think it won't make a difference. Now at least two of them had had to have a look at the consequences of that. I hoped they slept badly.

39. Monday 18 April

Hi Clint,

Eric came first thing this morning to bring me to the grave-yard and by the time he arrived I was dying to go, so I grabbed a jacket and we left. It was a lovely morning this morning – sunny with a blue sky and small white clouds, but it was cold enough.

Town was busy and I was nervous getting into the van – I mean, maybe we were in the papers again and stuff. But Eric said we weren't, and anyway once we started driving I sort of relaxed.

Do you know something, Clint? I was glad to be going to Tony's grave in a sad sort of morbid way but more than any-thing it was great to be away from those mad fuckers I was stuck with. The flat is beginning to be worse than any prison.

On the way through the traffic, Eric and me didn't say much. A few words about the weather. Another few about Spain and Peter. He never said a word about Agnes and I didn't bring it up. Eric knows all about it, of course, though he hadn't had anything to do with her coming. She bought her own ticket and isn't even travelling on the same flight. She's coming two days after us, which is something, I suppose.

On the way Eric stopped and bought flowers at a garage. Daffodils and tulips. They were lovely. Yellow and red and pink and all bunched up with these long flat dark green leaves. Remember how Tony loved flowers? Remember how his apartment was always full of them?

He used to say that the reason he loved them so much was because he was a pansy himself. Everybody always laughed when he said that but I kind of knew he was just saying it before anybody else got a chance. I miss him so much now that it's like there's a hole in my belly.

Eric parked the van outside the graveyard and led the way to Tony's grave. There didn't seem to be anybody around, which was good, but I was caring less by then anyway. I hate graveyards. It's like the air in them is actually sad, isn't it?

Eric stopped in front of a fresh grave. There was no marker on it but he said it was easy to find because it was right beside a huge white marble headstone that had a photograph of a laughing toddler right in the middle of it. I couldn't look at the picture, thinking it was possible that you or Glenn or someone like you had stolen his identity. At least his name wasn't Jake – I saw that much before I looked away.

Me and Eric stood in silence in front of Tony's grave. I laid the flowers down and in my head said a Hail Mary and that made me think of Mam. For ages after you died, every night when I was going to sleep I used to hear her voice from her bedroom saying those Hail Marys over and over and over.

I never said it to her but I knew she was saying them for you in case your soul was in trouble. You know, all the old-fashioned stuff about suicide and that – you know what she's like. I thought of asking her to say some for me, 'cos I figured you were probably all right but I was definitely in trouble. But I couldn't say it because it was embarrassing somehow that we could hear her praying when she thought she was alone.

That was what I was thinking about standing there in the graveyard beside Tony's grave and I was so wrapped up in it that Eric had to tap me on the shoulder. I jumped like he'd woken me up.

Sorry, Gina – I didn't mean to startle you. Is Clint buried up here as well? That's all I was wondering.

I nodded.

Will we visit the grave?

I nodded again and, taking a last look at the red and yellow tulips lying on the chocolate-coloured earth piled on Tony's grave, walked to the far corner of the graveyard. Eric followed me, never saying a word until we reached your grave.

Clint Brennan, nineteen years, Eric read in a loud whisper. I stared at the headstone and thought about nothing. Then Eric leaned forward and placed two red tulips that he must have taken from Tony's grave on the grass in front of the small grey headstone. He turned his head to look at me and smiled. 'Tony would want Clint to have some of his flowers,' he said.

I laughed then, suddenly feeling all right for a few seconds as I looked at the bright red of the petals on the green grass. We stayed standing there for a few more minutes and I even said a Hail Mary in my head for you as well and then we went back to the van.

The weather had changed while we were in the graveyard and we were just pulling out of the car park when the rain came.

The rain in Spain falls mainly on the plain, Eric said, waving at a truck driver who'd let him into the traffic.

I looked at him like he was mad and he started laughing and asked me if I was looking forward to going to Spain. I told him the truth, which is that I can hardly wait, and that made him laugh and he started saying we wouldn't feel the time now and by tomorrow night we'd be in Spain.

Jesus, Clint, can you credit that? Tomorrow night? I didn't say any more about what I was thinking but it was all along the lines of the sooner the better and then suddenly Eric brings up the subject of Agnes out of the blue.

Can I say something about Agnes? he says and I say, OK. Then he went quiet for a few minutes. After a while he looks sideways at me and says he's not trying to be mean or nothing and she's a nice woman but do we know anything about her?

I said no, just that she's Kelly's mother, and he shut up all over again. And then eventually he said, I don't like gossip but I think you should know that she has a bit of a reputation.

So I asked what kind – I mean, I bet I have a bit of a reputation myself in this town by now. He said that she was known for being involved in prostitution and stuff like that. Which makes sense when you consider that Kelly was in for being on the game. I told Eric and he nodded like he already knew. Then he started telling me more about Kelly and her mother: how it was a real high-class set-up – no standing on the Dock Road in white patent thigh boots.

I sat back in my seat and looked out the window at the rainy streets we were driving through and then I told him how I felt about her and how I didn't trust her – or any of them by now – and as soon as we were in Spain I'd be getting away from the whole lot of them. He asked if I meant Natalie too and I just shrugged and didn't answer. I mean, I'm mad about him, Clint, but he isn't Tony, is he? That's what I was thinking then but I didn't say it.

But it didn't matter – he kept talking anyway. Saying stuff about Natalie and how she isn't wise like me. That made me laugh. But he said no, it was true and that Natalie is a good kid really and you can see that by the way she minds the baby but she wants things to be a certain way and so she'll believe whatever she has to believe to convince herself that's true.

I kept looking out the window and didn't answer, 'cos I knew all that, but so what? Then I asked him what he wanted me to do and he said nothing, he was just saying that was all.

Then we were back in front of our building. He turned off the engine and asked if I was OK. I said I was fine and then he did all this coughing and says he knows he's not Tony but if he could ever do anything for me, just ask. Then he made me promise that I'd get in touch with him if I ever needed anything.

I leaned over and kissed his cheek and promised and said Tony fell on his feet with him. And he thought that was funny and grinned and hugged me and then we got out of the van and went into the building and up the wide staircase to his brother's apartment.

On the top landing there was a young blonde woman with a toddler and a buggy, speaking on an old-fashioned public phone. She was holding the kid by the hood of his jumper and he was squealing and trying to get away. She hung up just as we got to the top and picked up the small boy under one arm and the buggy by the handles. Eric offered to help her.

And she said no thanks, in this real flat Cork accent. Said she was grand – balanced – and that she'd probably fall over if she gave him the buggy. We all laughed at that and she went off and Eric opened the door of the apartment with a key. It was four in the afternoon and sort of dark on account of the rain outside. The flat was silent. I walked around, turning on lights and calling people's names, but there was nobody around.

I thought it was odd but figured maybe they'd all gone shopping with Agnes. They were all so fucking sure they were invisible with their disguises they were probably parading up and down O'Connell Street. I invited Eric to stay for some cheese on toast but he said he had to go back to work for a while and left after giving me another hug and a big kiss.

I love Eric but I was glad to be by myself. I made two slices of cheese on toast and a pot of tea and took it all into the sitting room. *Spiderman The Movie* was on, so I watched it while I was eating and then sat back on the couch and fell asleep.

I dreamed about Ray again. This time we were just talking and walking in a big green field, holding hands, but I woke up wondering: if I asked Glenn, would he get me Ray's phone number? I can always call him from Spain once I'm settled, can't I? Maybe he'd even like to visit.

The phone just rang there, Clint – just after I wrote the thing about Ray. Oh man, it was weird – really fucking weird. There I was, still half asleep looking at Toby Maguire's face and thinking he reminded me a lot of Glenn, and my phone rang.

I didn't recognize the number when I looked at the screen but I answered it anyway.

Gina? Gina? Natalie's voice shouted as soon as I pressed the button.

I sat up.

Natalie? I could hear a baby crying in the background.

Gina, you have to help us, please. I can't talk . . . Is Eric with you?

No. He left a little while ago. What's wrong?

Oh Jesus, Gina. Please come. We're—

And that was it: she was gone. I tried returning a call to

320

the number but it was withheld and wouldn't do it. Fuck it, Clint – what am I supposed to do? What the hell is going on? Maybe I should go outside and look for her, but where will I go?

I don't know what to do, Clint. *Help!*

Gina

40. Monday 18 April

I slept like the proverbial baby after my act of unlawful detention. The calm feeling I had when I went home stayed with me all the way to the verge of unconsciousness. I must have had dreams, but I don't remember. The exhaustion of the weekend spent sleeping on that hospital camp bed caught up with me and I didn't wake until lunchtime. In fact I was so exhausted I might have slept even longer if the telephone hadn't woken me. I searched blindly for the receiver.

'Rob. It's Janice.'

I sat up in bed and squinted at the radio alarm clock beside my bed. 'Jesus! Janice. What time is it? Rita was sick all weekend and I didn't hear the alarm . . .'

Janice didn't say anything for a few seconds.

'Janice?'

'Sorry – are you feeling OK? You're not sick or anything?'

'No, I feel great. Rested. Why?'

'Look, I'm sorry to be waking you up with this news but you need to come in if you can. There's been a bit of an incident and Seán is missing.'

41. Monday 18 April

Oh Jesus, Clint,

Things are really falling apart. I told you about Natalie ringing and all that. After I wrote it all out for you I felt a bit clearer about it and as Natalie still hadn't rung back by then, I rang Eric. Like I should have done in the first place.

But he didn't answer. And when he didn't, that sort of did my head in even more, because I was really up shit creek then. I tried sitting back down and writing to you but I couldn't settle, so instead I started prowling around the flat like an animal in the zoo. My head felt like it was on fire, trying to work out what was going on. I mean, it could have been anything.

First I thought they might have been arrested when they were prancing around town but then I figured probably not. Even Natalie wouldn't be stupid enough to ring me if they'd been arrested. I mean, what for?

Then I thought maybe they'd been in an accident or something and needed my help and that seemed like a good possibility but I had no idea how I was supposed to help when I didn't know where they were. Then the phone rang again.

Gina! It's me, Natalie says in this shaky half-crying voice, and I started shouting at her and asking her where she was and all that and she didn't say anything first and then she whispered, Look Gina, I can't talk . . . You have to help us.

Where are you? I said and I could hear Peter whingeing in the background.

Jesus, Gina. Natalie's voice was shaking like my hand now. She's gone mad and . . . Look, just come.'

Come where? Where the fuck are you? I said, shouting at her.

And she said, I don't exactly know the address.

So I said, Then how exactly am I supposed to find you, Natalie?

You might have to . . . Look, find a phone book or someone who knows where the Hendricks live – that's where I am.

I couldn't believe my ears, so I said to her, The man who was killed? That Hendrick? What are you doing there?

And she gave this big long sigh and said it was a long story and she just needed me to find them and something about someone – a woman – having a gun. And then there were voices and noise and stuff and the phone went dead in my hand.

I immediately tried Eric again. This time the message told me the phone was turned off or out of range. My heart was beating like a drum in my chest – I could actually feel it pounding against my ribs. It was horrible.

For a few seconds I couldn't think at all – just kept hearing Natalie saying *she has a gun* over and over in my head; and then I remembered she said she was in the Hendricks' house and my head kind of cleared a bit, so I ran into the kitchen and tore everything out until I found a phone book.

If I could find out where they were then maybe I could help them. But there was nothing there about any Billy Hendrick and I didn't even know his wife's name so that wasn't any good.

So I rang directory enquiries and asked if they could get me an address from a name. This snotty bitch said, No, look in the phone book, so I just hung up and tried Eric again. Same story. Phone off.

I tried Glenn. Answering machine.

All I said was, Glenn, call me back straight away when you get this.

Then I hung up.

Fuck.

I was really losing it by then, Clint. How was I going to find Natalie? Who the hell was the 'she' with a gun? Kelly? I kept thinking I didn't know what to do but I was fooling myself because I did. I just didn't want to do it.

Eventually I gave in and got the phone book and found the list of police stations and kept going until I found Henry Street. I punched in the number before I could think about it and my heart was pounding even harder and I felt like throwing up. It started to ring and all this stuff came into my head about jail and how I didn't want to go back and how they'd lock me up now and throw away the key. So I hung up.

I just couldn't do it, Clint. After I hung up I started the walking thing again. Walking and thinking. Buzzing, buzzing, buzzing inside my head. I mean, would they do it for me if the shoe was on the other foot? Do you think they would? No fucking way.

Kelly wouldn't even think about it. She'd toss her hair and say, Too bad, Gina, bad luck. And Natalie? Well, she might, but then she mightn't as well – she isn't the most loyal friend in the world, is she? Making faces at Kelly behind my back when it suited her to have Kelly as her friend instead of me. And now she rings me up and I'm supposed to risk everything to help her.

I went into the bedroom and took out the printouts Eric had given us and read all the details of the flights. Eight fifteen tomorrow night and I'll be gone on that plane. By midnight I'll be in Spain and my new life can start. I feel rotten about it but if I get pulled into this shit now, Clint, then I'll probably be back in Limerick prison by midnight tomorrow. I feel really shit about it but I just can't do it.

Love,
Gina

42. Monday 18 April

At first I thought I was still asleep and dreaming, but I got out of bed anyway and opened the curtains and looked at myself in the dressing-table mirror as Janice's voice was still talking in my ear. I was too confused to follow what she'd been saying so I asked her to repeat it. She did.

'Seán tried to call you early this morning.'

'I was asleep. Fuck – what did he want?'

'Caroline Hendrick called him to say she'd set up a meeting with Kelly Moloney.'

'Christ. When?'

'This morning, I think. It wasn't easy to get information out of Seán – you know what he's like – but he couldn't get you so he told me. Caroline seems to have set some kind of a trap for Kelly. She told Seán that Kelly had called, trying to blackmail her, and that she'd agreed to give her money if she came to her house at twelve o'clock.'

Now I was wide awake. I jumped on to the floor. 'And what did she want from Seán?'

'She wanted him – and you – to come alone to her house at noon and arrest Kelly Moloney. No squad cars. No fuss. Just you two.'

'He didn't go by himself?' I said, pulling on my trousers and shoving my feet into shoes, with my phone tucked in between my chin and shoulder.

'No – Hugh went with him.'

'So? What's the problem?'

'I've been trying to ring Seán for the past two hours. His

wife is looking for him to sign a passport form or something and she keeps ringing and they keep putting her through to me.'

'He's not exactly in Yvonne's good books at the moment,' I said. 'But I can't see the problem. His phone is probably turned off. Did you try the car radio?'

'Yeah – no answer.'

'And Hugh's phone?'

'No answer.'

'I bet there's a simple explanation,' I said, stretching to wake up my muscles.

Janice didn't answer for a few seconds. 'Maybe. Look, it sounds stupid but I have a feeling about this. I said it to Seán but as you know I'm not exactly his favourite person. I thought he should have been more cautious going in there.'

'And now you're worried?'

Janice laughed. 'I know, I know – probably just paranoia, but still.'

'I'll be right there.'

'OK, great. He might be back by the time you get here.'

'Knowing Seán there's some kind of a delay and he hasn't bothered his arse to ring it in.'

'I hope so,' Janice said.

'Trust me,' I said. 'I know Seán.'

I hung up and, pulling a sweater over my head, went down the stairs. In the kitchen I buttered a slice of bread and took it and an apple with me to my car. As I backed out of my driveway I suddenly remembered the night before and wondered if I'd been complained about yet. I didn't care.

I drove up my street. It was deserted. Everybody was at work – just an ordinary day at the coalface. Nobody at home except a handful of cats and a few burglar alarms.

As I drove, a thick drizzle folded the town into something

that looked like a grey gauze shroud. I hated this weather. Maybe I wouldn't bother my arse moving back to Cork when I left the force. Maybe I'd wait until Rita was better and then we could go and live somewhere else. I could go back to my roots in Spain. Or somewhere else. Anywhere with a blue sky would do.

I pulled into a sudden knot of heavy traffic on the main road and inched along towards the traffic lights. Tapping the steering wheel in impatience, I fiddled with the radio to find a different station. Something light. Something distracting. Listening for a minute, I gave up and dropped the glove box open to search for a CD. All the time moving at the treacle-slow pace of the traffic. What the fuck was the hold-up? It was hardly rush hour. Why was everybody out in their cars? The rain probably.

I tried Seán's number. No luck. He was such a bastard — never took anybody else into account. Like a kid — as long as he was all right he just presumed everybody knew it. Never bothered his arse checking in.

I looked at passers-by hurrying through the sheets of fine rain and wondered what their lives were like. What was it like to be an ordinary person who worked in an office or a bank and whose worst experience of man's inhumanity to man was being cut off when trying to find a parking space?

I thought about Billy Hendrick's dead body and his fucked-up life and wondered what Kelly Moloney had on the Hendricks that she hoped would be good for a few bob to use to run away. It had to be something to do with Dylan. The adoption was all legal and above board — we'd checked. Still, there might be something else about the adoption that never made it to the legal documents. So maybe she'd been blackmailing Billy as well. Was that why he had money in a briefcase?

If that was so, then why hadn't she taken it with her after she shot him? Surely it was a bit of a mistake to go to the trouble of blowing his brains out and then forget to take the booty?

But she was young – maybe she'd been spooked when she saw what she'd done and run off. I hadn't found him a pretty sight and I was some way used to looking at murder victims. I couldn't imagine what it'd be like for her. She wasn't much more than a kid, really.

I sighed out loud when I thought of all the shit that went on. The domino effect from Kelly Moloney's mother's fucked-up life which fucked up her daughter's life and would fuck up another generation unless something intervened to stop it. It was too depressing. I'd be glad to be finished with it all.

I wondered if maybe I should hand in my notice before I was fired. That'd be more dignified. Hopefully there wouldn't be any criminal charges. I didn't really care, though. It still felt as if it'd been worth it. I figured I should tell Seán what had happened. He deserved to hear it from the horse's mouth. Maybe after this we'd get a chance to go for a drink and I could tell him about what I'd done and what I'd decided. I owed him that.

43. Monday 18 April

Clint,

After I wrote the last piece to you, I was determined to get going. Time to move. Time to look after *mé féin*. Myself. Number One. I'd done what I could for them – they'd tagged along from the start and it looked like they were trying to pull me into some shit-hole with them and I swear I wasn't going to let that happen.

So I got busy. Agnes had insisted on giving me this suitcase, even when I wouldn't let her get me clothes, so I went and got it and threw my few bits and pieces of clothes into it. It was pathetic-looking, now, I have to admit. But I put in all my make-up then and that made me feel a bit better 'cos it looked good there.

I finished packing in a few minutes and that was a drag 'cos it meant I was off thinking again. But I knew it was a waste of time. I mean, I'm not a fool, Clint, and I knew I couldn't save Natalie and Peter – even if I wanted to. But knowing that didn't make much difference – I still couldn't stop thinking about them.

I was mad with Natalie. I still am. I mean, why did she go with them? Any kind of fool could see that Agnes Moloney was bad news. Why couldn't Natalie see that? Eric is right about her – too fucking busy believing what she wants to believe. Always the same.

I sat down on the bed beside the suitcase and tried to get rid of the sound of Natalie's voice in my head. She was frightened – I knew that. More than frightened, even. But then again, as I told myself, Natalie's an awful panicker. Maybe she was just panicking about nothing. She can be highly strung like that. Flies off in a mad fit for half nothing.

But I don't know, Clint. I mean, would even Nat be ringing me up like that for no reason? That's the thing that got to me eventually. I tried not to think about it. Got up and left the bedroom and went back to the sitting room and turned on the TV and a rapper with a red beanie hat looked at me with big brown eyes and shouted something about someone getting shot. I couldn't believe it, but I also couldn't listen to it, so I turned off the TV and sat down on to the sofa.

And that's when it happened. This hot pain filled my stomach. I did everything. Moved around. Bent over on top of it. But it was no good. It was like a knife in my guts and first I was telling myself it must be my period coming early but I knew it wasn't. I know that pain. It's the pain I got after you died. The very exact same pain.

You see, Clint, the problem is that when someone you know well dies it changes everything. Breaks the spell. You don't think any more that dying is for people who were never really alive. Nobody admits it, but I think that's what they think really until it happens to them. That's what it was like for me, anyway.

You know that people die and you really do know it unless you're a fucking eejit, but because you don't know them or don't know them well they're never really alive to you, are they? And then someone who was alive for you dies and you know it can happen any time.

So now what the fuck am I going to do? What if somebody really does kill Natalie and Peter? If only I knew where they are I could just ring the cops and give them the address and not get involved. And that's more of it, isn't it?

I mean, why didn't she ring the cops herself instead of ringing me if things are that bad? I mean, for fuck's sake, what good am I going to be to them? Who does she think I am that I'd be able to stop anybody killing anybody? Does she think I'm Jackie Chan or Buffy or someone and that I'm just going to be able to charge in there and beat everybody up and save her?

How did I manage to get into this bloody mess? If I'd just gone by myself that day – said nothing to no one – none of this shit'd be happening. Fucking stupid ass, Natalie. Always the same fucked-up junkie behaviour. Always in some kind of trouble. Kelly was right about her – how the hell did Natalie think she'd ever be able to sort herself out? I'd love to thump the head off her.

I know that there's probably nothing I can do and if there's some psycho with them they'll probably end up being killed anyway and all that'll happen is that I'll just end up back in jail and it'll be all for nothing. But then what if I do try to help and they're saved? What about that? I fucking hate this because part of me knows that if I don't try I'll never know if I could have saved them and that'll ruin my life anyway.

It doesn't matter that I didn't do any of it. For fuck's sake, I didn't even ask them along in the first place, did I? Now it is what it is, though, and if I don't do what I know I should do there'll be no magical 'new life' for me anyway, will there?

Look, Clint, I'll talk to you later. I have to go and do some serious thinking for myself.

xxx

44. Monday 18 April

I put on a CD that I'd been given free with some newspaper and disco music of the seventies filled my car and my head. I drove across the junction when the lights changed and made good progress until I got as far as Shannon Bridge. For some reason unknown to me the traffic had come to a complete standstill.

I looked at the grey Shannon flowing away from the bridge towards the sea and the tall buildings that faced it. Two huge yellow cranes swung bundles of building materials towards scaffolding-clad structures, delivering the where-withal to make even more tall buildings. The traffic moved and I crawled approximately one length of my car, and then we stopped again. I was starting to lose my calm attitude to Seán's silence and was on the point of calling the station when my phone rang. It was Janice again.

'More news?' I asked.

'No. Not about Seán, but a woman rang – a young woman. She wanted to talk to whoever was in charge of the Billy Hendrick case.'

'Did you talk to her?'

'She wouldn't talk to me. The desk gave her your name and she'll only talk to you.'

'OK. How do I contact her?'

'She's going to call me back in two minutes exactly. I didn't want to give her your number without speaking with you first.'

'That's fine. I'll talk to her. She might know something

334

useful about the case. We could definitely do with a break.'

'Thanks, Rob. Where are you, by the way?'

'Stuck in a huge traffic jam coming over the bridge. I don't know what's going on.'

'Roadworks on the Dock Road. Maybe you should just go directly to the Hendricks' house and have a look around?' Janice said.

'That's a good idea. I think I'll do just that and maybe this traffic will have cleared by the time I get back.'

'Talk to you later, Rob.'

'See you, Janice.'

As soon as I hung up I turned my car and drove back towards the Hendricks'. Kool and the Gang sang their little hearts out as I drove through a gap in the stationary traffic and swung up the leafy, tree-lined road that led to the Hendricks' house. My phone rang again and I pushed the pick-up button on the hands-free cradle.

'Hello?' I said.

There was no answer.

'Hello?' I said again.

'Is this Detective Inspector Rob O'Connell?'

'Yes. How can I help you?'

'It's my friend – she's in this house and there's somebody there with a gun and she rang me and needs me to help her.'

'Can I ask your name?' I said.

I heard a noisy scared-sounding breath. 'No. Please. I just want you to help her. You're in charge of the Billy Hendrick thing, aren't you? Well, that's where she is and there's some-body there with a gun.'

'Sorry – what do you mean "That's where she is"?'

'She's in that Billy Hendrick's house. I don't know where it is but I suppose you do.'

'And somebody has a gun?'

'Yes. Somebody has a gun.'

'Will you tell me your friend's name?' I said, pulling into the side road that led to Hendrick's place.

'It doesn't matter – just go there.'

The phone went dead and I turned left into the cul-de-sac and through the high gates. There were no cars parked anywhere on the gravel surrounding the red-brick house. I stopped and got out of my car and walked up the broad steps to the front door and rang the bell. No answer. I tried again. Still no answer. I walked back down the broad steps and had a look at the house.

As I paused the girl on the phone came back into my head. She had to be one of the escapees – but which one? And if Seán was here, he had a gun but he wasn't likely to start shooting innocents. It didn't make sense. I walked around the side of the house, my shoes crunching loudly on the gravel. The rain had stopped and the golden-coloured gravel looked like wet brown sugar.

At the back was a white painted door. I rapped on that – no answer. I tried the handle. It opened. I pulled out my .38, just in case of any nasty surprises, and walked into a small back hallway that led straight into a large, warm kitchen. The remains of someone's breakfast was still on the draining board of the sink but there was no sign of life. I kept going into the spacious main hallway and along the side of the huge staircase. Just as I reached the door I knew led to the sitting room it opened and Seán appeared.

'Jesus, man – where have you been? Where's your car?' I said.

Seán looked at me and I noticed that his face was paper white against his black hair. He was holding his left hand to his right shoulder and there was blood oozing between his fingers. He leaned heavily against the doorjamb and winked at me.

'Fucking whore shot me. I think I might need an ambulance,' he said through lips almost as white as his face. Then he folded at the knees, leaving a dramatic red smear on the white paintwork as he travelled down to the floor.

45. Monday 18 April

OK, Clint –

I did it. I rang the cops and held out until they let me talk to the guy in charge. OK. Fuck it, I'm still shaking like a leaf but at least I did it. I told him where they were, so now it's up to him. At least now they can find her and Peter and everything will be OK. And I wasn't caught – at least I can't see how they'd trace me – which is good!

I'm glad now that I did it. It was the right thing to do. I'm sitting here, by the window, drinking a cup of tea, writing this and looking out on to the street. The rain is thick outside – makes the air look grey when it's like that, doesn't it?

I can't help thinking about what's going to happen to Natalie if the police get her. I mean, I know they'll save her from whatever shit's going down but what about after that? They'll definitely take Peter away from her. That'll break her heart but it's better than them both being dead, I suppose.

Maybe that won't happen, though. Maybe she'll get away before the cops get there and then she'll get back here and we'll go to Spain and everything'll be OK. Sounds a bit La-La Land all right when I see it written down. But fuck it, maybe it'll happen – stranger things than that have happened to me.

I wonder where Kelly is? Natalie didn't say anything about her and I've just been presuming they're together, but maybe they aren't. Maybe Kelly is going to arrive back at the flat wanting to know about Natalie. I think I'll have a quick look around. Be back in a minute, don't go anywhere – ha ha.

Fuck it, Clint – you won't believe this. I went into my bedroom just there and had a quick look in the wardrobe. I never really looked at anything when I was packing my own case earlier. And everything is gone.

All the clothes that Agnes bought for Kelly – gone. Those shitty, ugly Burberry suitcases – gone. Then I had a look in Natalie and Peter's room. It was a mess, as usual. She hadn't even made the bed and the bedclothes were all falling on to the floor. But it was the same thing there as well – everything was gone out of the wardrobes.

I went back into the kitchen and tried Eric and Glenn again just in case they knew something – still no luck. And then it dawned on me. They left without me. I don't know why or how or where they were going but the bitches had packed up and left without me while I was at the graveyard. I started laughing then because the whole thing is so fucking ridiculous.

Those two had come along uninvited that first day when I took off. I didn't need or even want them to come and they've been nothing but trouble to me the whole time since we ran. And then they have the cheek to fuck off without me.

I know it was probably Agnes's idea but I don't really care. Fucking disloyal wagons. Especially Natalie. And that was more of it: ringing me up when she was in trouble and me – bigger fucking fool – risked my fucking ass ringing the Guards and all the time she'd been planning to leave without me. Do you know something, Clint? I'm an eejit. A total and complete fucking eejit.

After I realized what had happened I was raging, so I had to calm myself down. I marched into the sitting room and turned on the TV and tried to watch it. But I couldn't stop thinking about them. I sat there hoping that the Guards caught the two of them and locked them up. It was the least they deserved and I even decided that if they ratted me out I'd find a way to pay someone to beat seven kinds of shit out of them.

My stomach started paining me again when I was thinking about them and I felt so horrible and all alone. Not that there's much I can do about that, is there? I'd better get used to it. Anyway, I think I'm better off by myself. Better than being with two bitches pretending to be my friends and planning to do me down all the time.

I was thinking all that when the phone rang. I thought it was probably Eric or Glenn answering one of my messages. I couldn't wait to tell them what I'd found out. But it wasn't them. It was Natalie. The minute I heard her voice my temper flared up inside me like a match and I nearly hung up.

Fuck you! I shouted down the phone at her. Fuck you! You left without me. Well, you can just go and fuck yourself – I don't give a shit what happens to you or that other wagon.

And she's all crying of course and going, Please, Gina, don't hang up, it was Agnes's idea – she said it'd be safer for you too.

I told her to fuck off and she goes, Just listen, and then she's going on how Agnes told her she had contacts in Boston and they could get in touch with me in a few months. See if I wanted to go there with them.

Horse shit. Pure horse shit and I said it and said I was hanging up, and she was still crying and begging me not to. I asked her where she was and she said she was locked in the jacks and then she says, Hold on one minute, and I heard the sound of a toilet flushing and then the sound of running water and I wanted to hang up but somehow I just couldn't.

340

So I called her and she came back on and said she was pretending to wash her hands and if I didn't want to help her then maybe I could help Peter. So I told her then I'd rung the Guards and sent them to Hendrick's house and she said it was too late. They were gone. So I said, Too bad, there's nothing I can do about that, and I could taste the meanness in me on the tip of my tongue.

And I was just about to hang up and she says all this stuff about someone shooting two Guards and taking their car and dumping it and then making them all go with her. So I'm going, Who, Natalie? Who? And then she says it's Agnes.

Says she's gone completely fucking mad. Took someone called Caroline and her kid, Dylan, with them. Natalie says there's this other guy – Alan or Adam or something – and he's supposed to come with money or she says she'll shoot Caroline and her kid. She made the Caroline one ring him and tell him about shooting the cops so he'd know she was serious.

I didn't say anything for a few seconds and then I asked her about Kelly – where was she and stuff – and she said she was there as well. She's not mad like Agnes but Agnes is saying all this stuff to her about making things up to her and Kelly looks really weird. And then she's off again, crying and begging me to help her.

I said, Pity about you, Natalie – nobody made you go with them. And she said she was sorry about a hundred times but that she's afraid Agnes will kill her – and Peter too. And I said maybe she won't, but she said I didn't see her. Or see what she did already and please would I save them – she thought they were somewhere out by Meelick but they were in Agnes's house, she was sure of that. And then I hear her flushing the jacks again and saying, I'll be right out – a dose of the trots, that's all. And that was it.

So there I was back at the start. They left me and now they want me to help them. Again. Fucking typical.

I sat on the sofa for a few minutes after she was gone, thinking, and then I decided that whatever I did I wasn't going to be as fucking bad as them so I'd ring the cop again and tell him and then that'd be that. I still had his number on a piece of paper. But nothing is ever simple, is it?

I went to make the phone call and discovered my phone was dead. So I had to look for the charger – only guess what? I can't find it. I've looked everywhere. One of those wagons must have packed it either accidentally or on purpose.

I picked at the skin around my thumbnail until I made it bleed while I was trying to think of a solution to this one and then I remembered. There's a phone on the landing outside. So off I went into the hallway with my piece of paper to call that detective.

I was careful when I went out there. Had a good look around, but the whole place was empty and quiet. I picked up the heavy receiver to see if it was working and it was. Before I could think too much about it I punched in the number of the detective and rolled coins into the phone. The number rang and rang and I was just about to hang up when he answered.

It's me, I said. I rang a while ago. They've gone from Hendrick's.

I know, he said. I'm here.

She shot two Guards – Agnes, I mean. I think she killed them and then they took your woman Caroline and her young fella with them, like hostages or something.

Why are you calling me? he said and he sounded really angry. I felt like hanging up but I couldn't. He was all I had.

I need you to find them. My friend is with her, and the baby, and she thinks your woman is going to kill them.

What's your name? he said and he was still angry-sounding. I didn't say anything. So he said it again. What's your name?

Gina, I said then because it didn't matter. He wouldn't be able to find me anyway, would he? For all I knew he'd already been able to work out who I was. Gina Brennan.

And your friend's name? he goes then.

Natalie O'Rourke.

He didn't say anything for a second and then he asked me if I knew where they were gone to and I said kind of, that Natalie said they were in Agnes Moloney's house out near Meelick somewhere. Then he asked me was I sure it was Agnes who was doing the shooting and I said yeah and that Natalie said they were waiting for some guy to come with money and he says, What guy? and I said I didn't know – Alan or Adam or something. And anyway what difference did it make?

The real thing was that Natalie says Agnes is mad and she'll probably kill them all – even Peter. That was a mistake because then he's all, Who the hell is Peter? So I just said it didn't matter and that Peter is just a baby we found and Nat looks after him and then I asked him if he wanted a dead baby on his conscience. And do you know what he says to that, Clint? He goes, Why don't you come into the station, Gina?

So I go, Why don't you fuck off. Then I slammed down the phone.

That's it – that's what I did. Do you think I'm mad? Probably. Talk to you later.

Love,
Gina xxx

46. Monday 18 April

The ambulance had just left with Seán when my phone rang. Hugh Kelly's body was still lying on the floor of Caroline Hendrick's sitting room. There was no need for an ambulance for Hugh. He was dead. Shot square in the neck. Seán'd tried to tell me what had happened but he was in a lot of pain and slipping in and out of consciousness, so it was actually Gina Brennan who filled me in, in some kind of an intelligible way.

As I was speaking to her I noticed that the screen on my phone was displaying a telephone number, so I wrote it down. I could tell from the number that it was a landline somewhere in town. As soon as she hung up I rang Janice and told her what Gina had told me.

'Do you think they're in the apartment we were at?' Janice asked.

'No, she said a house and so I figured Meelick. Will you look up the address? Didn't you say we'd found it?'

'Yeah. Two seconds.'

Less than two seconds later, Janice was back. 'Two Towers, Meelick – that's the name of her house. I looked at the note about it and it says that it's two miles out the Garden Road in Meelick.'

'I know where that is.'

'Will I meet you there?'

'I think that'd be a good idea.'

'Don't go in until we get there, Rob.'

'Thanks for the tip, Janice.'

'Sorry. It's just – wait for us.'

'We don't even know if Gina Brennan is right – they might not be there at all.'

'Still,' she said.

'Janice,' I said.

She laughed. 'OK. Anything else?'

'Yeah. Here's a phone number. Will you see if you can get an address to go with it?'

I read the number to her and she repeated it back to me. 'I think that might be where the runaways are.'

'OK, I'll get someone on it. How's Seán?'

'I don't know. They said there was no point in going to the hospital with him. He was unconscious, anyway, by the time they put him in the ambulance.'

'He'll be OK – Seán is tough.'

'Hopefully,' I said, sitting into my car and raising a finger in farewell to the five uniformed policemen standing outside the front door of Caroline Hendrick's house. They all waved back. 'I'd better called Yvonne. See you in Meelick.'

As I drove away I scrolled through my address book, my heart pounding with tension. Baby-faced Hugh Kelly was dead. Just finishing his two years' probation and about to become a fully fledged detective – and a good one at that, but not now. Now his young wife was widowed and their new baby fatherless, and Seán was in hospital and some girl was going to be killed unless I could save her. For all their sakes I wished they had someone better than me to rely on.

I found Yvonne's mobile number and took a deep breath as I punched the call button. She picked up straight away and didn't say anything for a few seconds after I told her Seán'd been shot.

Eventually I heard her taking a deep breath. 'Are they bringing him to the Regional?'

'Yes.'

Another breath. 'I'd better go to the hospital, so, I suppose.'

'OK,' I said. 'I'll see you there in a while – there's some work I have to do first. Call me if there's any news.'

'I will,' she said and her voice was starting to shake. 'Thanks for calling me, Rob.'

'No problem.'

I hung up. I drove on to the main road and I was glad to see that most of the traffic had cleared. I continued out the Ennis Road, turning at Ivans' shop and heading out the Cratloe Road for Meelick at the LIT roundabout. I was pretty certain I knew where we'd find Agnes's house. I'd had a girlfriend years ago who lived on that road. As I exited off the roundabout my phone rang.

'Rob?' Janice's voice filled the car.

'Hi, Janice.'

'The call was made from town – 37 Oznam Terrace, near Pery's Square. The phone is registered in the name of the owner of three of the apartments, a Harry McGee, but he doesn't live there.'

'Great stuff,' I said, indicating to turn right at the Country Club.

'I think we should take reinforcements to Agnes Moloney's house,' Janice said. 'Two squads – armed, no sirens. Armed back-up.'

'That's fine with me. I'm almost there.'

'Me too.'

I looked in my mirror to see two Garda cars driving down the narrow country road behind me. Janice waved from the front seat of the first one. I laughed. Who was this woman?

'Look,' I said, 'I'm going to try to see if I can find Alan Hendrick.'

346

'Grand. Talk to you in a minute.'

Janice hung up and I rang the station to get a number for Hendrick's Solicitors.

Sheila Cunningham, one of the receptionists, answered.

'Hi, Sheila,' I said. 'Can you get me the number for Hendrick's Solicitors?'

'No problem,' Sheila said in her Tipperary accent. 'Is it true about Hugh Kelly?'

'Yeah, it's true.'

Sheila didn't say anything for a few seconds. 'His wife has just had a baby,' she said finally.

I didn't answer. What can you say?

'And Seán?' Sheila asked. 'I heard he was hurt.'

'Yeah, but I think he'll be OK.'

Sheila sighed a long low sigh. 'I'll get it for you now, Rob.'

'Thanks,' I said, looking at each house I passed to see if there might be some indication of a name. There were loads, but none was that of Two Towers. As soon as Sheila gave me the number I called Hendrick's.

'Hello, Hendrick's Sol –'

'Hello, Vanessa?' I interrupted. 'Detective Inspector O'Connell here. Is Alan in, please? It's urgent.'

'No, sorry, Detective. He left about an hour ago.'

Shit.

'Do you know where he went?'

'No. Sorry. He just said he wasn't sure if he'd be back today.'

'OK – thanks,' I said, and I hung up.

I rang Janice and told her and she let out a long sigh.

'Any sign of the house?'

'Not yet.'

'Don't worry, Rob – we'll find them and it'll all work out.'

347

I didn't answer – just looked at the houses along the roadside. My head was buzzing like a radio picking up forty stations all at once and I was trying to force some order on my thoughts before I found what I was looking for.

Two men had already been shot. One was dead. I had to be able to think before I approached that house. I forced myself to take deep breaths and tried to line up my thoughts so that the whole thing made sense. It was a waste of time.

And then I saw it. A big stone-fronted dormer-windowed house off the road. By the front stone wall was a huge timber sign with burned-out lettering announcing it as Two Towers. I stopped on the road outside, hoping I was out of view of the house. Janice's car and the other squad car stopped behind me.

'OK,' I said as I walked towards Janice and the uniformed men getting out of the two cars.

She handed me a yellow Post-it. 'The address of your caller.'

'Thanks.' I shoved the piece of paper in my pocket. 'OK, so. Let's go in.'

Janice looked worried. 'Maybe we should wait – we don't know what's going on in there, Rob.'

'I know that but maybe there's nothing going on in there.'

'Or maybe there's a mad woman with a gun running around in there.'

I nodded. 'Maybe. But I think it's better not to create a big siege situation if we can help it, don't you? I don't want to be the subject of a commission of inquiry.'

She nodded and shrugged. 'Still.'

'Look, will I go in alone?'

She laughed at that. 'No way.'

'OK, so, it's better to keep it calm if we can. The lads will cover us. Did they bring firearms?'

'Yeah.'

'OK, so.' I turned to the uniformed police officers standing behind us. 'Detective Long and I will go in first. We're not even sure this is the correct house, let alone sure that there's anything going on, so you wait here and stay awake and we'll see what happens. OK?'

They all nodded. Just then another car pulled up behind the squad cars and two men in jeans and jackets jumped out. I didn't recognize them but the flak jackets under their civilian clothes were a bit of a giveaway. They opened the boot of their car and took out two sniper rifles that looked like a Benelli and a Heckler and Koch but I wasn't sure. Seán knew more about guns than I did.

They walked towards us and shook hands with Janice, and she introduced me to them and told them to stay out of sight.

Then Janice and I turned and walked side by side into the front driveway of Two Towers.

'Emergency Response Unit?' I said as we walked. 'How did they get here so fast?'

'They were around. A drugs thing at the weekend. I knew they were in Limerick so I called them, just to be on the safe side,' she said as we passed a badly parked navy Audi.

'Dubliners,' I said, grinning at her. 'Seán is right – you come in here and think you know everything.'

She gave me a fake sweet smile as we reached the house. 'Was I wrong? I don't think so.'

There was nothing to see at the front of Agnes Moloney's house, but that didn't mean a thing. There were people inside. I could feel it.

'You ring the bell. I'll have a walk around the back,' I said to Janice and she nodded, her face serious now and full of concentration.

As I made my way around the side of the house I could hear the doorbell chime inside. Two Towers had a large enclosed back garden and a big set of sliding glass doors with a great view of the same. I walked close to the doors, removing my .38 from its holster as I saw Agnes Moloney sitting at a long pine table, calmly sipping from a big blue mug.

She didn't appear to have a gun, but that didn't mean there wasn't one, of course, so, concealing my weapon behind my thigh, I knocked on the glass with my free hand. She looked up at me and smiled and beckoned me to come in. I pulled open one of the doors.

'Agnes?'

'Detective – how nice that it's you. Come on in.'

I stepped into the bright Shaker kitchen. The doorbell rang again.

'Just a moment,' Agnes said. She rose, swaying slightly as she walked out to open the door. I watched her all the time – still no sign of a gun. She opened the door and Janice stood in the porch, her right hand out of view just like mine.

'Obviously I was expecting somebody, though maybe not quite so soon,' Agnes said as she came back into the kitchen with Janice. 'But I am surprised to see that it's the two of you again.'

She walked over to where a handbag was sitting open on a worktop and extracted a small Beretta. Janice and I immediately tensed and I held my gun tightly. But then she turned and walked towards me, holding her pistol by the barrel.

I put out my left hand and she placed it on my outstretched palm, and then returned to her seat at the table. The house seemed to be completely quiet and I wondered where in hell everybody might be and if the reports I'd had from Gina Brennan about hostages were even true.

But as Agnes had just handed me a gun – and I was betting it was at least the gun that was used to kill Billy Hendrick – I decided to play the game for the moment. Anyway, I had her gun. That was unless she had another, which I doubted.

Agnes rose, filled the kettle with water and switched it on, as if this was the most normal of social calls.

'You'll probably want to call your people,' she said, folding her arms and leaning against the black marble worktop. 'Alan is in the sitting room. I'm afraid he's dead.'

Janice looked at me and I nodded. She turned and walked from the room. Agnes didn't seem to notice. The kettle clicked loudly as it came to the boil.

'Tea?' Agnes asked.

I shook my head. She ceremoniously spooned tea leaves into a small flower-patterned porcelain pot and poured boiling water on top.

'I'm sorry about your friends back at the Hendrick place,' she said, smiling at me as she stirred the tea and replaced the delicate lid. 'That was Caroline's fault.'

'Caroline shot them?'

Agnes smiled. 'Caroline? You must be joking. No, I shot them, I'm afraid. She brought them, though. If she'd done as I'd asked nobody would have been hurt – well, OK, Alan would still be dead, but nobody else.'

Janice came back into the room and her pale face was even whiter than usual.

'He is dead, isn't he?' Agnes asked her.

'Yes,' Janice said. 'I called it in and I called the lads outside as well.'

Agnes listened to our conversation as she poured tea into a tall, fat-bellied cup that matched the teapot. She sipped at it immediately without adding milk and sugar.

'Earl Grey,' she said, looking at me with slightly unfocused brown eyes. 'I wonder if they'd let me bring some to prison?'

The doorbell rang and Janice went to answer it. The loud sound of feet and murmuring voices travelled to the kitchen, but Agnes was still calm.

'I killed Billy as well,' Agnes said, gently resting her cup on a saucer. I didn't answer. 'And I'm not sorry – I suppose you think that's terrible.'

She paused and I shrugged. That seemed to be enough for her.

'He raped Kelly,' she continued. 'I mean, I wasn't a great mother ever – I could hardly look after myself most of the time when she was a child. They took her off me. But you know that, don't you?'

'Yes.'

She looked into her cup. 'I've had a bit of a problem with the booze for most of my life.' She sipped from her thin cup and smiled broadly at me. 'I could do with a drink right now.'

I smiled back at her in spite of myself. There was something very engaging about her. She was like a child who is totally honest and open and not bothered with pretending. I watched as she bent down and produced a bottle of brandy from under the sink. She poured a generous dollop of it into her tea and took a long drink.

'Once I was sober I knew that I had to sort things out for Kelly. The thought of it kept me going when I was in rehab. Don't mind that shit they tell you about doing it for yourself.' She lit a cigarette and blew a stream of smoke up towards the concealed lighting overhead. 'The lies that bastard told about her . . . And she was only a child. A little girl. And a good girl at that.' She finished her tea and poured herself another full cup, generously laced with more brandy.

'So you shot him,' I said. Janice had come back into the room and was standing behind me.

'I shot him,' Agnes echoed. 'He was an animal, that man. He's no loss.'

'And the two Guards you shot at Hendrick's?'

Agnes sighed. 'Caroline thought Alan had shot Billy – can you credit that? Billy told her that if she tried to leave him he'd take Dylan. He said one simple test and he could prove he was his father and that she'd never get the child. She loves Dylan, I'll give her that.'

'I don't understand,' I said.

Agnes looked at me as she inhaled deeply from her cigarette. 'I wanted to get money out of Caroline for Kelly. It's the least she deserved – that woman took her baby. And if there's one thing I know, it's what it's like when someone takes your baby away. I rang Caroline up and we went there. I was going to put the girls on a plane tonight – that was the plan. But Caroline, the bitch, queered things as always. She called you people. Thought she could frame Kelly for the murder of that bastard Billy so she could protect her precious Alan.'

'So you shot the policemen.'

Agnes sighed. 'I'm sorry, but they tried to stop me. Jumped out and did all this macho shit. I had no choice – I had to keep going once I'd started.'

I shook my head.

Agnes's face became angry. 'You don't seem to be really getting it, do you? My life has been one big fucking nothing and Kelly paid the price for that. I thought if I could get her away from here – get her some money to start a new life – that'd be something.'

'And killing the Hendricks – was that for her as well?'

'Yes, actually – though not only for her. Maybe it was

353

more for me in a way. I mean, Billy was a total bastard but Alan was as bad. For God's sake, everybody knows Alan made Billy marry that bitch when that rich wife of his found out he was fucking her.'

She lit a cigarette and took a long, luxurious drag. Her face was beginning to crumble now as she allowed herself to remember. 'He ... he knew that Billy was having sex with Kelly – a child – and he did nothing about it. As far as he was concerned it kept Billy away from him and Caroline, and that was all he cared about.'

'You can't know that,' Janice said quietly.

Agnes looked at her. 'I know that he knew what was happening. I know that Kelly was a child when she lived in that house.' She drank the contents of the cup and refilled it with straight brandy this time, which she drank in one go. 'Caroline knew as well. I'd shoot that bitch in a minute except that Kelly said no. Said she was Dylan's mother.'

'Adoptive mother,' I said.

Agnes rolled her eyes skywards like a brazen teenager. 'Only mother he's ever had, I suppose.'

'So where are Caroline and Dylan now?'

'Upstairs in a bedroom. They're fine – don't worry.'

I knew by her voice that she was telling the truth. Janice left the kitchen and I listened to her footfall on the stairs. Agnes and I didn't speak as we heard the sound of multiple feet clattering down the wooden stairs. I looked out of the window at a robin on the windowsill and she lit another cigarette and drank her brandy as if she was relaxing at a dinner party.

'I can see that they were bastards, Agnes, but why kill them?' I said, just as Janice came back into the kitchen. She looked at me and nodded.

Agnes smiled. I noticed the slight cast in her right eye again, which made her seem as though she was focusing slightly over my shoulder. Agnes was a very beautiful woman in spite of the years of abuse she'd visited on her body. I could imagine that she'd been at least as beautiful as her daughter when she was younger. What I couldn't imagine was what she could have hated so much about herself.

'Kelly called him and he said he'd give her money. She rang me and told me, but I know that bollocks – I knew he'd want something in return. So I went there a bit early. I talked to him – tried to reason. You see, I think they should let Kelly be involved with her child.'

'And what does Kelly think?'

'Kelly's not sure how to manage the situation but I think that's best all round, don't you? It's always best. Mother and child – there's nothing like it. I said that to him – tried to talk to him about it – and, well, the bastard laughed.'

'So you shot him?' Janice asked.

Agnes shrugged. 'Not just because he laughed. He said other stuff as well about how they'd see to it that Kelly spent the rest of her life in jail – that kind of thing. I had a gun and he tried to get it off me and, well, that was that.'

'So it was an accident?' I asked.

She shook her head. 'No. Not really. I meant it. At the time I got a bit of a fright – I mean, I've never shot anybody before and it's messy, isn't it?'

She paused for a few seconds. 'So I took off, but since then I have to tell you, I'm quite glad.'

'But why did you kill Alan?'

'Once I'd killed Billy I knew it was the right thing to do – the only way to make it OK for my baby, to make he safe from those bastards – so I decided to kill him too. I just didn't think I was going to get my chance today. Today I thought I'd get the money. Then maybe tomorrow or the next day I was going to get rid of that other shit.'

'But why?' I said.

'Revenge,' she said after a few seconds of reflection. 'I'd have to say, revenge – plain and simple.'

'You know what they say: if you're looking for revenge, you'd better dig two graves.'

Agnes laughed a low throaty laugh. 'Good one, that. But it's fine. I'm ready to lie down in my grave now that those bastards are dead. Now that Kelly is safe.'

'Where is Kelly now, by the way?' I said.

Agnes smiled. 'Why do you want Kelly? She didn't do anything.'

'She escaped from prison.'

Agnes raised one eyebrow. 'Please. I murdered two men and you have me. Come on, isn't it about time you arrested me?' she walked towards us, holding out her joined wrists.

'You're not planning to run away, are you?' I asked.

She shook her head and smiled again.

'Then we won't need cuffs.'

She shrugged and walked with Janice into the hallway. I followed them, and as they left through the front door I walked over as far as the sitting room and looked in. Alan Hendrick was lying face down on the highly polished beech floor, his head in a pool of blood. My stomach turned over and I remembered the day he'd been grey-faced in my office pressurizing me to find his brother's killer.

I turned away and nodded greetings at the uniformed Guards all around the hallway. In an effort to distract myself from the image of the dead man in the sitting room, I fished in my pocket for the piece of paper with the address from which Gina Brennan had made the phone call. It didn't take a rocket scientist to work out that there was at least a slim chance that Kelly had gone back there. Thinking of Gina made me remember why she'd called me. I walked out of the house to where Agnes was just about to get into a squad car with Janice.

'There was another girl,' I said. 'Natalie. And a baby – I can't remember his name.'

Agnes looked at me.

'Where are they?' I asked.

She smiled. 'I don't know what you mean.'

'Natalie? A small baby?'

She shrugged. 'I've no idea what you're talking about – sorry.'

I stared into her brown eyes and smelled the mingled fragrances of brandy and Earl Grey tea and expensive perfume.

'They were with Kelly,' I said.

She smiled and got into the car.

I looked at Janice. 'I have the address you gave me. Think I'll swing by on my way back to the station.'

'Do you want me to go with you?'

I shook my head. 'You go with Agnes. I'll have a look at the building and see if I can find out anything. I'll call in for back-up if I think I need it.'

Janice nodded and got into the car beside Agnes. Agnes tapped on the car window and motioned to me to open the door. I did so.

'Let them go,' she said.

I shook my head.

'They have a chance now. What good is it going to do to throw them back into prison, for God's sake? They're hardly a danger to society. Come on, Detective. Have a heart – just turn a blind eye and let them go.'

I looked into her eyes. 'I don't know what you're talking about,' I said.

Agnes's mouth twisted in a sneer. 'Bastard,' she said, reaching out and slamming the car door shut.

The squad car started up and I stood on the gravel of the driveway and watched them leave. Then I got into my car and drove back towards town. The traffic was heavy again as I queued to get on to the LIT roundabout. I was tired. Really, really tired. Tired in my bones, as if I'd never again have energy. My phone rang.

'Rob?'

'Yes.'

'Hi, it's Maureen Jennings here at Árd Aoibhinn.'

'How's it going, Maureen – everything all right?'

'We were just wondering if you might be able to pop in to see us for a minute. Dr Yarborough the specialist is here. We need to speak with you.'

'Now?'

'If you can – she has to leave soon.'

'I thought she wasn't coming until tomorrow.'

'Change of plan. Any chance you could drop by?'

My heart sank at the prospect of meeting some po-faced doctor who was going to tell me all over again about permanent vegetative states and how there was no chance Rita was ever coming out of hers. But I'd known this day was coming – especially with the anniversary of the accident and the magical fucking year deadline. I'd be as well to get it over with, all told.

'OK,' I said, waving thanks at a young man in a truck who let me switch lanes. 'I'll be there in five minutes.'

Of course it took more like twenty minutes, but when I eventually walked through the doors of Árd Aoibhinn Maureen Jennings was waiting for me. She pretended she wasn't. Tried to act as though she was doing some important business with the receptionist. But I knew she'd been waiting.

'Rob!' she said and her smile was pulled at the corners as if it didn't fit her mouth. 'Will you just pop down to Dr Tuohy's office with me?'

She took off then and on the short journey to the office pretended to read the file she was holding in her hand. It was as if she didn't want to have to talk to me.

That was OK with me. I didn't want to talk to anyone. The picture of Alan Hendrick's ruptured skull spilling its contents on to Agnes Moloney's sitting-room floor was still too huge in my mind to permit casual chit-chat.

Both doctors were waiting in the office. Jerry Tuohy jumped up as soon as we walked through the door and introduced me to the famous Catherine Yarborough. I shook hands with her. She was very young-looking to be a specialist in anything. Short – maybe a tiny bit over five feet tall with clear, fair skin and caramel-coloured hair cut in a bob. Her eyes were older than her face, though. Dark blue – nearly navy – and kind. She smiled as we shook hands and then we all sat down. Except for Maureen, who stood with her back to the closed door.

'So?' I said, anxious to hurry it along.

Jerry Tuohy looked at me. 'Well, you know that Rita has been ill for the past few days?'

I nodded.

'I'm afraid it became more serious than we thought it was at first,' he said.

I stood up. 'Is she very sick?'

He took a breath. 'Yes, I'm afraid so – that chest infection seems to have turned into pneumonia.'

I started towards the door and Maureen looked at me.

359

Her face was drawn and there was something in it that made me turn back towards the two doctors, now standing as well.

'Look, Rob, I'm sorry to have to tell you this but Rita passed away about two hours ago.' Jerry Tuohy took a breath and I looked away from him at the specialist, this mythical woman who was coming to assess my wife. She looked pretty ordinary to me now.

'The change was sudden,' she said in a soft Donegal accent. 'Maureen noticed her breathing was worse this afternoon and we increased the physio. But there wasn't much of an improvement. We weren't all that concerned, which is why we didn't ring you, but we were considering a tracheotomy to help her breathe . . .'

She paused and I nodded and she fiddled with a pen. 'But then when we checked on her just a little while ago we found that she'd . . . she'd died. It was peaceful, though: she doesn't seem to have been distressed at all.'

I frowned so hard that I could hardly see; then I turned and walked to the door. Maureen Jennings stepped aside and I went immediately to Rita's room. They all followed me.

The room was silent, but that was the way of it always and Rita looked the same. A little paler than the day before but pretty much the same still, beautiful Rita I'd been looking at for a year. I touched her face with my lips and she felt cold all right, but still they couldn't be right. They always thought the worst, those doctors and nurses. They didn't believe in her as I did. It was just a bad turn. Just another fucking curve ball.

'You told me she'd be all right,' I said to Maureen, who nodded.

'I know I did. I'm sorry, Rob – I thought she would be all right.'

I looked back at Rita. 'Why didn't anyone call me when she got worse?' I said and after the words were out I could hear that I'd shouted them.

'We would have called you but it didn't go on very long. Isabel Kelly, one of the young nurses, found her – she'd already passed away.'

This was bullshit. I just knew it.

'I examined her this morning,' Dr Yarborough said, coming to stand close by me. 'I was concerned about her lungs and we were going to have her X-rayed this afternoon, and I told you we were thinking about a tracheotomy. But the deterioration was very sudden and very severe – nobody was expecting it.' The strain on her heart was probably just too much.

I looked at Rita and picked up her hand in mine. The fingers were stiffer than usual but the same. Still the same shape and size and colour and smell. The same fingers that'd touched me and held my hand and passed me cups of tea on a Sunday when we sat all day on the sofa reading newspapers and watching movies.

Nobody said anything; we just all stood there, me holding Rita's motionless hand and the other three looking at me.

'I'd like to be alone with my wife,' I said, without turning around.

I think they must have agreed because I heard the door close and when I looked around they'd gone. I saw then that all the tubes that had hung from the sides of the bed like umbilical cords had gone as well and someone had shoved the intravenous drip stand into a corner.

I laid Rita's hand back on the covers and then sat down on the bed and took off my shoes and socks. I even remembered to turn off my phone. Then I climbed into bed beside her and took her in my arms. Her body fell against me as I tried to lift her.

Eventually I managed to position her so that her head was on my shoulder and her hair was just under my nose. I kissed the top of her head and felt her weight against my chest and then I closed my eyes and imagined we were at home. In our bed. Sleeping after making love. I kissed her hair again and again and again, and all the time I kept my eyes closed because I knew as soon as I opened them I'd have to see the world. And inside me the bleeding began.

47. Monday 18 April

Clint,

Kelly and Natalie came back. I couldn't believe it. I'd been walking the floors wondering how I was going to survive if they were killed even if I'd done everything I could and then they just came in the door. Just like that. I didn't know what I felt when I saw them. No clue. First I felt happy and nearly even kissed them but it never got that far because straight away almost I was raging with them. Natalie hugged me hard but I just stood there like a board.

I can't believe it. I can't believe it. I can't believe it, was all she said, over and over. It was annoying. Peter was asleep in her arms and I rubbed the top of his head. I looked at Kelly. Her face was as pale as flour and she didn't seem to be full of her usual guff. Just sat on the sofa chain-smoking.

Natalie gave me Peter to hold and made us all tea. She talked non-stop. I wasn't able to follow all of it but I worked out that Agnes had really shot two cops. I didn't let on that I was shocked, even though I was. I wouldn't give it to Natalie to look interested. It didn't matter, though – she talked anyway.

She said that after they'd left the first house – Hendrick's, I think – they went to that second house – Agnes's house – and then someone else was shot, a man – I couldn't follow who. But Agnes didn't shoot any women. Not even one. Natalie stopped pouring the tea she'd been pouring and looked at me.

Maybe she just hates men? she asked me.

I said nothing.

But she wasn't really waiting for an answer from me, anyway. I know that's true because she just kept going. She said they didn't see that man being shot but they heard it. But they did see the first two – the Guards. Well, she didn't – she was in the loo – and luckily the small boy who was there, Dylan, was out of the room as well. But everybody else saw it happening. Kelly and this other woman Caroline Hendrick – the first dead guy's wife. I looked at Kelly, but she was staring at a spot on the wall and still smoking.

Natalie said that she saw one of the Guards lying on the floor but Agnes made them go into another room and that was grand with her – she didn't want to be looking at dead guys. That was when she rang me the first time, she said. She had Kelly's mobile. Kelly put it down and Natalie took it and hid it and said she was going to the toilet but she was really ringing me. Kelly never even missed it she was so wrapped up in her mother, so Natalie just kept it. So she still had it to call me from the second house.

Natalie lit a cigarette then as well and stopped talking for about two seconds. Then she started off again. Told me about the second house and how Agnes was all mad and wound up. She looked at Kelly when she said that but Kelly didn't even react. In that house they stayed in the kitchen the whole time, Natalie said. All of them. Your woman Caroline and the kid and all.

Then the man came and they heard voices in the hallway and a shot and Agnes came back in the kitchen and took Caroline and Dylan. That was the kid – really, really cute, according to Natalie, and about seven. Anyway, she took them upstairs and locked them in a room.

Natalie said she was guessing that – the locking-in part –

but she was sure it's what she did. Then Agnes came back downstairs, all normal again, and called a cab, to send Natalie and Kelly and Peter away.

Natalie said that she was worried, so she asked Agnes about the kid and his mother and she said they were fine. Then Natalie said she was thinking about it and she figured that maybe they were. Maybe she just locked them in a room but didn't do anything to them. That wouldn't be too bad for a seven-year-old, would it?

Then Natalie said, Look, sorry, Kelly, but your mother is a bit off the deep end – there's no denying that.

Kelly sort of woke up at that part. She didn't hurt them, she said. She wouldn't. She promised.

I felt a sudden kind of pain looking at Kelly, and the picture of the small girl and the rows and rows of sinks came back into my head. That was all she said, though. Just lit another cigarette then and held the cup of tea Natalie handed her. But she didn't drink it.

Do you think we'll be safe here? Natalie asked me, then all business. I didn't answer but this time she was looking for me to say something.

Do you? she said again.

I shrugged and said, How would I know? Maybe the police followed you here.

Natalie shook her head and rubbed Peter's belly. He was lying on the sofa between me and her and he made a kind of purring noise when she rubbed his belly like that. Natalie smiled at him and then at me.

She said nobody followed them. There were no Guards there – well, except in the first house, but they were shot, weren't they? So that meant nobody knew where we were, so it was all still OK and we'd be in Spain by tomorrow.

I just looked at her. Fucking wagon. And then I couldn't

take it any more and said they could just go fuck themselves that they left me and I had to help them and now was I supposed to pretend nothing ever happened. Well, tough, 'cos I couldn't, 'cos I'm not as good at pretending as them.

Fuck you, I started shouting at them then. Fuck both of you. I'm sorry I ever had anything to do with you.

Natalie tried to put her hand on my arm but I pulled away from her. And she started with the usual shit like, Agnes said it'd be safer – even for you.

And I said, Forget it. As soon as we got to Spain they were on their own and Natalie was all crying and stuff and saying could they stay in Derek Greene's house and I said no – they could stay in the house Agnes got for them.

And she says, that was in America.

And I said, Fuck off to America, so. And she said Agnes said it'd be easier with speaking English and all. Better. She said I'd have a better chance on my own as well and she was swearing a hole through a pot that she believed Agnes.

Kelly started laughing real loud then and we both looked at her. She was sitting back in the sofa smoking, all relaxed-looking. We stared at her, but she just laughed, and then she finished her fag and closed her eyes and went to sleep. It was fucking weird.

I got up and came into the bedroom here to write this but I don't know what we're going to do about any of it yet. There's no point in changing the plan we had, is there? I mean, it was a good plan, whatever they thought about it.

I think I'll talk to Eric when I can get him to answer his phone and tell him what happened. Then we'll probably just go ahead. It isn't long now. I can put up with them for another few hours and then we'll be going to Spain and that'll be that. I don't know what I'll do once we get there.

I can't really turf them out on the street, can I? I'd like to, though – bitches.

At least that Agnes one is gone. I hope the Guards arrested her. They won't be able to find us, though, will they? Not unless she tells them, and she won't because Kelly's here. I think I might get up and clean my teeth and go to bed. I'm not hungry. If I fell asleep then I wouldn't have to think about the shit until morning and then it'd be time to go to Spain. That sounds like a plan.

I probably won't get to write to you again until we're in Spain, so say hi to Tony for me.

Lots and lots and lots of love,
Gina xxxxxxx

48. Tuesday 19 April

I fell asleep with Rita and they left me there. It was probably as easy. When I woke up it was after twelve and Rita was really, really gone. I placed her body back on the bed and kissed her cold face and stiffening fingertips, and then I just left. It wasn't hard to leave, funnily enough, because now she was actually gone there wasn't much point in me being there.

I drove to the Regional and talked to the night nurse about Seán, but she wouldn't let me see him, even when I tried my 'I am a police officer' routine. She didn't care. Said he was very ill but stable, and when I asked her if she thought he'd be OK she must have detected something because she smiled and said yes, she thought he would.

I didn't know what to do then. I didn't really want to go home because I knew I couldn't sleep. I had no Rita to be with any more and I didn't really want to be with anybody else. I drove around for a while. It was a mild night. Dry and clear after all the rain. Rita loved walking at night – she'd have liked it. But I didn't want to think about her because I knew if I did I was going to have to start feeling as well and I wasn't ready. I parked and went into a late-night café.

The waitress was a fiftyish woman with the face of an aged child. Her hair was dyed jet black, which gave her the appearance of hardness, and it was fluffed out around her face as if that might soften the effect. Her lips were carefully painted a bright red and she sucked her tongue against her yellow teeth as she waited for me to make a selection from the menu. Eventually I decided on fish and chips and tea and bread and butter and asked the waitress if she had a newspaper. She nodded and went away, tiredly, to get me food and reading material.

There was another man alone in a corner booth staring out of the dark window into the street and a drunken couple sniggered loudly every few seconds on the opposite side of the café. I fiddled with the glass bottle of vinegar on the table and wished she'd hurry back. I was hungry. Empty. And my head was straying back to Rita and I wanted to stay away.

My food arrived and I concentrated all my efforts on eating. Then I slowly drank the strong tea as I read the newspaper. That got me through an hour but eventually I finished and it was still only just after one thirty. I paid for my food and left the café as a sudden influx of customers surprised the exhausted staff.

In my car I listened to a late-night radio station and tried to think what else I could do. I could go for a long drive, but long driving encouraged long thinking and that was the very thing I wanted to avoid.

Then I remembered the piece of paper still in my jacket pocket. I pulled it out and drove to 37 Oznam Terrace. I parked across the road and looked across at the red-brick terraced house. Nice investment, Mr McGee. Taking a quick walk over, I checked the names on the six doorbells outside the front door, but none looked familiar so I went back to my car.

Maybe Janice had come round here already and had a look for the girls? I doubted it. By the time she'd booked Agnes Moloney and dealt with all the shit it'd definitely be knocking-off time, and anyway I'd said I'd check it out, but then I'd been waylaid.

I considered calling her but I was pretty sure she'd be asleep, as it was forty minutes after two a.m. I'd wait. They were only ordinary runaways, as it turned out. Seán had been right. They weren't murderers. It could wait. I'd call her first thing and maybe she and I could go together.

I thought about Agnes Moloney and how she'd shot the Hendrick brothers. She obviously thought she was removing obstacles for Kelly. Knocking down brick walls so her child could progress. I sort of hoped she was right.

I looked at the house and watched as the last lighted window went black. Everybody was asleep. In bed, resting up, so as to get back in the fray first thing in the morning. I was starting to feel tired and thought maybe I should head for home. But I was afraid I wouldn't sleep, so I figured I might be better off if I just put back my seat and lay down in the car for a while. I'd listen to music on the radio and try to relax. Then maybe I could chance my own bed.

I settled down and closed my eyes, and the next thing I knew was somebody on *Morning Ireland* announcing the time as seven fifteen. I sat up and rubbed my face until I woke properly. I couldn't believe I'd slept for so long in the car, but then a year of sleeping on chairs in Árd Aoibhinn would train you to sleep anywhere.

But not any more. Rita's dead, I thought, and it took my breath away. My chest felt as if it was being crushed and I fought for breath. Eventually air seeped into my lungs and I slumped forward with my elbows resting on the steering wheel.

I felt like a man facing the back wall of a maze. There was no way forward – I was pretty sure of that. No way of getting out from where I was and now probably no point in going back either. What the fuck was I going to do?

The sudden opening of the front door of 37 Oznam

Terrace took my attention and I lifted my head. A tall, young woman with bobbed black hair let herself out and ran down the road towards O'Connell Avenue. She didn't fit any of the descriptions of the girls we were looking for but I just knew she was one of them. I considered following her but she was out of sight before I could make up my mind.

I leaned into the back seat and grabbed one of the newspapers with the photographs of the runaway convicts. They looked like children. Just then I saw the same girl turning the corner from O'Connell Street. She was carrying a two-litre bottle of milk.

Hoping she hadn't seen me, I went over to the door of number thirty-seven and pretended to be calling someone on my phone. When she reached me she smiled unsteadily as she raised her hand and put her key in the front door.

'Listen, I'm locked out,' I said and she paused and looked at me. 'I've been trying to call my wife but she's still asleep. Would you mind if I came in with you?'

She looked at me assessingly for a few seconds and then shrugged and opened the door. I thanked her and followed her into the small tiled hallway.

'Thanks,' I said. She waved and cantered up the stairs.

I stood still and listened. Two flights of stairs. OK. In the distance I heard a door slam and then I walked as silently as I could manage up the stairs. At the top of the second flight, in the small landing, was a public phone. To the right was a navy wooden door. I stood on the stairs and looked at it. Now what?

I knew as well as I'd ever known anything that our runaway convicts were in the apartment behind that door. I should call it in. Call Janice. Tell somebody.

I walked up the last few steps and knocked at the door. The same girl who'd let me in the front door opened the navy door now. Looking into her face confirmed what I already really knew.

'Gina?' I said.

Her eyes blinked fast but the rest of her face didn't change.

'Sorry,' she said. 'There isn't any Gina here.'

'Oh,' I said. 'Are you sure?'

She nodded and I could see that she wanted to slam the door but was doing her best to appear nonchalant. I looked into her face and that's when I realized she was facing the maze wall as well. The dead end.

I smiled at her and said, 'The removal men will be here by about half nine – ten at the latest. I don't think they'll be able to delay it any longer than that.'

Her eyes widened as she listened.

'Is that OK with you?' I said.

She nodded slowly.

'Half nine. Don't forget.'

'Half nine,' she echoed.

I waved and walked away. She must have watched me go down the stairs because I didn't hear the door close until I was back in the downstairs hallway. I let myself out and walked down the street. The town was waking up. Cars and delivery vans and the first wave of hurrying workers began to appear on the streets.

I got into my car and drove aimlessly, eventually ending up down by the courthouse. I pulled in outside the Potato Market and looked across at the stern stone façade of the court and thought maybe I should go somewhere else. I was bound to meet people I knew down here and I didn't want to talk to anybody. But I couldn't work out where else I might go, so I parked and got out of my car.

I didn't know where I was going – didn't have a plan. I

was just walking. One foot in front of the other stuff. A bell rang in St Mary's Cathedral and I could feel the sound of it resonating in my empty chest. And I walked.

People passed me on Nicholas Street. I could see their shapes but they didn't really exist for me. They were just part of the fog that was outside me, the indistinct material of reality that had no real substance – not like the poker burning its way into my guts as the reality of Rita's death spread through me.

Suddenly terrified I'd meet someone I'd have to talk to, I cut down by the museum and made my way to the riverbank behind John's Castle. It was a tiny, grassy place. Empty. No people. A used condom and some empty beer cans but no people. The day was sunny but the wind from the Shannon was cold. I stood at the side with my hands in my pockets and watched the river flow.

Across the river on Clancy's Strand cars queued and crawled on to Sarsfield Bridge. School. Work. Life. I looked towards the bridge and the town and everything looked as it always did on a Tuesday morning at eight thirty. Busy. Everything carried on like the river, even though my life had stopped. Maybe all clichés were true, then.

I sat on a vandalized bench, beside a vandalized rowan tree that was struggling to make a few leaves in spite of the battering it'd received, and everything inside me melted and I began to cry. Hot tears started slowly at first, running singly down my face, but as they came the pain inside me grew and more and more and more tears came and none of them was enough to ease the pressure in my heart. I lay down on the bench and curled myself into a ball as I cried, not caring where I was or who saw me. I was past that.

A low moan erupted from my body. I don't know how long I was making that sound before I heard it myself and even then I couldn't stop it. It really felt as if half of me had been wrenched off and I was left alive but was slowly and painfully bleeding to death.

Eventually, though, I didn't die just there and then. Instead I stopped crying and sat up. The river was still there, flowing in front of me, and the town was wide awake and open for business all around me. I thought about what next. What next? The big question made of impossibly hard, prickly substances.

After the accident, on the rare occasion when my defences had fallen apart and I'd let myself think that maybe Rita wouldn't be coming home, I used to imagine myself holding her body, unable to leave her behind me. But now that it had happened it was nothing like that. The body in Árd Aoibhinn didn't mean all that much to me any more. The thing was that my heart was broken because Rita was gone, not because she was there.

I sat looking at the Curraghgower Falls as the water sizzled past and imagined my dry-eyed demeanour at the funeral. The mourners and the family. Sad faces. Handshakes. My body an automaton I'd send along to pay my respects.

People would say I was holding up well. I could nearly hear them saying that it was a shock all right, a real shock, God help us, but he's had a year to prepare himself, hasn't he? Maybe it'll be an ease to him now that the ordeal is over. And that wasn't true. Rita'd only just died – but so what? She was dead now and I didn't care what anybody believed.

I thought of my parents and how sad they were going to be when I told them that Rita had died. They weren't really able for the tragedy of any of it. They loved Rita – and me. They were thrilled when we said we were getting married –

happy that we were happy. All they'd ever really asked from life was that their children would grow up and have lives and children of their own. Jimmy Boy had robbed them as well.

I looked at my watch. It was after nine. I took my phone from my pocket and switched it on and called Janice.

'Good morning, Rob,' she said so cheerily it hurt my ear.

I took a breath. 'Hi, Janice. Listen – do you remember that number I asked you to look up yesterday?'

'Oh God, right! I'd forgotten about that. Did you get a chance to check it out? Is it where the girls are hiding, do you think?'

'I'm pretty sure it is,' I said.

'Will we go and have a look?'

I took another deep breath. 'I think you should, if you get a minute. I don't think I'll be in for a few days, though, Janice – I wonder if you'd let people know and take care of things, if you don't mind. My wife died yesterday.'

I heard her sharp intake of breath.

'Jesus, Rob – I'm sorry. That was sudden.'

'Yes, yes it was. Anyway, I'll be out for a couple of days – you know yourself.'

'Of course . . . Jesus, look if there's anything I can do . . .'

'Thanks, Janice. I'll be fine but thanks. Talk to you later.' And then I hung up because I could feel the ball of tears in my throat growing. I turned off my phone again and put it back into my pocket. Then I went back to my car and drove to Maria's. It was time to tell people. People who'd cry and make me cry. I was ready for it now.

30 June

Dear Detective O'Connell,

I am writing to you care of Henry Street Garda station so I hope you get this letter. I heard that your wife died and I was very sorry to hear it and I wanted to write just to let you know how sad I feel for you. I also want to thank you for everything you did for us.

I know that when your people arrived at the apartment that morning you'd have found the blood in the bathroom and you probably know it was Kelly's – I've seen CSI. Anyway, she did that because everything sort of tumbled in on top of her – you know how it can be. But now she's all right. Good, even. Maybe you'd tell her mother if you get a chance? I'd really appreciate it.

Anyway, that's it. Mostly I just wanted to say that I'm sorry and also – though I know it's a bit different – I wanted to tell you that I know what it's like when someone you love dies. It's one of the worst pains in the world.

If it's any help I found it good to write letters – it's kind of like being able to talk to the person in a way. Anyway, I hope you find something to help you. I'll say a prayer for you that your heart heals.

Once again, I'm sorry and thanks for what you did for us.

All the best,
Gina Brennan

PS I'm having this letter posted in Limerick but I promise you we're no longer there. We aren't even in Ireland any more, so don't vex yourself looking for us!

Acknowledgements

I'd like to thank Alison Walsh and Patricia Deevy for all their advice, encouragement and editorial suggestions. In addition I'd like to thank my agent Faith O'Grady for her help, and Anne Askwith, Ann Cooke and Donna Poppy at Penguin UK for their cheerful, painstaking work on the manuscript.

I'd especially like to acknowledge the help of the Garda Press Office in helping me with the research for this book. They patiently answered all of my questions even though every question just led to ten more – I'm sure they were sick of me! In particular I'd like to thank, Sergeant Ronan Farrelly, Sergeant Brendan Walsh, Garda Lynne Nolan, Garda Gerry Curley and Garda Marie Egan.